EVERYTHING,
SOMEWHERE

EVERYTHING
SOMWHERE

DAVID KUMMER

Published by David Kummer

Edited by Marni Macrae
Cover art and design by Dark Wish Designs
Interior design by Jordon Greene

Printed in the United States of America

FIRST EDITION

Paperback ISBN 978-1-0879367-8-9
Hardback ISBN 978-1-0879372-7-4

Fiction: Young Adult Contemporary
Fiction: Coming-of-Age

TO MY MOM,
because she, to quote Tom Petty, has
"a heart so big it could crush this town."

O look, look in the mirror
O look in your distress
Life remains a blessing
Although you cannot bless

O stand, stand at the window
As the tears scald and start
You shall love your crooked neighbour
With your crooked heart

It was late, late in the evening
The lovers, they were gone
The clocks had ceased their chiming
And the deep river ran on

- W.H. Auden, As I Walked Out One Evening -

PART 1

A PLACE OF INCREDIBLE BOREDOM

1
HUDSON

There hadn't been a suicide in Little Rush for at least fifty years. Maybe that tells you everything you need to know. For a few years, I'd been keenly aware that I would one day break that streak. Like the moment before you hit a deer with your car, speeding on a backroad late at night. Inevitable. Beautiful. Raw.

It's not that I wanted the *feeling* of death. I never liked pain. Always avoided it, honestly. I once cut my thighs with a razorblade for about a week before I gave that up. When I realized that alcohol numbed everything more effectively, I went for that particular addiction rather than self-harm. I suppose it was the better choice, in a brutal sort of way.

Honestly, you could even say I feared death. But at the same time, I couldn't turn away from it. Talking with Willow once, I compared it to sitting on a train track. Not tied down, just of my own free will. With every night that passed, with every panic attack or breakdown, I could feel the ground shaking under my feet. See that swift-moving beast in the distance as it hurtled closer. Yes, I knew that death was coming for me. Faster than it does for most. I felt jaw-clenching fear but wanted it so damn badly.

Little Rush. That quaint, postcard town. I felt a disconnect from it. Everybody else, they found aspects to enjoy. They had places or people that rooted them. Not me.

All those people growing old and wasting away in the same spot for years... to me, it felt like they were settling, like they could've achieved something greater. Who would give up the world for a life of *this*? Not me.

I was gonna get out. But if I had to die here, I would take care of it my-goddamn-self.

All through high school, I thought about my funeral, probably more than was healthy. Especially the playlist. A set of songs that would capture my entire life. Maybe I'd start with Bon Iver. I wondered how it would affect the old people.

Honestly, I just hoped that Mason and Willow would stick around. Those were the only two people who really cared about me. They were the only two keeping me around. Not in Little Rush. Just alive in general.

o o o

"Hudson!" my father yelled from the first floor. I could barely hear him over the low hum from my window AC unit. The wooden stairs creaked as he moved up a few steps. "Go feed those chickens!"

I ground my teeth together. I'd been laying on my bed, head resting on a pillow, wasting away the first Friday of summer. This self-pitying, casket position served me well. "Mason'll be here any minute," I yelled back, not rude per se but definitely not happy.

I didn't want an argument with him. After a full day working outside, he was often on edge. There was a moment's pause. I closed my eyes and tried to really savor those last moments of rest. We both knew what would happen now. As a kid, I fought against doing any chores but eventually tired of my phone being taken away.

"Then you best hurry," he called back with a chuckle.

His footsteps descended those first few steps. I heard my mom arguing with him briefly, something about dirt in the house. My father made his way to what we affectionately dubbed "the mud room." Here, he would deposit shirts, boots, jeans, anything caked in mud or grass. Then Mom would wash it, and so the cycle went. They'd kiss after this, despite their twenty-plus years of kissing. I didn't think they ever had sex nowadays. After all, I'd remained an only child my entire life, though I would've liked a sister. Maybe she'd turn out less conceited.

My father seemed like a typical farmer if you barely knew him. In a lot of ways, I was the same. But I liked to imagine that we weren't so stereotypical on the inside. Maybe it was wishful thinking. Everybody in Little Rush had a bit of country in them, some more than others. I'd say my family was about average.

With this in mind, I rose from my bed and stared out the window. There was a large field of grass in front of our house, stretching out maybe a quarter-mile to the distant road. A chicken coop stood halfway, cheap fencing circling the squat building where those stupid fowl lived. I wasn't sure why we even kept chickens. We never had other farm animals. Never owned any pets. And sure, Mom used the eggs, but those were available at the grocery store just a few miles away. Our house wasn't far from town.

Down the stairs and trudging through the living room, I came to the front door. Every floor in our house was carpeted, save for the kitchen. There were a few fatherly dirt footprints leading down the hallway toward the mudroom. No wonder Mom had been angry. Hopefully I wouldn't have to scrub it clean later.

A brisk walk to the chicken's enclosure ensued, where I just had to scoop out some feed from a large plastic bag. A cup sat in the huge container. The sides felt like they were caked in ashes. I wiped the residue off on my worn jeans and turned away. Standing in the dark shade, I peered around at the small world that enclosed me. Chickens were clucking around my ankles, and the smell of feed and bird shit wafted to my nose.

My eyes snapped to the sun like a magnet to a fridge. Sinking in the distance, it made way for that perfect time of evening. The air chilled, the wind calmed, and the trees were a blend of yellow and green. No longer did stepping outside feel like wading into a sauna. No longer did the air stick to skin like a tight sweater from an estranged aunt. When the sun died off, when darkness fell and coyotes were cackling in the distance, the countryside came alive with shapes and shadows.

I breathed deep and made my way back to the house, all thoughts of chickens and chores gone. Mason would be here in an hour, maybe less, and I needed to shower.

As I reentered the house, I didn't look back over my shoulder, though maybe I should've. The gate swung open, pushed by the breeze, because I hadn't reset the lock. The chickens were already pecking near the opening.

o o o

Mason's sleek, red convertible probably cost five times as much as my ramshackle truck. Acknowledging Willow with a nod, I slid into his backseat and reached for my seatbelt. From the driver's seat, he blew a kiss to my mom, who stood on the porch watching me climb in. She rolled her eyes but blushed all the same before disappearing indoors. Dad had gone into the shower just a few minutes ago, or he probably would've watched me all the way down the driveway.

"I hate when you do that," I said with a touch of annoyance.

Mason glanced at me in the mirror, wearing that stupid grin on his face. "Gotta soften her up for when she finds you passed out 'cause of our drinking."

"Shut up," I murmured but couldn't help a smirk.

Willow, Mason's girlfriend and my other close friend, scrolled through something on her phone. She wore sunglasses and an average outfit for her — long sleeved crop-top and worn jean shorts. Even though she came from a fairly poor family, she always managed to dress stylish. Mason himself wore a Nike tank top, like always, and cargo shorts. I felt a little out of place with my blue jeans and dirty Cincinnati Reds shirt, but I always did around these two. They were like something from a movie, a real star couple. Or at least they had the attitude and bodies for it.

Mason accelerated down the gravel driveway. It wound around my house from the back and then made straight to the road. Trees younger than me were planted on either side, casting long shadows on the yard. The car bounced slightly as he roared through the shaded portion. These maples gave the entrance to our property a nice vibe. It was, truthfully, a real scenic place until you saw our barn and the tractor Dad spent hours fixing, enhancing, tweaking. That piece of trash.

"What'd you get for tonight?" I asked as he turned out of my driveway onto the narrow country roads that mapped my life.

"He got Coors," Willow answered.

"Disgusting," I said. They weren't that bad, but I loved to mess with Mason. "You never get good stuff."

"Shut up. You'll drink them, and you'll like it." He shot me a knowing look in the mirror, again with that cockeyed smirk and stupidly tanned features.

The two of them weren't so helpful for my self-esteem, but friends are friends. His tanned skin in that waning sunlight, dark curly hair, with stunning Willow beside him... I couldn't help noticing how impressively bland I'd become.

Without another word, I settled into the leather seat and leaned my head back. The wind rushed over me, throwing my stringy hair around and into my eyes. I smelled a bonfire somewhere nearby, a homely scent that carries for miles. The trees were golden, the air fresher than it had been all day. Overhead, there were no clouds in sight, just a brilliant, endless ombre of blue-to-orange-to-yellow.

The first week of June in Little Rush is the best time of the year (except for maybe October). In those first seven-to-ten days of June, the entire summer stretched before us like a cornfield beginning to bud. Little green shoots everywhere, and the dirt so soft you could almost sink in it. Each sunset more beautiful than the last, each morning a more refreshing birth. Days outside, nights by a bonfire. The occasional trip to a movie theater or bowling alley.

For teenagers like us, this summer held more promise than maybe any other. We were entering our senior year of high school, which meant we had more freedom than ever before. Everybody had their license by now, most of us knew the taste of beer almost as well as our fathers did, and the girls were the hottest they'd ever been. For someone like Mason, who already had his number-one option, that didn't matter too much. For me, on the other hand, it was a constant thought.

The summer held so much hope. There were kids who couldn't wait to get started in the family business, others who would work at McDonald's their whole life. There were some who might trek off to college and explore all the possible careers waiting for them. They were maybe five years away from a real job, but only one from that slice of perfect independence called university.

And then there were people like me. I had nothing to look forward to. I wouldn't be taking over my father's business because we had none. I refused to follow in his well-trod footsteps, working at the local power-plant and turning hay fields into profit on the side. But I also didn't have the money or motivation for another four years of school. I couldn't stay in this town and work at McDonald's for years. I had nowhere to go. No real assurance that I'd even be alive come next summer.

I thought about my funeral more than was healthy. Especially the people whose tears would moisturize my corpse. Especially the look in their eyes.

o   o   o

The convertible glided to a stop beside an old cabin deep in the woods. The back of it overlooked a small creek, while the front could have been an advertisement for a vacation rental. Mason grinned when he shifted into park and sighed like he always did when we arrived here. It was his father's, but Jedidiah Cooper hardly ever had time for it. According to Mason, he hardly had time for anything but work. This cabin had become our most common drinking location about two years ago, once Mason stole a key to the place. (Technically, it was a gift, but it was also sort of robbery.)

"Haven't been here in months," he said, brightening as he turned to Willow and I in turn. "You guys ready?"

"Don't get all nostalgic already," I said, climbing out of the car and smacking him on the shoulder.

The cabin didn't hold much inside. A large, open floor sitting area with two long sofas and a tiny television. It didn't have cable or anything, but it did have Netflix and Wi-Fi. There was a large bedroom down the hall, a bathroom jutting out from the side. A ladder in the sitting room led to a tiny loft area overhead, complete with a bed that had been there for years. Mason and I spent plenty of nights there as children. Back when his dad didn't work so much, and my parents were happy to let me leave anytime, as long as "Jed's got a close eye on you hooligans."

For us and our potentially disastrous drinking habits, the most enjoyable part of the cabin had nothing to do with inside.

In the back, a spacious, furnished deck overlooked a small forest descent to the creekbed. The porch had chairs for eight people and a large table in the center, all of it wooden and smooth. We could sit there for hours, staring into the depth of trees and listening as the creek gurgled by just out of sight. The oaky smell of that porch grew heavier as the alcohol infused us with a new sense of life and loss of direction. One time, about eight beers in, I'd stumbled down to the creek bed and lounged on the rocks for a while. With my back completely soaked and eyes brighter than the moon overhead, I'd bumbled up the hill again and slept outside on the table.

This memory and many others coursed through me at the sight of the porch. It really had been forever since we'd come here last Halloween. The evening felt crisp now, and the sky had morphed into a pale shade of burgundy.

I helped them unload the trunk of Mason's convertible. Thirty-six cans of beer —even if they were Coors— would be a good time. Along with a bottle of cheap vodka, which confused me for a moment.

"Since when did you drink vodka?" I asked, raising an eyebrow as Mason set it on the table.

He took a seat beside me. "Willow asked for it."

"She doesn't usually go that hard," I commented. The two of us were lounging on the deck, and she'd gone back to the car for something, so I didn't mind the momentary gossip.

"Me either. I'm… curious to see how wild she gets." A smile touched his face, a scheming look with just a bit of lust. I guess it should've dawned on me earlier why Mason wanted her to spend the night here so badly.

Should've brought my ear plugs, I mused. Maybe I'd just sleep on the porch again.

Willow returned from the car and chose a chair across the table from both of us. While Mason and I carried on talking, she extracted a pink shot glass with Bob Ross on the side. Then she grasped the vodka bottle by the neck and unscrewed the cap.

"Did you tell your parents you were staying overnight?" Mason asked, cracking open his first can.

I took a pause before I answered. We ogled as Willow downed three shots in quick succession and an eager look spread over her face. Her body shuddered as the sting hit her, and she winced, laughing. The sound echoed around us for a moment.

I answered Mason's question. "I didn't, but it'll be fine." Taking a drink of my own beer and screwing up my face on purpose, I said, "*Real* high quality stuff, Mason."

"You don't have to drink any," he said, calling my bluff. "I'll save it for myself."

"Whatever. Pass me another, will you?" And with that, I chugged the rest.

The minutes stretched before us. We told stories for a while, memories that we shared. Willow instigated some kind of toast to "the last good summer," a cheesy move but also powerful in its own way. All three of us said, "We need to do this again soon" a few times, each more slurred than the previous repetition. I retold the story of my infamous tattoo, the one I'd given myself in a drunken stupor with a friend's tattoo gun at some house party. That'd been almost a year ago, I realized. The last week before Junior year. Sloppy work, sure, but important to me.

The minutes lagged. It had been an hour, maybe two, when Willow checked her phone. I didn't feel completely gone yet, maybe eight beers in, not yet feeling the last three. Mason, who weighed more than either of us, hadn't even approached his wall yet. Willow had downed maybe five shots altogether, and her eyes were a bit loopy as she read whatever appeared on her screen.

"Oh my god."

I grinned instinctively, because at that point anything made me laugh. I exchanged a glance with Mason, expecting Willow to have some funny video to share. But then she went on.

"You won't believe this. Oh my god. You seriously won't believe this."

She looked up from the phone, wide eyes twinkling. She stared at us both and gripped her phone tight. The screen illuminated her face, gave it an eerie shadow, beautiful and mysterious.

"You gonna elaborate or not?" I asked, head starting to wobble. Or maybe the world was moving and not me.

"You're gonna say I'm lying," she said, taking a deep breath, "but I swear to god it's the truth."

"Jesus Christ, babe." Mason scratched at his head, running a hand down his sharp jawline and slight scruff. "Did someone die?"

"*No*. The opposite."

"Someone… was born?" I chuckled. "Not that big a deal. I'll bet you ten bucks it's a drug-baby if they're from—"

"Don't be mean. Just listen!" she said, tapping on the table. Her fingernails made a strange sound on the wood. Like one of those… those pecking birds. My eyes were drawn to the noise, but she continued. "You both know Bruce Michaels, right?"

"Pshh." Mason leaned back and shot me a grin, rolling his eyes. "Do we *know* Bruce Michaels? You kidding? He's my goddamned religion, he is."

"Never made a bad movie," I interjected, pointing a finger at Mason.

He nodded and pounded on the table. Then he shouted a line from our favorite Bruce movie with the accompanying accent. "Fuck you, rednecks!"

"He's moving here," Willow rolled her eyes. "Next week."

I stopped thinking. Stopped drinking, talking, everything. I just stared at her in disbelief.

"Don't do this to me right now," Mason said, sitting forward now. He shook his head slightly, amused. "Not when I'm drunk. I don't like jokes when—"

"I'm not kidding." She held up the phone, blinding us both with the light. First Mason read and then me. I couldn't stop my jaw from sliding open.

The headline read exactly as she'd said.

EXCLUSIVE: Bruce Michaels To Leave Hollywood! Moving to Nowhere, Indiana!

The short paragraph under it named the town, our town. Little Rush. I didn't even care how they knew. Just that they did. Of course, they might be wrong. We'd know soon enough, but even the possibility...

"But..." I glanced up at them. The air felt cold all of a sudden and my mouth drier than it ever had. Their faces were unresponsive, blurred. I couldn't focus on anything. "But... he's..."

"Fucking Bruce Michaels." Mason put a hand to his forehead and blew a raspberry. "Goddamn... Here? Really here? This isn't some... fake shit?"

"He's done acting then, yeah?" Willow kept moving her eyes between the two of us. She didn't show the appreciation or astonishment this situation called for. "He's... retired?"

"You think my dad'll meet with him?" Mason drummed his knuckles on the table, now full of energy. "I bet he will. What if he comes to my house? Oh my *god*, what if?"

I broke out in a wild, toothy smile at that moment. "What if I have a delivery to his house? He... he eats pizza, I'm sure? I'll get to deliver to him! That's literally insane!"

Willow rolled her eyes, sliding us each another can of beer. "Please get more drunk so we can stop talking about this actor. I shouldn't even have told you two."

"Fucking Bruce Michaels!" I exclaimed one last time, thumping my chest with a fist.

o o o

I had the hangover of a lifetime that next morning, but it didn't really matter. We went through the motions in sluggish silence, Mason and I. Throwing away the cans, checking that we hadn't knocked over anything inside. Willow slept through all of it, but we didn't feel like waking her. The two of us had never been so excited for anything. Ever. She didn't really understand. She didn't quite *get* Bruce Michaels like we did.

"He really retired then," I commented at one interval. We passed by each other, one going toward the trash can and the other away. I carried two empty cans, ants crawling around the lips. "I thought that was just rumors."

"I mean, he's done *everything*," Mason pointed out, walking by me. "He's got nothing left to prove, you know?"

But why here? Why not a nice mansion in Los Angeles? Or a coastal home in Florida? Why Little Rush? A river town in the middle of nowhere, an hour away from any real city. Farms everywhere, a single McDonald's, and our biggest store was an undersized Walmart. The most unique thing about this place? A winding river that made for great pictures but not much else. It's not like anybody ever swam in the Ohio River. If anything, people avoided the water itself and spent their time on the downtown sidewalk that ran alongside it.

"Maybe he wants to farm?" Mason suggested when we'd filled up one trash bag and I was shaking loose another. "Wasn't... wasn't he a farmer in that movie? I think we were in middle school."

"You're right!" I shook my head. I opened up the new bag and its floral scent permeated the air. "Yeah, maybe that's it."

That whole morning passed in a drag. Willow had reported "next week" he'd be here. What did that mean? Today, Saturday, marked the end of a week. So... tomorrow? A literal seven days from now? Somewhere in between? Maybe there'd be warning signs, like streets blocked off, a flood of reporters, other oddities. Old and decrepit Little Rush now buzzing with energy. But for the time being, we could only think of how this change might affect us personally. Forget the town; we wanted a piece of Bruce Michaels for ourselves.

"Can you imagine if we get to meet him?" I asked as the two of us climbed into his convertible an hour later. My skull still suffered from a constant drumbeat, but I managed to ignore it for the most part. Bruce Michaels, the cure for any headache.

Willow remained inside, working on homework, while I took my place in the passenger seat. She'd decided to take a few online college courses this summer, which boggled my mind. As expected, they kept her pretty busy. Mason said she did schoolwork every morning for at least two hours. I didn't even know what she was taking, nor could I relate to that dedication.

Mason planned on dropping me off and then coming back for her, probably for that round of sex he didn't get last night. We'd been too worked up to think of anything like that. The two of us, anyways. I had no idea what Willow thought. She'd acted a bit peeved.

"Would be crazy." Mason swerved out onto the country roads, a mere ten minutes from my house. Tapping his fingers on the steering wheel, a devilish grin broke out on his face. I didn't know what he'd imagined, didn't really care. A feeling welled inside. My own imagination, wild dreams.

"Really would."

o o o

Who would have thought that only twenty minutes later, I'd be kneeling on my bed, staring out the window with crushing despair. Intense ache, somewhere just under my heart, near that sloppy, drunken tattoo I'd given myself a long time ago.

Just take me there, it read.

From the moment Mason had turned onto the gravel driveway, sped between the trees and toward my house, this sensation had been building. The instant I'd seen their carcasses strewn across the yard, white feathers in clumps of bloody meat, I'd known I made a terrible mistake. In the middle of the yard, the gate stood wide open, leading right through the fencing around the chicken's enclosure. Maybe the most important part of my chore, and I'd forgotten entirely.

"Oh shit," I murmured. The convertible rattled past an area of the yard that looked particularly gruesome. "Oh man, I really…"

Mason stared wide-eyed at the brutality in front of us. He gave me a pat on the back as I struggled out of the car with heart racing. I didn't know where this would lead. What kind of punishment would be dealt. How much did a few chickens cost? How many did we even have?

Had, I thought. *Have no longer.*

The door to the house creaked open as I stepped inside, hoping they would be asleep. Maybe enjoying a late-morning nap. Maybe Dad in the barn with the tractor. But no, they were seated at the kitchen table, a phone laying before them and a man's voice droning from the speaker.

"I'll call ya back inna bit," my father said before abruptly hanging up.

Four eyes stared at me. Two different emotions, but neither of them pleased. I shifted uncomfortably, hoping they couldn't smell the alcohol on my breath. That would send them over the edge.

"Stayed out, huh?" my father started, voice choking. Clearly holding back whatever he wanted to say. "But ya... ya couldn't take time to do yer fucking chore right, huh?"

"Henry..." My mom placed a hand on his forearm, but it was no use.

He stood from the table and stepped closer. Towering over me, really. He had the look of a real man, a farmer. Broad shoulders, heavy chest. Thick, coiled arms and tanned skin. His eyes were piercing as I tried not to look away. He'd never hit me before. Would this be the moment?

"Get... get up to your room. Don't let me see your ass down here rest o' the day," he snapped, stalking away into deeper realms of the house.

His massive form disappeared around the doorway. I heard him rummaging in the mudroom, pulling on boots, and then the screen door slammed as he marched outside. His therapy, I supposed. Messing with that tractor.

My mom bowed her head and shuffled past me. Scolding me in a different way.

And so, I slouched to my room and knelt on the bed for a while, staring outside. The AC unit hummed, blowing cold air on my torso, freezing my heart. The room around me felt vacant now. The record collection meant nothing. The cluttered desk, all my posters, deflated basketball. All of it nothing. Just objects that I'd give up in a heartbeat.

For a brief while, I'd escaped this town, if only in my mind. I'd dreamed of stardom, of the fame that would soon settle upon Little Rush and our baking sidewalks. But the truth couldn't have been farther.

Even Bruce Michaels couldn't save this town. I had no clue why he'd ever set foot here. A man who'd done real, important things. Had a life with purpose. Maybe I should've been jealous of that. Maybe I should've hated Bruce Michaels. But I couldn't help adoring him.

My eyes focused on the trees across the road, far from my bedroom window. That forest went on as far as I could see from here, the tops reaching for a blue sky they would never touch. Could never dream of feeling.

I didn't think of myself as a particularly messed up person. No more than your average alcoholic, undiagnosed, self-destructive teen on the verge of adulthood. But when I fell asleep soon after, I dreamed of a large cliff and of myself. In Mason's car. Driving over the edge at ninety miles an hour.

2

WILLOW

If dating Mason taught me one thing, it was that people who admired sunsets were super annoying. They thought every glimmer of the sky deserved applause, like nothing beautiful ever took place on terrestrial earth. Both of the boys were like that, but Hudson even more so. The three of us were alike in a lot of ways, but those two never got over their love for sunsets.

The river struck me as a more beautiful and awe-inspiring sight. Consistent, strong, and dangerous. Unlike the sun, an object we could never aspire to, the river was *right there*. A physical place, shared by generations and people groups, one that we had the privilege of seeing daily. So many people walked by without acknowledging the simplistic and incredible. But then again, you could say the same about Little Rush. If the river was the forgotten treasure of the town, maybe we were the forgotten river of the country.

My relationship with Little Rush was confusing. I loved the town. I admired so many streets and views and places. The memories I had were irreplaceable. The drunken conversations at Mason's cabin. The time I convinced Hudson to try a cigarette. All the trouble I achieved in school, even without those two, and the anxiety leading up to each August. But that summer, right before our senior year, brought so many questions for us. After high school, what then? To stay or to go? Build a life here or pack up everything, catch the first train to anywhere?

The trains didn't run anymore. They hadn't in decades. But it would've been cool, and it made for a nice thought.

It's not like I had some fantastical idea of the town. I grew up in poverty. My parents were divorced, and I almost never saw my younger brother. I got a job at fifteen and walked to it each day for the first year. But even I couldn't ignore the intrinsic beauty found in this forgotten corner of the world. The feeling of a magnet, somewhere under these streets, and each day it pulled just a little harder. Something here wanted me to stay, wanted desperately. There were days I resisted and other times when I didn't.

I find it amusing that for everybody in Little Rush, part of your personality is how you relate to the town itself. As if it's that friend with a bit of a reputation, and what you think of them defines you, too. I guess when put that way, Little Rush is magnetic after all. It's gorgeous, witty, layered, and nuanced. None of which I think about on a daily basis.

No, on a typical day at my dad's apartment, I wake up and glance outside first thing in the morning. Peering through my window, an alleyway, and down two intersections, I can just barely make out the Ohio River. Fog billowing from its surface and covering downtown like a blanket.

A magnet. Just have to give in.

o o o

I opened the convertible door and gathered my backpack. With a heave, I threw it onto my shoulder and bungled out of Mason's car. He watched me wordlessly until I stood on the sidewalk, shifting in place. My eyes were locked on the ground, shoulders hunched, like an ashamed child dropped off at school in the morning. Only this was my home, my dad's apartment, and I shouldn't have been so embarrassed.

"I'll see you," he said, one hand resting on top of the wheel.

I still didn't look up. I didn't want to see the way his eyes lingered on the alleyway, on the buildings all around us. The way his brows would furrow in confusion and he would pull away slowly from the curb. Only a few seconds later would he peel his gaze away from the rundown apartment buildings and the muggy alleyway. It happened every time he dropped me off, and I knew he didn't mean anything by it. Nonetheless, it nagged at me.

"See you."

He revved the engine and started away from the curb. "I love you," he called over the noise.

My chin rose, and I saw him offering a hopeful, empathetic smile. "Love you too," I said, voice dull, before turning away to face the alley. This reality, in contrast to his sleek convertible. My life.

My dad's house was only two streets from the river, but that's important. The first one, directly beside the Ohio and with all these neat lights next to the sidewalk, was really just for tourism and businesses. Few people lived there. More like a place to view the river than an actual road.

The one up from that, First Street, was the "wealthy" section of downtown, if such a thing existed. Those people could see the river from their fourth-floor windows, from their balconies, and really appreciate that postcard-view firsthand.

Second Street, though, was my own, my dad's. Full of alleyways and cheap apartments and the occasional homeless person. A real divide. We could see the river between buildings, if you got the right angle, but not quite feel it. We were the closest you could get in Little Rush to feeling "boxed in."

My mom lived in an affordable housing community up on the hilltop, just off Rush Road. My younger brother lived with her, but I rarely ever saw him. Even when I stayed there, he spent the days in his room or with my mom. I don't know what caused the distance between us, but it continued into his grade school days. I had too many other worries to pay it much thought.

I never liked the hilltop or Rush Road as much as downtown. That was the four-lane road with pretty much everything. The one with McDonald's, Wendy's, the movie theater, the Chinese restaurants, Big O Tires, all that stuff. It eventually led to the Kroger and Walmart, our only *real* stores. The street speckled with billboards and chain restaurants and no sidewalks. Mom preferred that modernized section of Little Rush, much different than downtown, but it's not like she had a great living setup. Those apartments were the cheapest option in town, full of dented cars and disarrayed people. The kind of place that nobody talked about but everyone knew by name. "Liberty Apartments," they'd whisper and grant a side-eyed scowl. My younger brother was too little to know about all that. He didn't quite understand the stigma attached to it, but he would soon enough.

That kid would grow up without a dad, since my mom's ex had left a few years back. He'd be the poor kid, the one whose locker they searched for drugs and whose car broke down once a month. I knew what that felt like, and I hated that things would be the same for him. But one way or another, we all had to adapt, survive.

Each parent had advantages, of course.

At my dad's, there was a little hippie shop nearby that sold sticks of incense, singing bowls, stuff like that. And a chalk sign outside, always real decorative, where somebody wrote amusing or passionate or insightful quotes. I remember a particular one. "Keep believing in the feeling, and you'll be just fine." I always loved that one. It stuck with me for some reason.

My mom's apartment also had benefits. She never cared

where I went or when. She let me do whatever I wanted. And, of course, living in those apartments near Kroger offered so many memories. So many ideas and formative experiences. I'm thankful for my time there. I really am. They were life-changing, and a big part of that is because of her.

I guess that's where the disconnect started between me and Mason. He lived in this real nice house a few miles from my mom's. His whole neighborhood had a kind of sparkle to it. Matching mailboxes all the way down, set in ornate brick formations. Expensive cars anywhere you turned. Lawns so manicured they were irritating. Clearly the sort of place with a homeowners association. And the people living there... Business owners. Regional managers. One or two pastors. The Blough family —whose dad was the only guy with money like Jed Cooper. Pretty sure Mayor Johnson even lived in that neighborhood. Mason Cooper fit in perfectly.

He had a life set up for him. He'd take over his dad's business, probably. Easily. Whereas I... I slaved away my summer with three online courses, two of which were business-focused. I had to work my ass off, climb out of my parents' rut. Not only that, but being a woman and aiming to work in the business world wasn't exactly... ideal. I had nothing set up for me. Not a single step. My future was a wild jungle, and I had nothing to cut through it apart from my own self-taught skills.

Mason's neighborhood looked down on those living at Liberty Apartments. On "poor." And yet I felt like the people at Liberty had certain characteristics those people didn't. Some they passed on to me. Toughness. Integrity. I didn't know if it was a conscious thing or just the way we all filled our roles. But some of the conversations I had... It's undeniable that those in Liberty had just as much potential, just as much "talent," as those with all the money. Only they could get help for things like addiction or debt, and we couldn't.

Again, I didn't think about any of this on a daily basis. And yet when I did, when I got sucked into that black hole of spiraling thought and self-doubt, I couldn't help but compare Mason's situation to my own. Especially to the times when we lived at Liberty. Back then, I walked everywhere. That sidewalk between our apartment and Kroger set the scene for most of my pre-high school memories.

Like the kind, old black guy who always rode his bike to Kroger and back, one hand holding groceries and the other steering in wild movements. He always grinned at me and my friends, even threw us packs of unopened gum sometimes. He had this crazy look in his eyes that *now* I'm pretty sure was drugs, but back then I thought he just loved his life. I never learned his name, though. Not sure I ever had a conversation with him. Two or three dozen times, he threw us bubblegum. I loved that about him. There weren't many black people around town, and I do wish I could've talked with him, just once. But in hindsight, I'm glad I never knew his name. It would've made what came next even worse.

The day he swerved into the road and flew into the air. His bike a twisted mess, his body lifeless on the ground. A pool of blood. I remember those details. Remember feeling intense pain in my stomach. The horrible coincidence that I'd been walking by. And then nothing more.

I often wondered what that man would've become, if only he got the necessary help. Such a genuinely good person, held captive by some surface-level addiction. I would've liked to be friends with him. Wished I could help.

Mason and even Hudson didn't understand. They never would. The former was a rich boy, though I didn't hate him for it. I honestly loved him. And the latter was a farm boy. Not rich by any means, but he didn't go hungry at night. He had a job because he wanted one, not out of necessity. I started working when I got tired of a grumbling stomach keeping me awake.

They had families in Little Rush. Roots. A history. I had nothing.

They never walked beside a field of knee-high grass, trudging two miles in triple-digit heat just to buy that night's dinner. And they never had to choose their food methodically because when food stamps is the menu, picky isn't an option. They didn't form integral, childhood friendships that ended when that middle-schooler went to juvie or died from lack of health insurance. I wanted to leave town more than anything. I wanted to find a place where I could make a better life, where I could have a better home. Somewhere out there, I wanted to go. I just didn't know where yet.

Everybody had reasons for wanting to leave Little Rush. The thing is, most people also had something holding them down. For me, I had nothing. Except for Mason and the town's magnetic pull.

I'd never been one to give up my dreams or my style or my beliefs just to appease somebody else. I didn't conform. It was something I promised myself time and time again. But it's difficult, I guess, when it's somebody you love. That conversation is harder to have.

Swimming with an anchor chained to your leg is no fun. Especially when the tide is rising. And god dammit, that thing rises fast entering senior year.

Just believe, I told myself as Mason's car disappeared around a corner. I glanced in the other direction, toward the hippie shop, and wondered what the sign said today. *Just believe.* I stood on the sidewalk, beside the mouth of an alleyway. Halfway down, a rusted door, then a staircase, then my dad. *Keep believing in the feeling and you'll be just fine.*

3
JED

We thought of Little Rush as home, as the place we would grow and marry and raise children and die. We thought of it as the town which had everything, just enough of it. I still remember the night Lucy and I went on our first date. The downtown road illuminated by streetlights, her gorgeous, 80's style hair. She could've been a model, I swore it then and always would. Back then, in simpler times, we could just enjoy the city. We didn't have to think about leaving versus staying or about the way our children would rattle the caged walls of this old town.

Mason and his friends weren't what you'd call perfect kids. They were wild. They drank, they got in trouble, they ran around late at night doing god-knows-what. But all of that... I expected it. I could relate to it, understand in a way. The part that I couldn't quite get, the part that really drove a wedge between my son and I... The way his eyes locked on every sun setting behind every dilapidated barn, as if they were clues to a mystery I didn't know of.

Business consumed me, and yet I could never pull away. Because of it, I didn't see as much of him as I wanted. And when I did, he was standoffish, uncomfortable, vacant. He felt trapped, by Little Rush and by our family business. He didn't say it, wouldn't admit to me that he did, but I could tell. And I had absolutely no clue what to do about it.

This inability caused me great distress. In every other area of my life, I didn't have this… mental block. In business, I could get shit done. More than anyone else in this town, save for maybe Blough, I could honestly call myself a self-made man. I practically built this house, started this family. They depended on me, and I never let them down. Perhaps that's why I found work so… relieving. It was my comfortable place, an area I excelled at and knew it. The whole town did.

This little town, without a spark for so many years… and then such electric news? Bruce Michaels. The famous, the self-aggrandizing, the hardened vet of Hollywood's battlefront. From LA to Nowhere, Indiana, the headlines read. And sure enough, Tim called me not long after to confirm the news. As the mayor, I expected him to have more info. But, alas, no luck. Nobody knew why or when, only that it *would* happen. Bruce Michaels, larger than life itself, had sold his mansion and chosen Little Rush as his new home. What a mess it caused me.

An onslaught of messages began with my elbows resting on a pile five-papers deep. Static from an old radio near my ear lulled me into a daydream. The pen fell from my hand, landed next to my buzzing cell phone. Text after text. Person after person. Even at my home office, I couldn't escape them.

    #: Have you heard?
    #: This is huge news! For everyone!
    #: Ad deal?!?!?
    #: Where's he moving? One of YOUR properties???

Sometimes, I wished I had never bought that first restaurant. A pizza restaurant. That's all. And now… this.

Don't get me wrong. I worked for everything I owned, worked hard, in fact. A fairly large house, a cabin on the Rush Creek, three really nice cars. The ability to retire in another six or seven years. My money— I earned it right here, in Little Rush. I owned four restaurants, including the best pizza place for miles around. It had this weird half-pizza sticking out from the roof, something like twenty feet wide. It was enormous and that really brought people in, I guess. Once that business brought in some cash flow, I invested in properties at first. If the pizza restaurant was my first genius move, my second had to be the stocks.

A good friend of mine, owner of a local bank company, got bought out by a larger organization. He told me ahead of time, just enough for me to throw myself all-in on the stock market. It went better than even I expected. That local bank, one of the few traded on the NYSE, boomed soon after. I had the intuition and the gumption to invest everything into it. Idiotic amounts… and it erupted from there. All of a sudden, I had more money than I knew what to do with. A normal man would stop there. Only I doubled down, and so my fortune is different.

Real estate, apartments, properties. That was the only way to build up real wealth in a town like Little Rush. I had no doubt that in one of the bigger cities, my net worth would be laughed out of the building. Not here. I had over a hundred properties now. The four restaurants might be my public front, but they were pennies compared to what I've achieved.

And it's not like I'm a stingy bastard. I donated money to the local high school, to kindergarten tee-ball teams, to local business ventures, to charities, to the downtown food bank. But maybe it wasn't enough, and maybe it wasn't worth it.

Day after day, hour after hour, I poured over documents. I spent most of the week and a lot of the weekends buried in paperwork, phone calls, emails. My home office flooded with binders full of plans, scrap sheets of ideas, to-do lists, phone numbers to call. This work, my comfortable process. A to-do list that never ended, nor did I want it to. In a home I felt quite proud of, this office was my only real safe place. Outside, there were relationships, emotional cues, gray areas. In here, numbers, black and white, profits. A lifetime of work gone by, and yet another lifetime ahead. The chair worn down by the shape of my body. A small radio next to my desk, where I'd often have the weather or the local news. Sometimes it just emitted a low tune from the local music station. I let it play. Just to stay connected. Just to feel like a part of Little Rush.

All the money I made, I funneled right back to that complicated city. And what a city it was.

Little Rush. A beautiful mess of contradictions. For somebody like me, who lived here so many years and saw the city way back in the 80's, I could appreciate it more than Mason or any of his friends. By the time I realized what the empty factories meant and the way the landscape was shifting, all that remained of peak Little Rush was stories.

The old folks at the breakfast grill were eager to tell them. The men who sat with my father, late into the night, were desperate to share their tales. Like an ancient language, the last of a dying culture were relentless in explaining, in passing on, in preserving what they knew. To his credit, my father always listened, always lit their cigars, and another and another until the hours burned into nothing but ash. The city, nothing but ash.

Those old folks told him stories, and through him, they told me. Stories of a town where the factories weren't empty and the railroads were active, even bustling. They'd been reduced to scars on the land now. Vacant tracks that teenagers roamed, smoking and drinking and everything else. I did it too. I was just as wild. But I saw those railroad tracks in a different light as age gnawed at my bones. They were nearly holy, and me their reverential patron.

The factories were almost all decrepit. Around them, the lawns grew tall, and their walls were barren, sun-bleached, fading. On the hilltop, they could blend in with the wild landscape. Up there, the modern stores and restaurants and churches were built among the ruins of that old town. Abandoned factories are easier to ignore when they're just a blip on the side of a road, and beyond them more fields anyways. But in downtown Little Rush, the factories were unavoidable.

They filled blocks at a time. Broken windows, leaning doors, missing bricks. So much of downtown had been preserved, those buildings were right at home, in a sense. The architecture mixed well with the surrounding streets. The walls were the same, sidewalks beside them untouched and cracked. You could almost picture it. Workers that filled those buildings, dripped sweat in them, slaved away their lives in them, even stepping on those same sidewalks as me. It all blended together, times and places and stories. Only, the factories were forgotten. They served no purpose but for the teenagers to run wild in. A sort of modern wilderness, you might say.

Every once in a while, somebody came along, sure. Some out-of-towner who bought up the place and fixed it, transformed it. They were turned into nursing homes or business centers or even a factory once again. But those moments, those victories, were few and far between. There was no point in razing the buildings, either. And no point in leaving them up. They were ghosts, and also the ghost town. Life bubbled around them, in Little Rush, but it was something like large stones in a creek. Water gushes around, against, and over. The stones are unmoved, stepping stones for the gods. And for teenagers in the forest.

My phone buzzed again. I ran two hands over my face and took a deep breath, trying to focus. Deep breaths. The memories faded of that lost city and of my father. Both of them buried nearby. And based on his lifespan, who knew how long until I'd join them?

I lowered my eyes to the screen, saw the text. The name didn't matter. Just another name. Another adult, struggling with their bills and kids, who worked under me... and was probably a better person.

#: By the cemetery? Are you KIDDING me???? Why not that new house near the river??

A grin spread across my face, almost against my wishes. They were all so... excitable. Old enough to understand the magnitude of the news. Young enough to feel that energy coursing through their bones. But I knew better. I knew about Little Rush, more than they could.

Maybe Bruce Michaels is a big deal, at least for now. And he will be for a few weeks, maybe even a few months. I told myself that and knew it was true. With time, though, even the brightest of stars would fade in this empty sky of a town. He would move out or he would stay, but either way, he'd be forgotten.

I had to ponder the question though. I couldn't help it. The eccentricity of the decision... Fascinating.

Why *did* he buy the house near the cemetery? I could guess the answer. It was far from the river. Far from Main Street and the courthouse. Far enough from Rush Road, the lifeblood of the hilltop. Way out there, that field of gravestones is lonely. That entire area on the edge of the city limits. Like a distant galaxy yet to be colonized. And his star moved toward that blank stretch of sky, away from the other constellations. To be alone. *Maybe that's the point.*

I returned my attention to the to-do list and the pen that I'd dropped. Despite my childlike wonder, it would be irresponsible not to capitalize on this surge of attention. This town would get a boost, alright. I needed an ad campaign with Bruce, something to bump up business another notch. I also needed a few well-timed posts, a tweet, something that *might* go viral. And merchandise. Shirts with Bruce and with my restaurants. Lots and lots of shirts.

Before any of this, I'd have to meet with him. Ideally, Bruce would stop by for dinner one night, and we wouldn't make a big deal of it. Just a quiet, home-cooked meal. Isn't that what he wanted here?

To achieve this goal, I direct-messaged his Twitter account as soon as the news broke. (I already followed him, but then again who didn't?) Three times that week, I sent him a short, brief explanation of my role in the community and my intentions for meeting him. None of them were even opened, so I gave up. Over the next few days, I resigned myself to an in-person introduction as soon as I got the chance. Not that it stopped me from checking Twitter, praying for an update.

"When's he moving in?" Lucy asked me one day from her recliner in the living room. Her interest was genuine but also nonchalant.

She didn't quite understand how important this whole deal was to me. Even after years of marriage, decades even, she hadn't taken much interest in the business side of our life. I didn't blame her. In fact, I admired it. To enjoy Little Rush as a town without one eye always on the factories, on the railroads… That would be sublime. Lucy could look at the river and see a postcard, as it was meant to be. I would, from the same view, see a forgotten industry, a source of income that had dried. The rising, falling demons of Little Rush.

"Nobody knows," I recited the answer I'd given dozens of people already. "Whenever he wants."

"How does no one know?" she asked skeptically, setting down her cup of morning coffee. She leaned back in her recliner and stared at the ceiling. "What about his real estate agent? Or Mayor Johnson?"

I shrugged my shoulders, kept my eyes fixed on the television that cycled through the same news. "Nobody. Guess we'll have to wait and see."

o o o

My fingers tapped away on the pure screen of my iPhone. I felt Lucy's eyes across the dinner table, glaring at me. Mason's chair, to my immediate right, squeaked a bit as he reclined. They were both looking at me now, without a doubt. The dining room set so nicely, a real piece of work. Better than your average weekday. A chilled bottle of wine on the counter. And yet I slouched there, on my phone, typing away like some teenage girl who won't get off a screen.

"Jedidiah."

I always hated when she used my full first name, but she already knew that.

The dinner was nice enough. It's not that I hadn't wanted it. I just hadn't had *time*. Right when I'd taken a break from "work stuff" (as I described to them) and called for us to eat the delicious meal, Henry started texting me. The poor guy never picked a great time for phone conversations. At least he knew how to text now. That was improvement from three years ago.

"Jedidiah," she said again, my wife's tone a bit more terse.

"Sorry, sorry." I finished the sentence I was texting and glanced up. "Henry. You know."

She rolled her eyes. Mason shifted next to me, ate a cooked carrot from his fork with overly lazy movements. I guess this meant he didn't want to sit any longer. Then again, neither did I.

H: Guys at the plant today were crazy bout the news.

I chuckled at Henry's response. I never understood how he did it. Working forty-plus hour weeks at the power-plant, along with those fields where he grew that particular grass that turned into hay when you cut it. I never understood his farming, not how he had time for it or even the process. The guy was an animal, absolute hog. One of the best men I'd ever known, truly. Great wife, great kid, great house. Just a *great* guy.

H: Been meaning to ask. Chickens got ate few days ago. can I borrow 100 bucks from you? need to buy new ones, new fence. maybe another chunk $ for tractor part?

When I read that message, I powered off my phone and stuck it in my pocket. Henry didn't often ask for money, not unless things were really bad out at the farm. My eyes lifted to find Lucy glaring outright in my direction. I tried to play it off with a simple smirk and shrug, but no use. She didn't shake her head in disgust, but she might as well have.

"So..." I cleared my throat, glancing around, checking Mason's expression without being too obvious. He didn't look angry or even annoyed. Just apathetic. Maybe that was worse. "How's... your guys' day been?"

"You would know if you ever left your office," Lucy said through her gritted teeth, eating a sliver of steak from her fork. She chewed it the way she wanted to chew me out, barely holding back vitriol.

I turned to Mason, saw him slouching. He had the same dark hair I had at his age, with short curls that accentuated his best features. Sharp jawline, bright eyes. I used to be like that. I used to look almost the same, minus the abs. But I'd lost touch with that version of myself and with him.

"How's..." *How did I forget her name?* I cleared my throat, held up a hand. "Sorry. Um. How's... Willow?"

He didn't recoil. I'd gotten the name right, at least.

"Fine."

"You two... keeping everything wrapped up?" I tried to smirk, give him a little nudge to play off my terrible joke.

His nose wrinkled, and he stared at me like a wild coyote when you try to pet it. Wanting to fight. Wanting to run away. Wanting to have never come down this trail.

"Can I go, Mom?" he asked at last, giving me the side of his face. Not even a glance.

"Of course, hun."

He marched to the sink, dropped his plate in, and disappeared toward his room. Not a single word to me. Not even a look. Probably off to text Willow right then, tell her what an ass I'd made of myself. What a stupid thing to say to him. Not even remotely funny.

"Why'd you do that?" Lucy asked. She leaned on the table, elbow propped against the surface, chin resting on her palm. Her eyes were pitying. I hated that. "Are you really an idiot?"

I wondered the same as I cleared the table after dinner and washed the dishes. Dreaming of my to-do list, with new boxes to check each hour. The lights around our immaculate house popped out one by one. Lucy turned them off on her way to bed. Mason was already asleep or at least in his room, pitch darkness. I didn't even dream of barging in. Not once.

She fell asleep without me that night. I stood at the window for a while, looking out over the neighborhood. Not far from our house, it turned onto the four-lane road and McDonald's. Some real shops. But here, a mile from Little Rush, we lived in the "rich people's neighborhood." That's all I'd become. The rich man who had nobody. Nobody but his money.

What was that Beatles song? Something about money and love. I tried to hum it as I dropped into my favorite recliner. Cost me almost two grand, that damn chair. But I still couldn't remember the words.

4

LITTLE RUSH
THE REPORTER

She slunk out of the restaurant, cell phone at the ready. Standing on the sidewalk, she glanced in either direction at the downtown landscape. Her hair was pulled back tight, and she wore sleek glasses. Among people like this, she stood out in every way. The streetlights were dazzling, marking large, bright circles on the sidewalk. There were stragglers passing by in either direction, mostly couples and groups of shopping-women, as she referred to them.

Without a word, Gina snapped a few pictures with her phone, just to document it all. *This town is adorable,* she decided. A cute little place. The view of Main Street was really something. Little shops all along the edge, some vacant ones where dreams had died and "For Rent" signs were the only tombstone. Her eyes wandered over the scene, taking in every block, tongue against her lips. The air was so fresh, so much different than the city. Any city.

A car roared past, honked wildly, and a man yelled something at her. Obscene, without a doubt. But then again, she was wearing a knee-length skirt in a rural Indiana town. It's not like these people were *civilized*. She could take care of herself here. If any of them dared touch her, she'd make sure they regretted it. You can't just do that to a woman, not one with power. She'd make them pay.

Gina walked with no destination, toward City Hall in the distance, because she might as well stretch her legs on a gorgeous night like this. As she passed small groups, some of them giggling, she tried to throw back her shoulders and keep her head up. There was something intimidating about these small-town people, more than those in huge cities. At least in New York, everything blurred together, all the faces and noises and smells. But here, each one was distinct, each one noticeable, and the people far too familiar.

"Another one," a teenage boy chuckled as he strolled past, pretty girl on his arm. "Dumbass paparazzi."

And then a man approached her, clearly drunk from thirty feet away. His hair was balding, ears were extremely red. He had a gut but also those farmer-arms, the kind of peculiar strength and body ratio that comes with long days of manual labor. He licked his lips. The reporter stopped moving, crossed her arms.

"Hello, pretty lil' lady," he said, sticking out a hand for her to shake. "How's the"

"Nope." Gina tried to brush past him, but he shifted in front of her. "I said no," she repeated, this time with force.

"Wha's such a pretty lil' lady as yourself doin' alone?" He smiled, and it was repulsive. So much green where there should've been white. "You're in needa lil' company, sure?"

"Listen." Gina took a deep breath, brushing a loose strand of hair behind her ear. Adjusting her glasses, recrossing her arms. "Just don't. I've slept with women who would send you spinning with just their feet. 'K? So get out."

Right on cue, a patrol car turned onto Main Street and drifted by them. The officer in question never even turned, but the mere sight of him was enough to de-escalate. The man in front of her glared for a moment, opened his mouth to say something, but then turned his back. He shuffled away after that, a wounded dog. She watched him for a moment, rolling her eyes. If this became a nightly occurrence, she'd just stay indoors.

Abandoning her stroll down Main Street, Gina returned to her apartment building. It was a bit sketchy, a second-floor place with a staircase to reach it. The door was in an alleyway that smelled like dead rats. But it was something. All the hotels were booked. All the "dumbass paparazzi" moved in a few days ago. But she waited, didn't rush, because she didn't need a hotel.

The apartment was a minimum three-month rent, and her cabinets were stocked with cheap noodles and canned foods. She'd fade to sleep each night watching the local news coverage. Waiting for her phone to blow up with any news of Bruce. The rest of the reporters and journalists were in the same boat, but she was different. She'd rented an apartment. She planned on being here for a while.

This is it, she had told herself as soon as the headline bounced around her Twitter feed. Bruce Michaels moving to Little Rush, Indiana. What a bizarre move. Everybody wanted to know why, but nobody could ask the right questions. Nobody had the right sources.

This is it. My big break.

Gina had something none of those other people had. Not the national ones, not the locals. None of them.

She had potential. She had character. And she knew where to dig for dirt.

5
BRUCE

The town wasn't what I remembered. I guess that makes sense. The streets were the same, in a way, and most of the buildings. But there was something off about it, foreign. Like an old song rediscovered after years away. I knew all the words, still, and every guitar strum. But it felt different, because I had changed, though it remained the same.

Those memories were all foggy. The scenes that danced around the edges of my mind, from that summer here so long ago. Warmer days. Everything felt bigger then. All the streets now seemed thinner, the buildings less monstrous. The memories of a child, muddying my mind.

I couldn't be sure about Little Rush. Couldn't be sure about anything, really.

As I stepped into the tiny house, my back to the winding road that brought me here, I took a deep breath and tried to taste it. The atmosphere, the essence. This musty home smelled like mildew, probably drifting up from the crawlspace. It clung to me like a haunting, followed me as I stepped across the groaning floors and through the echoey hallways.

The carpet underfoot was an ugly red color, and I enjoyed it. The walls were barren. Dead flies covered the windowsills in each room. My eyes wandered as I walked around, as if stepping through a time portal. Everything exactly as it had been. The sitting room held an ancient-looking couch that faced the door and a small television to the side. The kitchen was past that through an opening. I remembered it well. To my right, a conjoined bathroom and bedroom. This was my entire world. I would live out my final days here, just like him.

This is what I need.

I stood in the sitting room for a while, waiting for something, anything. I could hear them outside, sitting in their cars, others crawling on the ground like flies to rotting fruit. The reporters, the cameras, the journalists. They were the bane of my existence. They were the darkness that I could never outrun. A part of it, at least.

After a while, I hobbled to that sagging couch and grabbed the remote. When the television flickered on, I met my own face. The local news channel. I grimaced, turned away. It was that old clip they played so often— from a few years ago.

"I really love it here," the electronic me said, voice barely audible over the thrum of bass guitars and crowds cheering. We were back-stage at one of those music festivals over in California. All these summers later, I couldn't remember which one. There had been so many. "I can't see myself ever leaving. Cali's where it's at!"

I muted the television and left the room. What a difference time could make.

When I entered the kitchen, I stared out the window and observed my property. Not technically mine, but close enough. The only house for a mile in either direction. The only living soul, and yet surrounded.

This house —my house— sat next to a cemetery. There were dozens of rows, almost a hundred tombstones. All shapes and sizes. Crosses, squares, curved tops. Loose, baking grass strewn across the face of some from yesterday's mow. I wouldn't have to do that work, at least. I didn't have to care for this land. Just occupy it.

Maybe I would take a walk that evening, once the flies outside had flown. I would read each name and think about that lost being. Make special note of any tombstones with quotes and ponder what my own would be. It could be anything, really. Anything except for one of my movie quotes, one of those films.

Incredible how I could sum up my entire career with "those films." A stint in Hollywood lasting decades; countless awards and appearances. So many women and directors and co-stars.

People always clap for the wrong scenes, the wrong lines. They didn't understand. This... this was important. This was my greatest role, my greatest scene. I'd never done something like this, so impulsive and brash. Giving away all of *that* in search of something *here*.

I was going to find it. I wouldn't leave here in vain. This town would be the final set. I wanted to integrate myself, become a vital part of it. Observe them in their daily life, become one of them even. The fans in California... I'd grown bitter toward them. Those people... they'd buy bottles of my piss if I sold it. But here, in Indiana, I could find hard-working families, true innocence and integrity. And maybe, just maybe, I could learn from them.

The afternoon faded outside my window as I rested on that dilapidated couch. With each breath, I drank in the mildew home and grew more assured that I'd done the right thing. My ears overflowed with a television show, accompanied by an irritating laugh track. I hated television. I hated movies. I wanted the opposite of that.

My only relief was the photograph sitting in front of me on the dining room table. The image that stared back at me, a peacefulness I longed for each and every moment. The most important thing in my house.

Dinner was nothing. I wasn't hungry. My gaze wandered to that graveyard every so often, and I longed to run my fingertips over the rough stones. To leave this near-empty house. I purposefully wanted it like this. The moving crew did exactly what I'd said. A sparsely furnished dwelling, everything as I remembered. From that summer so long ago.

And one of the idiots left a note on my counter. I felt like I'd paid them enough to leave me alone. They moved all my stuff fine. *Now leave me alone.*

The note read: *So happy to have you here, Mr. Michaels. You'll love Little Rush!*

As soon as I found the note, I had touched the tip with my lighter and watched it curl into a blackened heap.

o   o   o

I woke up hurting that next morning, bad. When I came to, I found myself on that old couch, the world swimming around me. Sunlight streaming through a crack in the curtains, setting fire to my eyes. I groaned, rolled over, but sleep danced away as I pulled the blanket over my aching corpse.

Must have been drinking last night.

At this point, I didn't even enjoy it. I should've tried pills, honestly. Something to shut off my brain but without the hangover effects. Up to ten years left on this rotten ground — I didn't want to spend them all with a throbbing headache and aversion to sunlight.

I needed to explore. It was my first day here. Whatever the future would bring, I had to make the most of this chance. Run some red lights. Flip off people. I already knew the way things would go here. I could break any law. I could probably kill someone, and nobody would touch me.

I'll consider it.

Maybe I'd go for a walk. Just through the forest. Feel that

underbrush again, run my palms over the bark. The trees had grown so much since that summer here. I wondered if the old path still ran nearby.

When I sat up, though, I caught a glimpse out the window. I fell onto my back, defeated. The paparazzi. It would be impossible to leave, at least until night.

I had fragments of memory from the night before, long after I'd been drunk. I could remember the door opening and shutting. Had I gone out to the cemetery before? Had I seen those names and —more importantly— his?

I felt bile rising in my throat. Another nasty effect of the bottle. I didn't *want* to be an alcoholic anymore, but, at this point, what difference did it make? Maybe it would help having locals to drink with, if only I could find some.

6
HUDSON

I knew I shouldn't think all this. There was nothing truly wrong with my life. I wasn't oppressed, I wasn't poor, I wasn't stressed. If anything, I had the most normal, complacent, comfortable existence possible for a teenager in Little Rush. And yet there were days when I'd wake up and whisper, "Today, I'm gonna do it. I'm gonna kill myself."

A cruel twist of fate that on a day meant to honor my father, I spent every moment possible away from him. Each one more painful, each one pushing me closer to the edge.

Father's Day passed in an unimportant manner, but at least I wasn't alone. Mason texted me that night and said Jed had sulked around the house all day and been in his study all afternoon. In other words, it didn't pass very well at the Cooper household. From what he told me, Jedidiah didn't seem like a great guy, but then again, what did I know. It wasn't like my father and I were on the best of terms.

Dad had the day off from his real job at the power-plant, given that it was a weekend. But of course, he couldn't *not* be working. Most people saw it as an admirable personality trait. I had to disagree. It was irritating to watch him drive that tractor late into the evenings. Mowing down those seas of wavy, waist-high grass, his tractor churning in perfect paths, a large arm sticking out from the back where a complicated mower slaughtered everything in its way. He'd called it a drumming mower, but I didn't know the significance. For a few days after he cut the grass, he would tinker with the tractor, spend more time inside, or just longer shifts at work. And then for a day, he'd spend every waking minute driving the tractor again, this time with an attached baler, dropping these huge cylinders of hay in his wake. Our property would be covered with them, round bales that dotted the landscape. All of it unsettlingly different from just a week prior.

When I was a little kid, my father would move all the cylinders close together, and I'd jump across them, run around them, as if exploring a new city I'd discovered. Then I got too old for that stuff. Maybe for excitement altogether. Older, more isolated, and more self-centered, even if I struggled to admit that last one.

Those circular bales sat for another day or two in the barren fields. Meanwhile, I'd be forced to help Dad as he drove a different kind of baler and a long trailer on the back. We would churn out around two-hundred square bales in one evening. These came from a different field, sectioned off by fencing. That was usually the extent of my work with him, and we rarely spoke. He would drive; I would grab the square bales and throw them onto the trailer where I stood. I'd gotten good at it over the years. Didn't need much help. My hands burned like hell each time, though, and I'd have blisters for a few days. I guess it was better than sitting inside, watching him. For at least that one day, I'd feel a kind of connection. Us working together, sweating in that godawful sun until it sank and our slickened arms froze in the evening winds. Those sunsets truly were amazing. And watching the land transform as we worked… awe-inspiring.

That particular summer, though, Father's Day was a round-bale kind of day. When I sluggishly descended the stairs around eleven, he'd already been on the tractor for at least three hours.

He didn't come in until dinner, a quicker-than-usual meal, and then disappeared outside once again. I wasn't sure what Mom did all that day. Maybe she didn't mind as much. To me, Father's Day had always been about me and him, our connection with all its frayed wiring. I expected him to go out of his way, make time for me. Perhaps I should've done so for him. Instead, I kept to myself and pounded my head with music to drone out the roaring sounds of farm equipment.

That day, I wished for sickness. A fever or something. That always made me sleep better. I used to have a bottle of vodka in the bottom drawer of my desk. Also would've done the trick. Problem was, I'd finished it a few weeks ago and never bothered asking Mason to hook me up with more.

My mind refused to stop working, kept grinding away at what little sanity remained. As my father cut down his fields of grass outside, I felt like somebody else had taken a tractor inside my brain and done the same. My glass panes were cracking as I lay in my bed and stared at the dull ceiling overhead. Watched the fan whipping around, shaking just a bit. I could almost hear it, almost, but the music overwhelmed me. I started to feel like I'd jumped into an ocean. Like I was drowning underneath that pale light, in my own comfortable bed.

There's nothing wrong with you, I chide myself. It was the truth. My parents weren't divorced. I had a nice house, big yard. I rose each morning to a warm sun and lay down to a chilled moon. I had two close friends, hung out at Mason's cabin, drank pretty much anytime I wanted. Sure, I wanted to leave. I was desperate to. But for Little Rush, my life was pretty much perfect.

So why did I hear it? The blaring train horn as it closed the distance between us.

Some days, I felt terrified of death. Anytime I drove at night, I'd be scared of cresting one of those narrow, country hills to find myself in a head-on collision that did the trick. But then I'd get home, and I'd wrap myself in the darkness of my room. And then I'd imagine death and how it fit me like a tailored suit. If only I had the balls. If only I knew a painless way to do it.

If there were a button, I would've pushed it. I guess if that were the case, a lot of us would be gone. Things that used to be fun were just annoyances, and things that were annoying made me feel insignificant. There was nothing I could change, nothing broken I could fix. And so, I lay in bed for hours, drowning and blind, swallowed each day by the weight of invasive normalcy.

On Father's Day, all of this happened per usual. I thought a lot about heroes. That's what the day honors, right? And I realized that the old saying was a lie. We weren't the heroes of our stories. Most of us couldn't even pretend that. Instead, we were victims of every tale we told. It vindicated our worst actions and gave more meaning to our good deeds. Because all of us, we never did anything worth shit.

I was the victim of my own story. I had been assaulted by an average life, and I was aware of it. This fact, instead of comforting me, only made the hatred inside bubble to a spilling point. It only made me burn.

While my father worked in the fields and my mom worried about family-stuff, house-stuff, bill-stuff, I laid in my room like an entitled piece of shit and felt overwhelmed in a Queen-sized bed. I realized that I hated myself.

The town was a cage around me. I would feel better if only I could leave. I was somewhat sure of it.

Somewhere out there was a better place, an existence that suited me. For now, the only thing about Little Rush I respected was the town's complete apathy. Maybe the town reminded me too much of myself. Insignificant. Damaged. The all-consuming blanket of undiagnosed depression. I wanted something more than that. No, I *needed* something more. Because if I stayed, Little Rush was gonna kill me.

7
WILLOW

I guess the only thing we really had was that river. The water almost never made for bad scenery, as it reflected the deep greens of the rolling hills on either bank. The bridge, too, was especially photogenic. Even the power-plant, downstream a bit, seemed to entice people's cameras.

Standing on the brick sidewalk, which ran along the riverfront for about a mile, Little Rush was a blissful place. The little street lights that ran next to the sidewalk at night, the beautiful darkness of the water. All of it worked to distract from some of the grimmer realities downtown held. The poverty, the shops closing, the crumbling buildings. I loved downtown, honestly, but for somebody like me... it was hard to not look past the river and see all the issues. Maybe I should've ignored it, but there's a difference between people who live with rats and flies in their house and those who don't.

Though on days like this, I did my best to look away. There were times when I just tried to soak in the energy around me, the perfect parts of Little Rush that deserved admiration.

The three of us were crouched deep in the trees, far enough that nobody on the outside could see us or the cigarettes we held. I took a seat on the huge log that we usually ended up at, while the two boys stood and continued talking. In the distance ahead of us, I could see the old baseball field and the hill behind it. This scene had become so familiar to me that at times I forgot to appreciate it.

This place held a rustic charm. The baseball field was still usable, thanks to decent upkeep, but nobody ever took advantage of it for that sport. You could follow a little staircase up the hill behind it and reach a tiny gazebo, with walkways branching out in all directions. This little park became ten times as beautiful in the fall when leaves were resting on the ground and the colors were vibrant, but just as before nobody seemed to travel here. Occasional dog-walkers or runners would traverse those stone paths. For the most part, people kept away from this area. Which made it ideal for smoking, especially down in the forest. I suppose living downtown had its perks, since I knew about all the cool locales such as this.

"At least it doesn't smell like sewage here today, right?"

Mason turned to face me, grinning. He was trying harder than usual with me today. He had a cut-off on, shorts that were tighter than usual. We made eye contact. I grinned, a little fake, but it was fine. His eyes dropped to my lips, to my boobs. Didn't matter what I wore, I guess. I was in a baggy sweatshirt with the sleeves rolled up. I mean, come on. But he always glanced. Usually smacked my butt, too. I didn't mind often, and it was playful, cute. Sometimes a bit much, though. He wasn't getting sex that night either way. Just not on my to-do list. Not to mention the loads of homework I'd been putting off from the college courses.

He didn't notice, but I rolled my eyes. Took another drag from my cigarette. Sometimes I hated boys, even my boyfriend. It felt like every time we hung out, the three of us, we were just sitting somewhere either drinking or smoking. Was this all we had around here? A long game of waiting?

"How was your Father's Day?" Mason asked, focused on

Hudson again. "I usually hate Mondays, but this is *way* better than yesterday, at least."

They traded stories about their awful experiences, not bothering to ask me. I wasn't surprised. They always thought of it as a "Son's and Father's Day," it seemed. They didn't always remember I, too, had a dad. I, too, had issues with my parents. But it was fine right then. I just wanted to enjoy the taste of the cigarette, listen to the rustling of the trees around us. I thought for a moment I saw movement near the gazebo but lowered my eyes again when nothing happened.

There was something a little off with Hudson that day, but I tried not to pay too much attention. He didn't look any different. Same dirty jeans, worn t-shirt. He was just slouching a little, kind of dead. More self-absorbed than usual— they both were. But I'd always made it a goal that other people's bad moods wouldn't ruin my happiest moments. Not even Hudson. Though I couldn't help but worry.

"Hope my dad can't smell this," he mumbled, staring at his cigarette like it was some kind of tumor. Then he took another long inhale, holding it in his lungs. Breathed it out, the smoke fading into nothing as it floated away. "He'd be livid."

Mason nodded and tapped some ashes onto the log next to me. "You know how many times my dad's told me to 'never smoke?' Probably... a dozen."

"More than that for me," Hudson said. "Goes on and on about... about cancer and stuff."

I smirked at them. Held my own a little more expertly. They'd only been smokers for about four months. I had them beat by three years. Since Freshman year, pretty much. "You two are sissies."

"I didn't say I'm scared of cancer," Hudson snapped. "Just that my dad is."

"You aren't afraid of cancer, huh?" I leaned back and

observed him with my arms folded. "I don't believe you."

"Why should I be?" He stared at me with a little animosity. The tree branches behind him made a nice backdrop for his defensive expression. "I'm not afraid of dying. I don't even wanna live to…. like fifty. I *want* to die young."

"My dad's almost fifty," Mason pointed out, "and he's doing fine."

"Shut up." Hudson crushed the cigarette butt into a nearby stone and left it there. "You know what I mean. Everybody… gets something bad when they get to that age. Diseases and stuff." He lowered onto the log as well so that Mason was the only one left standing. Hudson's shoulders pulled back that way he always did when he was about to say something kind of hurtful or offensive. "By the time you're fifty, you're just a bunch of tumors waiting for one to turn cancerous and kill you. I wouldn't say that's a person with much potential."

"Well if that's your logic, nobody has much potential," I countered, finishing my own cigarette and smashing it against the log-seat.

He nodded. "I accept that."

Mason crushed his cigarette and they each took a piece of gum that Mason had brought. A spray of cologne, a change of shirt. They were very intense about the whole process, like television spies preparing for a mission. I was surprised they didn't have a theme song and everything. I chuckled, watching them, and felt none of the same anxiety. My dad was a huge smoker. The entire house smelled like it. I could bathe in a sauna of cigarette smoke and it wouldn't make a difference. When I was at my mom's, different story, but I usually didn't mess with smoking when I stayed there. Not as many good spots on the hilltop, anyway. Downtown, the options were endless. I even smoked in the old, abandoned factory once, with all the smashed windows facing the river.

"I thought I'm supposed to feel... happy or something?" Hudson questioned as he pulled on a fresh shirt. "From nicotine."

"Dunno." Mason leaned against a tree, hands behind his head. "I never do from smoking."

"Alcohol's better," Hudson muttered, returning to his seat on the log. He kicked at the ground and sent a few leaves flying into the air.

Mason sighed, resting his head on the tree trunk. "Are we gonna mope around forever or talk about the big news? I mean, come on... Bruce!"

I groaned and smacked myself on the forehead dramatically. "Please, god, no. I'm sick of it. Every single night on social media—"

"Come on, Willow." Hudson stared at me now, some life in his eyes again. "It's *huge* news for the town."

"Why do you think he moved by the cemetery?" Mason asked, the question directed more to Hudson than me. He even leaned closer in that direction.

"No idea."

I was content to let the boys have this conversation to themselves. I could care less about the famous actor. In fact, I kind of disliked him, but my interest was piqued, nonetheless. "Didn't the last guy who lived there die sleeping in a chair or something?" My eyes traced both of them, searching for reactions.

"I think you're right, actually." Mason stroked at his chin, where he liked to imagine stubble. "I think my dad *did* say that one time."

"Just hoping he'll order pizza." Hudson got a dreamy-eyed look and smiled with his eyes lowered. "That'd be so cool to meet him. Maybe get an autograph."

"I seriously don't get why you love him so much." I couldn't hold back any longer, and I might as well tell them straight up.

"I mean... he's in all these stupid, high-brow movies. Like who does he think he is? That one about the high-class lawyer and the... the prostitute or whatever? There was some *real* sexist bullshit in that one." I saw their mouths open at the same time and added, "Don't deny it!"

"That's the whole *point*," Mason urged, his hands actually clasped together like in prayer.

"This guy's like a role model," Hudson continued. "He's just... so *important*."

"I always wanted to be like his character in *The Bandit*," Mason admitted. He looked at Hudson now mainly. I was once again a bit on the outside. "I mean, that guy's *hot*. That's really the look I'm going for, you know?"

"You're both ridiculous." I sighed heavily, not trying to hide it, not caring if they could sense my frustration. I actually hoped they would. I was really sick of hearing about this Bruce guy. To my knowledge, he'd never done any great philanthropy, never supported movements I really cared about. He'd been in some "deep" movies that mainly focused on male audiences. He was almost in *Fight Club* or something. That was his kind of acting, the kind of guy he was, and I really didn't care for it.

"You just don't get it." Hudson picked up a small rock and threw it. We could hear it ripping through some leaves as it made an arc, dropping at the edge of the trees and rolling a few feet onto the baseball field.

"You know what he is?" I said definitively, "He's just a knock-off Brad Pitt who prefers Tarintino-style movies."

The wolves jumped at my throat after that, so I decided it was time to head out. We all made our way out of the trees and around the baseball field. As we traversed the staircase, I glanced behind us at the trees and sighed. The boys continued with their conversation even as we moved past the gazebo, over the walking path, and onto one of the downtown sidewalks.

Hudson's beat-up truck was parked about two blocks away. I kept to myself while they talked, glanced upward at the sky just to see what it had transformed into. In Little Rush, there wasn't a lot to see. Everything became dull after a while, familiar, and there were no real tall buildings. Maybe that's why I looked at the sky so often, even if I didn't want to. At any given moment, the sky would take up half of my vision, sometimes more. I couldn't help but observe.

We made our way to the parking lot, which was situated on Main Street. Hudson gestured across the street where a vacant storefront held a "For Sale" sign.

He asked, "Is it true your dad wants to open a fancy restaurant there?"

"Who the hell knows anymore," Mason groaned as he climbed into the front seat. "Guess he'll buy just about anything."

He shut the car door harder than usual. I slid into the backseat and lay down, feeling a bit of a nicotine buzz now. The other two had only smoked one each, whereas I burnt through three. As Hudson pulled out of the parking space, I closed my eyes and sank into relaxation.

I thought about speaking up but decided not to. A few times before, I'd mentioned ideas regarding Jed's businesses, whether it was a promotion or an ad campaign or even a cool new place he could open. Mason always shot them down for whatever reason. After a while, I gave up mentioning anything. I liked to think I'd be a pretty good business owner, if I ever got the chance. *Maybe I'll open a bookstore or something.*

Hudson turned onto Main Street and progressed toward my house. I stared up at the truck ceiling, my back against the firm leather seats, lost in thought.

There are things I hated about this town, for sure. I got the impression that adult women had a much harder time gaining respect, at least in the business sense. They were all expected to stay home and have kids. And, of course, the town was pretty conservative, with a few hardcore racists and sexists. It bothered me at times.

o o o

"Let's live in the suburbs," I whispered to Mason, leaning my head on his shoulder and staring out at the dark river.

Night had fallen quickly. We were both sitting on a park bench now, down on that first sidewalk that overlooks the Ohio. The dark water glittered with stars, reflecting everything above it. The whole scene took my breath away, like peering into a second nighttime sky. In the distance, I could barely make out the hills of Kentucky and the collection of lights from houses over there, cars coming and going. They had a nice Dairy Queen, too.

"Oh, yeah?" Mason replied, stroking the back of my head, running his fingers through my hair.

"I think we should." I closed my eyes and imagined it. A nice house on a street full of them. Some neighborhood where the skyline of a nearby city towered in the distance. It didn't have to be far. Just an hour away, down near Louisville. That would be plenty good.

"Maybe we will," he said. "Who knows what the future holds."

This answer didn't really satisfy me, but at that moment a cloud passed by and the moon emerged, brighter than ever. I couldn't tear my eyes away, so I let that sight entrance me entirely.

Despite all the ups and downs, there was something about Little Rush that kept me close. Something different. There were a lot of somewheres, a lot of greener pastures, and yet there I was. Still trying to figure out why.

8

HUDSON

I underestimated what a sight it would be. The house stood in solitude, a small structure next to the county road that led away from Little Rush. Most wouldn't even call this a part of the city, but when Bruce Michaels lives somewhere the borders can stretch a bit to include him.

As I approached in my truck, I noticed the reporters crouched next to their vehicles, some even wandering into the cemetery. Like an army waiting to invade. I felt a pang of guilt for Bruce, a desire to help in some way, but that was impossible. Nor was it my job. Me, a pizza delivery guy, had nothing to do with this. I just had to drop it off and try not to freak out too bad.

From the driveway of his home, I could see the water tower in the distance, those letters bold against the dirty-white surface. LITTLE RUSH. It was one of the few structures that you could see from pretty much anywhere. Even the power-plant's massive towers down by the river became invisible when you traveled this far away. That water tower, though, stood against the reddening sky. A reminder that I could never get far enough away, that I would live my whole life in its shadow.

Once I was in the driveway, I had to take a deep breath. They were all watching *me*, now. I hated the stupid work hat I reluctantly wore, but maybe it was a blessing. I didn't need all those people with cameras seeing my untamed mess of thin and wild hair.

Stepping out of the truck brought an uncomfortable rise in temperature, even at seven o'clock. With the pizza in hand, the exterior of the box hot and greasy, I started to sweat. I didn't look at the reporters or the cameras. I couldn't tell if they were taking pictures, but I hoped not. Only a few paces led to the doorstep but it felt like an eternity. The house exterior was white-painted brick and grimy. I knocked a few times on the door.

I shifted on the balls of my feet. There were footsteps inside, shuffling. The handle turned, and the door swung inward. There he stood. Broad, godlike. He wore sunglasses, only adding to the intimidation. His hairline was receding, making his forehead huge, but he didn't even try to hide it. Why should he? He actually embraced it. His hair was slicked back, eyebrows furrowed. The lower half of his face was a polar opposite to that smooth skin. His chin and cheeks were covered with a beard, thick enough without being excessive. A gray color, just like his hair. His shoulders were slouched a bit, arms crossed, standing wide. Wearing a bathrobe, I thought, or something similar. I couldn't look away. It felt like I was a mortal and I'd approached Zeus on that mountain where he lives, whatever it's called. And he struck me with lightning.

"Pizza…" I stammered, my fingers digging into the sides now, pressing so hard I almost poked through, "… sir."

"Thanks." His voice was gruff, incredibly so. Like he was doing it on purpose almost. It was so weird to see him now. Otherworldly. He wasn't in character. He wasn't aiming for anything. He was just a *guy* who ordered *pizza,* and it was so humanizing. Bruce Michaels. As real as can be.

I forced myself to let go of the box as he took it. Bruce turned for a moment, set it somewhere I couldn't see. As his body shifted, I noticed the coffee table behind him. Completely barren, except for a dark bottle and the back of a framed photograph.

As he dug in the pockets of his bathrobe and pulled out a twenty-dollar bill, his body blocked the scene once again. He extended the note, wrinkled and in a ball, but I gingerly accepted.

"Here's this." There was a tiny smirk on his face as he closed the door. "Keep the change."

"Thank you!" I bit my lip to stop from shouting it.

No more words were exchanged. None were needed.

When I faced my truck again, I didn't even see the reporters. There was nothing important to me but Bruce. The trees were beautiful with night approaching, the way the road stretched out endlessly. I admired the barren land where they'd been meticulously cut back to make way for power lines, like some kind of natural tunnel through the wilderness. I was completely content, as free as those treetop canopies, swaying in the evening breeze.

My eyes touched on the water tower, that godforsaken beacon, like a lighthouse drawing me to shore. I remembered where I belonged. Those dirty roads of Little Rush. Bruce would scorch the earth with his fame if he ever set foot there. Would set fire to the water tower. The whole town. If he wanted to, he could. I marveled at that power. That ability. To leave, to come, to destroy, anyone anytime. What a man. *What a man.*

o o o

I followed the road back toward town, winding next to fields and over a tiny creek. That water tower remained always in the corner of my eye, those words even brighter now with the sun's aid. The road disappeared before me. I'd driven this so many times before. Once you drive like that enough, every country road is the same. It's all just dirt and asphalt. Eventually it merged into the four-lane spinal cord called Rush Road.

This section of Little Rush, the hilltop, was a typical Anywhere, USA. This was the true source of my despair. Besides the movie theater and bowling alley, each with their own rundown charm, there was nothing. A common late-night activity was hanging out with friends in the movie theater parking lot or a McDonald's booth. We had a pretty big hospital, though. That was something. That hospital was probably the biggest building I'd ever been in, since my family never traveled. Checkups, shots, everything took place in that hospital, all through my adolescence.

I guess if you wanted to have a kid, it was nice you didn't need to leave town, because nobody truly *left*. Your kid could be born here, live here, and die here. A comfortable, average life, all within a few square miles. What a godawful idea.

Bruce Michaels, he probably never felt this type of entrapment. He spent his whole life in sprawling Los Angeles or in the skyscrapers of New York. It still didn't feel right, having him so close. At any given moment, less than a dozen miles from me, from my house. It was both invasive and invigorating.

Maybe I'd only ever see him through delivering pizzas or chance encounters around town. Nonetheless, simply his presence affected me. It was torturous to think about the freedom he possessed, the ability to change his life and his setting on a whim. And at the same time, weren't we similar in the end? We were both stuck here, at least for now. I could bask in that connection, though it was thin and probably temporary.

Rush Road flooded my vision at that point, and I had to concentrate on the few stoplights and braking cars ahead of me. All the important buildings were along this four-lane road, and the various backroads branched out from there. Those took you to fields, rectangle-shaped and bordered by thick trees. I imagined that a long time ago, there had been a huge forest, untouched, and then some giant took a heavy square-shaped tool. A tamper or something. And that's how they got the fields. Just smashed down the trees into perfect plots of geometric land.

There were houses dotting the countryside out there, the occasional Dollar General or weird gas station with a name I'd never heard of. A local grocery store not far from my house, but milk was twice as expensive as the DG. Like I said, it was all good for nothing, nothing but driving at night, nothing but sunsets. That's all we had out there. At least Mason lived in a nice neighborhood on the edge of town, and Willow bounced between her downtown dad and her hilltop mom. Me, I was just a "country boy" who hated every bit of the stereotype.

The only things I felt in control of were my job and my music. I loved weird indie music, as opposed to my father's country, because it made me different from him. I loved my pizza deliveries because I got to drive all over the place.

Bruce Michaels. That old man could go anywhere, be anybody, and he would never feel boxed in to a stereotype. He had invented a new kind of person, in my opinion. Formed a permanent change in American culture, at least to some small degree. Few people could claim that. Not many lived in such close proximity to that kind of person, either.

There was something about Little Rush that made me want to drive forever in a straight line, taking any road I could, just chasing that fleeing orb of light. Little Rush filled me with this sense of despair, but also energy. There were days when I just wanted to go somewhere, that way or that way or I didn't even care. And other times, I wanted this town to be the thing that killed me, because it already did slowly.

Having him this near only inflamed all of my desires. I'd wanted to run before, and now I wanted it more than ever. I'd longed for freedom, but now that longing consumed me in every way.

I hoped that things would change with Bruce around. I

hoped that *something* would be different, anything really. Maybe Little Rush would grow on me, turn out bearable, with the great Bruce Michaels as part of it. But all I'd seen so far were reporters, and I hated reporters. That wasn't a change. Just another reason to leave.

9
BRUCE

Sometimes I do believe there's a heaven or something. It's hard not to in a place like Little Rush. In California, in Hollywood, there's so much to see and do that nobody takes the time to glance upward. Out here, though, there's only the sky. Only the clouds and colors and their formations. When the sky looks a certain way, the cloud layers are almost like a staircase to whatever hides up there.

There are times when I can almost… believe it. But it doesn't matter in the end, I guess. Heaven or not, I sure as hell won't ever get there.

Every time I ponder questions like that, my mind travels back to the church revival and what I felt that day.

I hadn't even wanted to go, but my grandpa had been a religious man and I never dared to argue with him. He clung to that old church long after I would've, long after my grandma died of breast cancer. That's the whole reason I came out here to Little Rush. That entire summer wouldn't have happened if not for her untimely death. I would never have moved out here to live with him, in this very house I now owned.

Some people would say a house like this was haunted, but I knew the truth. My grandpa had lived here for decades, thrived here even, but I only saw the decline. After my grandma's death, he was never the same man, and I witnessed all of it. He'd already been a ghost. When he died, he had no haunting left.

"You go on up there," he had said to me, gesturing at the front of the church. The pews around us were full of men and women and children, all of them breathless with anticipation. The pulpit absent for now, the church quiet, but soon it would be roaring.

I took my place with the other young boys, all of us immature and unsure. Few of us were there of our own accord. Almost all of us had followed parents or grandparents, pulled along by the leash of childhood. And now we waited for the moment that would define our days, maybe even our weeks.

After the hymns swelled and died, after the low prayers and the raised voice of the traveling pastor, he spread his arms and welcomed us to the front. As teenagers, we knew this was coming. We'd all heard stories of these revivalists, of their impassioned and fiery tongues. I had told myself earlier that day, as I walked into the sanctuary, that I wouldn't rise from my seat, that I wouldn't listen to his call. But he'd done his job well and I couldn't control what I felt.

Others around me rose and went to the front. They knelt in prayer and sobbed, joined by their families. I remained, looking on in envy, wanting to follow them into that great unknown. I almost walked down that aisle, truly. But I didn't, and that's all that counts.

I don't believe in a god, and I don't believe one ever helped my grandpa. He fell apart that summer. I cherish the memories. I cherish what's left of him in my mind. But I don't agree with what he told me, whenever the topic arose.

And yet... when I remember that church scene, there's a feeling of guilt that gnaws at me. An idea in my mind that maybe it was the beginning. Maybe that's where I went wrong. It seemed like ever since, in every way, I'd been a plague on this earth, a curse on those who knew me.

The more I drank, the more I realized. This house was haunted, indeed. I was now the old man who lived in the house. And just like him, my time grew short, the moments were fleeting. He chose religion as a temporary raft. But I had none.

o o o

Their beady eyes and those flashing bulbs never seemed to leave. I could remember the lightning bugs here in Little Rush from that summer years ago, but so far I hadn't seen any. They'd been scared away by those brighter pops, the cameras with their photographers, the notepads with their scribblers, always stalking the edge of my property.

I'd been sitting in front of the television for probably an hour, and the pizza box lay on the table in front of me, half-eaten. My stomach was just starting to hurt. I knew I'd eaten too much, but I didn't really care. I'd throw it up later with the whiskey anyway.

Next to the pizza box and empty whiskey bottle, I tried to focus on the framed photograph, but my eyes wouldn't adjust. Everything had gone too blurry now, so I returned my attention to the stupid TV.

I couldn't even focus on the screen because through the window I could see their flashing cameras. What the hell were they even taking pictures of? When would they leave? It'd be pitch black in an hour and I wanted to sleep. Wake up, yet again, and wish that I could just sleep forever, in every sense of the phrase.

Dirty bastards. Should call the cops on them.

When it became too much to bear, I ripped the curtains completely shut and paced around my sitting room, seething. The couch smelled awful when I first arrived but I was getting used to it. I even slept on it a few times, whenever I was too drunk to crawl into the other room. Sometimes the bedroom was just too dark and cold. I preferred this sleeping arrangement, with the television flickering throughout the night, the hours swirling by as I slid in and out of intoxicated dreams. Felt like some kind of trance.

It was a sensation I could only compare to a wave pool. My head ducked under, I emerged and caught a breath of air, then under again. All the world bubbled around me and splashed in my mouth. The waves never ceasing. Not until morning brought sweet, temporary relief.

The cameras popped again. I could see them, even through the curtains, just barely.

I wished I had a gun. I'd love nothing better than to take aim at a few of those reporters. Man or woman. I didn't care. I probably wouldn't even hit them. Never been a good shot. Never had much practice. But just the act of shooting at them, that might cheer me up. God knows I needed it.

For a moment, I leaned against the wall and stared through a crack in the curtains. Their bodies shuffled outside like ants consuming crumbs from a dinner plate. Sometimes chatting with each other. The latest news, maybe, or a story idea. The constant buzz of information that seeped into my brain and under my door. The droning static of social media and voices I didn't care about. I leaned there for a while longer and started to think, let my thoughts drift out from the walls.

To grow old in a coffin. That would've been ideal. Somewhere with darkness and quiet. Somewhere to think and to forget everything I'd lost, everything I'd done. Somewhere they would never find me. Where the truth would never come out. That was the goal, after all. This tiny house, this lost town. This was meant to be my dark coffin. Yet they had reached inside with their slimy hands and wrung my neck.

Looking for respite, I turned to my television, but it acted as a mirror. There was nothing as awful as a mirror that came out of nowhere. My own image flitting across the nightly news, some headline about my future plans. Little Rush had grown obsessed, like a needy lover. I grabbed the remote, and with a tiny pop, the television program extinguished.

Then I opened my phone, checked Twitter, the only social media I maintained. I didn't even have an account, not one that I ran anyway. There was one with *my* name that some agent controlled. I didn't follow it, never even looked. I used a faceless account, a username with many numbers. Yet I saw my real name trending on the list of topics. "Bruce Michaels" near the top and then "Michaels Moves To Nowhere?" a little under that. A few hashtags that I didn't really understand. When I refreshed my feed, the first post I saw was of my own face. Another surprise mirror. I chucked my phone across the room where it bounced off the couch and onto the floor.

A sudden anger swelled inside of me, and I turned to the door. I grabbed the doorknob, closed my eyes, shuddered at the images that leapt into my brain. To grow old with the nighttime instead of in this early dawn...

I swung the door open, stepped outside, and threw my arms in the air. Exposing my whole body as if to beg, *Shoot me. Shoot me now.*

"Fuck you!" I screamed as loud as I could. My voice was hoarse, choking. A reminder of the years I'd lost. Their cameras flashed like a volley of bullets. I flipped them off with both fingers. "Fuck you all!" I yelled again before storming back inside and slamming the door behind me. I wished it would've splintered, just a little.

10
JED

Cynicism was the constant throughout my daily life. Little Rush was my home in a different way than everybody else. Some people had roots there, some really deep. Family ties. Memories. All that. Some people had ancestors who were a part of the Underground Railroad when it bubbled in downtown Little Rush all those generations ago. Others had grandparents who came back from the wars and settled there. So many roots.

But, in a sense, none of them were as deep as mine. And I don't mean that in a boastful way. It was a curse as much as a blessing. My business. All the restaurants I operated, the countless properties I owned. Each one a thick rope binding me to that town, for better or for worse. So much of my money tied up, my fortune contingent on the Little Rush housing market. Maybe that's why Mason seemed to hate me. A potential reason, at least.

I did love Little Rush. It was a beautiful city. Peaceful, quiet, with just the right amount of big brands and local-owned. The right mixture of people. Democratic, Republican, rich, poor. To me, there was no city quite like that. Nothing as perfect. Nothing so simple but complex.

That's why the predicament with Bruce Michaels fascinated me. What would happen when you took somebody like that, with no roots and a completely different background, and threw him into this stew? There were so many different angles to the situation, nuances impossible to decipher. The only way to find out was to wait and see. Would the mixture be like oil and water? Would Bruce turn to steam like pouring rain on a scorching hot sidewalk? Would he blend seamlessly?

These thoughts are what I wanted to dwell on. I wanted to ponder these, sit for hours and dream. But instead, work called, as always, and I was never one to refuse. If my prosperity bound me to this town, then the mundane activities of my day-to-day life bound me to my home office. The door shut. Desk covered.

They were strewn everywhere on my desk. Project folders, restaurant receipts, phone numbers to call, tenants to chew out. A calculator, a calendar. A to-do list that I would never escape, that grew each hour. This tunnel had no light at the end, yet I didn't mind the darkness. It calmed me. I reclined in the chair for a moment and let my gaze wander to the ceiling. A pale lightbulb and a black fan spinning overhead. The closed door acted like a barrier against the tide outside, one that rose each day and threatened to spill over.

I glanced at my cell phone where it lay on top of my desk. I could hear the faint static of an ongoing phone call over the speakers, the only noise apart from that overhead fan. I tried to control my breathing. There was silence on the other end. It'd been sitting on my desk for nearly half an hour, the call on speaker mode. A pressure building just behind my eyes, a throbbing drumbeat against my skull that would soon turn into a sharp, blinding pain. Dealing with people frustrated me to no end. I much preferred numbers.

"What about Campaign Two?" a voice said at last. One of my many advisors. We were supposed to have a meeting today in person, but I'd canceled it. Switched to a phone call. Maybe that explained her irritation.

"I told you. I don't like it." I squeezed my hands tighter together. My eyes shifted to the desk, the flood of paperwork and tasks that could comfort me. Planning ad campaigns was the worst part of this whole ordeal. Promotional discounts, changes to the menu, anything to get a burst of revenue. Summertime was our key season, the time we raked in the most. Years ago, when I only had to worry about managing the pizza restaurant, I quite enjoyed these meetings. I could be creative with the campaigns, invest myself in them, really set the mood for the whole Little Rush season. But now, with six restaurants in total, a general store, and over a hundred rental properties, each meeting took a greater toll than the one before.

"Jed, listen. It's mid-June and we —"

"No." I smacked the desk loud enough that she'd hear it and shut up. Understand my frustration. "I'm not gonna run some half-assed ad or change the prices unless *I know* that it's profitable. Nothing you've suggested is!"

There was silence again. I took a deep breath and prepared my half-apology. We'd reach a decision, of course, but I had to vent some of this anger first. That's the way it went. My employees understood. I never imagined myself as an excellent boss, but every so often, I realized I'd become a total ass.

Then the door to my office opened, slowly. I glanced in that direction and found Mason standing, a hand still on the doorknob. His eyes scanned the room, the messy desk, my bookshelves. He didn't leave right away. My eyebrows rose.

"Kate, we'll talk tomorrow." I hung up the call right away, flipped over my phone so that I couldn't see her text when it came. Without hesitation, I directed my attention to Mason who still waited, still hadn't said anything. I guessed he needed a push. "Sorry. Business... stuff." I tried to form a different expression, one more endearing and less serious. "What's up?"

"Um..." He cleared his throat and gestured at me. "Henry's

at the door. Says you're going with him?"

"Oh, right." I stood from my desk, hurrying out from the office. "Completely forgot." I thought I should probably change, put on something more comfortable. Mason stepped aside as I passed, a bit reluctant. Odd. I didn't have time to think, though. I was rushing toward my bedroom when he spoke up.

"I was gonna ask…"

I stopped on a dime and turned, still uncomfortably conscious of my expression. He was standing by my office door still. The hallway and living room behind him were empty. No sounds of Lucy. For the first time in what felt like weeks, Mason's eyes were directly on me.

"Yeah. Sure… What's up?"

"I need…" He smiled a little, the way you do when things get awkward. "You know, you're in a rush." He waved a hand, and the smile grew but it was different now. It was something not quite genuine. Maybe disappointed. "Never mind."

"No, no, it's—"

"Nah. Nevermind."

He turned his back to me then and marched into the depths of the house. I didn't feel comfortable calling after him. I *was* in a rush. Each step he took was another punch to my chest. I wondered what he would've asked. If it was important. If it would've… helped us.

I dressed quickly with that widening gulf in my mind. Mason and I stood on different sides of a chasm that neither wanted to jump across. There were no bridges. There were no ropes. Just a deadly descent.

I wished I could be like Henry. Him and his son, that was an honest relationship. They were hard workers. They were tan, dirty, farmer-guys. I wanted that. I wanted all of it. I wanted to feel soil on my hands and instinctively know what each farm instrument did. That guy, he didn't sit through meetings. He just *did* stuff. A great family, beautiful land, just a few miles away. Here I was, stuck in a neighborhood where all the mailboxes were the same, all the cars were nice. Not as nice as mine, sure, and the houses weren't as big. But sometimes I wished, I dreamed, that mine could be smaller. That it had a garden in the backyard. That I mowed my own grass.

If I was the typical businessman, owner of many properties and obsessed with the town's economics, then Henry was a typical farmer on the surface. Sure, he worked his fields and owned a tractor he always tinkered with. Had chickens up until a few weeks ago. But he also worked at the power-plant, got along with all the factory guys. He held discussions better than most, retained a lot of the characteristics that had made us friends way back in middle school. He might've been a farmer by occupation, but I got the sense that we were more similar than different.

I always envied him for his lifestyle. Henry had a *real* job, and he farmed his ass off on top of that. Hay, mostly, bundles and bundles of it. He once tried to explain the whole process to me, but it made as much sense as cash flow and organization design did to him. I enjoyed it, though, every chance I got to spend time around him. To feel that bit of country lifestyle rubbing off on me. It helped to get out of my preppy house, spend a while with a close friend, a hands-in-the-dirt kind of guy. An honest, true, honorable man. I couldn't find many of those, not even in Little Rush. Certainly not in the mirror.

I emerged onto the front porch five minutes later and Henry was there. He was chatting with Lucy, who had a wide smile. He had always been charismatic. Swear to god, he could take my wife if he wanted to. He just has that look about him. He attracts. He really does. Somehow.

"I about thought you'd make me go alone!" he exclaimed as the door swung shut behind me. I offered him a shrug and kissed my wife. She disappeared into the house, saying quick goodbyes to us both, though I wished she would've stayed just a bit longer. Sometimes I missed her on busy days like these.

Henry led the way over my step-stone path to his beat-up truck. He climbed into the driver's seat after wrestling with the door handle for a minute. I felt a tinge of guilt. Compared to my cars, this thing was worthless. I really wished I could help him. Really wanted to give him a loan or something. He asked, occasionally, but only when things were really bad for him. It took some humility for a guy like him to ask, and I still couldn't do it. They say loaning money to friends never works out well. And besides, I wasn't in a great position at the moment. Most of my wealth was in properties, so it wasn't like I had cash to spare.

"Did I ever tell you this reminds me of your truck from high school?" I slid into the passenger's seat. The fabric was ripped in places and had that distinct smell of old seats that've been rained and sweat on countless times. The dashboard wasn't anything impressive. It didn't have any of those buttons my new Jeep did. I wasn't sure his AC even functioned.

"This rust-bucket's about as old, innit?" He grinned at me and reversed into the road. "My tab's on you tonight?"

"Of course. Are you gonna pay for the cab?" I asked with a coy smile.

"No cab, nah. I'll drive us back no problem. Never got a DUI, never will." He chuckled and took off down the road, the engine rattling and brakes squealing. But Henry didn't seem to mind or even notice.

"Jesus Christ, you have no idea how badly I need this." I leaned back against the headrest and breathed in the old truck. Again, my mind was filled with that image. Henry on a tractor in his field, the sun setting behind him. I wanted that sensation. I wanted that ugly tan line he had mid-bicep and that uncompromising strength developed over so many summers. I wanted to worry about money, just a little, and have to drive a rickety truck.

"Anytime, pal. That's how it goes." He reached for the dial, turned on some country song I didn't know or care about.

I hated country music, usually, but with Henry, it had a nice feel to it. Henry's the kind of guy you want to be but know you aren't strong enough. You know you couldn't do it. But the idea is nice. One of those ideas that refused to leave, that dug into my brain the entire evening.

So many stressors and worries. I wanted to talk about Mason with him. I wanted to ask about Hudson, how he was doing. But those weren't things that grown men talked about. These weren't farm-topics. Sure, we would be at a bar and not his farm, but I knew how Henry was. Those weren't topics for us.

I only knew one way to truly decompress, to forget. A dozen beers with Henry over the course of three hours. But even that didn't help tonight. I couldn't quite forget. If anything, the alcohol just added more weight. One of these days, it would all crush me.

11

HUDSON

I crouched at the edge of the trees, peering into the evening half-light as the reporters started to file away. Back into their cars, back down the winding road to where distant hotel rooms waited. Mason lounged beside me, his back against a tree trunk, smoking a cigarette. I felt too nervous for that. We weren't in any real danger, but this still wasn't "legal" per se. Stalking somebody's house, even Bruce Michaels.

"Looks like rain tonight," Mason said with the cigarette dangling from his lips. He typed something into his phone and then stuck it in his pocket. Probably texting Willow.

I grunted in response. I didn't care much about the weather. My eyes were straight ahead, on the house.

"Remind me to put up my convertible roof, will ya?" I heard him rummaging for something. Probably the pack of cigarettes. "Do you want one of these?" he asked. "Willow showed me 'em. I actually like this sort. Don't give you that sticky feeling when you're done with it."

"No." My eyes caught on the water tower in the distance, peeking over the trees. Beyond it, I could just barely see plumes of smoke rising from the power-plant, though the towers themselves were covered by trees. That expansive setup was right next to the river, along one of the four winding roads that led to downtown Little Rush.

That's one thing interesting about the power-plant. A tunnel of smoke rose from it at all hours of the day and night. I'd guess that stuff rising was probably steam in reality, but it looked a lot like smoke. On the really overcast days, that stuff just drifted up forever. Mingled with the thick, gray clouds. It looked sometimes like the power-plant itself churned out the clouds. That's what I used to think as a kid.

The water tower, much closer, split the cloudy sky. It didn't stick up far, but I usually managed to find it in the distance. I'd always wanted to climb it, honestly. Always thought about it. There was a little ladder built into the side and all. I wanted to get up there, touch those bold letters. Watch the entire town at once. See what that hill looked like, the one leading downtown. If you drove down it, your ears popped, but I wondered if it really looked so steep from a water tower. I'd always wanted to at least try. It's just one of those things, I guess.

"I'm glad those reporters left," Mason commented. He shifted again, cracking a few sticks. He was always relaxed, didn't matter where we were. I hardly ever saw him lose his cool or even act nervous. "Thought they might see us." He paused for a moment to light a cigarette and wonder aloud, "Is this... illegal? What we're doing."

"Dunno." I shrugged and did so honestly. When the house still showed no movement, I settled back next to Mason and reclined against a different tree. It was nearing dark, and we were far enough into the trees that we were effectively invisible. Nobody came to a cemetery this late, anyway, especially not a tiny one on the outskirts of town. "Doubt he would report us, you know? I'm sure people... do this all the time."

Mason grinned and so did I. We both knew that was false. *Normal* people didn't stalk somebody's house. But then again, *normal* people didn't *get* stalked. And Bruce Michaels was anything but normal.

"This is a kinda nice spot." Mason seemed to detest any form of silence. He was always the one to break it, to force conversation. "For sitting and smoking, you know?"

"Whatever you say." I picked up a fallen leaf and traced the veins running through it. "I just feel nervous, really."

"Eh, relax, man. You need a smoke." Mason again extended the box to me, but I declined. He scowled, pocketed it. "That guy, he won't do anything if he happens to see us. And how would he even? He's probably watching TV or drinking himself to death."

"I mean, he didn't *seem* depressed when I gave him the pizza." I realized, as I spoke this thought, that first impressions meant nothing. *I* probably seemed fine on any given day. But of course, that wasn't true. Maybe Bruce Michaels fit in the same boat. That gave me a little hope, a sliver of light.

"Never know, though, do you?" Mason raised his eyebrows. I imagined him as some awful kind of philosopher, the drunk guy who sat at the edge of the bar and recited half-poems. That'd be an amusing role for him.

It was after nine now. I felt pretty confident the storm would hit within an hour. I had no desire to be stuck out here with torrents of hard rain smacking us. Then again, I didn't want to go home. My father and Mason's were out drinking, as they put it. I don't think they ever actually got *drunk*. I couldn't imagine Dad or Jed hammered, but maybe a little tipsy. They would also make nice bar-philosophers, solving the world's problems over a few beers. Maybe that's what they did to relax. Adults were weird once they got to that age.

When I thought about them, I remembered an important question that I kept forgetting to ask. I turned to Mason, trying to sound casual, but he probably heard the wobble in my voice. "Have you asked your dad about the... um, cabin for this weekend?"

He wrinkled his nose, pointed at me with his glowing cigarette. "I said stop asking me that, man. I'll deal with it. Just... haven't yet."

"You better ask." I shot him an irritated glare. "Don't cancel again."

"We're gonna have the party, okay? Don't worry." He sighed, threw his head back. "Geez. What're you so caught up on it for?"

"Just looking forward to having an *actual* party for once," I said like no big deal. The wind picked up a little and threatened the coming storm. "I mean, people *are* actually coming to this one, right?"

Mason grinned and rubbed at his chin. He did that sometimes, like he thought he had facial hair. He barely had anything, but I guess it made him feel hotter or something. He was already an annoying sort of handsome without the fake-beard mannerisms.

"Oh, they're coming. I got *tons* of girls to agree, and that's all you need, Hudson. If the girls come, the guys follow." He held up a hand with just his middle finger extended. "Party rule number one."

"Shut up." I threw a tiny rock at him, missing by an inch.

"That was probably a piece of someone's gravestone, you idiot." He shook his head and put out his cigarette on the base of a tree, a mischievous twinkle in his bright eyes. "I know why you're actually excited for the party. You're hoping to get laid."

"What? Not even... no." I batted a hand through the air. "I just wanna get drunk."

"You just wanna get *laid*." He wore a half-smile, that cockeyed expression. Hated that.

I sat up abruptly and peered through the darkening cemetery toward the small house. "Hey, did you see something there?"

"Don't change the subject."

I settled back again, huffing, and crossed my arms. He'd called my bluff.

"I get it, man." Mason laid a hand on my shoulder and added a melancholy note to his tone. "You're just a lonely, horny teenager. It's okay." Then his façade cracked and he chuckled. "You're finally hitting puberty."

"Shut up!" I couldn't help myself from laughing as I punched at his arm. "I hate you."

"Listen, man, you've just gotta find the right girl. You know, like me and Willow, she's into some pretty wild—"

"Shut. Up!" I grabbed a handful of leaves and threw them, but most drifted to the ground like bubbles. "You're like... Jesus, stop. I don't even know what to call you." I rolled my eyes and turned away from him, holding back a smile.

"I'm just saying. I mean, your bed is the most comfortable place I've ever—"

"Oh god!" I closed my eyes and shook my head. "If you're not kidding, I'm *going* to kill you. You son of a—"

"I kid, I kid!" Mason threw his hands up in defense, chuckling. "Don't be so gullible."

"Might kill you anyways," I murmured. "If I ever had to talk about my sex life with you," I fought back a yawn, "I'd just die right then. Just combust into flames immediately."

"Ah, you're so vanilla." Mason put his hands behind his head like he'd recline in a hammock. His eyes turned upward, to the tree canopy and the stars just beyond. "You do need to get laid soon. You've got too much built-up tension. You're a bomb waiting to go off, you know that?"

"Thanks, Dr. Phil." I considered throwing something else at him, but the moment passed. We sat there without speaking, each of us lost in thought. He was probably dwelling on Willow. I tried not to be jealous of them, or of him in general, but it was hard at times. He had such a large house, never had a job. All through high school, he'd just been coasting, pretty much. The only thing he really *tried* for was his appearance. Just too goddamn attractive. It made me hate him a little, that and his money. And now he'd been with Willow for, what, over a year? And she was just jaw-dropping some days, in appearance but also in the way she acted. I'd never met someone so… electric. Of course he got to be with her. It just made sense.

I was a side character in that story. Everybody in Little Rush knew Mason, and most people knew Willow too, or at least what she looked like. Me? I was the farm boy. I was the kid who didn't get invited to stuff. I was the one nobody thought of when they had an extra movie ticket. That was me. And somehow, I still ended up with Mason as my best friend. It could be a pain.

The wind smacked even harder now. I was about to mention it, suggest we head out, when I heard something in the trees behind us. I thought Mason did too because he gave me this wide-eyed expression, this fearful look. It could be literally anything out here. A coyote. A bear. Some farmer with a shotgun. Anything.

I turned around and so did Mason. And there he was, standing with broad shoulders and fists clenched. I could barely tell it was him in the darkness, but there was no mistaking that silhouette. I would recognize him anywhere. Just by the way he stood.

"Run, Hudson!"

Mason took off right away, heading toward the road. His car was parked about a quarter-mile away in the driveway of some abandoned house. He was heading in that direction. But for some reason, I couldn't bring myself to move. I just toppled backward, onto the ground. Mason had fled in an instant, his feet churning the earth, and I knew he wouldn't turn back.

"I… I'm sorry, I didn't…"

"Get up, will ya?" Bruce Michaels barked at me, extending a hand.

I grasped it, felt those gnarled calluses and the years that had carved into his fingers. Then I was standing in front of him, our eyes meeting for only the second time, but it was a face I'd watched for countless hours. He observed me, my clothing, my hair. Took a sniff.

"You been smoking?" he asked.

I shook my head. He, on the other hand, smelled like alcohol. Had to be slightly drunk, at least.

"Damn. Was gonna ask for one." He clicked his tongue and motioned for me to follow. "How long 'til it rains would you say?"

I didn't move. I tried not to look too shocked. This conversation had already lasted longer than expected. "Um... forty minutes?"

He nodded and chewed on his lip. His head swiveled to either side, and then he gestured into the trees where an ill-traveled path curled away into the forest. "Think there's anything interesting this way?"

"Um..." I turned around, just to see if Mason had stopped running, but he was nowhere in sight. It was getting dark, sure, but I didn't feel afraid of this man. I would have *loved* to walk down a trail with him. Bruce Michaels, after all. But I still didn't feel quite... comfortable.

"What do you say we find out?" He raised an eyebrow and a smile tugged at his lips. With that, he took a step past me, toward the barely-existent route.

I still didn't shift my feet. He sighed, maybe irritated, but I didn't care. "You aren't gonna... call the cops?"

"Jesus, no. Just want someone to talk to." He cocked his head like some bird. "Don't tell me you're refusing?"

I lowered my head and followed him after that. He was

right, after all. There was zero chance I'd refuse a conversation with Bruce Michaels. I'd been dreaming about this for years. Always wanted to meet him. I assumed it would be in an airport or something, but instead, I would wander a forest trail next to him. Who would've imagined?

He led me into the trees, stepping through the underbrush. The cemetery to our right disappeared as the forest consumed us both. The storm rumbled overhead, and I could only pray that it would hold off for a while longer. Night crept closer as we crunched our way down the path, toward a part of Little Rush I'd never known.

I thought about turning back, and maybe I should've. I didn't know what he had planned or even who he was, really. But something pushed me on, something in the way he limped along, almost like a wounded animal.

"What about my friend?" I asked before we were truly gone into the depth of the woods.

He shrugged and brushed a branch out of the way. "Text him to come back in, say, thirty minutes." His eyes were straight ahead, almost as if I didn't exist. His expression so weary, his skin wrinkled. Bruce Michaels, worn and old, almost decrepit. But I couldn't turn away. He was everything I'd ever wanted to be.

12
LITTLE RUSH
THE ROBBERS

"You got any more of them… what's-they-calleds from earlier?" Curtis crumpled a Milky Way wrapper and threw it on the ground. He leaned back in the chair.

June looked on, rolling her eyes. She could barely hear them as the wind picked up, assaulting their small apartment's single window.

"Edibles." Randy crossed his arms and slipped a plastic bag into the pocket of his jacket. "Got no more."

"You's lying, you piece of shit." Curtis pointed a finger at him, narrowed his eyes, but then let it drop. He leaned even farther back in the rickety recliner until it nearly tipped over.

Randy and June were seated on a couch, older and shabbier than any of them by a good measure. It was rugged and had pieces of the back sticking out at odd angles, but it'd been free. Their apartment, too, wasn't the prettiest thing. A second-story place, few blocks up from the river. The curtains were torn in places and the walls an ugly color. Likely some mold in that one corner. But they made it work.

It was comfortable enough, though June had to resist the urge to shout whenever they got into their childish arguments.

The three of them were sitting in front of the television, with the first thunderstorm in weeks pounding outside. The relentless torrents of rain forced them to turn the television up every so often. It sounded like the storm only worsened as the hours passed. But in reality, it didn't bother them much. The three of them tuned out everything but the news, which once again bubbled with promise. Bruce Michaels, living here for half a week now. What a few days it had been.

This was the most promising news she'd had since the debacle with the drug dealers. Back when June had first met the two of them, they'd tried to work as drug mules between Cincinnati and Louisville. Trouble was, the real serious dealers didn't trust people like them. With the added weight of these two, June couldn't ever make it work, and so they'd suffered through odd jobs and random thefts. Anything to get by.

"No work tomorrow, eh," Curtis chuckled, relaxing with both arms behind his head now.

The other two didn't answer right away. June's eyes were locked on the television, entranced. She didn't like Curtis much when he got in these moods. Anytime he took edibles, he started to talk a lot. He rarely acted high, just annoying.

"Nice, free day, eh," he went on, fishing for any kind of response. June noticed his eyes were locked on the two of them, though she didn't answer.

"Speak for yourself," Randy grumbled. "Got two more shifts at Krogers this week and another at the Shell."

"Kroger, no *s,*" June corrected him, not bothering to turn. Her voice was always emotionless, eyes focused ahead. She'd become a leader of sorts to them, ever since they moved in here two years ago. "Don't you two forget about this weekend."

"Won't forget," Randy assured her.

Curtis raised his eyebrows. "Say what? What's 'is weekend?"

June glared at him for just a split second then stared out the dark window. Rain beat against it so loudly now that she thought it might crack in places. Storms always sounded worse up here, in a rickety apartment that would even shake from a big truck rolling down the street.

"Tell him, Randy," she said at last.

Randy cleared his throat. "The... the, um... which place's it?"

"The goddamn ice cream shop, Randy." June punched him on the knee, not in a kind way, and stood from the couch. It lifted a bit as she rose. None of them weighed much —they couldn't afford enough food to— but the couch was so old a mouse would've made a difference.

"I remember!" Curtis clapped his hands together and gestured at June. "We robbin' that sucker, right? Don't you worry. Won't forget this time."

June paced to the window and placed a hand on it. Her nose pressed against the glass, the rain splattering less than an inch from her eyes. She knew the two men watched her for a second, but their eyes returned to the television, a nightly comedy broadcast from some big city.

She couldn't help but feel exhausted. The two of them would never know all the weight pressing down on her, all the roles she had to fill. These dimwits, relying on her to move forward, to survive. They would never understand. She needed a big score and soon. Something bigger than they'd ever done before.

June stared out into the darkness, watched the rain drip down the glass. Somewhere out there, a few streets away, lived her mother. She'd have to stop by soon enough, drop off another wad of cash. The problem was scrounging enough. Insulin prices continued to rise, and her mother's condition only worsened. Who knew how long she had now. Months, maybe, or even a few years.

But if she got caught... June knew that jail time for her also meant a death sentence for her mom. The woman couldn't work, could barely get out of bed. All her underlying conditions only made things worse. June closed her eyes and tried hard not to imagine her mother in bed, frail under the blankets, her fragile body wasting away. And all the while, these two idiots were constantly forgetting plans.

"Least this show don't have that laugh track, amiright?" Curtis commented.

Randy shrugged. "Dunno what you mean."

"Boys, I've been thinking…"

In the window's dark reflection, she saw them both face her. She could see the excitement in their eyes, the rapt fascination.

She kicked at the carpet, scuffed against it with her bare toes. A quiet frown. She opened her eyes and took a deep breath. These next words were important, the way she would phrase the kernel of a plan.

"We been wearing these damned clothes for too long, don'tchu think? And we… we're living in trash, boys. Really digging ourselves a hole. These little jobs, these stores… we're gonna run out of places or get caught. You wanna go to prison?" She turned to them now and saw both men shaking their heads in fear. June crossed her arms, squinted a little. "But I got an idea, boys. I really been thinking. I think this is our *shot.*"

Neither one of them answered. June formed two fists and began to grind them against each other. Her determination deepened and a mischievous wrinkle touched the corners of her eyes.

"Michaels. That's the key. That man… he's got more money than we've all three ever had combined."

Randy nodded, stroking at the thin chinstrap of facial hair he wore. Curtis rubbed at his head, brain churning nearly as loud as the rain outside.

"I say we go for the big fish. Forget these little jobs. We don't gotta steal straight cash, see. We can... take something valuable. Sell it. Hell, that man's surely got enough in his wallet to top what we've done in six months!" *And enough for Mom,* she thought to herself.

"You think so?" Randy leaned forward. His shoulders were tense, breathing irregular. The couch moved as he stood. "You think it's possible?"

"Boys, we gotta do this." June nodded at them both, tapped her bare foot against the carpet. "We gotta rob Bruce Michaels."

13
BRUCE

The kid and I wandered through the forest, following an almost invisible trail that I could barely remember. Sometime long ago, I'd come this same way, only then I was in the other role, even younger than this kid. It'd been a summer similar to this, and I had acted the same way, tentative but curious. Farther and farther we traveled, the trees swallowing us, the sky overheard growing darker and angrier.

We emerged at last into a bit of a clearing, the end of our travels. A sharp descent lay ahead, plummeting down the side of the valley. I took the next steps gingerly, trudging through high grass, walking in the footsteps of a man long gone. The forest had grown dense around us, but ahead... an opening in the trees showed a majestic sight.

"What is this place?" he asked, sounding worried.

I didn't turn back to face him. Instead, I pushed forward, found myself standing on a platform of bricks and stone, older than I could have ever guessed. The trees were gone just ahead of us, clearly a manmade overlook that had been forgotten with time. This place had once been glorious. Years ago, when I'd first stepped foot here, there'd been a functioning trail that led down the hill. It was too long for me then, even more so now, and the entrance had been lost to weeds and bushes growing freely. If I could've walked it, though, that old trail would eventually bring me to the edge of downtown Little Rush. One journey, across two settings and a steep descent.

At this point on the hilltop, we could stare down at the Ohio River, even see the power-plant in the far distance. The river in all its glory, winding into the far horizon. My grandpa had told me then what I wanted to tell this kid now. That there were few spots where such a sight existed, the Ohio River bending three times and disappearing around the final turn. On toward Louisville, maybe, or some other forgotten town like our own.

"Have you ever been here?" I asked him after a moment of silence. Weeds and grass had grown up through the brick platform where I stood, but I could almost remember a time when it had been much cleaner here. Well-tended.

"No, never." He stood next to me now, admiring the same view. "It's beautiful."

Even under the weight of the coming storm, I couldn't help but smile. No matter how many clouds were overhead, no matter the rain that would soon batter these trees, this sight would always bring me joy. One of those places where the wilderness is perfection.

"Do you like this town, kid?" I asked him, turning my head just a fraction to gauge his response.

"It's Hudson." He chewed on his lip for a moment. "And I suppose so."

"As a pizza guy, you probably know a bit about the place, huh?"

He shifted in place and nodded. "I suppose."

"I don't know much about this town," I lied, hoping he would trust me. He had no reason not to. "Figured I'd like to have a real conversation tonight, instead of passing out drunk." I shot him a wavering smile.

"Know what you mean." Hudson crossed his arms and

didn't look away from the bends in the river. I couldn't tell if he really was that focused on it or just didn't want to make eye contact. I didn't blame him either way.

He couldn't have been out of high school, and yet he talked with the sort of dreary tone that I'd expect from someone much older. Someone who had his share of drunken nights and hungover mornings, who knew what it was like to drink because of pain and not for fun. *Stop reading into him,* I chided himself. *This kid isn't you.*

"You graduated yet?" I asked him, trying to gauge the kid's age. He could've been anywhere from sixteen to twenty-two, for all I knew.

"Course not," he said, smirking a little. I could see it in his eyes. *Stupid question,* he was thinking. "If I'd graduated, I wouldn't be here."

I waited a ten-count before pushing forward with the conversation. In the lulls between words, my eyes were inevitably drawn to the river and town spreading out below us or the gathering clouds overhead. They continued to build as the world grew incrementally darker. Soon enough, we would be standing in the midst of a thunderous assault.

I finally brought myself to ask, "So you're planning on leaving, then?"

Hudson narrowed his eyes at me and hesitated, as if deciding whether to go ahead with the conversation. I had no doubt that he would. One of the few perks that came with being me. People, when addressed, would never refuse to answer.

"Course I am," he said at last. "And it's not 'planning.' I *am* leaving."

"So then you *don't* actually like this town?" I didn't look at him this time. I wanted to give him time and space to think. He was the first local I'd spoken to, and I found myself intrigued by his feelings for Little Rush itself. Everyone here had largely different experiences than me.

"It's fine and all." He shrugged and stared at his feet. Maybe at the brick foundation we stood on, with grass fighting its way through the cracks. That was a downside of being me, I supposed. People would answer, sure, but they'd almost never make eye contact. Especially not when you're an off putting old man like me.

"Elaborate, if you don't mind." I closed my eyes for just a moment, inhaling the forest scent as the wind picked up slightly.

He huffed. "It's a fine place. We have some stuff. Like the pizza where I work is good. My friend you saw, his dad actually owns it. Dad works at that power-plant down there." He pointed at the view in front of us, but I already knew what he meant. "And we've got nice downtown shops and all, but mostly... I guess it's just not for me." He looked up now and actually gestured at me with his hand. "Whatever you see in it, right, that's what I hate about it. You came here because it's small, and that's why I want to leave."

"I came here because I threw a dart at a map and it landed," I corrected him, adding another lie. He finally made eye contact with me and I thought for a moment he would call my bluff.

"See, I wish I could do *that*," Hudson went on. "But if I live here, I'll never be able to. I just wanna get out there and go places."

I added with a touch of humor, "Places are overrated. And..." A pause, then pushing forward. "I'm just playing devil's advocate here. But, see, what if you can't find what you're looking for out there? Huh?"

Hudson's eyes drifted away again. "What does it matter? I won't find it here, either way. I mean... do you think you'll find whatever you're looking for? Have you?"

At that moment, the sky overhead gave a particularly dangerous grumble and I glanced up to find it had grown to a deep, dark purple. The clouds were menacing, and the walk back a bit farther than I would've liked, so I turned and started on the path.

"Let's head back," I said, emphasizing the direction with a nod of my head.

Hudson followed after me, kicking at the dirt as he stepped off the bricks. When we'd gone a few paces, he said, "You never answered my question. About what you're looking for here."

I smiled at the resilience and took a deep breath. "What makes you think I'm looking for something?"

"You left LA. You gave up on acting. I don't know why, but I know those are the..." He took time with the next phrase. I could tell he'd dwelt on this matter for some time before our chance encounter tonight. "The actions of a man who's searching."

"Let me tell you why I picked that house, Hudson," I said, pointing in the vague direction of it, though we couldn't yet see its grimy exterior. "Maybe that'll help."

"Sure." There was a noticeable raise in his voice, probably because I'd addressed him by name. It was probably a dream of his. Average people have such flaccid dreams.

I went on. "I moved here because of the cemetery, believe it or not. I'll end up there and I don't have much time left. According to my family history, anyways. I guess you could say it's a... reminder. We're all going there, really, but I'm closer than most." I ran a hand through my hair and felt how sparse it'd become. It unnerved me how I was opening up to this kid, and yet I couldn't resist, not now. "I'm almost to the end of the race, you might say. I've just got to see it through."

"But why give up acting?" Hudson insisted. "Why retire?"

"Just didn't like what I was doing anymore." I could feel my heart beating weaker with every step, feel my knees threatening to give out. Nothing could terrify and comfort me like my own mortality. "I'm here to talk about you, not me. So, tell me. What are *you* looking for? From... from one searcher to another," I added with a hint of a smile.

"I'm looking for..." A dignified pause. Another break to contemplate his next words. This kid spoke like a much older man. Like a friend I'd once known. "Somewhere better."

"Somewhere better, you say?" I chewed on those words for a moment. The route stretched out before us, another five minutes at least. Maybe more. If the storm would just wait, it would all be okay. "Have you thought about the possibility that there *is* nowhere better?"

Hudson grinned a little, and there was youthfulness in his expression. "You really think Little Rush is the best? No way."

"Maybe it's the best for a certain kind of life."

"I don't want that life, then." There was an air of finality in his voice. No doubt at all. It troubled me. "If this is life, I don't want it."

The trees were rustling louder now, the wind threatening to pull them away. Clouds overhead had built to an unimaginable depth, and I knew that any moment now they would soak us. Yet Hudson carried on, his face aglow, just content to be here. And for the first time in months, I felt the same. Like he had unlocked some part of me that was better, that could live here in peace. His own doubts had made me certain. Little Rush would be my home, if only for the end.

My grandpa had done the same. Had embraced the town in his final years. And if I was him, then Hudson damn sure fit the role of a younger me. There was so much about him. His mannerisms. His way of speech. The way his eyes were always dancing on the horizon, searching for a deeper meaning to it all. It unnerved me, really, how similar I had been. What I had become.

"Have you ever thought, Hudson, that maybe we aren't

searchers?" The house was in view now, and I wanted to share one more thought before we departed. "Maybe we're both... running from something, instead. The goal isn't to find a place, it's to escape from one. We're both trying to escape. We just have different finish lines and different demons chasing us there."

He granted me a half-smile. I couldn't tell if he was really thinking it over or if I'd lost him along the way. I wouldn't blame him. It took me years to realize. For someone his age, life was still potential and purpose. But for me, I saw everything clearly.

We were standing at the forest's edge now. A short walk among the tombstones, and I would arrive at my front door. I could see an unfamiliar car on the side of the road, engine on. Some kind of convertible with the roof up. I assumed that would be Hudson's friend.

The drops started to sprinkle us, first landing on our cheeks and then our shoulders. The aroma started to grow, the kind that only a good storm can stir up. A scent of earthly beauty and nature at peace. Rain was different in Little Rush, like everything else. More pure, more cleansing. I'd missed it. I needed it.

Hudson stood outside the trees, staring at me. We were facing each other for the first time, man-to-man, eye-to-eye. And now I saw him in an entirely different light.

"And for you?" He turned the question back on me, the way I'd hoped he wouldn't. But also the way I wanted him to. I needed him to ask. I needed the chance to confess, even if I never would. "What are you running from? In LA?"

"I don't think it's in LA," I said in a moment of honesty that shocked even myself. Now the rain had picked up slightly, and it splashed in my eyes. Gave me an excuse to glance down, avoid his piercing gaze. What a switch in our roles. What an interesting kid. "I think what I'm running from is... somewhere in here."

The words tumbled out before I knew them, before I understood them. But the moment they leapt from my tongue, I knew they were true. I touched my chest with two fingers and brushed them across the slightly damp fabric. Then I added, in a whisper, barely audible over the building storm, "And I'm not sure if I can escape it."

14
LITTLE RUSH
THE REPORTER

A little house in the middle of nowhere, perched next to a field of stone. Just beyond it, a youthful cornfield spread out, only dirt and tiny stalks for now. She maintained her position by the road for a while, camera at the ready, but no opportunity presented itself. Bruce had closed all the curtains to his house and probably locked the doors. As the sun rose and then fell, they all waited for any movement. None came. The other reporters grumbled to each other, some reminiscing with old colleagues. But Gina, she kept her distance. They were here for different reasons. They had no connection with her or her developing story.

She noticed when they turned away or gave her suspicious side-eyes. She recognized that feeling. They were intimidated by her, no doubt about it. Gina would be flattered, usually, but right now she only felt irritated. She had the kind of looks they wanted, sure, either to be or to fuck. She stood out in a crowd. But none of that mattered. They were competitors, and they would stab her in the back without hesitation.

I'd do the same, she thought with a chuckle.

Most of these camera-laden maniacs were from magazines or websites that functioned the same. Gossip this, rumor that. She hated the lot of them. Fake journalism, phonies. They didn't dig into anything, didn't even think for the most part. They would snap the picture, send it to their boss, and a team would create some storyline from the mess of photos. They weren't good for anything. And they got in the way of *serious* work, like hers.

Gina leaned against her car, sitting in the grass. From this point of view, she could see the others, crawling around the cemetery like rodents, trying to find the right angle for their camera. Maybe hiding in hopes that Bruce would peek through his curtains. Their strategy made no sense. They were being too obvious, too upfront. Gina, though, she'd formed a better idea. Sitting away from the mess, observing, she calculated, and her lips twitched.

As soon as these idiots cleared out of Little Rush, she'd make her move. Bruce Michaels couldn't resist a woman like her. Not with her legs, her lips, her authority. She would use every tool.

Those maggots crawled through the tombstones, across the sacred space of local families, without a care. Gina looked on in disgust, narrowing her eyes. This crazed mass of media was a plague on the town. The longer she stayed here, the more she understood why Little Rush was so adverse to the widespread coverage. Bruce Michaels, for all his fame, brought a cloud of flies with him to each new stop in life.

It makes sense, Gina thought to herself, watching as they buzzed closer to the walls of his tiny home. *Skeletons in the closet and all that. I suppose skeletons attract flies.*

But if that was the case, one could say only she, Gina, had the right reasons for being here. The only one who knew about the skeleton, who could see this course through to its grizzly and bloody end. If they were flies, then she was the huntress.

Gina picked at the blades of grass around her as she contemplated him. Like a twinkle always hovering in the corner of her vision.

Guys like Bruce Michaels, they moved to small towns for an

assortment of reasons. He moved to Little Rush because here, he didn't have to obey laws. He could do *anything.*

But for Bruce, time would soon run out. Even in Little Rush, he couldn't do just *anything.*

Not when I'm around.

She smirked and clambered back into the car. A different day, then. When the flies had cleared away and she could inspect the skeleton more easily. Then, at last, everybody would know the true story of Bruce Michaels.

15
WILLOW

How many times had I found myself staring out the window, down at the scarcely-trod streets below us? My dad's apartment looked out on one of the many downtown streets where the sidewalks were cracked and the people too. This view always disturbed me a little, made me want to run away. Then I'd peer between buildings at the river, and that would settle my spirit.

"How soon you leaving?" my dad called from the other room. I glanced in that direction to see if he was coming down the hall or just shouting. There were no footsteps.

"Few minutes," I answered, raising my voice when he didn't appear. "Can I have gas money?"

I'd gotten so used to the smell, I didn't even notice when he smoked. Only when he talked could I hear that faint distinction in his voice, whether holding the cigarette between his teeth or having taken it out. Regardless, he *was* smoking once again. It scared me that I couldn't even smell it. Not a great sign.

He responded, "No cash," and that ended our conversation.

I'd started to lose track of the days since we had that experience at the cabin. How long had it been since Bruce Michaels encroached on our regular lives? It felt like an eternity, truly. It had to be at least a week, but could've been as many as three. All I knew was Mason's party at that same cabin would be a fitting bookend to this chapter of our lives. The media would move on. Bruce Michaels would morph into just another old man around town. And we'd face senior year of high school, just like everybody else in the region, famous actor nearby or not.

I packed my bags, the usual way, and prepared for the trip to Mom's apartment. It infuriated me, how she lived ten minutes away, just up on the hilltop, and yet I had to pack multiple bags each weekend. I jumped between the two places, back and forth, hilltop and downtown, like a horse being whipped on two different sides. The weeks were sluggish, especially in the summer. My only marker of time was the bags I packed and the familiar roads I drove. Between parents, between lives really. Torture.

The only benefit of my mom's was that she didn't ask many questions. She didn't mind me spending the night with Mason at his cabin, although I hadn't told her about the planned party. As far as she knew, we were just "hanging out" with Hudson, usual stuff.

It confused me. How could my dad live this lifestyle and still obsess over my location? Any time I left the house, he demanded answers. Where was I going? When would I be back? That kind of stuff really irritated me. When people couldn't just trust me to do the right thing. It drove me mad. Not to mention, living with my dad is likely what got me addicted to nicotine. He didn't give me much in life, I guess. Trust issues and a nicotine addiction. Plus gas money, sometimes. At least here I didn't have to worry about my younger brother. It was much easier to push him to the back of my mind, as cruel as that sounds.

I wandered out from my room, a backpack hoisted on my shoulders and a duffle bag in each hand. I could've left the backpack if it weren't for my courses, which required lugging around a computer and four huge textbooks. Dad was in his recliner, watching one of the national news pundits I tried to avoid. He wrinkled his nose as I entered the room. Not that he meant anything bad, but he never loved when I left for Mom's. The same was true vice versa.

"I'll see ya later," I mumbled, waving to him as I passed through the room.

"See ya."

There was no reason to go over schedules because we both knew when I'd be back. Exactly a week from that moment, I'd walk in the door, and he'd probably be in the same position, savoring his weekend off from whatever job he filled. It changed, month to month, but I only noticed because the potato chips were different depending on his income.

I descended the thin staircase and reached the main floor. Ahead of me, the door led out to a dark and musty alleyway. To the side of me, a hotel-style door, complete with peephole and knocker, but it was actually our downstairs neighbors. They were nice enough people, never complained about my dad watching the television so loud. Or the smell of smoke. They weren't exactly role models, either, but nice enough.

My car was always parked outside on Second Street. I think they named it that because it's the second numbered street up from the riverfront. I'm not even sure what street *was* right by the river, because nobody used its real name. Everybody would say, "The pool by the river" or whatever, and everyone knew where that meant.

The only nice thing about downtown Little Rush was the exit or the entrance. Whether I drove up the hill or down it— always beautiful scenery. Especially at night, with the lights of downtown flickering either in the mirror or my eyes. The hilltop buildings were more spread out, like a normal rural city, and there weren't as many street lights.

With each pass up the hill, I could feel the end of that summer pressing against me. Senior year of high school meant...

well, everything. Choosing a college, a career, a future. Leaving my family behind. I had too many choices on a day-to-day basis to think about the vast possibility of "future." It was funny how people always described it as a good thing, full of potential. Hudson, too, would talk about his future, where he wanted to end up. But I didn't feel the same. I didn't want to leave Little Rush, and at the same time knew I had to. College, career, life… it wasn't here. Little Rush was the place you were born and left, or maybe you retired to and died. Nobody *lived* here. You were either coming or going, never staying. Not forever. A train station town.

There were moments, though, when I imagined a sort of life here. A forever here. And on trips up and down that hill, I didn't hate what I imagined. I actually enjoyed it.

I couldn't help but wonder, at certain moments, what the town would look like in ten years. When my younger brother would enter high school and meet his own friends, attend his own parties. The kid didn't have much impact on my life, but he did force me to consider the future. The kind of world developing around me. I hoped things wouldn't be too different. It felt sometimes like everything good, everything natural, was fading away. Just for him to catch a glimpse as it vanished.

On the way to my mom's apartment, I stopped at the Dollar General. Right when you reached "the top," where the roads leveled out and weren't twisting through a slanted forest, a Dollar General awaited, sort of welcoming. But then again, those things were everywhere in southern Indiana. If stores ever came to life, Dollar Generals would dominate this part of the country with their cheap products and empty shelves, no doubt about it.

Climbing out of the car, I remembered I should pick up bananas, the cheapest anti-hangover/anti-puke solution known to womankind. I also needed a couple Kool-Aid gallons and other drinks to mix with the copious amounts of alcohol Mason purchased. He said he knew a college kid, back home for the summer, who bought him everything, but still. It was really a *lot* for a side-market transaction. Maybe Mason had a fake ID he wouldn't tell me about.

I'd hoped that weekend would mark the end of a weird segment in our lives. That everything would return to normal, mostly. I'd had my share of the abnormal, the surprising, and now I wanted to enjoy this last month of summer vacation before staring down what lay beyond graduation. Wherever the road took me, Little Rush or New York, I wanted to savor moments like these. Like walking into a Dollar General and making eye contact with the cashier, who knew exactly why you needed five gallons of Kool-Aid and a dozen bananas.

That's the funny thing about moments, though. The harder you squeeze them, the more slippery they become. And then, before long, you've lost them entirely.

16
JED

Each morning, before preparing for the work day, I drank half my coffee and then left the house to check the mailbox. This time of year, the grass was covered in dew, the sun glaring directly in my eyes. Our neighbors house across the street would've blocked it had they built a taller attic. Maneuvering along the driveway in my sandals, careful not to step in the grass and soak my feet, I drank in the sight of our little neighborhood.

Once at the mailbox, I did a quick glance down the street in either direction. There were often cars leaving for work, the men in suits or similarly nice outfits pulling away for their various occupations. Some of them had wives who perched in the doorway, waving them off, dressed in a robe. Some had teenage sons also leaving for their shifts at any of the various establishments around town. Those high schoolers with their summer jobs. But me, I stood alone at the mailbox, observing the same, mundane routines every morning.

"Hey there, old man!"

I had just opened the mail slot when I had to stop and turn. The man waved at me from across the road, standing next to an identical mailbox. Everyone in this neighborhood had the exact same, all set in ornate stone that rose from the ground. Each house looked nearly identical, the same architecture and same color palette. Some were larger, some had nicer cars, but we were more similar than different. Each and every one of us.

"Morning, Carl," I called back, nodding at him. I turned back to the mailbox and stuck a hand inside, discovering a few letters and a small package.

"Crazy stuff about Bruce Michaels, huh?"

I rolled my eyes with my back still to Carl, but turned around to oblige him in a short conversation. I'd always felt a soft spot for him and his wife, ever since they lost their son to a summer camp accident a few years back. That whole situation had disturbed me. Not just the loss itself, but the town's reaction and especially this neighborhood's. Despite the cooked meals delivered and the baskets of gifts and the warm letters, nobody ever went to visit Carl's house. Nobody checked up on them, not after the funeral. Neither did I, of course. But it still didn't sit right with me. That sort of cold dissociation.

"Really is," I responded, granting him a smile.

"You'll be having him around for dinner, I assume?" Carl's eyes were intent, and his meager grin did nothing to hide his true intentions.

"Not sure."

"Well… if you do, be sure to say hi from me. I'm a… a big fan and all."

Carl blushed a little and hid it by digging through his mail. As I'd expected, he wanted to meet Bruce. Everybody did. I would surely get more questions like this, but maybe, if possible… maybe I could grant Carl's wish. Just to be thoughtful, for once.

"How's your boy doing?" Carl called to me, straightening up again. His eyes didn't give away any emotion now.

I always felt a little uncomfortable when he asked about Mason, wondering just slightly if he felt some kind of… jealousy or bitterness. Mason had attended that same camp, after all, years before Carl's boy.

"Just fine, thanks." I gestured back at the house with my handful of mail. "I best be going. Lucy's waiting."

"You take care, alright?" Carl wrinkled his nose and glanced in either direction. With nobody in earshot or driving by, he took a few steps into the road and said in a slightly lower voice, "Heard there's some... big party this weekend. Friend of mine said his daughter's been talking with friends about it. Not sure where or anything. Just thought you'd wanna know."

"Thanks, Carl." I nodded at him and escaped back to the house.

Just before I reached for the doorknob, I turned around to see Carl in his own doorway. Back to me, facing inside, he touched the wall with a hand and collapsed against it. His body breaking down into gentle sobs. I averted my eyes and caught on a house down the street, where an older man sat on his front porch, smoking a cigarette. I recognized the man but couldn't decide on a name. Something about his appearance struck me. The way his eyes roamed, not unlike my own. Maybe we'd both run our course here.

As I turned away from the landscape of wealth and uniformity that had consumed me, I couldn't help but think to myself that all of us were the same here. This segment of Little Rush, we faced the same difficulties and the same fears. Even Blough and I, though we didn't get along. Even Carl.

We were sons of great men and of terrible ones, but we had become neither. There were no heroes and no villains. Just existence, breathing dying, in the name of nothing. All for nothing. What a generation to call my own.

o o o

That evening, I found myself sitting on the porch, surveying the neighborhood from a chair, but to my dismay, the older man down the road hadn't reappeared. I had no cigarettes or even beer, but it still felt like a comfortable night to exist out here, watching people drive by.

The front door opened, and Mason hurried out, stumbling a bit when he saw me.

"Just heading out." Mason stepped off the porch.

I asked, "So, you all just... hanging out?"

He glanced over his shoulder. Moving toward his convertible, keys in hand. He had the roof up, which seemed odd. He always kept it down, especially on sunny days like this. But I didn't want to press him. I didn't want an argument or even that look he shot me anytime I pried.

"Yeah. Just hanging." He opened the driver's door and stared at me. Something on the tip of his tongue. Then he swallowed.

I knew this wouldn't be just a normal night. He never *asked* if he could use the cabin. He always just told me his plans. But yesterday, he'd actually asked. Something would be different tonight, then. Combined with the rumors Carl had shared, I had to wonder about some party. Not at my cabin, I hoped.

Behind him, the backdrop stretched in all directions, a quiet, suburban neighborhood. The wealthiest of the town in our meager glory. Matching mailboxes and glimmering cars. Freshly paved driveways and pristine lawns. The sun would finish its hour-long dive and the darkness would swallow us all. Each of us, the adults, looking on at a sky that signalled the end of another day. And soon our children would free themselves, drive their cars into the distance. Would they ever return? Could we stop them if we tried?

Sometimes, I felt incredibly connected with the rest of the houses. With these other men of wealth and nothing else. We were all proficient and efficient, all of us successful. Yet in the matter of children and wives, we couldn't be more helpless. I supposed we were just modern men.

"Just stay safe and all," I said. I took a sip from the glass of water in front of me, set it back down on the table next to the newspaper I'd considered reading.

We maintained eye contact for another moment. He nodded, a faltering smile, and then climbed into the car. I watched as he backed out of the driveway and turned onto the main road. I felt pretty confident they were throwing a party, with many more than just him, Willow, and Hudson. I also knew there would be plenty of alcohol. Just had a feeling. I mean, by his age, I'd taken my share of drinks. But it didn't abate that sinking in my gut. I hated being lied to, by anyone, but especially Mason.

His car disappeared from sight and I slouched into the house. Lucy had taken off an hour ago. She and some friends were spending the night in a hotel, then going to something the next day. I didn't know or care. For the first time in a few months, I had the house to myself.

Funny how things change. As a teenager, I'd have given anything for a night alone in a house this big, this expensive. Now I hated it. The walls closing in. The different paintings beginning to spin. The carpet opening to consume.

As the door shut behind me, I took a seat at the kitchen table and stared at the blank wall. I could see it now. Mason, partying. Mason, having sex. Mason, an unexpected pregnancy or an alcohol addiction, or both. Would I hate the girl after it happened? Would we ever talk again?

We weren't that different, really. I did all the same stuff as a teenager. This town hadn't changed much since then. Only, my friends and I got drunk in someone's dilapidated house downtown instead of a well-off cabin. Not only that, but in our free time, we'd bike around for hours downtown, visit some of the local shops, especially this one guy who sold soaps. Every day, we'd go in there and torment him. Just cause a scene. Get drunk at night, spend the morning hungover. At least we went to church, though. Mason hadn't been to church in years. Then again, neither had I.

As teenagers, my friends and I spent more time hunting than drinking, truth be told. I never felt like alcohol dominated my teenage years. Smoking was just casual, too, and still accepted. I gave it up pretty easily. I wasn't even sure if Mason smoked or not. If any kids did now. I didn't know much about "kids" in general. Until Mason started high school, I hadn't known the disconnect between me and people his age. As soon as he turned fifteen, that all changed.

Maybe that's why we never had another kid. Henry thinks that's the case. Him and his wife had talked about it, but they had trouble the first time around anyways. Lucy and I... we didn't talk much about stuff like that. It wasn't a good thing, but just one of those losses you can't win back. There were moments for stuff like that, to commit your relationship, ensure you're both communicating well. That moment passes, though, and by the time you realize it's too late.

I'd always wanted a son. We agreed on that, at least, and then it actually happened. Lucy had her own reasons, but me... I wanted to have those man-to-man conversations. With someone I'd raised, cared for. I wanted that deepest of connections. And now, I felt nothing. Nothing but fear, anger, desperation, loss.

Mason had slipped so far away. What did I have left? A small fortune of assets, some businesses, an empty home?

Lucy would probably leave me soon if things didn't change. It's not like we'd been happy. The more success I got, the farther I drifted from my family's rowboat. But I, with the huge ship, could do nothing about it. I couldn't move. I'd been anchored in this hurricane ocean. The distance between our two lives began to stretch. I wanted nothing more than to be on that smaller raft.

I'd face life-threatening storms on the sea if only I could have them. Worth more than this gigantic vessel.

My chin smacked the tabletop as I let my head fall. This table had cost me more than some people's cars. And now, my tears dripped onto the expensive wood I couldn't even pronounce. I don't know how long I cried, and, like most things, it doesn't matter. Tears never stuck around for long. They evaporated and left behind empty spaces.

In the richest house around, there was nothing alive. An elaborate vessel, and I was tied to the mast. We were sinking, sinking, sinking.

17
HUDSON

I'd never been a fan of parties in the traditional sense. Whether they took place somewhere I was familiar with or in a house I'd never been to, I disliked the actual "party" aspect. The techno lights, the throbbing bass notes, playlists that weren't really in my wheelhouse. Lots of people swaying, sweating. The girls were always dressed sexy, the kind of outfit where you really *want* to start a conversation and more, but you're also aware they're way out of your league. Well, that's how it was for guys like me. Other dudes, like Mason, they could bang anybody they made eye contact with.

The guys. That's another thing I hated about parties. They were always dressed awkwardly and stood that way, too. Some wore jeans, others cargo shorts, and others went all in for that "cool" look, like something Kanye would wear. I guess. I don't really know cool guys or what they're supposed to look like, but it sure as hell isn't what high school boys wear to parties.

So, yeah, parties sucked. Or at least, the stuff everyone else liked about them. But I did enjoy the atmosphere, as long as I stood a few feet away from it. The human connection, sort of an energy charge. Just being where everybody else was, seeing what they saw. I always felt alive, even a bit happy.

Mason's cabin held innumerable lights, flashing everywhere,

almost blinding. And the floors pounded with bass vibrations emitting from two huge speakers. He had the full party atmosphere, complete with a DJ, some college kid. He really just chose the songs, didn't do any actual DJ-ing, but wow did some people think he was cool. Girls, too. Those damn college kids.

Willow looked absolutely stunning, a kind of sexy that nobody else could pull off. The "I'm taken but I know I'm beautiful" kind of sexy. Mason did his best, but for the first time she really *looked* out of his league. I think he knew it, because he kind of sulked around the place for a while. He drank even more than I did, which never happened.

That's another thing about parties. I couldn't really get as drunk as I wanted. When I'm alone or with those two, I liked to drink enough that I could *potentially* die. Entertaining, in a way. Wondering if I'd wake up on the floor or in a hospital bed. Or if I'd even remember the night. At parties, that's a no-go. I just casually drank, loafed around the corners of whatever room I found myself trapped in. I *did not* dance, not even in that quirky, sarcastic way. Not even when drunk.

I would describe myself as the wallpaper of the party. There were a few of us, really. Occasionally, I'd see the others, dressed very much like me. They didn't look quite as sad, though, and they sometimes fist pumped when the right song came on. But altogether, we formed the wallpaper. We were the conversation topics that couples used if they wanted to avoid awkward pauses. We were the comedic relief that "cool guys" mocked to impress more attractive girls. We marked the boundaries of any given room, and, sometimes, if there were enough of us, we could even dictate the room where everybody flocked to. Nobody likes to be in a room without wallpaper to distract. Things get too real.

I did my best for Mason. And I enjoyed myself to some extent. For as much as I claim to hate parties, I really like the atmosphere if I'm away from it. Like outside, on the back porch. I can feel the energy of the crowds without having to talk. For the first hour of the party, I strolled from room to room, downing a few beers. I actually played a game of beer pong, which was a first, but this one cute girl didn't have a partner. Needless to say, we lost, and I never spoke to her again. But I guess that experience had its own charm, a good story to tell. I knew I'd eventually have to start liking parties, so I figured this summer was the time to change.

Mason took, by my count, seven shots in the first thirty minutes. And I spotted him with three separate beers. This meant he was pretty much wasted by the time eleven o'clock rolled around. I'd been waiting for this moment, when the whole world descended into a thick darkness. I could sneak out and leave. I had it all planned. But then Mason started to worry me.

"Come on." Willow clutched him by the arm, dragging him across the room toward me. Her hair was a little frazzled now and she kept pulling down the back of her skirt. As they approached me, struggling, she let out a huge sigh and pretty much threw Mason at me.

"What's up?" I looked at Mason. His eyes were doing a little dance of their own, swaying over the room, sometimes wide and other times narrow. I'm not sure I'd ever seen him this drunk, at least not while I was this sober.

"He won't stop," Willow grumbled. "Keeps grabbing at my ass and punching other guys in the shoulder. I swear, Hudson, I'm gonna hit him." She looked at me with crazy eyes, shaking her head.

I believed her. "Let's just hold off on that." I turned to Mason and touched him lightly on his cheek. "Hey, dude. What'chu looking at?"

His eyes were across the room on a group of three guys. They were all dressed in button-ups, pretentious ones, and didn't have any girls draped around them. The one in the middle, who had similar features and build to Mason, kept pointing at things around the room and snickering. The speakers, the couches, even the table where another college-aged student served beers and shots. Whoever this guy and his goons were, they'd caught Mason's attention without much effort.

"That son of a bitch," he breathed, now gripping my forearm so tightly I winced. "He brought them? I swear... I'll..."

"Mason, come on." Willow rolled her eyes and tried to pull him backward. He struggled against her for a moment but then relented.

As they turned to leave, I whispered, "Willow, who's that?"

She glanced over her shoulder, frowning. "One of the Blough boys. Him and Mason don't... get along."

The crowd swallowed them at that point. I stared in bewilderment as they disappeared. I knew the Bloughs, of course. They were the "other rich family" of Little Rush. I'm not sure who coined that phrase, but it fit. If there was a successful, local restaurant that Jed Cooper didn't own, you could bet money the Bloughs did or would soon. They even lived on the same street. This Blough kid had a similar build as Mason, maybe a bit wider, and he also had the blackest hair I'd ever seen, cut tight. Besides that, him and Mason were identical in almost everything. No wonder the animosity, then. But how come I hadn't heard about this before?

That thought nagged at me as I wandered through the rooms. The idea that Mason had taken up a different confidant in Willow. Of course they knew things about each other I never would. And I guess it made sense that she knew more about Mason's dislikes and hatreds. To be fair, I hadn't told him about my walk with Bruce, and I didn't intend on it. That conversation felt private to me. Mason didn't fit in with us. He wasn't a "searcher," or whatever term Bruce had coined. No, I wanted to keep all of that to myself, and it made sense that Mason did the same for a few things.

All the same, up to this moment, I'd never felt like a third wheel to them. I think they did it on purpose, always including me in stuff... *too* much. Never ignoring me whenever we hung out. Willow hugged me all the time, kissed me on the cheek, all that. I just felt like we were... just three good friends, and those two had a different level of friendship. I guess I should've realized, at some point, that things would change. They always did. I only hoped it wouldn't cause any lasting issues.

With two beers in hand, I navigated my way through the crowd of bodies and emerged onto the familiar back porch. There were only a few people out here. One couple made out to my left. Two boys stood just ahead, leaning on the railing and chatting, like my father and Jed would've done. Maybe these were two old-souls. I turned to my right, where I knew a bench rested against the wall, but even there I found someone. One girl, dark hair in a bun, a pale crop-top that accentuated her darker skin. She stared off into the distance, a lonely kind of way. I assumed that meant "don't talk to me."

For a moment, I thought about going back inside. But the air out here felt so nice, so cool on my skin. Not at all like the heat waves pulsing inside, the dank stench of spilled beer and body odor. I even enjoyed this peaceful darkness, unlike the throbbing lights and sexualized atmosphere of every room inside. So I made a move. I sat down next to the strikingly beautiful girl.

She turned to me and smiled, just a little. I could tell she had an incredible smile. I didn't think I'd ever seen a face like that. The kind where you just *know* every inch of her is incredibly gorgeous, even if you don't look at her body. Just that face. That's all it took. A piece of wallpaper had been ripped away from inside, and now I took my chance.

"Hey." I stuck out my hand. *Jesus Christ, a handshake? Is this a job interview?*

The girl, to her credit, glossed over this awkwardness and shook with a soft, gentle grip. "Hey. I think I recognize you. What's your name?"

It took me a moment. Even her voice just floored me, especially sitting this close to her. But I finally said, "Hudson. You?"

"Layla."

Something about the way she said that, I instantly wanted to lean over and kiss her. I figured, however, that this might border on sexual assault and definitely wouldn't make for a good first impression. So I just tried to play it cool, tried to ignore the squelching sounds that emanated from the other side of the porch.

"You mind if I... sit here?"

Layla's almond-colored eyes sparkled. "You already are."

"Right. That." I grinned, sheepish. At that point, I would usually recoil into my turtle shell and escape down the hill. But I resisted this urge. "Don't really enjoy... all that, so..." I gestured a hand at the cabin, at the blaring music, at the sea of grinding bodies beyond the wall.

"Me either. Not really my scene, y'know." She shrugged and granted me another one of those cute half-smiles.

In the moment, that expression sounded like a really witty statement and only attracted me even more. I wanted to press on, get a real, wide smile out of her. So I launched into one of my many stories about the cabin. I told her about the time I got black-out drunk, wandered down to the creek, and just laid there for a while. She didn't interrupt me, didn't even laugh really, but her lips did part and show off her flawless teeth.

"So you know the guy?" Layla nodded toward the cabin. "Whose party this is?"

"Yeah. We're good friends." All the air deflated inside of me.

My chest shrunk a solid inch. I tried not to sound like it, but I assumed this meant the end of my chances. Every time a girl asked me about Mason, that meant she was into Mason. I prepared myself for the usual, "he's taken" apology, and then I would make my graceful exit to the creek. Alone.

"So... is he gonna miss you?" Her grin shifted a little, something more devilish. Layla went on in a teasing sort of tone, "If you're... gone for a bit?"

"Don't think he even knows I'm out here," I answered, leaning closer. That sounded like a good answer. Should I put my hand on her knee or something now? Kiss her?

Layla, thankfully, took the reins at that point. Maybe she sensed that I was gonna fall on my face or maybe she was just the kind of girl who liked to take charge. Either way, I didn't care in that moment. I felt wildly magnetized to her, more than I had to any girl in a long time.

"You wanna show me that creek from your story?" she said in almost a whisper, tugging on the bottom of my shirt. "I'm not quite drunk, but it still sounds nice."

"Absolutely." I stood up right away. Together, we moved off the porch, into the trees.

o o o

The creek was nothing impressive, especially not at night. There really wasn't much to see in the daytime, just an inch or two of water that bubbles over the stones and pebbles. Sometimes I'd catch sight of a frog or a snake down there, but usually at night just crickets. And tons of them. Their constant chatter overwhelmed the brain until you learn to tune it out.

Layla followed close behind me as we moved through the trees. Down a gentle, sloping hill, we held onto tree branches for balance and shuddered anytime something brushed against our legs. Snakes are cool-looking and all, but I've never liked them.

Layla didn't mention anything specific, but I could only imagine she felt the same way.

We reached the creek and stopped dead. The quiet, trickling water and those chirping insects were the only noises. I glanced upward, trying to glimpse the moon and stars through the treetop canopy, but wasn't able to. When I turned back to Layla, she'd stepped closer. Her hand touched my hip and then my back. I pushed against her, my fingers on the bare skin of her stomach and sides, feeling just above her skirt,

"There's just something about you…" she said, biting her lip now. God, that killed me. "What'd you say your name is again?"

"Hudson." I reached up with one hand and brushed her cheek, her collarbone. "But it doesn't really matter."

"Dunno." Her voice dropped to a whisper. It had an edge, where she sounded almost out of breath, but I recognized it as desire. That really got me. I didn't think I'd ever had somebody so beautiful seem so genuinely into me with such passion. "Maybe… I'll need it later."

Then we kissed. I couldn't say who started it and to be honest I didn't think much about the kiss at all. Just that my lips were wet all of a sudden and I felt a different tongue in my mouth. I realized, at that moment, how awkward it really is to kiss somebody. Layla wasn't my first, not by any means. I mean, I'd *had* sex before. Just not a ton. And not a ton of girlfriends, either.

"I want you so bad," she murmured, pulling off her crop top in a swift, seductive motion.

It caught on a branch and hung just above her. I smirked, my confidence building. She kissed me again, relentlessly, and tried to undo my pants. I had to help out with that and sat down on a grassy area. In the meantime, she unclasped her bra. Then she pounced on me.

Laying there together, the grass sticking to our sweaty backs and bare flesh, Layla attacked my lips over and over, ran her hands across my entire body. I tried to return the favor but kept jerking around anytime a sharp rock dug into my shoulder blades or ankles. She would chuckle and wait for me to reposition, then go at it again with the foreplay.

We moved around for maybe ten minutes, at most, from the time her bra dropped to the moment she reclasped it. It just happened that way. Before we actually did anything, before I even took her underwear off, she just kind of... tossed herself beside me on the ground. We kissed for another minute or two, but she stopped pushing forward, and I didn't take control. Once I realized my mistake, I just didn't feel like correcting it. Sex is weird in that way, I guess. Sometimes it happens, and then sometimes the moment just dies.

Our candle flickered and then reduced itself to melted wax. Layla stood up and redressed, mumbling something apologetic. I tried to answer, but my jaw refused to budge. She did a kind of half-wave as she left, back toward the cabin. I watched her silhouette disappear into the dark trees, moving into those sparkling lights up on the hill. The cabin party still raged on. I could almost hear the music, if I really tried.

It was a shame how things ended with Layla. I wasn't sure I could even label our encounter "things." For a brief moment of time, maybe half an hour total, we shared a place in the world. We explored the creek bed, we tasted each other, and we danced on the ground. Then she vanished. I knew I'd see her again, of course. In Little Rush, you always see everyone. But I didn't expect us to ever speak or even acknowledge each other again. That's the way things were. A lost chance. An empty ending. I knew I'd have to tell Mason and Willow eventually. God, that would be embarrassing.

A part of me understood that I could've forced her into it. I was stronger, in a position of power, and I could've gone through with it. I almost wanted to, for a moment. The alcohol buzzing inside, hot blood coursing through me. But I shook the thought away almost as quickly. That wasn't me. Not even in this drunken state. Layla deserved better than that. Whatever we had, it'd simply sizzled out, and that was something I'd have to live with. I wasn't a forceful person. I wasn't bad... But then again, would a good person even have the thought?

I remained in that patch of grass, wearing only my boxers, for probably an hour. The effects of the alcohol slowly dripped away. It was a miserable experience to go through, the whole process of sobering in silence. I preferred sleeping it off. But emerging from a drunken stupor, inch by inch, with my back covered in grass and sexed-up blood coursing through my veins, was really a miserable experience.

Jesus Christ, I wish I had a cigarette.

I didn't want to go back to the cabin, of course. It really wasn't for me. I told myself I'd head up soon to help clean and all, but I didn't. Not for an hour or so. Maybe longer, I couldn't be sure. I knew the party lights were still sparkling when I rolled onto my stomach. Without knowing why, I planted my face in the grass, wet with dew. I closed my eyes then and let the sounds of the forest really consume my brain. I tried to connect with the natural world around me as much as possible. I really did. But my mind kept returning to the topic I hated.

Sometimes I was lonely. And sometimes I mistook this decrepit emotion for wanting love.

I wasn't the kind of guy to sit around and ponder "love," whatever that really meant. But for that brief stint, laying naked in the forest, I couldn't stop. I came to some pretty profound revelations that night but knew they'd slip away the next morning. All I had were the facts.

I'd never had a serious girlfriend or even a really hot girl like Layla show interest in me. In the end, she hadn't been any different. All of them, even the ugly ones, they got to know me, and that was the problem. Once they understood a bit of me, they ran away. At this point, I couldn't blame them.

Bruce, though... Bruce Michaels never had a problem with girls. He could have any girl he wanted, because everyone wanted him. In the grass, in the dark, I thought about him. In his prime, he'd probably fucked anybody he wanted. Probably still did, I considered. All sorts of hot and electric and freaky girls.

If I could be more like him, I told myself, dreaming. *If only I looked like him.*

In the end, I just wanted recognition. I wanted somebody to appreciate me on a deeper level. Somebody who loved the weird spots of my body and the flaws in my character. Somebody who made me feel a little less fucking suicidal.

It's this town, I convinced myself, breathing in the fumes of the creek and the taste of the dirt. *There's nobody here for me. Nothing here. It just isn't for me. The girls, the whole town. If I can just get out of here, maybe it'll be okay. Maybe I'll be okay.*

18
WILLOW

I heard the scuffle from the other side of the room. I'd just poured vodka and pineapple juice into a thermos and turned away from the alcohol table. It started with some "oohs" and "get him!" but already I had a sinking feeling. Something like this could ruin the whole night.

I surveyed the scene quickly, tried to peer through the slowly expanding crowd of people. The funny thing about fights at parties is that everybody knows and also everybody is unaware. They all stared on, gawking, probably hoping for some punches or a headlock. Something exciting, full of action. But this same crowd of teenagers kept dancing, swaying, talking to their partners. Like they existed in two worlds at once.

"You son of a bitch!" Mason roared from somewhere in their midst.

That did it for me. I sprinted toward the crowd and started shoving my way through them. Sweaty arms and chests, hand-locked lovers, it all parted. I scratched and clawed my way to the front of the pack and saw them.

Mason, drenched in sweat, cheeks red, stood opposite the boy from earlier, Blough. Nobody ever called him by his first name, for whatever reason. Probably because last names carry more significance when your dad owns a third of the businesses on Main Street. They eyed each other dangerously, each with clenched fists. I held my breath for a moment. I probably should have rushed in, pulled Mason away, but something stopped me.

I'd never seen him this upset, this agitated. Especially not at somebody from our high school. I didn't understand. And I couldn't tear my eyes away.

Maybe a part of me wished Hudson would come running out and join the fight, or at least stop it. I didn't feel comfortable doing so. And I should've, really. I could hit harder than any of these bystanders, especially Hudson. But I didn't get involved.

"Do it!" Blough stepped forward, puffing out his chest.

They were both really tan and you could tell they worked to keep up appearances. I think one of the girls behind me got really turned on by the two "models" fighting, because she kept moaning a little and taking shallow breaths. Swear to god, people are weird.

"I'll break your fucking neck," Mason shouted. He shoved him, not hard but enough to move them both a bit.

Blough just grinned, crossed his arms. Not a great defensive move, but I guess he didn't expect things to escalate much farther. "Get outta here, pretty boy. You don't want a fight."

Mason narrowed his eyes. "You don't fight without your group of retards, do you?"

"Mason!" I exclaimed, my eyes wide. I'd *definitely* never heard him call someone that before, not in a few years. I felt a tinge of anger myself.

He didn't seem to hear me. He only scowled. Blough was sneering, arms at his sides now and fists clenched again.

"Don't test me," he breathed.

Mason went on. "Wanna call your mom? She's probably fucking your neighbor's brains out as we speak. What an ugly old bitch."

Blough shoved then, almost enough to topple Mason.

Everybody oohed, and I caught my breath. Then Mason pushed back, dug his heels in. The two were locked for a moment, each wrestling for a better position, clawing. The pulsating music hadn't stopped. It made a weird soundtrack for the fight. The lights dazzling us, the smell of cheap beer and spilled booze. For a moment, I took in the whole scene at once like a single photograph. Appreciated it. Wild, youthful fun. Then the glass of my picture shattered.

Blough landed a punch to Mason's midsection. He doubled over, coughing, out of breath. I lost my own at the sight. For just a split second, he stood defenseless. I expected this blow to end the fight. It didn't.

Just as the beat dropped in some awful techno song, Blough struck again. He caught Mason right above the eye with a sideways swing and then again on the jaw with a nasty uppercut. Mason flew into the air —I swear he did— and then dropped to the ground on his back. I could already see the blood above his eyebrow. The crowd shrieked, backed away from the body.

"Oh my god!" I leapt forward and knelt beside him. He groaned and didn't open his eyes. It didn't look as bad as I thought, but it would all probably bruise. This would be some tough explaining to his dad.

"Fucking cunt," Blough spat. I didn't know if it was directed at me or Mason or both. Then he called, "Let's get outta here," and stormed toward the front door with his group of stuck-ups.

The rest of the crowd waited for a few moments, watching me kneel beside Mason. I finally glanced up and yelled for them to go. Once, twice, maybe three times, I lambasted them. "Party's over!" or something along those lines. All a blur after that. The hatred boiling inside me, the anxiety over Mason's injuries. Everything felt clouded, foggy.

People started to filter out, taking beers with them as they went. I lashed out at a few, but it didn't matter. I was preoccupied. It took me a few minutes, but I eventually gathered Mason, leaning heavily against me, and we trudged to the back porch. He groaned with every step, and his head slouched to one side. When we reached the colder air outside, he took a deep breath and winced.

"Get outta here," I snapped at the stragglers on the back porch. One couple was making out to the left and two guys were chatting against the railing. They all lowered their heads and shuffled past me. One of them, carrying about seven beers, tried to sneak by. I reached out a hand, grabbed his shirt. "Leave them or I swear to god I'll castrate you."

I don't think he knew what it meant, but my tone managed to explain. He set them on a bench and shuffled off the porch, back around the house. They would all be gone soon, I hoped. But I did question where Hudson had wandered off to. Maybe he'd left. He certainly hadn't been inside, nor out here, and despite his best attempts I didn't think he enjoyed the party that much.

Mason plopped into a deck chair and leaned his head back. I ran back inside, cursed at some remaining people, then located a paper towel roll and glass of water. Once I handed those to Mason, I took a seat beside him. He started to dab at the cut above his eye. I just fidgeted with one of the rips in my jeans. He didn't say a word, not a thank you, not an explanation. I mumbled something about "I thought you stopped calling people the r-word," and he sort of mumbled an apology. But besides that, no words were spoken. We just sat there for a while, the sweat drying on our bodies, absorbing the chilled night like a refreshing drink.

"What happened in there?" I asked finally. I turned to him. I couldn't see well in the dark, but the moon offered just enough light. There were tears on his cheeks, I was pretty sure. "You don't talk like that, and you never... fight."

"Just lost it," he muttered. "Hate that guy."

"I know, but never... never like that." I sighed, then propped an elbow on the table and leaned against it. "Gonna be tough to explain those bruises to your dad." A feeble shot at humor, but I had to try.

"No kidding." He murmured, but I could hear a hint of amusement.

"Your first fight?" I asked. I knew the answer.

"Yeah."

"Didn't go so hot."

He laughed a little. "Shut up."

Another few moments passed. The air grew increasingly chilled, or maybe my skin just cooled off. There were no voices anywhere, no cars pulling out of the driveway out front. For another five minutes, we waited there. Everybody would have gone by now. We were alone. I didn't expect the aftermath of the party to be like this, but that was part of the appeal. When you throw a party or go to one or get really drunk in general, you never know how the night will end up. You just wait and see. There wasn't much else to do around here, anyway.

"How drunk are you?" I asked him, breaking our silence.

"Not much." His words weren't slurred, just groggy. "That punch really sobered me up."

"Figures." Another brief pause. Sometimes I hated conversations with him. Not the most forthcoming of people whenever I broached serious topics. "Seriously, though... why'd you get involved like that?"

He shrugged. "Couldn't ignore him."

"Bad excuse," I persisted. "Try again."

"I just *hate* that guy, babe." He groaned and pressed a hand against his forehead. Probably a searing headache. I'd expect so. "He acts like... like he runs the goddamn town."

"Mason, honey." I tried to smile, tried to dip my words in

some amount of empathy. "I don't think you understand how similar you two are."

"No, I do, I really do." He paused. Dabbed at his forehead again. Took a deep breath through gritted teeth. "I know we are and maybe that's why I hate him so much. I see stuff in him that I don't like. All the parts of me that I want to ignore. He's them."

"I get it." I reached out, placed a hand on his knee. "Next time, though... Don't lose."

He smirked and turned away from me.

Seconds blending into minutes, and the scenery remained unchanged. No signs of Hudson. I pushed him from my mind. Just Mason and I, alone. The party had been a success, at least, even with the fight. Though I didn't enjoy having to sheep-dog Mason, keep him out of trouble. I didn't expect him to throw another one, not now. He'd be too embarrassed, too stuck on his fragile masculinity. It was times like these I wished for another girl friend, somebody who could relate on a different level. I had a few from work, but people generally avoided me. Another downside of living at Liberty Apartments.

"I think we should move near Louisville in the future," I said, replaying the fanciful conversation we had many times before. My hand rested gently on his thigh and I smiled. "Like the suburbs, you know?"

Only he didn't respond like normal. He just stared into the distance, grimacing.

I glanced up at the stars, as if they would offer me some level of support. They did not. "I think we should go away for college. Somewhere like... California or New York. Maybe a Carolina."

He still didn't answer. I thought I might have to repeat myself. It sort of worried me that he didn't respond, since usually we breezed through this topic. Maybe I shouldn't have mentioned it, not after the rough night for us both.

Mason turned halfway, glancing at me. "Why?"

"I think we need to... to get away from this town. From people like Blough." I cleared my throat. "And it'll be good for you."

"My family's here," he said. His voice sounded really dead now. Lacking of all emotion. Hollow. "My dad's business. My friends." He took a breath, maybe to steady his thoughts or maybe to buy some time. "What about... what if we just went somewhere in state? Like IUS? Or maybe, like, Evansville? It's cheaper and all."

As if money was ever a concern for him. "But... Mason..." I couldn't smile at this point or even muster a cute laugh. "It'd be good for us. To live a little, you know. Experience something else besides... Little Rush."

"I know, but there's so much here I can't leave." He drummed his fingers on the table, but his voice held no energy. Just hopeless resignation to this fate.

"Are you being serious?" I folded my arms and turned away, holding back a torrent of words. I wanted to yell, get in his face.

"Sorry, babe."

I didn't answer this time because I chose not to fight, even if I wanted to. Not with him bleeding all over the table. Not with us both in a post-drunk, bitter mood. But it was one of those things where I knew a fight was coming, one way or another. Maybe in a few days or maybe in a month.

People always say you shouldn't date seriously in high school because you'll both have different plans for the future. I didn't believe them until that point. And I really dreaded the fights that would grow from this disagreement. But either way, I wouldn't be the one crying about it.

Mason shut me down again later when I tried to bring up colleges. I suggested a compromise, somewhere like Ohio or Illinois. Somewhere in between. He didn't give me a real answer. The same bullshit as earlier. And for the first time in probably a year, I started to have my doubts. That's how I remained as we drifted off to sleep.

He'd always had a side to him that I didn't enjoy. A more sarcastic, drawling tone that sometimes crept to the forefront. Mason was by no means the ideal man or my dream guy. He might've had the body of Mr. Perfect. I mean, damn, who doesn't enjoy abs? But something about his personality, you might say, or his nature. Just... something off.

Did I think at times that by choosing Mason and sticking with him I'd settled for less than what I wanted? Even deserved? Sure. But so was everybody in Little Rush. This rural town felt like the edge of the world in some ways. On the coldest of nights, lost in the wild cornfields of southern Indiana, you might have to throw your hopes on the fire just to keep it burning. Just to stay alive. Settling wasn't the worst thing in the world. You just have to... become okay with it.

Not that this realization relieved my aching heart. It sent me spinning. I wondered if we would make it after all. I wondered if we would have that wedding we dreamed of, those kids, the careers. We'd seen eye-to-eye on most things up to that point, but I knew the topic of college held a much deeper truth. He wanted to stay, and I wanted to go. Whatever the reasons, whatever the pros and cons, it boiled down to that simple truth.

If someone came up and asked whether or not we'd stay together, I wouldn't have known what to say. I would only have my doubts, my creeping suspicions. Little Rush had always been my home, had been my whole world. It had been the place where I met the person I loved more than anybody or anything else. A place of complex people, astounding scenery, hushed adventures in the local Walmart.

At the elementary school we all attended, the playground had a chain-link fence around it. As early high schoolers, we'd sometimes go there on weeknights and climb over top of it. On the swing set where we spent our childhoods, we once again wasted away countless hours. Talking about life and about the future and how much trouble we'd get in if we were caught. We even managed to break into the school one night. I snagged my leg on the fence and ripped a hole in the sweatpants I'd worn, but it didn't matter. We'd roamed those dark hallways for hours. I had smoked a cigarette, sitting at a teacher's desk, and then made out in the corner while the others played hallway bowling. That night, one of the best I ever knew.

In a sense, Little Rush was that chain-link fence. Sometimes you just have to jump it.

This town, for all its glory, had always been a place best suited to those with patience. A place of virtue, sure, but rarely excitement. No, Little Rush, my home and my undoing, for all its pain and soft-spoken goodbyes, was a place of incredible boredom.

PART 2

A PLACE OF
EMPTY DREAMING

1

BRUCE

Only moments before she arrived did I realize I had to hide it. With a quick glance out the window, I snatched the photograph from my coffee table and carried it away into the bedroom where I hid the thing under a pillow. A secretive location. And, truth be told, I never planned on removing it from that spot ever again. Just in case. They didn't need to know, and most definitely not her, a journalist.

When she did finally show up, the woman took a hesitant first step into my house, not that this surprised me. Her eyes were wide, darting all around, and she clutched a small purse tight against her side. The journalist had a youthful glow to her, despite her age. The shorter-than-normal skirt didn't hurt, either. She couldn't have been more than thirty-five. After all, the local paper wouldn't send anybody *new* for this assignment.

"Thank you again, Mr. Michaels," she addressed me once I'd closed the door behind us. She beamed, looking around the simple sitting room, her eyes fixating on the couch against the wall. I'd left an empty beer bottle on the table and quickly disposed of that.

"No problem."

With the bottle in the trash can, I reentered the sitting room and found her inspecting the window curtains. An odd journalist, this one. Overeager, a little too pleased. I cleared my throat, and she turned around, that smile wide as ever. I couldn't help but grin a little. She had a certain air to her that felt familiar. Maybe something in the way she stood. More like me than any other person in this town.

I went on. "I've been wanting a... an interview like this since I moved in. But waiting for the..." I caught myself before I said *paparazzi*. Maybe as a journalist she would find that offensive. "For the out-of-towners to clear out," I finished.

She nodded appreciatively and extracted a small pad from her purse. Her eyes arched just a bit, and her lips opened an inch. I noticed for the first time how red they were. Matching the color of her tight top. Surely not all journalists dressed like this? I hadn't seen another woman in this whole town quite as attractively intimidating.

"So... I..." I struggled to collect my thoughts under the weight of her gaze. I could feel myself changing a bit. Opening up. To her, to the town. "We can sit here, I'd say." I gestured to the couch and then to the flimsy folding chair across from it. The coffee table rested in between the two, barren.

"That'll do." She took her place in the folding chair, shifting uncomfortably at first, but then settled back and crossed her legs. Pulling out her notepad and leaning forward a few inches, the skirt rose higher up her leg than I think she realized. Or maybe she realized perfectly. What a woman.

I leaned back on the couch and observed her more intently. She had a darker tan than most people around here and no pale lines to be seen. Her hair was dark, pulled back, and she wore sleek glasses that gave her the aura of wicked intelligence. Sharp cheekbones and lipstick completed the look. I wondered where in Little Rush women like her were hiding. Surely, I wanted to visit that place. For a guy my age, porn held no real enjoyment. I needed the real thing.

"Mr. Michaels," she started, but I cut her off.

"Call me Bruce." I gave her my best, sly smile and added, "I insist." Flirting, if it could be called that. It felt good, or at least not bad. I felt like a human again.

She nodded then and scribbled something on her notepad. "Bruce. I just have a few questions if that's alright." Her eyes rose to meet mine, a reassuring curve gracing those perfect lips. "Won't take much of your time."

"Take as much as you please." I extended my arms to either side, opening up my whole body. Times like these, I wished I'd kept up my physique over the last few years. All those workouts as a twenty-something, all those crunches, good for nothing in the end. At least I didn't have a beer belly yet, not a noticeable one. "And what do I call you? Just so we aren't... strangers."

"Gina," she said. Something about the way a person says their own name. It can tell you a lot about them. She said it kind of cutesy, real quick, like she didn't often go by her first name. An air of intimacy, then, between us. A good start. "You understand why I'm here? Interviewing you?"

I shrugged. Thought about pulling out a cigarette. Would that impress her or scare her off? As a woman around here, she'd seen plenty of guys smoke. But then again, I didn't see a wedding ring, so maybe the guys around here didn't check all her boxes. No smoking, then.

"The local paper wants to run a lengthy article in next month's special edition," she said. Her pen hovered just above the lined surface, like a cocked gun. "I'll start, I suppose, with a simple question. *Why* did you move away from California?"

"LA, baby." I chuckled. "Not *just* Cali. And... I'd say a few reasons."

She laughed politely. "Go on."

"Well..." I cleared my throat, fidgeted with the seams of the couch. Without a cigarette or a drink, I didn't know what my hands should be doing. "I'd say... I got bored of the movie industry. No, truthfully. Just couldn't find anything suited for me."

Gina chewed on the butt of her pen for a moment. "So is that why you've had so few appearances in recent years?"

"Eh, suppose so." I kicked my legs up onto the small table. I could fall asleep in this position, really. Instead, I found myself gesturing with one hand. "I like to make serious movies, see. Don't even *consider* one if the runtime is under two hours. Not a single role. So, yeah, maybe that's why I got bored of the whole scene. Not enough movies like I wanted." I pointed at her. "See here, these people... they want me to be some Steve Carrel old man type, right? Nah. I'm not. I'm more... serious." I smacked my fist against my chest to emphasize the point. "I really *do* things."

"Are you aware critics have attacked you for that stance in the past?" An eyebrow rose as she waited for my response. "Some might say you have a... self-aggrandizing attitude."

"Ah, fuck 'em. That's what I always say about that." I batted a hand through the air. "Maybe it makes me a bad person to meet, I dunno. I don't care, either. I do real, meaningful work, see? Who cares what they think. *I* know the truth." That felt great to admit. I hadn't spoken on this topic in years. I guess the attention was nice, especially coming from somebody like her.

"Interesting," she mumbled, scribbling a few lines on her notepad.

I grasped the remote, which had been laying on the ground, and pointed it at the television. "You want some... some background noise or something?"

Gina didn't answer. She just kept writing, so I flicked on a rerun of some half-hour comedy I didn't care for. A perfect illustration for my points, I thought. This garbage, cable television stuff.

"What appealed to you about Little Rush specifically?" she

asked at last, raising her eyes from the notepad to me.

I shrugged again. "Dunno. Just chose at random."

"Hmm." She wrote something with sharp movements. I wondered what that meant. "So no... prior relatives here? No history?"

I scowled at her without meaning to. "Nope." I never liked when journalists did that. When they asked a question and then felt the need to ensure you were telling the truth. If I wanted to lie, asking again wouldn't stop me. And when talking to a small-town journalist like this, lying was the best option.

I thought I saw her chuckle just a bit, but I couldn't be sure. She went on with the questions for another fifteen minutes, and I quickly lost my infatuation. All the questions, variations of the same stuff. Why had I chosen this house? Why had I been so secretive moving in? What did I miss about LA? What did I like about Little Rush? Did I feel like I'd made the right decision? All stuff that I didn't want to trudge through, but I *had* agreed to this whole thing.

The longer she went on, the more irritated I became. It felt like hours, sitting there with her. Even when she bit her lip a time or two, I didn't feel anything. By that point, no attraction to her. No primal desires. She'd been just like all the others, just stupid people asking stupid questions. Sure, she had a nicer body than the rest of them, but that didn't mean much. Back in LA, I could fuck somebody *twice* as good with zero effort or care.

"I have one last question, Bruce," she said. Gina stored away the notepad into her purse, which I found odd. If she really had another question, wouldn't she want to write my answer down or something?

"Go ahead," I said, still reclining on the couch.

She stood up and grinned, but it was different this time. Less cutesy, more prickly. The way her eyes cut into mine, void of any emotion. Just cold orbs that swam in the tan sea of her face.

"I have a friend that you might know," she began. "And I wondered if I could maybe... get an autograph?"

I cocked my head, unsure where this was going. "I can sign something, yeah. Like a magazine." I started rummaging in my pockets for a pen or a sharpie. "What's his name?"

"*Her* name." Gina hesitated. "Madeline Suso."

"Oh. Um... sorry." I tried to force a smile, feeling panic rise in my stomach and throat. "I'm actually... in a hurry, I have to be somewhere. You know how it is."

Our eyes met for a second, and she pierced into me. That face, so entrancing to me earlier, now glowed with mischief. I refused to look away, to even budge. She nodded once, slung her purse strap over a shoulder, and turned away to the front door.

"Nice chatting with you, Bruce," she called over her shoulder, easing her way outside. "I hope to see you again before too long." Then I was completely alone.

The remote flew across the room before I could control myself. It smacked the wall and dropped to the floor, two batteries rolling out to either side. For a moment, I sat there, shoulders hunched, seething. *Deep breaths,* I told myself.

I rested my forehead on the coffee table and grabbed a handful of my hair. Her car churned to life outside and then sped away, back to town. Gone for now.

She'd been lying. I had no doubts anymore. Not a Little Rush journalist, no article in next month's paper. No, that scheming bitch was something else entirely. Something more sinister. A trap.

This in itself didn't unnerve me. I'd had plenty of lying, filthy bitches investigate me, and even confront me. What really bothered me was the name. The one nobody else should've known. The one that I didn't want any connection with.

I did know a Madeline Suso. And god dammit, I'd done my best to forget.

2
HUDSON

"So you really tried to take on the Blough kid?"

I chuckled and glanced at Mason. He lay completely still in the bed of my truck, a beer bottle in hand. The moonlight glinted off its dark surface and off those dazzling teeth as he smiled. I took a sip from my own and set it down. I leaned to the side and took a moment to observe the stars. With the sun finally absent, the outside world felt decent again, not sticky like earlier.

In Little Rush, there'd be a certain kind of humidity and heat that only came after a heavy June rainstorm. For a day or two after, it'd be so hot that every time I stepped outside it felt like walking into a sauna. Only there was extra light glaring in my eyes and I was fully clothed instead of draped in a towel. The air thick as fog, and the entire day I'd think, *This is the hottest weather I've ever felt.* Eventually that all subsided, only to return with a vengeance at the next thunderstorm.

"I really did." Mason chuckled finally. After a weekend to recuperate, battle scars were easier to laugh at. He shrugged his shoulders and downed the rest of his beer. "Hand me another."

I obliged and dug through the cooler full of ice and bottles for a minute. "Only a few more."

"Which of us is gonna drive home?" he asked, eyebrows raised.

I took a long gulp. "Pretty sure this is our home, now."

"Touché."

My truck sat at the edge of a field, one that nobody had used for a few years. If you knew where to look, a little dirt path cut off from the country road and let out to this spot, right next to the trees. We came here every so often when the cabin was being used by his dad or whenever we just liked the idea of getting wasted outside. It also made for a great place to smoke weed, but we rarely had any.

The forest rustled briefly as some deer emerged and pranced across the field. They paid us no mind, and we didn't call out or anything. The beautiful animals went their own way, and we stayed in our spot, watching them for a moment. Soon they were out of sight, into the darkness and through the other side of the clearing, just as they'd come. A slight rustle and then empty space.

"What happened with you and that girl?" Mason asked me after a long pause. He didn't glance my direction. In fact, he stared completely away. That's how I knew he was hesitant to bring it up. "You never really explained. Just said…"

"Nothing scandalous." I laughed, and it sounded more jaded than I intended. "I almost wish it had been. The truth is, we were just making out. Down by that creek, you know, on the grass? And then… I dunno." A fresh drink bought me a moment to organize my words. "It just kinda fizzled out. Can't really explain it."

"Shame." Mason picked up his empty bottle and stared into its glass depths. "She's pretty hot. *Way* out of your league, man."

"Trust me, I'm aware." I leaned back and let out a deep, exasperated sigh, the kind that Mason would usually make fun of. Something held his tongue, though.

If only to change the subject, I remembered the ten-dollar bill in my pocket and extracted it with some effort. Mason watched me, eyebrow raised, as I writhed around for a second. Then I pulled out the wrinkled, dirty bill and offered it.

"Here," I explained, "this should cover my booze for tonight."

He batted a hand through the air and shooed the money away. "I told you, stop trying to pay me for this. You're doing me a favor by just being here."

"That's bullshit, and you know it." I narrowed my eyes, but when he wouldn't budge, I stuffed the crumpled money back into my pocket. "Thanks, though. Honestly."

He didn't answer. Neither of us felt very emotive.

Mason never let me pay him back for alcohol. Not even back in our freshman year of high school and the summer immediately after. Over that timeframe, we spent countless nights here. Those days, when Mason had his license but neither of us held down jobs, were some of the best. Carefree, dripping with potential. The first time I ever tried alcohol was in this field, when an older kid bought Mason a bottle of vodka. I always hated that stuff, and Mason would poke fun at me for it.

Then, once we discovered beer as a suitable drink, the nights really got wild. Two or three times a week, we'd lie to our parents, make up some awful excuse, and escape here. Sometimes, driving back at two or three in the morning, we'd feel on the brink of death. Drunk driving on a country road, the lights swimming around us. Mason, hands on the wheel, really had to focus. I would just lean back in my seat, enjoy the night air, the potential that any moment I might not exist any longer. It didn't hurt that this beer bliss didn't cost a cent.

We spent hours in this field, talking about nonsense. Before jobs, before girls, before any actual problems. Thinking about adulthood. Sorting through our fears and our overwhelming dread. Mason, back then, was more open to these kinds of airy, philosophical conversations. We both agreed on one thing. That we could feel the unavoidable weight pressing on our heads, threatening to crush our bodies into paper. Something about growing up. Something about the world shrinking in on you. It all just pressed so hard.

Back then, we spent many conversations on this topic. Together, Mason and I had decided the best way to fight this feeling boiled down to two goals. Stay young and stay wild. We were immature kids, really, and it was a bit embarrassing in hindsight, but I didn't hate the memory.

As Mason and I carried on a flimsy, unimportant conversation, I realized that we had both failed. Terribly. Since we decided on those goals, Mason had become a gym rat, obsessed with the physical, reluctant to step away from this stage where we'd grown up. And me? I fit a different set of descriptions. Depressed, lost, wild in a harmful way. In reality, though, I had tightened. Formed a suit of armor around myself and refused to open. At least Mason could enjoy life. At least he felt emotions intensely and… lived. I didn't do either. I failed. Now I could almost imagine death, like a wild animal in the clearing, creeping near my truck bed.

A pause fell over our conversation. I couldn't remember who had spoken last and didn't care. To avoid the dark thoughts growing in the corners of my mind, I breached the subject we'd been dancing around for a few minutes. "What about you and Willow? Things still… good?"

"Suppose so." He tapped on the glass bottle now, then rolled it up and down on the truck bed. It made a weird noise, rumbling against the aluminum. "She said something, though… about wanting to move away. I dunno how that'll work."

"Right." I set aside the beer bottle for a moment. Number five or six, I couldn't remember. But I could feel the alcohol, without a doubt, and wanted a few minutes of clarity for this conversation. Then I would blackout, sure. "You don't want to, I assume?"

"I really don't know." He held the bottle up again, admiring it. Mason gets really intimate with beer bottles once he drinks them. I don't understand it. Not any weirder than biting fingernails, I guess. "I want... her. But I also want... everything I have here. You know?"

"Right, yeah." That wasn't entirely true. I wanted nothing here. I wanted to leave as soon as possible. But I guess Little Rush had a bit of charm. I could relate to his struggle in some ways, but really more to Willow.

Without warning, Mason chucked the bottle high in the air. It arced away from us and crashed to the ground somewhere in the field. I could hear the glass shattering, but muffled. Then he leaned back fully, crossed his arms, and huffed.

"Sorry," he murmured. "I know you hate when I do that."

"It's fine." I cleared my throat. I did hate when he littered out here, but he'd mostly cleaned up that habit. Honestly, since getting with Willow, he'd cleaned up a lot of habits. "You know what I think?"

He turned his head and eyed me.

"If this was my last day alive," I said, picking up my half-full bottle, "you know what I'd do? Just come out here, get drunk as fuck. And run around naked."

Mason chuckled at that, and I broke into a grin.

"Not tonight, please," he said. "If that girl ran away from just you in your boxers, I can't imagine—"

"Shut up or I'll cut you off," I said, laying a hand on the beer cooler.

"I'll beat you up." Mason sat up woozily and pointed a finger at me, his smile more radiant than it ever got when sober.

I raised my eyebrows. "Oh yeah? Wanna lose two fights in one week?"

It had been months since we drove out here and spent the

late hours drinking, the early hours drunk. Just the two of us. No worries, no cares. The talk usually turned to girls, and Mason would inevitably discard a bottle or two in the most dramatic fashion. But it felt comfortable. That was more than most days could claim.

The hours wore on and on. We waited breathless for the sunrise. Coming down from our drunken mountain, neither of us were shy about our emotions in that moment. We each longed to watch it peer above those trees and paint the sky with brush strokes too godlike to truly emulate. We waited for what felt like an eternity, the conversation shifting and dying altogether at times.

I felt bad, in certain moments, for not telling him about Bruce. I knew, deep down, that I should share that experience with Mason. We'd both loved the actor for so many years, it was wrong to keep him to myself. But Bruce had chosen me to share that conversation with, not Mason. Maybe it was a jealousy thing, like I finally had something Mason didn't, or perhaps I just worried about being that open with another teenager. Whatever the reasons, I held my tongue. What did one more regret matter on a pile that had grown so high?

And I knew more soft regrets waited in the future. College approached. Adulthood. Career choices. Marriage, funerals, children. A world of mistakes made and lived with. If I was a sponge and alcohol the squeeze, so many regrets would pour from my body. And it only got worse with each passing year.

Mason ached with questions. I could see it in his eyes that whole time, sitting in the bed of my pickup. He struggled, already, with so much. To stay in Little Rush or stay with Willow? Could there be a compromise? Did he have any choice in the matter? Would he run his father's business well?

And myself, I stared at the sky that early morning, looking for my own answers. Would I really be trapped here, to a factory lifestyle or a job I hated? Could I ever leave this place, even if I desperately wanted to? And if I stayed, would I survive?

When the sun did finally rise, it found us both asleep on the truck bed, snoring loudly. Beer bottles scattered beside us, one of them having spilled. My bare heel in the liquid puddle. Two caged teenagers, a glorious sunrise, and the fog rose from the ground like the regrets we'd been avoiding all our young lives. But there were no answers in the fog and there was no help in the sunrise.

3
JED

Main Street was the hub of downtown Little Rush, with most of the stores and restaurants, along with a plethora of loft apartments and houses. It could be imagined as two separate areas, with Allen's Burgers serving as the link that connected them.

The eastern half was mostly commercial spaces. Stores lined both sides of the street, with a smattering of restaurants, coffee shops, a few inns, a nail salon, and everything else that made up the tourism center of the city. There were elegant churches with their steeples jutting into the clouds, an ornate fountain set just off Main Street, and the large courthouse, marking the end of this area where the road shifted into a highway. From there, it ran across the Ohio in a wide bridge and vanished.

The western sections of Main Street were almost entirely houses, along with a public school that'd seen better days. All the buildings were different shapes and colors, the only common denominator being their age and similar architecture. When driving through downtown Little Rush, it was evident that little had changed in the past century. Other than the vacant factories, mills, and windows with "For Rent" signs, most things were preserved from decades ago.

Conjoining these two worlds was a brick building that'd

been in operation for almost a hundred years. Allen's Burgers, a staple of downtown, and one of the places I found myself all too often, never for a good reason.

They called them sliders, the tiny grease burgers that were served on chipped plates. This restaurant had a distinct smell like nothing else in Little Rush. Just walking by outside, you got a whiff of it. Very effective marketing. I wasn't sure what the oldest restaurant in town was, but it had to be way up there. It'd been around since I could remember. And since I could remember, I'd been a regular.

Allen's Burgers was just a blink along Main Street but packed a punch. It was the go-to for hamburgers, when you wanted good ones and not McDonald's crap, especially for teenagers wandering around at midnight. It was about the only thing still open that late other than Taco Bell on the hilltop. Allen's had also been serving breakfast for a few years and the same crowd would filter in. Everybody came to talk, to laugh, and to enjoy food that felt like a blood clot as it dropped to your stomach.

As a high-schooler, I'd spent many evenings there, even a few afternoons whenever I'd skip the back-half of the school day. Allen still ran the place back then and could be found on any given day. Flipping burgers, serving sodas, teaching new employees how to use the clunky old milkshake machine. He and I struck up conversation easily. I think those meals were the first time I envisioned myself as a businessman. He convinced me I could own a restaurant, actually succeed, if only I stuck it out through high school and applied myself in college. So I'd done just that.

Allen was the kind of guy everybody knew by his first name. I'd see him around town, every once in a while, and at the local high school basketball games. Never got into any trouble. Never had his name run through the mud. An all-around good guy.

Still, we all saw it coming after his retirement. Once he gave up the restaurant, Allen only lived another six months. That may have been the best-attended funeral I ever witnessed in Little Rush. More people showed up than for the previous mayor when he'd died. They held Allen's at the biggest church in town, but even that couldn't fit everybody.

"Hey there, Jed. Long time," Sondra called out as soon as I stepped in the door.

I waved at her and chuckled. The door shut behind me with a jingling of chimes, and then aromas blanketed me entirely.

There were two seating areas at Allen's Burgers, each with its own entrance door. One was a typical dining room, with ten tables, four chairs at each one. They were all retro-looking, cold metal, old-fashioned ketchup and mustard on the tables. The second area, where I preferred to sit, was bar-style, with about a dozen stools along a counter. Same deal with the retro look and everything, but a bit more personal. The workers were always talkative, the crowd interesting, and an unused jukebox sat in the corner, giving off a nice vibe.

You never knew what kind of crowd would be at Allen's on a weekday evening. I wouldn't be there myself, except that Lucy and I had ourselves a pretty serious fight about two hours earlier. The topic wasn't important because honestly *every* fight was the same. We bickered about how often I worked, though that never came up word-for-word. Other problems bubbled to the surface. We yelled, and she cried, and nothing ever got resolved. This time, though, she'd announced her intention to make popcorn for dinner and told me to "get the hell out or get back into your study." I had no intentions of working, so I left the house and strolled around downtown a bit. When I finally felt hunger gnawing, the smell from Allen's brought me around.

Tonight, there were only a handful of us seated at the counter. A teenage couple all the way down, farthest from the door. Then, a few seats away, a middle-aged man sat hunched over his burgers like precious gold he had to protect. Another few seats down, two older men with white hair were engaged in a passionate debate that took up most of the room's air. These three types of people were spaced evenly down the bar, and I had no interest in debating the white-haired men or crashing a date, so I took a seat next to the quiet one.

"The usual?" Sondra asked as I located my stool.

I nodded at her and settled onto it.

"Coming right up, honey," she quipped, and set to work on my order. She snapped at a young woman passing by to get me a Coke.

The gentleman beside me turned on his seat. He already had a plate of two sliders sitting on the countertop with what appeared to be relish piled on. His hands, clasped around a large mug, were rough. I recognized his dark shirt and blue jeans as the typical uniform from one of the factories. He extended a cold, damp hand to shake mine, and I could read his shirt. "Rush Industries."

"How's it going?" His voice hit like gravel, probably a smoker. His hair was dark and thinning, with a battered IU ball cap on top.

"Fine." A different waitress I didn't recognize handed me a soda, and I thanked her quickly. Then she disappeared into the recesses of the kitchen, probably to a table on the other side. I turned my attention to the man, who I didn't remember from the typical Allen's crowd. Then again, it was easy to miss people. "Eat here often?"

"Nah." He took a long gulp of beer and set his mug on the counter. Wiping his mouth, he elaborated, "Usually out with some buddies." A grin broke out underneath that messy beard. "I seen you around here, though. Couple'a times, I'd say."

I shrugged and took a sip from my Coke. "Can't deny it."

He squinted at me for a moment. "You're the... the one who owns the pizza joint on the hill?"

I nodded, watching his expression closely. People asked me that question often, in different ways. Sometimes I owned the pizza place, sometimes I owned the apartment complex by the river, and sometimes I was just the local rich guy— "but not Blough." He would always receive a little more recognition than me, given his sons were bigtime athletes at the high school. Mason, not so much.

The man raised an eyebrow and tapped on the table a few times. "You see here, I've got a question for you. Heard a rumor the other day and it's been burning at my brain. Maybe you'd... know something 'bout it."

I set my drink on the counter and folded my hands into a tent-shape. It would probably be something about Bruce. That's how all these conversations had gone recently. But I had nobody else to talk to and might as well indulge the man's inquiry. "Maybe so. What'd you hear?"

He grinned wide at that point and studied my face. His eyes were full of newfound hope, and his left leg started to bounce on the floor. "I heard about some ATV company gonna buy up the old hilltop factory. By the highway. I was... just wondering if you'd heard it too or not?" He cleared his throat and added in a hurry before I could speak, "Just, see, I been looking for a nicer-paying job, and I hear them ATV manufacturers are real nice money if you got some experience."

Sondra brought my sliders out at that moment, which spared me from answering him right away. We exchanged pleasantries for just a moment before she bustled off. I took my time applying ketchup and mustard, finally turning back to the man once I had a response ready.

"Haven't heard anything about that, no, but doesn't mean much. I'm not well connected with the factories."

He sighed, and his chest deflated a bit, but that glimmer in his eyes persisted. "Ah, well. Thought I'd try."

The man left a few minutes later, without ever telling me his name. I watched him go, a sad smile creeping onto my face, and then the door shut. I realized it had grown remarkably dark outside. *Maybe I should head home.* I ordered a milkshake for Lucy, a small peace offering, but she really loved Allen's peanut butter ones.

Maybe I should've told the man the truth. That no new ATV factory would be opening soon, and I most definitely would've heard of such a thing. We already had an ATV place on the hilltop. I didn't know if he'd forgotten this fact, overlooked it, or purposely ignored it. Whatever the case, I allowed him to carry on that night with a little bit of a hope. I didn't know if I'd done him a favor or an injustice.

I contemplated that man as I left Allen's Burgers and strolled back toward my car. People like him had so much faith and hope in this town. They hadn't resigned themselves like me. Not that I didn't appreciate Little Rush. I loved it. Every bit of it. But those people, they still hoped for a kind of vague grandeur. Factories opening again. A population that grew. Young people moving back instead of away. Hell, they probably hoped for trains to return someday.

I'd been like that once. As a child and a teenager and the years I spent away in college. Even when I first moved back and bought the pizza restaurant. During that time of my life, I'd also hoped for Little Rush to prosper. In different ways, maybe, but still growth. I didn't know what I gave up that hope for. I still wanted good for the town. I also didn't like the change that crept its way inside. Every time a chain restaurant replaced a local establishment, I felt a pang of fear. Every time an old landmark fell to disrepair or the city razed an old building, I lost sight of the town I'd grown up in.

I also feared change, because for Little Rush that meant leaving behind something great. Something worth remembering. Maybe I'd just given up hoping for good change at all. I didn't see any point in dreaming of a large business moving here. Just not feasible. I didn't even wish for a population surge anymore. I'm not sure what I wished for.

If time could freeze and Little Rush could remain exactly as it was forever, I think I'd be content with that. This, sadly, was also not an option. Businesses sink. People die. The cemetery fills. The young people leave. And the rest of us would be left watching. Time moved so slowly that it was hard to tell. Was the town burning down around us? Or did Little Rush actually *need* a bigger fire?

I had a sudden idea on my way up the hill. With Lucy's milkshake sweating in the cup holder, I stopped by the Walmart and purchased a brand new iPhone. The only place in town I could even buy one. A gift for Mason. If anything could repair relationships, it had to be milkshakes and iPhones.

I didn't linger in town for long, mainly because I didn't want to hand my wife a liquefied shake. But I did savor my drive home. Often, I forgot to look around when I drove. It was so easy to keep my eyes fixed on the yellow lines that blurred as I raced from place to place, using music or a podcast to distract me. That night, however, I turned off the radio and inhaled the scenery. Up here, it didn't feel the same as downtown, but held its own beauty.

The sky darkened as I drove. The air dropped about ten degrees, so that when I stepped out of my car, I could fully appreciate the weather. June afternoons in Little Rush could kill you, but then the temperature cooled, and it became perfect. The clouds bathed in deep purple and the fields swaying in gentle breezes. My house wasn't far from Rush Road, of course; it wasn't like I lived in the country. But almost there. I could sort of see it in the distance as I pulled into my isolated neighborhood.

There were no bad thoughts as I stepped into my house. Just a wide smile and hope. Hope like that factory worker. He wanted a new business to open. I just wanted to mend a relationship. Well, two of them.

Here goes the first step, I told myself as I let the door swing shut behind me.

I found Lucy asleep on the couch, mascara tears dried on her face. For a few moments, I stood there as her chest rose and fell peacefully. I realized the milkshake in my hand had melted entirely, so I chucked it in the trash

I visited Mason's room next. Not home. I remembered now that he wouldn't be around tonight. Something with Hudson, I guessed. I couldn't even remember. I'd been on a phone call when he told me. I saved the iPhone, set it beside my bed. Maybe I'd give that to Lucy. Maybe I could at least fix that.

I tried to lay down that night, alone, ignoring the cold side of our bed as best I could. For all I knew, Lucy had calmed down and forgiven me before she fell asleep on the couch. Maybe everything would be fine in the morning. I tried to convince myself of that, on a California King mattress all alone. Maybe I should've let her get that ugly dog for Christmas. Having a dog would be nice for these moments.

When sleep wouldn't come, I trudged into the living room and took a seat in my recliner, near Lucy's sleeping body. She looked so beautiful, with the mascara dried on her cheeks and her hair like a torrential hurricane. Her shoulders rising and falling, simple movements. Her right foot would twitch sometimes, and she would smile in whatever dream had taken hold. Something better than reality, for sure.

"I don't blame you," I muttered, wishing she could hear me. But at the same time, I didn't. "It's not your fault... that we're like this. It's just been a really stressful few months, is all. We're gonna be okay, Lucy. We really are, I think."

She didn't respond, of course. Her eyelids didn't even flinch. She just held that same, vacant smile. I thought maybe, somewhere in her dreams, she was looking at me that way, the way she used to. Lovestruck teenagers, running around Little Rush. Taking walks over the bridge, skipping stones on the Ohio River. She had always loved the river, always appreciated it more than me.

I remembered the time when we found a more secluded spot, over by the forest that grew along one section of the bank. Nobody ever went there, at least not at two in the morning. Lucy had birthed the idea. She'd been wild in high school. Incredibly sexy. Out of this world.

She hadn't told me exactly what she had in mind that night, but we walked down there, cutting through the trees. The Ohio River spreading before us, dark rippling water stretching across to the silhouette of a hillside. We stood at the water's edge, the cold river lapping against our ankles. Lucy raised her eyebrows and granted me a seductive smile, then... she just stripped. Completely naked. I did the same after some persuasion. And we went skinny dipping in the frigid Ohio River. What a night. What a year, really. God damn, she'd been everything I could've wished for.

Watching her sleep on the obnoxiously nice couch, I felt like a different person. Like we were different people in a different city. This couldn't be that same Little Rush where we'd been wild, explored the world and each other. Savored everything, dreamed of big plans, done things that would make us blush to even mention now. Where had that spark gone? Had we lost it? Had the whole town lost it?

"I always hate when we fight," I whispered again to Lucy. "I hate it so much. And I know it's my fault..."

She didn't wake. Now I really wished she would. I wanted

to admit all this. I wanted to open up. Or at least spend a night remembering the wilder, teenage years we burnt through together. Maybe if we could just think about those, reminisce... maybe it would help us now. Help us to get through this. To compromise. Solve our problems over a nostalgic night and a bottle of wine.

"Tell me how I can do this, Lucy." I leaned forward, head in hands. I took a few deep breaths in that position. In an ideal world, she would wake up, pull my hands away, kiss me gently. But I didn't live in an ideal world. I lived in Little Rush. "I swear to you, I'm trying. God dammit, I am."

4
BRUCE

"Everybody's gonna forget as soon as you're gone."

His words caught me off guard. I'd been staring at the gossip magazines next to the candy bars. One caught my attention because it showed a tiny picture of my current house, out by the cemetery. It also showed that pizza boy, Hudson I think, on the night he'd delivered to me. Intriguing.

The grocery clerk had just finished ringing up my items. He was starting to bag them when he mumbled that sentence under his breath. Barely audible over the beeping scanners and the rattling coin drawers from all around.

I glanced up to find him staring intently at a container of sliced turkey. A gruff old man, the kind who often found jobs at Kroger or Walmart, which seemed to be the only major stores around here. The kind who probably wanted to retire by now, but something had happened to keep him working. My father had been the same way. Went back to work after the economy collapsed in '08. Only he'd died a few weeks later. This old geezer kept chugging along. He certainly looked older than my dad when he'd died, but then again he'd had all sorts of medical complications. The kind that threatened me any year now.

I ignored the cashier and started to collect the grocery bags. There were only six, so I could manage without a cart. When I'd snatched the last one and held them all, he cleared his throat loudly. I glanced up to find him staring intently at me.

"You're one stupid sonofabitch to come here," he mumbled, as if to himself, but the way he glared ensured I was his target. Then he turned back to the next customer and began ringing up their items, no more words exchanged.

When the groceries were packed into my car and the strip mall had shifted into my rearview mirror, I spent ten minutes driving home in a daze. I passed a collection of apartment buildings that were run down and crowded, judging from the cars in the parking lot. A long sidewalk connected it to the Kroger and Walmart intersection, and a worn sign named it "Liberty Apartments." Looked like the kind of place that trailer home residents dreamed of. I couldn't stand the lot of them.

Then I drove by the huge hospital, the only newish building in Little Rush as far as I could tell. I couldn't help but wonder if my cashier would end up there before long.

Maybe he'd just lost his mind and would spout rude comments to every customer nowadays. But I doubted it. What he said felt very much targeted at me. I hadn't run into anybody like that around here. Nobody seemed to openly hate me. Quite the opposite. Anytime I went out on the hilltop, there were people gawking, some of the brave ones asking for autographs. This one kid brought a poster of my first movie and asked me to sign it. His dad stood behind him, smiling just as wide. It felt, in that moment, like the entire town adored me, all generations. I suppose that wasn't true after all.

I hadn't come here to be loved, so that didn't really bother me. I only wanted to blend in, to become one of the locals. And anyway, I'd had plenty of people hate me over the years, from critics to shunned lovers to actors who lost roles. In LA, I'd become an expert at forming shallow friendships and deep feuds. That's just the way business went.

No, what bothered me about the man's first statement was the timeliness of it. What is acting, after all, if not an attempt to be remembered? Sure, we shine a light on characters and historical figures who shouldn't be forgotten, but we also strive to preserve our own legacy. I used to be obsessed with that in my early days. Wondering how people would remember each film I had a major role in. Maybe that's what caused me to be so picky over the years. In the end, it didn't matter. Critics found things to hate. Audiences found things to love. And decades down the road, none of it would matter. It already didn't.

Even here. Even in Little Rush. That's what the cashier's statement forced me to realize. Even in a place this obscure, I wouldn't last forever. They might talk about me years down the line, maybe point to the small house, maybe tell stories about my reckless driving and... shadowy eyes. In reality, though, they would all forget. Even here and even me.

Maybe I should've bought the magazine that showed the pizza boy and I. It would've made a nice gift, if I ever saw him again.

As I pulled into the driveway next to my small house and looked around at the scenery, I made a promise to myself. One of these days, I'd go walking downtown. I'd take a break from the gravestones, the trees, the endless fields. Breathe in the air of a small city, a historical landmark. I couldn't remember a single thing about downtown Little Rush other than I loved it. I'd loved it back then as a kid, and surely I would love it again.

The problem with downtown, though, is I might run into that Gina woman. The journalist with the seductive eyes and the name I couldn't forget, didn't want to remember.

Chuckling to myself, I struggled out of the car and carried grocery bags into the house. The familiar doorway greeted me as I stepped inside and made my way to the kitchen. This place had finally started to feel like home. I didn't want that Gina woman ruining it all, not just now.

I laughed again. I'd thought of something when I first glanced at those magazines. What covers would people make if they found out about Madeline? It would spread all over the country, surely. Every single magazine and newspaper. Oh, the headlines. I could imagine them now. I could already feel them tearing away at me. That would hurt. It really would. A physical pain like nothing I'd ever felt before.

A few people hated me now. But just imagine... if that story got out...

5

WILLOW

One oddity about Little Rush is that when high schoolers went on a "date," it usually meant walking around downtown and checking out some of the quirky shops that lined Main Street. Unless you were going to a movie or bowling, that's pretty much the most entertaining option. They were all local, each shop a unique experience, and they were most responsible for the enjoyable atmosphere of Main Street.

There were a handful of restaurants, sure, like the deli where I never ate. Mason's dad owned that one. A coffee shop, too, where I spent many more hours. It had changed hands a few times over the past ten years. And of course the famously greasy Allen's Burgers, the kind of place older people ate regularly but I couldn't stomach as anything more than a guilty pleasure.

For me, that's about all Main Street consisted of. Shops and food. Maybe a more mature observer would notice things I didn't, but most of the other buildings were no use to me. I had never and probably would never enter them. They were for stories that others would tell or maybe for pictures, just filling in the setting.

The stores themselves are where I spent most of my time. They varied wildly, which made it all the more fun. Some dealt in soaps and lotions. Those smelled excellent, and that was honestly half the reason I shopped there. Other places sold antiques, old baseball cards, ancient gaming systems. These were fun in their own nostalgic sort of way. I bought a GameCube one time, the kind my dad had years ago, but never played it. I suppose I should've.

My favorite kind of store were the random ones that sold clothing, among other things. Most of these also had a section for antiques and knick-knacks in the back, but the front was all clothes, shoes, jewelry. There were also graphic tees, retro looks, the kind of stuff you might find in a Hot Topic, but way better and more obscure.

Off Main Street, there were a smattering of other places to visit, like the store near my dad's apartment. They sold singing bowls, incense. I bought an awesome Baja hoodie there. Cost me like twenty-five bucks, and I wasn't exactly drowning in money from my Kroger job, but worth it. And of course they had the ever-changing sign out front, which I loved.

There used to be a grocery store downtown, dad told me, but it closed a while ago. Unlike my mom's apartment, where you could walk to Kroger, we didn't have many options at my dad's. Unless you wanted to drive to the hilltop, the only food you could buy was from a restaurant or Circle K.

Then again, downtown Little Rush wasn't meant to exist on its own. If you took away the hilltop, I don't think the collection of streets by the Ohio would last. There just wasn't enough. People, stores, food, anything. But maybe it could, who knows. It'd clearly been around a long time. Just looking at the sidewalks or the abandoned factories would tell you that.

There was something about downtown, though, which drew you to it. Especially if you're a hilltop kid, like Mason. For him, downtown was something of a spectacle, a place to visit when the urge struck you and then to ignore for a few weeks. Most of the people up there thought along those lines. Maybe that's why we still didn't have a grocery store. Why did we need one, after all, if we were just for amusement, an eccentric younger brother that served no purpose other than tourism and the occasional art festival or boat race?

In this way, Mason and I ended up downtown one evening. We'd gone to see a movie at the theater on Main Street. Some action flick that I didn't much care for, but Mason enjoyed it thoroughly. He always fell for that Vin Diesel, ultra-macho crap. But it was still a compromise. I got to pick the theater, and he chose the movie. Not that there were many options. The Ohio Theatre was the only choice downtown; we had one other on the hilltop. Of the two, I would choose this downtown setting every time.

The Ohio Theatre had the same entrance and marquee as the pictures from maybe a century ago. Like perhaps, once upon a time, it had been grand. Now, the ceiling had leaks and the carpet smelled its age. In the upstairs theater, half the seats were broken, and I swore to Mason I saw a mouse one time. (He didn't believe me.) The main room —with maybe a hundred seats— never filled up. It didn't help that the Ohio always got movies a week later than the place uptown. Despite the lower prices, despite clever advertising, despite the comfortable feel of it, there had been rumors for a year or two about the Ohio closing. I remembered this every time I entered and the lady in the ticket booth shot me a worn smile while she extended two ticket stubs. Or when the lights dimmed and the curtains slid open, straining against their own weight.

How many summers had I spent there as a child during their free movies? How many tiny popcorn trays had I devoured in a more innocent time? Maybe that's all the theater really held. Nostalgia. But wouldn't that nostalgia have worn off after dozens or even a hundred trips? It seemed like each one only deepened my love for the place, my unexplainable admiration.

The things we're drawn to, I guess, are never what we expect. And there I was, all the same, a smile so wide it hurt. Just from seeing that familiar lady with her tickets.

"Enjoy the show," she said. Her voice was so genuinely sympathetic that it felt like I'd spoken with the ghost of my grandmother.

"We will," I answered, beaming, trying to express in those two words my genuine thankfulness. For her, for the Ohio Theatre, for the brief escape it offered me.

It felt, to me, like an integral spoke at the center of the downtown wheel. The kind of place that glued everything together. A place that, if allowed to sit empty, would be like cutting out the very heart of Little Rush. Every time I saw a movie there, each time I enjoyed their wildly salty popcorn, it reminded me a little of why I stuck around. I could've run away and all. Not like my parents would ever chase me down. But the Ohio Theatre was the physical representation of why I didn't. I was a dog tied to a tree. That stupid old theater was why I couldn't quite run, even though I'd severed the leash. And even if I called it stupid, I meant I needed it.

"I hope they don't close that place down," Mason said as we exited. The sky had darkened now to a deep blue. The sun would set within the hour. We stood there for a moment, under the theater's massive marquee, and drank in downtown Little Rush as night fell.

"I didn't realize you liked it that much." I grabbed his hand and led him away from the double doors. There were actually many glass doors, probably around sixteen, but only four were ever unlocked. I wanted to see this place in its peak, with all sixteen open, but that time would never come again, I expected.

"It's just... a good time." He chose these words carefully. We started walking down the sidewalk toward the frozen yogurt shop like usual. I felt him squeeze my hand a little tighter. "Can't ever miss a good time around here."

This phrase struck me as not quite right, but I ignored it. My eyes scanned Main Street. The streetlights were on now, granting everything a more comfortable glow. Something like heaven. I bet heaven has lots of streetlights.

Most of the shops had their doors propped open, breathing in the beautiful evening, the perfect temperature. People strolled by us in either direction, most of them chatting to a loved one or a friend. Few walked alone at this hour. Even if they did, they would grin wide. On an exquisite Friday night, the first day of July, it felt like the entire city had descended on Main Street. There were just the right amount of people. Enough that you didn't feel alone, not so many that you were crowded.

"Wanna walk around a little before we head back?" I asked him. The yogurt shop was in sight now, but I didn't feel much like sitting down. I just wanted to explore, to bathe in the postcard view. Every once in a while, these days came along. They always caught me by surprise but never disappointed. Like everything clicked into place, at last, and the world could never get any better.

"Sure." He had a vacant glint in his eyes, but a happy one. I expected he felt many of the same emotions.

"Wanna skip the fro-yo and come back when it's dark?"

He nodded and gestured back the way we'd come. "We could walk down and check out some of the shops. I think the soap one closes soon."

I spun toward him for a minute with an inquisitive smile. "You never wanna go to the soap shop... What's up today?"

He shrugged. I grabbed his other hand and narrowed my eyes, pressing for an answer.

"I just... feel really good. You know?"

I planted a kiss on his lips, something I didn't often do in public. I noticed his surprise, because it took him a second to kiss me back. "I do too." Then I pulled away and took his hand, leading him toward the collection of shops just past the theater.

The differences between June thirtieth and July first are quite subtle in some ways, but to a high schooler, the shift is more noticeable than ever. All through June, there is a safe wall between you and the next school year. July, with its full thirty-one days, is a barrier against that tidal wave. It's the beginning of summer, with promise and watermelons and infectious pop music. On July first, there's a shift. That's really the perfect word for it. School is, all of a sudden, right around the corner. The heat is beginning to wear on you. Most people have a tan if they're going to get one. Have a job if they need one. You can count the rest of summer in a matter of weeks, and those weeks on one hand.

For me, entering my senior year of high school, this feeling is amplified by a thousand. Not only is school creeping closer, but so is graduation. College. Decisions. Career. Moving out. Independence. Debt. All of that, the biggest tidal wave to that point in life. The summer before senior year is the most important of them all and also the hardest to hold onto. It's the most fun, since everyone has their license and most of your friends are into the whole drinking thing. But it's the easiest to miss, because it hits so hard and doesn't slow down.

Fitting, I guess, that on the first day of July, we were exploring downtown Little Rush. Clinging to each shop that we entered and browsed. Holding to every step of sidewalk that disappeared beneath our feet. The air had a touch of mischief, of cars with steamy windows and clothing on the dashboard. Of stealing a Coke bottle just because you could. That night, the beginning of the end, I felt more like a wild, angsty high schooler than I ever had or ever would. Mason, with that twinkle in his eye and his bulging chest muscles, was the same. I could tell, and I never wanted it to end.

"I'm kinda hungry," I said at last, rummaging through a rack of sweatshirts outside one of the clothing stores. "Let's ditch this place and hit the yogurt shop."

Mason glanced at his phone, presumably to check the time, and agreed. We grasped each other by the hand and made our way toward that end of town. He pointed out one of the shops as we passed, where they were giving out free wine and cheese samples.

"Think they'd give us one?" he asked, chuckling.

"Doubt it, but we can try in a bit."

In ten minutes time, we returned to that spot, each of us holding a bowl filled with frozen yogurt and toppings. I'd wanted to work at the frozen yogurt shop last summer because they had cute shirts and all my friends went there, but I settled for Kroger because it paid a little better and I didn't have to pay for gas money getting there.

We approached the store giving out samples, pleased to find they were still open. Although it was nearly ten o'clock, the crowd downtown hadn't dispersed much, and all the doors were reluctant to close. Not only did it feel like an amazing time to be down here, but surely they were raking in above-average profits. For instance, Allen's down the road had a line outside waiting to order.

"Babe, look." Mason nudged my arm.

I ate what I had on my spoon and then glanced in the direction he pointed. There were a few people outside the shop, looking the other way and conversing. I turned to him and cocked my head. "What?"

"That's Blough."

I looked again and saw it now. The boy in the middle was indeed the Blough kid he'd tried to fight. I grimaced and opened my mouth to protest whatever he'd thought of doing, but it was too late.

"Wait here," he said with a devilish expression. He gave me a "shh" finger and then moved ahead.

I thought about stopping him. I really did. But then I remembered that Blough had called me a "cunt" and nearly broken my boyfriend's jaw. So, I settled back on my heels, eating frozen yogurt like theater popcorn, and observed. What the hell. This was a night for impulsive, wild action.

Mason worked his way through a small crowd, quickly but quietly. Then he gripped the bowl with two hands and lifted it. I gasped as I finally understood his plan. In one movement, he turned the bowl upside down and planted it on Blough's head. The yogurt dripped everywhere. Through his hair, onto his shoulders, probably in his eyes. Mason crushed the bowl on his head, eking every last bit onto the boy's scalp, and then whipped around in my direction.

"Run!" he bellowed, fighting back laughter. As he cut his way through the crowd of people, I saw Blough turn around, his cheeks inflamed and jaw clenched. The three boys around him flexed their muscles and started chase.

I made the crucial decision to drop my bowl. It splattered on the ground, but by that point, I'd darted into an alleyway, Mason's footsteps echoing after me. He caught up and we ran together, faster than I had in a long time. Fast enough that I felt my sides aching. Mason couldn't contain himself. His laughter echoed off the brick walls and back to us, amplified. I joined in.

We reached the street and made a sharp right. They were behind us, without a doubt, and we had to navigate our way through various streets. Mason sputtered something about "lead the way" and I knew this also meant "because you know downtown better." I obliged and took the lead. We darted into another alleyway, back to Main Street. This sharp maneuver may have lost the yogurt-head and his cronies, but just in case, we kept running.

People darted out of our way and stared with wide eyes. I didn't bother trying to explain. Their expressions, though, brought on another fit of laughter that clawed at my heaving sides. After two more blocks and a near-collision with a Jeep pulling onto Main Street, I led Mason across the street and into another alleyway. We ran straight until we reached Second Street, made another left. Only after two more blocks, a right, a left, and two more did we slow to a walk and check our surroundings.

Only then did I comprehend how dark it had become. How menacing each shadow around us felt as we strolled through a part of town with no light. The air felt crisp now, sweat trickling down my neck, and I struggled to catch my breath.

We'd arrived in front of a wealthy-looking house not far from the bridge. We could see the river as we crossed between buildings. For a few minutes, we kept our eyes peeled and our ears attentive for any footsteps or voices. Nothing jumped out at us. I felt pretty certain that my sharp decisions and doubling-back would've lost the boys. They were hilltop kids, anyway, and probably didn't know the shortcut I'd taken. Not to mention, Blough's buddies were large and not in great shape. Sure, they could break your nose, but they couldn't catch you to do so.

"What a rush," Mason exclaimed at last once we both felt comfortable in our escape. He turned to me, his wide smile visible in the darkness, and extended a hand. "Thanks for coming with me."

"You owe me a bowl of fro-yo." I leaned my head against his shoulder for a minute. This wasn't comfortable to do while walking, so I stood straight again. "Wanna go across the bridge?"

"Sure."

The bridge in its newest iteration, having gone through extensive repairs in our sixth-grade year, had a nice sidewalk for pedestrians on its right side. Complete with an outer railing and a barrier from cars, it felt relatively safe as long as you didn't fear heights. Pretty easy for someone to jump off, though. That would've been traumatic to witness on a night like this.

We turned in that direction a few blocks later, toward the bridge. This area didn't have many people walking around, nor were there lots of cars. But it was a calm darkness now, the threat having dissipated. To me, anyway. I'd been all around this city at nighttime, causing trouble with friends in middle school. I actually had my first cigarette in the old, abandoned factory nearby.

"Feel like you got good payback?" I asked him.

He chuckled. "I'd say so."

"Me too." I slapped him on the butt playfully. "What are we gonna do after the bridge?"

"Thinking I might do you." He grabbed my hand again, his touch soft. "How's that sound?"

"Can't go to my house," I reminded him. "Dad's not working tonight."

"So back in the old car?"

"Guess so. Mine, though," I insisted. "Yours is too cramped."

We had a few spots around the city that were optimal for midnight makeout sessions. I'd never forget when my grandma had told me, toward the end of her life, that she and my granddad got it on by the old state hospital. Back then it was no longer in use but not torn down yet either. I didn't have the guts for anything that spooky.

"You know what I think?" Mason asked.

We were about two blocks from the bridge now. The cars were sparse at this time of night, but one zoomed by every so often. Definitely over the speed limit.

"What, hun?"

He paused longer than normal. "I think I wanna marry you

soon."

I stopped walking, and he did too. Probably hoping I would jump right in with a "for sure" or something. And I considered it. It had been a great night. A perfect one. We were gonna top it off with sex, and judging by the look in his eyes it would be exquisite. But I couldn't just let a comment like that slide. Not when he'd refused to even consider my side of the whole college situation.

"I do, too." I took my own pause and frowned a little. "But you know I don't wanna go to college around here."

"I've been thinking about that," he said. And then he smirked.

That must be… good? "And?" I didn't mean to sound rude. Maybe I hadn't.

"I think… maybe I could leave." He grabbed my hand again and led me toward the bridge once more. The entrance to that pathway looming closer, the headlights coming and going just to our left. "Maybe I could move away from Dad. Figure things out with him. He can't expect me to stay here just because of his business, right? I mean… I'm my own person."

"You are, yeah."

"And I know it's something you want. And I totally get that." He kicked at the pavement, scuffed his heel. "I want it too. I want to be with you, somewhere out there. But you understand that it's hard for me to let go of this place, right? It's gonna… take some thinking."

We stood at the entrance to the pedestrian sidewalk. I leaned over and placed my hand on the railing. A long, steep climb in front of us. Unforgiving ground under our feet.

"It's hard to leave a place like this." I didn't resist when my eyes dropped to the road itself. Glancing just to his side, observing as the cars rushed past. One coming, then a moment's pause. Another would fill its place on this side of the river. "I get that. It's hard for me, too."

"And if I can't..." He sighed, rubbed his forehead with a fist. "Is that... it?"

It for us, he meant. The end. I knew that anxiety well, probably better than he realized.

"I don't think so." I lifted my gaze and reached out to touch his side. "I'm in love with you. Wherever you happen to be."

"But you don't wanna be here anymore." The way those words left his lips, he almost sounded hurt. "I know it's true, and I feel that. But I also... don't."

I stepped forward and hugged him. The kind of hug where my arms wrapped around his neck and I squeezed until he couldn't breathe. A desperation in my grip. A great and expanding fear. The July first kind of fear.

"I wanna marry you," I whispered into his ear, my lips touching the tiny hairs. His own smile spreading into my shoulder.

"I want you to be happy."

He meant it. That, to me, was enough. Enough for tonight.

We seperated again, still holding hands, and I turned my attention to the bridge. There were no cars now. Just a shadow hanging over it. A distant silhouette of hills where Kentucky's reflection of us rose into the air. Did they also feel this weight? Were there two identical versions of us, just on the other side, waiting to meet? A different world, over there. A different reality. Just crossing the river felt like such a huge step in that moment. Leaving this bubble. Leaving this innocence, this atmosphere.

"I'm kinda tired of walking," I said. I shrugged and pulled his hand closer to my waist. "Can we just head back now?

"Sure, babe."

Our footsteps echoed away from the bridge, back toward Main Street, toward the lights we had almost escaped. When we emerged into the heart of the city, I caught a glimpse of the Ohio Theatre, those bold letters on the marquee. The message on it struck me as important now, whereas earlier I'd ignored it easily.

Two names I didn't recognize had been married. Congratulations! sprawled just above them. And under that, the showtimes for this week's movies.

In that instant, I didn't think I could leave Little Rush. No matter how much I wanted to. No matter how much I loved myself. Something about that bridge appeared too daunting. Something about that theater too much like home.

"You alright, babe?" Mason asked.

I realized I'd been standing in place for at least twenty seconds, staring into the darkened lobby of the Ohio. A part of me wished someone in there would stare back. If only so I didn't feel alone.

I nodded quickly and took his hand, following toward the car.

6

HUDSON

I'd never experienced the impulse that sent me barreling toward Bruce Michael's house. Something about seeing myself on Twitter in a viral picture... it shook the nerves. I didn't know who had taken the picture, what their intentions were. I only knew that I hated it. Nobody knew my name or anything. It wasn't like they'd found my Twitter account and started following me. No, my life had, thankfully, been pretty much unchanged by the photo. The only difference? I couldn't scroll through the wasteland of internet anymore without staring at my own face.

It had been a simple image, taken from a crouched position, I think. One of the reporters, no doubt. It showed me, in my work outfit, standing on Bruce's porch. The picture caught me handing him the pizza box, a shy expression on my face. Bruce, to his credit, wore the typical, irritated mask he put on for any public occasion these days.

Mason: Have you seen that pic? It's everywhere man.

I didn't care to respond to his text. Instead, I jumped into my battered truck and roared away from my house. It took about fifteen minutes to reach Bruce's house. The entire time, my thoughts were churning. I felt a sort of dulled anger. Probably because I couldn't confront the reporter himself. Instead, I'd chosen to lash out at Bruce. Only I didn't know his number. So I would do it face-to-face.

That's what I told myself, anyway. I texted Mason my plan, right before pulling out of my gravel driveway. When I arrived at Bruce's house, parking behind his expensive Jeep, I checked my phone quickly and saw his response.

Mason: I think you just wanna see him again ;)

With this nagging thought in my head, I stepped out of my truck. I started to walk toward the house, eyes narrowed. Only then did I notice him in the cemetery.

Bruce knelt in front of a large gravestone, hands in his lap. His eyes were reading the words, I think, or maybe just staring at the rough surface. Either way, he hadn't noticed me pull in, or didn't react like it. I waited for a moment, thinking I might go ahead and leave. The scene felt intensely intimate, the kind of haunted peace I didn't want to disturb. Then his head turned to me and a slight smile broke on the man's weathered features.

His beard had grown even more haggard since I last saw him. He had dark shadows under his eyes. When he clambered to his feet, Bruce groaned, and I could hear his knees crackle even from across the yard. He didn't move toward me, though, so I had to make the initial approach. Treading between headstones and stepping over an empty beer bottle that lay in the grass, I came face-to-face with my idol once again.

"Thought you'd show up," he said with a rueful chuckle.

"I don't wanna see myself all over Twitter. Not ever again. And *especially* not as your 'pizza boy' or whatever." I crossed my arms and lifted my chin, trying to sound as defiant as possible. The truth was, my anger had dissipated. As soon as I lay eyes on his crumpled frame, kneeling next to that gravestone like a wounded animal, I couldn't bring myself to fury.

"I don't like to see myself either," he pointed out. He rested a hand on the waist-high tombstone beside him and leaned against it.

"Well... Okay, then." My voice faltered as I realized I had nothing else to say.

"Know what, kid?" He eyed me over and clicked his tongue. "You remind me of myself at your age."

I couldn't hold back a grin. I felt stupid when I thought it, but this might have been my proudest moment. The compliment meant more than anything, coming from the man himself.

"I hope to god you're not," he added.

I furrowed my eyebrows. When I didn't answer right away, Bruce rummaged in his pocket and pulled out a cigarette. He lit it deftly and started to smoke, right there among the dozens of buried corpses. The moment struck me as odd, the entire situation really. Standing in a cemetery, shooting the shit. Not my preferred setting.

"Why do you smoke?" I asked it before I could stop myself. Feeling like this question was too open-ended, I added a potential response. "A friend of mine does a ton, and I just don't get it. Never feel much. Does it help with stress?"

He chuckled, blew smoke from his nose, still leaning on that grave. I wanted to shift my position, read whose stone it was he'd been so interested in. His body managed to block it, though, intentionally or not.

"Is that what you think?"

"I'm..." I didn't like having the question switched around on me. I hated when people did that. "Not sure."

"To answer your question, no. Not really. Nowadays, I do it so I can die a bit sooner." Bruce stepped closer to me, shooing me backward. The cigarette smell hit me. I thought how cool it would be to sit and smoke with *Bruce freaking Michaels*. That would be the peak of my life. It would've been... perfect. "Let's get outta here," he said, gesturing me back toward the house. "Don't wanna get caught smoking on someone's grave."

"Get caught?" There were no cars out here, rarely ever were. He'd picked the most isolated spot in all of Little Rush.

"Paparazzi," he said in a wise tone. "Never know when they might show up."

Once we were both outside of the cemetery, standing a few yards from his back door, Bruce settled his attention on me again. The cigarette dangled from his lips as he stuck both hands in his pants pockets.

"You wanna... come inside? Chat or something?" he asked with slight hesitation. "I got nothing else to do."

I mulled over the offer. Wondered what his actual motives could be. Surely, he didn't enjoy my company. Maybe he had other questions about the town and wanted to grill me on them. Or maybe he was hoping the paparazzi would swing by for another unsolicited photo op. The headlines had all been fairly positive, after all, in regard to our picture. Stuff about "Bruce Michaels is just an average guy" or "Bruce Michaels returns to his roots and orders local." Really sickening stuff, the way people could interpret one man ordering food. I guess the paparazzi were all dick-suckers for certain actors.

"I..." A deep breath. "I really can't. Have to get back for dinner." This was the truth, after all. Mom had nearly been finished cooking when I left the house and had probably completed the meal prep by now.

He nodded and shrugged one shoulder in a kind of "who cares" way. Bruce gestured at my truck. "Next time, then. Feel free to stop by anytime."

I wandered to my truck and opened the door, feeling his eyes on my back. An offer like that, to come over whenever, had too much weight to process in the moment. A standing invitation to Bruce Michaels' house in the middle of nowhere. If I hadn't known better, I might think he had some creepy fascination with teenage boys. But I imagined the paparazzi would have some knowledge of that, if true.

"Sorry about the picture," he called as I climbed into the driver's seat.

I glanced over toward him. He stood at the corner of his house, cigarette between two fingers. His eyebrows were furrowed, as if he'd been wrestling with the decision to call out or not. His sympathy appeared genuine, much as I could tell. An honest-to-god apology.

Without words to really express what I felt, I shot him a cringey thumbs-up through my open window. His warm smile let me know that he understood. In return, he gave me a thumbs-up too, before ducking inside without another glance in my direction.

I drove home without music, trying to think. To figure it out. Were Bruce Michaels and I... friends? Could I ever consider somebody that much older a "friend?" That didn't feel like a natural step in any relationship between a sixty-something star and a high school senior. Again, the thought occurred to me that Bruce had some weird, perverted fascination with high school boys. Hadn't Michael Jackson? It wouldn't be unprecedented, then. On the drive home, I decided I would ask my parents over dinner, see what they thought. Surely, if there was any danger, my own mother would be the one to put her foot down and end things where they stood. I didn't have to take her advice, but it'd be nice to hear it, nonetheless.

The water tower danced to the left of my vision as I drove into Little Rush, down the road with restaurants and billboards and stores on either side. Finally, I turned onto a country highway leading to my own house, and the water tower fell into my rearview mirror. I wondered if Bruce felt like a mortal man in its shadow.

As I pulled into my driveway, my phone lit up with a text. I parked and opened it.

Mason: how'd it go with bruce? when's the adoption ceremony and everything?

I replied with something snarky and shoved the phone into my pocket. For a second, I sat in the driver's seat, staring at my house. Through the window, I could see my mom setting the table for dinner, her shoulders hunched over and body moving as if in slow-motion. Dad was nowhere to be found. I imagined him sitting on the couch, worn out, muddy. I guess we had a lot in common, too. Both of us self-centered, oblivious to others, stuck in our own heads.

I didn't want to be like these people. I had wanted to be like Bruce. But even he turned out too good to be true. Just another fake person I'd conjured in my mind. Behind that mask of fantasy, an old man with nothing but the weight of a full and costly life. I had overestimated him. All of them.

That nagged at me as I stepped out of the truck and approached my house. My initial anger at the viral Twitter picture returned. Bruce Michaels... A lonely guy on the run. I didn't know what from, but maybe it didn't matter. He had nobody here, nobody in life. I almost felt bad for him. Even *he* didn't have things figured out. Even *he* couldn't escape pain and creeping depression. We really were similar in more ways than I thought. Only instead of comforting me, this fact ached. I didn't want him to be like me. I wanted him to be superior, god-like, ascendent. And if Bruce Michaels didn't have it together, I felt certain that I never would either.

One of these days, I would climb that damn tower. Just to prove I could, even if I didn't have it all together. Just to see the world from such great heights. Maybe none of these fucking adults had the strength, but I did. I would.

o o o

My parents took long drinks from their water glasses, staring at each other in silence. I'd just finished my story, about Bruce's apparent interest in me. While they had some sort of non-verbal, eyes-only conversation, I picked absentmindedly at the roast beef on my plate. An untouched ear of corn lay beside it, soaking in the juices. I always hated when meat had this much juice, but to complain about Mom's cooking would be a death wish.

"I mean... you're a real unique kid," my father said. He glanced at my mom for some kind of support. I didn't care much what he had to say anyway.

"Very true," she agreed.

"So... what?" I set the fork down and scratched at my chin where my reluctance to shave resulted in straggly, irritable hairs. "You think he's alright to... to talk with?"

Dad sipped again from his glass, a nervous habit I'd noticed a long time ago. Anytime we were having a conversation and he didn't know exactly what to say, he would take a drink. This meant that, over the course of an average-length dinner, he would fill up his glass three or four times.

"I think there's... some benefit, right?" He pointed this out in an annoyingly vague tone.

"Maybe you two could go out for coffee sometime?" Mom suggested. I had a feeling this would be her idea. She was a big proponent of "coffee with people" lately and had convinced her own friends to go multiple times a week. Between her coffee dates and Dad's work, I often found our downstairs empty in the mornings.

"We don't even have common interests." I grabbed my own glass of water, about to take a drink, and then set it down again. I didn't want a habit identical to my father.

"But think how much you could *learn* from 'im," Dad insisted, leaning forward just slightly in his seat. "From a man like that!"

"I can't learn anything from him," I mumbled, grabbing the

corn from my plate and staring into the yellow kernels. "He doesn't know anything."

My parents both frowned. Mom said, "Be nice, now. He's a very experienced, intelligent man."

I deserted dinner soon after this remark. I said that Mason, Willow, and I were shooting off fireworks that night for Fourth of July. Probably out at his dad's cabin or a field nearby. They obliged and told me to be careful, the way they always did. Funny how they imagined fireworks were more dangerous than an old man who lived alone in a cemetery. That's the kind of stuff horror movies were derived from.

Just before dusk, I pulled out from the driveway once again, this time heading for Mason's house. He, supposedly, had bought a hundred dollars of fireworks and had "another great story about the Blough kid" that he needed to tell me, but only in person.

I didn't want to go. I wanted to be alone on a night like this. Or maybe talk to someone. But those two weren't much good for conversation recently. They had fixated on each other, as I knew would happen eventually. And my parents... they weren't worth a thing. They were no help. Not my peers, not adults, and so I had nobody.

An old, wandering actor as my closest thing to a confidant, and after only two conversations. I hated the idea of it. Hated what all my relationships had turned into. Completely one-sided. I got nothing from any of them, and that wouldn't change any time soon. If only Bruce could be what I needed... but even he let me down. Just like the rest.

The fireworks around town had already started by the time I reached Mason's neighborhood. I sat in his driveway for a moment, watching them in my mirror. Emotionless fireworks, in my opinion. I felt nothing. No excitement. No joy. I knew that I'd have to put on a mask for Mason and Willow, since Fourth of

July fireworks at the cabin had become a tradition of ours in recent years. The ride out there with them would be gut wrenching. Not a single part of me wanted to exist.

Should've just said I felt sick, I chided myself as the door to his house opened and they exited, holding hands. *Not a complete lie.*

How many times would they make out tonight while I tirelessly set off the fireworks? How many moments would they spend locked in each other's embrace while I hoped, against all odds, that one firework might light too quickly and explode right into my face? Killing me, perhaps, but at least granting me the gift of blindness.

It hadn't happened, not yet. Maybe this would be my lucky year.

"Fucking Bruce Michaels," I muttered, climbing out of my truck. Mason and Willow had already reached his convertible. I closed my eyes and tried to steady myself, flip a switch in my mind. But that old man refused to fade from memory. The crippling knowledge that he wouldn't be enough for me, that nobody could pull me from this darkness, not even him. Maybe it was too late for both of us.

BRUCE

I stumbled around the cemetery, the entire world darker than I could ever remember. Maybe it was the alcohol. I kept tripping over the gravestones, blindsided by each one. I would fall to the ground, dirt clinging to my knees and elbows. Stare intently at the name carved into each one, shake my head with disgust. And then I'd have to struggle to my feet once more.

Not this one. Not this one.

Overhead, there were fireworks. Off in the distance, to the left and the right, every direction. Most were those damn rednecks with money to spare. Some were the official city fireworks, exploding over the Ohio River, sent up from some barge. These were the spectacle everybody gathered to watch. People lined the river downtown and crowded into clearer spaces on the hilltop. Many brought picnic blankets, waited around for hours, spending their time in conversation with friends and neighbors. In a few of the locations near the river, you might find live bands and free water stations. I remembered it all too well from that summer here, decades ago. I had no urge to relive the experience.

It had been fun as a young teenager. Exciting and new. The fireworks here weren't that great, but the atmosphere couldn't be topped. So many families all together. Love-drunk school kids locking lips in the excitable glow of the explosions. The air popping with each burst of color. Those ringed patterns, all different shades of the rainbow. Beautiful stuff, I guess.

"Fuck you!" I now yelled with each burst. Every time I heard them or felt the ground shake under my bare feet. They would go on for a few seconds and then a brief release from the noise. I took deep, painful breaths and tried to steady myself. But the explosions commenced anew, and I collapsed over another tombstone.

"Where *are* you?" I begged, touching each stone as I crawled past. None of them were right. None of them were the one.

I understood on some level that the sky had never been so beautiful. Fireworks were the closest we miserable humans could ever get to creating stars. In the cities, where you never saw the pure nighttime sky, the fireworks *were* the only stars. Out here, they were just add-ons to an already-gorgeous celestial dome. Little sparks of human joy shot into the ether. The closest we would ever come. But none of this comforted me.

I knelt on the ground for a moment, pressed my head against the wet grass. I could envision those country roads and some of the neighborhoods, smoke drifting over the thin streets. So many cheers and whoops and swigs of beer. Fireworks, hotdogs, patriotism. The smoke expanding and growing as more people started their own celebrations. Cookouts, bonfires, grills.

"Answer me!" I screamed at one plot of grass. Nobody ever did.

The crowds would cheer. Sometimes I thought I could hear them from my graveyard. It must have been my imagination, because as soon as I tried to listen, the sounds were gone. Replaced by wind tickling the treetops, a gentle breeze in my ear. Then the fireworks once again, pounding against my temple.

I would eventually take up my own residence in this field. Like a crowded parking lot, I couldn't be sure where. But my battered car most definitely would find its way in between two yellow lines and there I would rest for all eternity.

Could the dead hear fireworks too? Were they as annoyed as me, or did they find this noise a relief from the dreadful silence underground?

"Fuck you all!" I lashed out at one of the smaller markers, swinging my foot in a wide arc. It dislodged from its spot in the ground and toppled flat. I stomped for a minute on the person's name, a woman I would never know, whose family I had never met. Her peaceful rest defiled, like my own.

Hours of searching, of crawling, of crying. None of the names were right. I had seen the correct one earlier. I had touched the letters, said a prayer for the first time in years. That boy had interrupted me. Hudson. Where had he gone? To shoot off these goddamn fireworks with that friend of his? Or had he stayed home, like me? Did he hate them, like me?

Not the right one. Not the right one.

Long after the fireworks had ceased and the calendar had flipped to July fifth, I collapsed on top of the correct grave. With my arms spread out and my face against the ground, I imagined him laying in a similar position, six feet under. Seperated by dirt and by death. I reached out for his name with one hand and traced the letters again. Silence all around me. The air turning cold as I ingested it.

The sun would rise on my body in that same, lost position. Clutching at a name I could never live up to, a legacy I would never reach. The kind of person you can't just copy, a life that money and fame don't buy.

"Take me," I whispered when the sun did rise, another harsh day breaking on my weary frame. "Hurry up and end this."

8
HUDSON

I couldn't help but marvel at the simple beauty of it. This structure went ignored every single day by countless people. Looming overhead at all hours.

The plain, white water tower stretched high into the air above me. Those bold-type letters on its pale side. LITTLE RUSH, they shouted. For miles around, all the way to Bruce Michael's house even, you could see it. Not that anyone ever took the time to look. It was just background to them.

No, this water tower meant nothing to so many people. Some of them probably weren't even aware that a thin, cruel ladder dropped on one side. An eternal temptation. Sure, it was likely meant for maintenance and other professionals to climb, always with some kind of protective gear, bungee cords, whatever those people used. But I just couldn't ignore that ladder. Each time I spotted the LITTLE RUSH, my eyes shifted just to the right, to the steel bars leading upward. If it wasn't meant to be climbed, then why the platform up above, a full circle of railing around the tower's bulbous girth? If it wasn't meant to be climbed, then why did I keep dreaming of it?

I stood under the water tower, my face pressed close against the chain fence. I could've breached this easily. The fence only stood about ten feet tall and there was nothing on top to prevent me from simply pulling myself up and over. One of these days, I really would do it. I would get inside this cage and climb to the very top of the world. The sky always looked so beautiful behind the tower. How would it look when I stood up there? How would Little Rush look? Would the ground swell and sink underneath me like a giant human chest, full of life and heart? Or would it just sprawl out in all directions, the small town as a choking cage?

For a minute, I tried to count the rungs on the ladder. Imagined actually gripping them, one by one, trying not to look down. Heights were never my specialty, but I also didn't fear them. Not as much as I feared being down here.

It would have to be a dry day. Any slippery sections, a wrong foot placement, and I would tumble... soar down, down to my end...

Not here. Not in Little Rush. I would give anything to die somewhere else. I would give my life willingly, if only to die in a better way, a better spot. Somewhere out there.

My phone buzzed, and I glanced down. Mason texted that he was leaving his house, heading downtown. I trudged back to my truck parked on the side of the road.

The neighborhood around me swam into focus once again. The setting of the water tower. This magnificent structure buried in a part of town that couldn't be any less impressive. Barren, cracking streets; homes that were cold to the touch, lacking any welcome. With this neighborhood in my view, the sky no longer appeared beautiful, but distant and foreboding, like a thundercloud expanding in the distance until it covered the entire horizon.

I left the water tower behind and made my way to the truck. It waited for me expectantly. Once I'd settled into the seat and started the engine, I took a few deep breaths. I couldn't go home now. I'd already promised Mason and Willow that I would spend the evening with them. Eat dinner somewhere, probably walk around. Willow loved just existing in that space, any given downtown street. I'd rather have stayed right here with the water tower.

LITTLE RUSH, it roared at me. LITTLE RUSH. The cage.

o o o

"Man, you should've seen his face." Mason threw his head back in laughter once again, clapping his hands together.

Our time downtown had instigated a second telling of the frozen yogurt story, in all its vivid details. Mason stopped every few sentences to burst out, rub his hands together, hold a palm to his forehead. He added any number of dramatic movements. Willow, for her part, didn't participate much in the telling and only chuckled whenever Mason turned to her. Besides that, she simply moved beside him, taking occasional sips from her straw.

With my own to-go drink in hand, I followed on the other side of Mason, closest to the street. As he told the story, we made our way beside the river.

Dinner had been a quick stop at the Chinese restaurant and then a brief stint at a table outside, where we ate. With loud cars rushing past and all of us famished, conversations were sparse and not long. I spent most of the meal gazing into the distance at passers-by, wondering if I'd see anyone I recognized. On Main Street, it was impossible to avoid familiar faces, so there were at least five characters I knew. None of them noticed me, or at least didn't say a thing.

The crowd was nothing spectacular this evening, not like the story Mason told, of a Main Street packed with people and ideal weather. For now, the heat chipped at my resolve, and the crowd appeared as normal. Mostly teenagers passing by in groups of four or five. Some families with little ones in strollers or clutching at Mom's hand. Twice, some boys zipped by on skateboards, sticking out their chests, wearing determined expressions.

"Not many people down here," Mason observed. Only then did I realize his story had come to its long-overdue end.

Willow reached down and held his hand, perhaps as a thanks for finishing the tale. "I thought there'd be more. It's really nice weather."

Really nice, in my opinion, was an exaggeration. Just because it was hot and cloudless didn't make the day nice. It could've been about ten degrees cooler, or at least not flirting with triple digits. *That* would've been decent.

The weather had some benefit. For a weekday eight o'clock, there were a surprising number of high school girls. Something about the sun in downtown Little Rush acted like a magnet for them, specifically the attractive ones. Wearing crop tops, jean shorts, any number of hairstyles, flirtatious smiles, and whatever else the current fashion called for. They would storm Main Street and especially this sidewalk along the river. Their eyes would glance over and with tiny smiles pass by. Those little grins haunted me until the next girl would do the same. I'd wonder, *What does that mean? Is that a you're-cute look or how-disgusting?*

"Why don't you ask one of these chicks for their number or something?" Mason said, as if reading my mind. He smacked my shoulder lightly. Even without turning, I could imagine his confident, self-assured expression. "No harm in trying!"

"Nah." We passed by a trash can and I threw my empty drink into it. "Don't feel like it." I stuffed both hands in my pockets and trudged along beside the couple. Unsteady third wheels tend to bump along in the worst ways.

"Why not, man?" Mason moved his shoulder like it had a hitch, but I recognized this as a subtle way of pointing. There were three girls coming toward us, all of them with twinkling eyes, tanned legs glistening in the waning sun. His voice dropped now that they were closer. "How about one of them?

I'm serious, it doesn't hurt to try! Right, babe? *We* would know, after all..."

We were dangerously close to story-time again, only now it would be a retelling of however he'd asked out Willow. I decided that a third account of the Blough kid's misery would be my preference over this new idea. As I opened my mouth to steer the subject away from "babe," Willow took matters into her own hands.

"Whatever."

That single word, spoken with such apathy, forced Mason to turn his attention on her. We crowded to one side as the three girls passed. I felt their presence brush against mine, just barely, and a chill ran down my spine. I would've liked to ask them, in all honesty. I would've been thrilled to spend time with them. But I couldn't bring myself to try, so the moment fled.

"What's up with you?" Mason squeezed her hand.

"Nothing."

She'd never been the jealous type, as far as I could tell. Willow herself was plenty beautiful, maybe not in the same jaw-dropping, fashionista way as these girls. They were on a different tier, one that only money could achieve. Willow, for all her attractiveness, didn't have the right makeup or clothes. I didn't blame her for feeling uneasy, though. And I'd never say any of this to her face. I was sure it would've come off as pretty dickish, even cruel.

Whatever the reasoning, I decided I didn't want to be with them, not anymore. I felt a kind of dullness, like I recently had so many times in their company. The sort of emotion that just weighs you down until you want a park bench where you can be alone. Nothing about this brought me joy. Exploring these well-worn streets with a couple who didn't quite understand me. It had been so long ago, in my mind, since we'd relaxed at Mason's cabin. Even the party, only a few weeks in the past, seemed ancient.

I only felt emptiness now. No real joy. I existed because I had to. I'd rather sleep forever.

"You're real quiet today, Hudson."

I glanced up. It had been Mason who spoke, but they were both eyeing me.

"Just tired," I said. What a cliched lie.

Mason shrugged and turned away, but Willow held my gaze for just a second longer. She called my bluff without even speaking. Then she too focused elsewhere.

"What do you say we head over to the railroad tracks?" Mason suggested.

Neither of us answered, and so he continued leading us straight down the sidewalk. Behind us, the bridge towered, casting long shadows. My truck was parked back there. *I could leave,* I realized. But I didn't.

"Ever walked up all the way?" Mason's conversation pieces kept coming, despite my numbed brain and Willow's reluctance to answer.

"No," she responded to this one.

"Well, it's pretty neat," he went on. "There's this one section where the rock walls on either side ..."

He went on to describe how the railroad tracks, which started near the river, could lead you up the hillside and emerge next to one of the main roads. According to him, the journey would be worth the energy spent. I figured this wasn't true.

I looked to our left and focused on the river. This scene, which I'd witnessed time and time again, held nothing for me. The hills of Kentucky rose on the other side, covered in trees. The water flowed by us, heading nowhere in particular, carrying limbs and trash along with it. On this side, a gentle sloping bank led from the sidewalk down to water's edge. A short, grassy descent, all that separated me from floating away.

Everything had lost what once made it beautiful. The colors were pale and dark. The sky bland. Nothing exciting. Nothing to prevent me from stepping into the road and flying into the air as a speeding car tore through my body and my life.

"I'm gonna... head back, I think." I spoke hesitantly, afraid that I would stumble over the words. My head felt extremely light now, like a tangible fog. My eyes refused to focus on anything in particular. Like some veil had fallen over the world, nothing appeared quite clear. Maybe I just needed to sleep.

"Alright, man."

Mason smacked me on the back and said something else, but I didn't hear. Willow's eyes pierced mine as I turned away from her and lowered my head. The entire world filled with static now as I strolled back toward the bridge. But also, in a way, toward nothing. Like the river, just in a general direction.

It's a casualty of being me that on certain days I don't talk much. In these moods, I prefer to stay at home, to listen to music. Anything but socialize. Anything but be out in downtown Little Rush. And yet, I found myself in that exact situation. Clutching for a lifeline. I knew that things weren't going to improve in Mason and Willow's company. I just didn't feel like ambling around the city and chatting. They could do whatever they pleased. I needed... to go.

As I lumbered in the direction of my truck, there were multiple girls I passed by and with each one, I glanced up, expecting myself to speak. Maybe just ask their name, try not to say anything awkward. But every time, we slipped by each other, eyes aligning but no words spoken. Then they too were gone, and I had drifted farther down the sidewalk, following the river. It felt like my feet weren't even walking, yet the ground moved past as a treadmill.

For whatever reason, I became hypercritical as they passed. I began to notice their flaws instead of their beauty. Maybe their smiles weren't white enough, just a tinge of yellow. Or their hair too frail, too thin. Their lips, shaped weird. Their makeup too fake, an imitation of reality. I would narrow my eyes at each high schooler and trudge by. Funny enough, I didn't see any of my male peers. But then again, I wasn't looking.

I glanced up and found myself underneath the bridge. Standing in the shadow of the monumental structure, I took a deep breath and closed my eyes. Feeling a wave of relief wash over me. Everything felt okay, now. The ground wouldn't swallow me. My ears no longer buzzed with static. I could return home, do nothing at all. Listen to music and sleep off this weird fog that had blanketed me.

Or I could cross the bridge.

"Hey, there."

I felt the hand on my shoulder, recognized the voice as female. Familiar, too, though I couldn't place it. Not with a name or a face or even a general opinion of the speaker.

"Hudson, right?"

At this, I turned around. Standing there — her lips slightly parted, as flawless as in my memory — Layla dropped her hand. She shifted back a fraction, as if I'd embarrassed her in some way. Her joy didn't falter, though.

"Yeah." My arms flailed for a second, as I didn't know where to put them. Crossed? Hands in my pockets? Around her?

"Do you wanna... walk across the bridge with me?" She asked the question, unsure, with her right heel bouncing on the ground.

I noticed this and then looked up to meet her gaze. "I was actually about to head home. I'm... kinda exhausted."

"Oh, alright." She grinned, trying to play it off. "I just thought maybe we could walk. I've been meaning to talk to you..." Her voice faded. It was her turn to appear uncomfortable, unsure how to stand.

"Let's... talk here," I suggested, trying to sound kind. I'd decided to cross my arms and did just that.

A car whizzed past and honked loudly at us, probably for standing so close to the road. Neither of us moved a fraction. Our eyes were locked in place, my hand itching to grab her own. Instead of acting, I just waited for her to speak.

"I'm sorry... about that night."

About leaving me naked by a creek, she meant. About promising so much and delivering on none of it. For an instant, I felt bitter. And then that subsided, back into my dull existence. I felt nothing once again, just an understanding. We had both been drunk. Shy. Overly confident of what we could and couldn't do. She'd made the mature decision to wait, to not hook up. I should've been admiring this, not begrudging her.

"It's okay." Simple words for so much thought.

"You sure?" she asked. When I nodded and tried to soothe her with a grin, she took a deep breath, chest rising and falling. "So..."

I felt just a sliver of something once again. Desire maybe, or something like the potential for happiness. I once again appreciated her beauty, her dark and flawless skin, her almond eyes. She didn't wear a crop top this time, nor did I feel sexual tension like at the party. And still, I could almost feel her body on my fingertips again. Almost touch the curves and hear the way those clothes slipped off her graceful form. All of it rushing back, waves of sensation.

Despite myself, I grinned. "So."

"Would you wanna..."

The world paused for a moment. The crowds of people had almost disappeared now. The sidewalks were empty in every direction. The river void of color. Still holding our breaths in the bridge's shadow like any moment the structure may fall on us. Everything so gray, all around us. Except for Layla. She remained vibrant, full of hope.

"...try this over again? Maybe go on a date?"

How can you fall for one person so instantly after barely thinking of them for weeks? How could one smile, one flicker of light in an iris, one slight touch of her fingertips, transform me so completely?

"I... yes, please, of course."

Layla kissed me on the cheek after that, and this somehow covered my arm in goosebumps. We'd made out before. I'd seen her body almost completely naked. I'd longed for her as she disappeared back toward the cabin and wished, at times, that I would have never met her in the first place. And yet, a simple, second-long kiss on the cheek. It sent my heart into a tailspin.

"Here." She pulled out her phone and tapped a few times on the screen. "Gimme your number."

As Layla added me into her phone, I felt a shiver through my legs. The cold shadow of the bridge had deepened since the last time I moved. It had been days since I felt alive, since I had been more than a barely-functioning corpse. The way that Bruce looked is how I now felt. I just wanted to escape whatever spell had taken hold of me. To be normal.

Maybe this, with Layla, could be the first step.

9
LITTLE RUSH
THE ROBBERS

June stood in front of them next to a posterboard that would've been better suited as the base for a schoolkid's presentation. Only this poster, rather than having pictures of animals or proof of research, contained plans. A diagram of Bruce Michael's house, lines drawn on the picture, as well as their names. Some of the marks were dotted, others zagging lines, and some straight ones. In front of this display, June stuck out her chest and crossed her arms, looking triumphant.

The darkened television behind her made no sound. The air conditioning unit had turned off when the apartment hit its set temperature of seventy-eight degrees. A bit on the warm side, Randy and Curtis lounged in tank tops, shorts, and bare feet. Curtis had taken to picking at his toes, both at the fuzz that got caught in between and also the nails which had grown too long.

"Christ, will ya stop that?" Randy lashed out, missing by an inch.

Curtis, propped on the couch alone, had sprawled out across the whole length. Bent in an awkward position, he worked at the toenails with his fingers, sticking out his tongue in concentration.

"Ain't doing you harm," he mumbled, continuing at his task.

"Swear to god I'll punch you!"

"Boys!" June clapped her hands together, and their attention turned at once. Both sets of eyes were now locked on her and the poster. She grinned, gestured at the diagram, waiting for their comments.

Curtis, of course, spoke first. "I... don't get it."

"You don't get anything," Randy murmured, although his own face balled up intensely, like he too couldn't make out the details.

"This line is you, Curtis," June began explaining, pointing to a section of the poster. It showed the yard in front of Bruce's house, closest to the road and his driveway. Then she moved her finger to the side where the tombstones sprawled. "This is you, Randy. This line." Finally, she scratched her nail against the final line at the back door of the house. "This is me."

"How we gonna... take his stuff?" Curtis asked, now rubbing at his head. "He won't just give'r up now, will 'e?"

"Good point, really." Randy cocked his head, still studying the poster.

"Guns. Or knives, if we can't get guns." June's toothy grin still hadn't dissipated. She observed the two of them with wide eyes, raised eyebrows, and a "ta-duh!" tone of voice. "Boys, this is really gonna work. I swear. The big fish!"

Their excitement didn't quite match her own. Soon, they were clambering to watch television, a baseball game or something equally boring. Uninterested, June collected her presentation and retired to her bed. Miffed, she grumbled at them while heading out of the room. Once in bed, her mind began to race. With the poster standing against her wall, she couldn't help but sneak glances in its direction. The other two were in the living room, hollering and hooting anytime something exciting happened, but June's mind stumbled its way through countless scenarios. So many possibilities. Split-second choices she'd have to make.

By the time exhaustion overwhelmed her, June had a concrete plot. Impossible to mess up. Impossible to be caught. Bruce Michaels lived way out there, after all, far from any major roads or other houses. An ideal spot for a robbery. It helped that nobody could hear him scream.

The plan had to be foolproof. Her mother's life depended on it. The future of these two numbskulls. This was their ticket out of here. And her ticket to a better life, whatever that meant. Bruce's valuables and money would open so many doors for all of them.

"We gotta do this," she repeated. "We gotta do this. And we will."

She couldn't help but imagine it. The three of them, cruising down the interstate in a sleek car, cops on their tail. That would be it. All she'd dreamed of. And if they really got away with it? The wealth of a millionaire actor?

Her mind couldn't help but wander. Think about what her mom had said last week. A trip to New York. That's all she could dream of. And it was June's goal to achieve that for her. Maybe not right away, but someday. She'd take her there someday. Make it a reality.

This final score would be the end of this business, without a doubt. She could pay her mom's insulin costs for a long time afterward. Maybe June would get a normal job after all this. Integrate into society as something other than a thief. And these two, they'd be on their own. Out of Little Rush. Out of her life.

It had to work. And it would. She'd give anything to ensure it.

10
HUDSON

With shoulders hunched forward and elbows resting on the table, I stared dead-panned at the entrance. The air hung heavy with smells of garlic, grease, and fresh-from-the-oven pizza. Every so often, a server would pass by the booth and wink at me. One of the guys stopped and made a thrusting movement. I knew it had been a mistake coming here. It was never a great idea to go on a date at the place you work, but Layla had suggested it.

For a few days, ever since our unexpected meeting, we'd been texting almost non-stop. My phone, usually barren, now lit up every few minutes with a new text. Then, once in our beds, we stayed up way too late texting and said "goodnight" half-heartedly, ready to pick up the conversation as soon as our alarms went off. The previous night, right after we'd agreed on this date, we video chatted for the first time. Layla wore a low-cut tank top and somehow had seen my eyes drop to her cleavage. She responded with a sly grin and a not-so-subtle removal of her shirt.

Suffice to say, I had no qualms as I pulled into the pizza restaurant and took a deep breath, composing myself. That weird half-pizza sticking out from the roof brought a sense of comfort. I'd spent countless hours in this building, knew it like the back of my hand. So, strolling inside, I stuck out my chest and assured myself things would go excellent. We were playing on my home turf, after all.

When I entered, though, Layla was nowhere to be found. Even though I arrived two minutes after six, she hadn't shown yet. I'd been forced to ask one of my friends behind the counter.

"Hey, Jimmy, I'm just... looking for a girl. Same grade as us. Layla? You know her?"

"That cute black girl, huh?" Jimmy grinned far too wide. "You on a date, huh?"

"Is she here or not?" I crossed my arms and glared over the register.

"Nah. I'll let her know you're here. *If* she shows."

From that moment onward, I'd been in a booth alone, eyes trained on the entrance. A quarter past six, by that point, and I'd already downed one soda. When Jimmy brought me a refill, he narrowed his eyebrows, as if some question ate at his insides. Silence prevailed, however, and he disappeared after that.

Sitting in the booth, I got a few texts from Mason. He'd messaged me right before I came here, something about "let me know how it goes." This time, he offered a little more detail.

Mason: Be drinking with babe at the cabin. text when you're free. good luck!

And then, a few minutes after that.

M: Wanna swing by after your date?

I didn't answer either of these. The thought of driving out to his dad's cabin didn't appeal to me. Neither did retelling the course of my date to a drunken idiot and his girlfriend who wouldn't care. Being with them in any capacity was unappealing. We'd drifted apart over the previous two weeks, ever since the party. I couldn't quite put a finger on the reason. They *had* sort of clung to each other in the aftermath and started doing things like this. Drinking at the cabin, sans me. Going on walks downtown, sans me. Being a third wheel was painful enough. Being a third wheel in the process of falling off hurt even more.

From my booth, I could see the television, where a baseball game played at low volume. I could hear noises from the kitchen, the typical clattering cutlery and voices of a busy pizzeria. The local radio station played over the speakers, nearly drowned out by conversations from surrounding tables. Lots of couples tonight, more than usual. Even two middle-aged men openly holding hands. I hadn't thought there were any gay couples in Little Rush.

My eyes shifted to the television. In the bottom right, the time had just turned six-twenty. I told myself that I'd give her ten minutes and then be out of here. Again, I checked my phone, hoping to find something from her. Even an apology and asking to reschedule would be enough. Instead, just another text from Mason.

A notification popped up, something from Twitter. I clicked it on and resigned myself to ten minutes of *this* before leaving. I could check my feed at least, just in case any other pictures had surfaced of me and Bruce. Since the pizza delivery incident, I hadn't noticed anything, but that didn't mean for sure nothing would.

"Oh my god, I'm so sorry!"

I glanced up and saw her approaching. Layla, breathless and out-of-sorts, hurried up to the booth. She stood, as if afraid to sit down. Her graphic t-shirt was wrinkled, one sock folded over itself in haste. Her hair had been pulled back in loose braids. She wasn't, by any means, the image of preparation. At the sight of her, I grinned and gestured to a chair at the table.

"Don't worry. I haven't ordered."

She took a seat and threw her head back almost right away, letting out an exasperated sigh. "Ugh, I feel awful, Hudson."

"It's honestly no big deal." I looked around for one of the servers, hoping that we could finally order. I'd worried myself into quite an appetite. "Everything okay?"

This thinly veiled request for an explanation went over fine, and she launched into a story, interrupted by Jimmy coming to take our order. (This ended with a wink and another thrusting movement when Layla couldn't see him.)

According to her, she'd started off running late, leaving her house just before six. Her mom needed help carrying groceries inside and then watching the baby while she prepared dinner. Layla, the oldest of six children, tried to throw on some make up and hurried through everything. Then, she got stuck behind a tractor on a two-lane road with no good places to pass. And finally, she'd driven past the pizza restaurant on accident twice and had to circle back.

"I guess I should've realized from the... that pizza thing sticking out of the roof," she finished, smacking herself on the forehead. "I've just never been here, so didn't know what to look for."

"Really?" I asked, shaking my head in disbelief. "You've never been here?"

She shrugged. "Never. We don't eat out much. Too many siblings and all. Too expensive."

It struck me as odd that myself and Mason were both single children. Even Willow only had one brother. I didn't usually consider siblings, since as an only child and a senior in high school I had no reason to. But I was sure that would've meant... well, more responsibility.

Layla's drink arrived, and our conversation turned to the pizzeria itself, being her first time. She commented on the memorabilia hanging beside us. The wall adjacent our booth had been covered with newspaper articles, pieces of basketball nets, a football helmet, all stuff from the local high school. I wasn't sure if Jed Cooper had decided on these neat touches or if they were somebody else's idea. Either way, the sports-bar aesthetic served the restaurant in a nice way.

Through some off-handed comment from Jimmy, Layla discovered that I worked here. She launched into questions about my job, what it entailed, did I enjoy it. I played along with this typical first-date game and asked her some as well. Turned out she'd only gotten a job recently, now that her eleven-year-old sister could watch the kids. She'd been at the movie theater for about five months and offered to get me discounted tickets sometime.

"Well, if you're paying, I'll see just about any movie," I offered up, taking a sip through my straw. "Maybe... date number two?"

"Maybe so." She kicked my foot under the table playfully. I didn't know what she meant, but it felt nice to talk so casually with someone. Someone new.

Maybe that's what irritated me whenever I spent hours in Mason and Willow's company. It was sort of the same feeling I used to have riding in my father's truck between him and my mom. Like in every conversation, they weren't ever fully talking to me. I only had a portion of their attention, never the full thing. With Layla, her eyes were only on me, her words directed only to my ears. Having somebody's full attention, somebody so beautiful, felt really nice for a change.

Maybe that's selfish. I pondered this as we talked, thinking it might not be a good thing I needed so much attention. But a date wasn't the time for that speculation.

The pizza and breadsticks arrived. Conversation lulled as we ate. Neither of us felt comfortable talking while chewing. Mostly, we resigned to exploring the other tables with our eyes, watching some of the couples. We would comment on them, sometimes rude but also genuine compliments. Layla took a particular liking to the gay couple who rose to leave.

This act of people-watching teamwork churned away the better part of an hour. When the pizza had turned into crumbs and our drinks were only ice, I glanced at the television screen and found that we'd been sitting longer than I thought. Plus my isolated half-hour.

Layla checked her phone, presumably for the time. She looked back at me with a thin, thoughtful smile. "You know, I just realized I *did* know you were a delivery guy. I remember that picture of you and Bruce Michaels from a while ago."

"Oh, right." I tried to force a smile. "Yep, that was really weird."

"Do you talk to him much?" she asked, leaning forward a bit, really leading the conversation now. "Or was that just a delivery thing? I didn't know if... maybe he asked for you specifically or something?"

"Or something, yeah." I cleared my throat and started to scoot out of the booth. "I'll be right back. Bathroom."

If she understood my sudden leave of absence, she didn't show it. I hurried away from the booth and into the restroom. The cramped space smelled like cherries. I noticed the air freshener resting just below the mirror. For a few minutes, I stared at myself in the glass, at the almost-stubble on my chin.

Deep breaths, I told myself. There was nothing malicious in her question. She'd enjoyed the date. *So did you,* I snapped. *Just a question.* She'd remembered it, not been thinking about it. She didn't *come here* just to pepper me about Bruce.

And yet, it almost felt that way. Like this whole date was a scam. She'd rejected me at the party, seen my picture with Bruce, and only then decided to give it a go. It made sense. It made perfect sense.

I didn't *want* to be associated with that old man. I didn't *want* him hanging over me. There were enough shadows here in Little

Rush without an extra one. I once thought of Bruce as an idol. Him moving here was the coolest thing. And now, his presence just gave me another reason to run away. Another regret in a life swamped by them.

My phone buzzed. I almost didn't pick up. It was probably Mason, now sufficiently drunk. God only knew what he would text this time. But when I did finally extract the phone from my pocket and read the name, it wasn't Mason.

Dad: Don't want to interrupt your date. And don't freak out. I just wanted to let you know that I won't be staying at the house tonight. I'm with Mason's dad for a few days.

My mind drew a blank at this text. None of that made sense. For a few days? I mean, he'd stayed at their house once last year, when Jed and him were too drunk and didn't feel like calling a taxi. Mom hadn't been too happy. But for a few days?

The next vibration brought few answers.

D: Your mother and I had just a small argument. We just need to cool off. Well I need to. Everything's okay, promise buddy. Just wanted to be open with you and all. We're just taking some time to think.

To think.

Taking some time to think.

What the fuck did that mean?

My own parents. My farmer's tan, workaholic dad and my faithful, relentlessly kind mom. Taking some time to think. About what? A divorce? God, would it be like Willow's parents, where her dad had really gone south afterwards? I didn't want to be that... that nineteen-year-old with parent issues, a fresh divorce. Jesus Christ, at least wait until I graduated high school! Not right now. Before I'd even settled on a future.

I stormed out of the pizzeria, shooting a glance at Layla. I could only offer her a small wave, mouth the words, "I'll explain later!"

I'd already left cash on the table to pay for the meal. No reason to return. I would text Layla that night, maybe. Give her an explanation and say sorry.

No, I wouldn't. I didn't owe her an apology.

I slammed the door of my truck and felt the engine rumbling. Shifting into reverse, I took one last glance at the window beside our booth. Layla stared back at me, her eyes wide, confused, hurt. I couldn't bear the sight, so I slammed on the gas and then maneuvered into the road. As quickly as possible, I fled the scene like a murder had just been committed.

There's nothing quite like leaving a person behind. No feeling that can touch every part of the soul like that. Grief and power. That image swam in my head as I sped toward my house. Of Layla, staring at me, not knowing what she'd done wrong, not understanding why I had to desert her.

Maybe I would text her. I probably did owe her that much.

Neither of my parents were home when I arrived. Without those texts from my father, this wouldn't have concerned me at all. Now, it sent me into a fit of rage.

They owed *me* an explanation. They needed to stay for *me*. And they'd left me behind. Just like I'd done to Layla.

I ran inside the house, closing the door so hard that I thought it might break. I called out once for my mom, hoping she would answer, already knowing she wouldn't. For just an instant, I stood in that house, completely alone, and thought about calling Layla. Maybe she would comfort me and come here. Maybe she'd understand these feelings and these fears. Were her parents divorced? God, I didn't even know the answer.

Mason. No, I never seriously considered calling him.

Instead, I hurried to my room, shut the door behind me, and locked it. Then I grabbed my desk chair and wedged it under the doorknob.

Five minutes later, with a bottle of vodka sitting cap-less on my desk and a notepad directly beside it, I considered writing a suicide note. Or I could just stare out the window for now and grow increasingly more drunk, closer and closer to making mistakes I would regret tomorrow morning. If that morning even came.

I didn't have the guts to kill myself yet. I already knew how the night would end.

Taking some time to think.

11
LITTLE RUSH
THE JOURNALIST

Gina rested her eyes for just a split second, savoring the darkness in contrast to her laptop screen. She shifted in an uncomfortable chair that came with the apartment. Her laptop, notepad, and a collection of newspapers from across the country were spread out on the desk. This apartment, while spacious enough, felt more like an oversized hotel room than a living space. Perhaps because she still hadn't unpacked, even after a month of living here.

The fireworks had finally died off just half an hour earlier, even though July fourth itself had been nearly a week ago. Something about little rural towns like this gave her a peaceful rest. A town where people had nothing better to do for days afterward than shoot off more fireworks, prolong the hotdog celebrations for as long as possible. She didn't hate this about Little Rush. In fact, she appreciated it. Hoped that tomorrow night, it would continue. Although eventually, she knew, it would all end.

Soon enough, she would leave this town, not likely to ever return. And in her wake? What would her impact be on this motley collection of neighborhoods, and on Bruce Michaels himself? Those questions remained a mystery.

Gina opened her eyes again and re-read the email she'd typed out.

I hope this finds you well, the message to her editor started. *I've had a chance to talk with Mr. Michaels under the guise of a local reporter. While I couldn't obtain any concrete answers to my questions, I did manage to piece together a few things. Including the girl.*

While he denies any memory and is reluctant to broach the subject, there is no doubt. Mr. Michaels remembers Ms. Suso. Even more, I can confidently say that his purpose in coming to Little Rush has been avoiding the memory of her, perhaps avoiding an investigation exactly like this one. In my opinion, we should press on, dig deeper, and unearth more about this hidden agenda before we move to publication. Discover what else Bruce —she deleted this and changed it to— *Mr. Michaels might be hiding.*

For all we know, there could be more out there with similar stories. If there are, and if they're willing to step forward, then we have to include them in our publication. To do otherwise would be both dishonest and a huge detriment to our public image.

The email went on for a few more paragraphs. It dove into more specific details, tidbits that would make for a compelling study on Bruce Michaels as a man, as a monster. As Gina read through them, she cringed at parts and reworded a few sentences. She'd been slightly drunk, she realized while reading the whole thing back. Drunk with anger. Outrage, even. Now, after another two weeks, she found some... not sympathy. Nobody could have sympathy for what this man had suffered, not after what he had done. She just felt like there were pieces missing. Things that didn't add up.

She wrote something along these lines at the back-end of the email, stressing her desire to push deeper into Bruce's story. Again, she found an instance where she'd called him by his first name, not the more formal term "Mr. Michaels." Having fixed that and a few other typos, she completed her parting thoughts, asked for advice, and wished him well on the other projects their magazine juggled.

When this email had flown into the abyss, she closed the tab. The screen switched to her personal email, where she noticed a new message. From Madeline Suso.

Her editor and the magazine higher-ups in general didn't know about these private communications, and hopefully never would. Officially, her relationship with the girl —no, not girl; Madeline had graduated from college by now— had ended a month ago. When their series of interviews and coffee dates had ended, and Gina herself bought a plane ticket to Louisville, she hadn't expected to hear from the young woman again. Gina focused her eyes on this no-name town, but then Madeline emailed. Gina answered the inquiry, but not on her work account. She took it to her personal Gmail and the conversation developed, slowly, over the last few weeks.

I just wanted to say thank you, Madeline had written.

Gina read the words, a skeptical smile touching her lips. Unsure what to think or what to believe of the young woman's facade.

It continued. *I hope my emails aren't annoying you. I don't mean to do that or anything. I'm just curious how the story is coming along. Has anyone else stepped forward yet? I know you told me not to get a lawyer yet… I'm trying my best to hold off. But the settlement they offered is so… much. I could pay off my student loans with that! It would just make me feel so much better if I know there are more like me. Do you know anything about that?*

I also wanted to ask if you're positive that you told your boss not to include my name. I don't want to be involved with this thing, not any more than I have to. I'll… I'll do the court stuff, like you asked, and I won't take a settlement for now. But I don't want to be in the article. I don't… I don't even know… I don't want Bruce to get life in prison or anything… I just hate that people think he's this great guy and he's really… You know what I mean, right?

Thank you again, Gina. You really seem to get me. Just please make sure they don't include my name, and I'll do my best to stay strong over here. I really just want to be normal again. To have my life back. Thank you for helping me.

Each time Gina read the young woman's messages, her heart filled with something like pity and wrath. She sensed the power she held in these months of investigation, of decisions. The ability to wreck somebody's life. Someone as powerful as Bruce. But also, in a sense, the inability to stop what she'd set in motion.

She hadn't told her editor to avoid using Madeline's name. And she'd told them all the salacious details, everything that made for a front-page story, maybe for weeks in a row. Sacrifices had to be made

This haunted her as she powered down the laptop. Watched the Google screen flicker into nothingness. Then she whipped it shut, turned back to face her empty apartment.

The ability to wreck somebody's life. To decide if he deserved it. To paint the story as cruel or as ambiguous as she wanted. But then again, the inability to save Madeline. She'd done what Gina suggested, refused the settlement over and over again. Not knowing it soon wouldn't be an option. Not knowing that she'd get no money out of this now.

But what she hadn't told Madeline is that her life would never be normal after this. That was out of their control now. Once more, the young woman had lost her innocence and control. Only this time, Gina herself had been the one to take it.

Gina fell back onto her bed, covering her face with a pillow. Trying to block out a thought which had tortured her for months.

Is all of this justice for her? Or profit for me?

12

HUDSON

They found the middle-aged man in his apartment, hanging on a noose that he made from a belt. I didn't recognize his name when I saw it in the paper, and I immediately forgot it. But the story stuck with me in a way that few news-related items did. Not because of the suicide itself. Though that was peculiar enough, for sure.

I'd always thought it would be me. The first one to kill himself in this town full of on-the-edge people. The edge of sanity, that is. The edge of a mountain, where you just might jump one day. I lived on that edge, spent my days peering over it at the chasm below. In my mind, suicide and I were on a collision path. We were bound to lock arms one fateful day and dance ourselves to sleep.

It's not to say that I felt angry at the man. I didn't, exactly. But I did feel betrayed. Fate had betrayed me. Given up the spotlight to this middle-aged nobody. A man with no future. A man who nobody would miss. That cut right into my heart when I read the story. The realization that a streak fifty years in the making had been wasted on this.

His divorced wife and estranged kids might miss him, sure. In a forced sort of way. But besides that, his death left no more impact on the world than his life had. A waste. All of it, a waste.

Would my own dad end up that way if my parents really divorced? Would I one day read about him in this same section, just a paragraph of words?

These were cruel thoughts, and I took no pleasure in them. But I also didn't resist.

To my surprise, nobody else noticed the correlation. Bruce Michaels moved to town, and within a few weeks somebody had killed themselves? No, not a coincidence. A cause. When somebody as bright as Bruce moves into a town like Little Rush, everybody feels a bit... overshadowed. I felt it myself. Continued to suffer under that feeling. This guy, this nobody, had given up. Had extinguished his light entirely.

I wondered, laying in my bed that night, if he had scars like I did. On his upper thigh where nobody could see. I wondered if he felt the same insatiable aching for pain and then instantly regretted it. If he had ever thought about suicide before, even tried it. If he had looked at the bridge and considered jumping. Stared down a cliffside and imagined his body bouncing off those rocks and exploding like a motherfucking Fourth of July celebration.

These were cruel thoughts, and I didn't enjoy them. I couldn't even remember that week when I cut myself daily. The urge passed with a fresh Monday, and I'd never touched that razorblade again. Threw it out, actually. But the impact was permanent. On me, on my skin.

In my dark bed, alone, in a house without a father, I wished I hadn't thrown it out. I wondered if my mother would come home, try to enter my room. Finding it locked, would she wonder if I'd gone through with it? Finally —what's the expression— kicked the bucket? And, whenever I groaned my way downstairs for breakfast, would she be disappointed to see me?

Most people would forget about that man and about his

unfortunate end. I wouldn't. I remembered him, thought about him weekly at least. There were nights when I pictured myself in his position. There were nights when I wanted to be.

I wished I could have read his suicide note. Pondered his final words.

What would mine have been? In his situation, in his shoes?

Bruce Michaels is a star that burns too bright. Why fight the inevitable? Why persist?

No, those weren't very good. They made me sound like a dick. But they weren't the dumbest I'd ever thought.

I liked the final line, at least. Honestly, I mean… why persist?

Mason and Willow had each other. They were in a fine place. Better than fine. Those fuckers would probably get married by next summer if I had to guess. It wasn't like they needed me any longer. Even if they *thought* so, they definitely didn't.

Besides, they could find a new friend. Maybe even couple-friends.

And my parents? Would they even stay together? Divorced adults don't need kids. Especially not one in college, accruing debts he could never repay. No, they truly would be better off without me. They might not even notice if I simply slipped to the other side. They were both busy people with a potential divorce and everything. Who knew what to call it. Who cared.

Besides, they could eventually make a new kid. Maybe it wouldn't be quite as fucked up.

Layla. I'd given her a chance, hadn't I? First, at the creek. I'd honestly *tried* to give myself away. She'd rejected me. Left me drunk, naked, alone. Maybe that's how I'd die, too. But then, I picked myself up. I did better. We had a pretty good date, in my opinion, until I ran off like an asshole. No explanation. Didn't even text her that night. She had every reason to hate me, to think about and curse me.

Sadly, I knew she wouldn't. Worse than being hated, I would

be forgotten. Just another failed boyfriend. A funny story for the next one to hear.

With all these thoughts in mind, I climbed into my truck with complete intention of killing myself. I made up my mind. I would drive downtown, park underneath the bridge again, and then walk onto that pedestrian sidewalk. Get out near the center where the wind smacked against your cheeks. Then I would jump and hope for the best. Or the worst, depending on your point of view.

When I started the engine, it comforted me. I imagined this would be the last time the old truck ever answered to my touch. My final trip. What a run we'd had together, the old junk bucket. Imagine a truck outlasting you. Jesus, I couldn't have been more pitiful.

"I will follow you into the dark." I sang the words in a shallow, throaty tone, so I turned the radio up until I couldn't hear my own voice. Or my own thoughts. Death Cab for Cutie assaulted me in all directions, blaring through my speakers. Who, exactly, would I be following? That question left unanswered, I roared away from my home. They certainly wouldn't follow me.

When I reached the end of my gravel driveway, I turned right and sped up. I had to make it there before I lost my nerve. I could feel it draining away already.

I ended up parking in a field, the same one Mason and I got drunk at from time to time. The place where I'd first considered death out loud and with a close friend. I pulled the truck over and waited. For a sign, for encouragement. Banged my head against the steering wheel a few times, hoping it might bleed or knock me out entirely. The song ended, and I restarted it.

After five times through, I backed onto the road once more and returned home in utter silence. To a house with no father, but at least not a house of grief. Not yet.

The moment had passed. The wave had crashed. Perhaps we were all better for it. Waves would come again, though. Endless storms in a place of empty dreaming.

PART 3

A PLACE OF PASSING MOMENTS

1
JED

For a time in my life, before the pizza restaurant made a profit and I hit it big with stocks and rental property, I was a normal person. Just a young man with a girlfriend and a minimum-wage job. Growing up in the 80's, running around with friends, no cell phones or Netflix or any of that stuff.

There were only a few days that I remembered. Mostly, it was all a blur, but a few moments stuck in my brain. Like the day that Lucy and I went skinny dipping in the river or my first time getting drunk with Henry. My first experience at the boat races. A lot of firsts.

Everything was so different back then in Little Rush. Not booming, by any stretch, but lively. It felt like the city hadn't fallen asleep yet, like we were holding onto the past. That wore off, naturally, and we became the sleepy river town of my adulthood. But for a time, it felt electric. For a time, I couldn't ask for anything more.

Maybe I should've seen it earlier. The way cities and relationships fall apart. There's always warning signs. In high school, you never see them. Even after, it's easy to ignore. But everything crumbles eventually, some over decades and some over hours. Growing up was the easy part. It's forced on you. But figuring out what to do next… that was the struggle.

o o o

It had only been a few weeks since we graduated high school, but Henry was already fully integrated. I could see it in his eyes as we wandered downtown Little Rush, both of us stumbling just a bit. He had already given in to adult life. Had become one of them. A forty-hour worker, already a job at the power plant.

I had my suspicions that he would never leave town. He looked too much like his coworkers. An ill-kept mullet, scraggly mustache. He wanted to fit in there, had tried his hardest. And one of those days he just might.

The two of us emerged from one of the old factory buildings, shading our eyes from the sunset. I shot him a grin and wobbled up the sloping sidewalk, back toward Main Street. The energy in the air was palpable, potential for something more.

It had been just days since the festivities died away. Only forty-eight hours earlier, the riverfront had been swollen with crowds and tents. A hundred thousand boat-racing fans showed up every year. The annual Regatta, broadcast on national television, the only real spectacle around here. For us, back in high school, the drinking started on July first, peaked on July fourth weekend, and continued for days after the boats disappeared. Now, freshly graduated, the tradition held.

"Can't imagine a crowd bigger'n this," Henry had said on the first day as we neared the huge crowds. They were lining the river as far as you could see, young and old, single and families. All of them raucous, all of them entranced by those boats zipping by on the water's surface, faster than life. "Can't imagine it gettin' any smaller, neither."

I'd agreed with him at the time. Now, days later, the crowds had mostly dissipated, and the boats were long gone. The river ran empty once more, the shores littered with wrappers and beer cans and broken lawn chairs. A few people were loitering there, taking their time. The fireworks on Fourth of July had brought another crowd, but even those sparks in the sky were absent. Now, Little Rush had fallen asleep. Its normal state of being.

We followed that sidewalk up toward Main Street, laughing at the stupidest of topics. It was a familiar trek by now. That empty factory building held countless beer cans and foggy memories. It was one of the few places two young men could really escape to. Leaving it behind, we usually wandered up to Allen's Burgers where we'd sober up with greasy burgers and cold sodas.

"Can't believe we both have girls now, huh?" I slapped him on the back as we waited for a car to pass by. Then we crossed the street and continued walking. "Almost like we're adults or some shit."

"I dunno." Henry chuckled and avoided my eyes, keeping his gaze straight ahead. "Probably gonna dump Laurie inna bit. She's at the Ohio, waiting for me, y'know?"

I furrowed my eyebrows. "Did something happen?"

"Nah, nothing much. Just... isn't working out."

We arrived at Main Street, and he glanced across the road, where the Ohio Theater waited, lights shining and doors open. There was a line of people funneling inside. Somewhere in that mess, Laurie waited for him, unaware of the heartbreak he brought toward her. Things might not be the greatest between them, but both were gonna hurt if he did indeed dump her.

"I don't think I'm ever gettin' married," Henry mumbled as we strolled in that direction. He would cross the street for the theater, and I would carry on, but for the time we were side-by-side.

"Oh, yeah?"

"No girls here for me." Henry glanced over at the theater and deflated. "This'll suck."

"If it makes you feel any better, I'm not sure Lucy's the

marrying type."

"What makes you say so?"

We stood at the crosswalk now, waiting for the light to change. "She's a bit... wild." I couldn't help but grin.

He smirked and rolled his eyes. "Never thought you two would be an item, true. But you're so vanilla it might wear off her crazy."

Henry left me at that point. I didn't question if he really should dump Laurie, because I didn't want to get involved. I had my own girlfriend to stress about. A friend of Laurie's, in fact. Lucy would be around to pick me up in a while, so I maneuvered a few blocks down and took up residence at Allen's Burgers.

I moved into the restaurant, waving at the familiar faces. "Hey there," I said, pushing my way to a seat at the counter. Once I took my spot, every stool had been filled, and there were a few people against the wall, waiting on to-go orders. For Allen's, this was a pretty typical crowd. He could've used some more seating, I always thought.

"Regular?" Allen slapped a hand on the counter in front of me and showed that wide, toothy grin.

"And a milkshake," I added, beaming. "For my lady."

o o o

"Hey, babe." I hopped into the passenger seat of Lucy's car, putting the milkshake into her cupholder. "Got this for you."

"Ooh, nice. Thank you." She leaned over and kissed me, then pulled back onto the road.

Allen's Burgers and the whole downtown quickly receded into the distance. Night had almost completely fallen. I didn't ask questions because I'd learned better than that with Lucy. The whole night had been loosely planned up to this point, but now we were headed god-knows-where.

She started up the winding road nearby that carried us to the hilltop. I hadn't expected this since we rarely went on dates that weren't downtown. Maybe the bowling alley, but it didn't feel like that kind of night. As the trees sprinted by my window and Lucy's small car fought its way along, I leaned against the headrest and closed my eyes.

"You know Henry's gonna dump Laurie tonight?" I started. "At the movies?"

"Oh, yeah?" She chewed on her lip and laughed somewhat darkly. "Funny thing. Laurie's gonna do the same to him."

"What? Why?" I glanced over, but her expression betrayed nothing.

"Says he's a dickhead sometimes. Can't say I disagree."

"I think he's just..." I let the sentence die off, because I didn't know how to frame my thoughts. Henry was certainly lazy at times. Maybe an underachiever. Maybe even a dick. But I still wanted to be friends with the dude, at least while we both stuck around here.

In Little Rush, long friendships were a novelty, and you couldn't be too picky. For me, anyway.

Lucy continued driving and led us out past Rush Road and into the country. We passed through a small neighborhood on the edge of town where all the wealthier people lived. Travelling on, into the darkness and uncertainty of the countryside, Lucy started to grin in the mischievous way I'd grown so fond of. I resisted, still, the urge to ask questions. Letting the journey spread out before me, a few feet at a time, just like the twisting country road in her headlights. Over hills so quickly that my stomach dropped, wincing anytime headlights passed. Lucy always drove pretty fast, but sometimes it scared me more than others. I guess that was true about a lot she did.

At last, she swerved off the road and into a gravel driveway. I opened my mouth at this point, but she placed a finger to my lips. With the other hand, she navigated down the driveway and parked next to a massive, half-constructed house.

It struck me at first how isolated we were. There were no homes for probably a mile in any direction, not even tilled fields. This house, three stories tall with a wrap-around porch, looked to be half-finished. There were walls undone, the structure mostly bare-bones. I didn't know exactly what she had planned, but Lucy hopped out of her seat eagerly.

"What're we doing here?" I asked at last, standing next to the car still.

She popped the trunk and dug around for a moment, pulling out a twelve-pack of beers and a bottle of vodka. Lucy held one in each hand and shrugged. Her eyes met mine, and I felt my knees go weak as she said, "Just having fun."

I carried the alcohol inside and found one room with the floor mostly done and a rough carpet laid down. While I unpacked the drinks, she brought in a large blanket, a lamp, and a bulky boombox radio. I stood against one wall, running a hand over the rough surface, looking around at the unfamiliar setting. I'd never been inside a house like this before. Not this size or this unfinished. But I tried to keep an open mind for whatever she had planned.

Lucy plugged the lamp into a socket, which apparently had electricity running. She winked at me. "Lucky for us it's on, I guess." Then she spread out a blanket on the ground, started the music, and opened the vodka bottle.

I started drinking right away, and it only took me a little bit to get sufficiently brave. Once I'd opened up a bit, Lucy convinced me to dance with her in the harsh light of that lamp, with an empty and creaking house around us. I grinned so wide, felt a rush of excitement with every turn of her body. The alcohol crept more and more into my bloodstream, and with each passing minute, Lucy grew more stunning. She had this glow about her, a liveliness that I'd never touched before. The kind of person who would take you to an empty house and dance.

"Give me your pocket knife," she said about an hour in. Both of us were sweating by that point since the house had no air conditioning. She'd taken off her shirt and now danced around in only jeans and a bra. When she extended a hand, I gave her my knife with some confusion.

"Come on. Don't be nervous." She grabbed my hand and led me toward the nearest doorway. With a giggle, she opened it and started carving into the frame. I twitched, thinking about stopping her, but Lucy turned back and reassured me. "It's okay. I won't put our names or anything."

She worked for a moment, humming to herself. Then she handed me the knife and stepped back. "Your turn."

In the doorframe, barely legible, she had cut the word: *someday...*

I moved forward, knowing exactly what to put next.

"I'm gonna live in a house this big, you know that?" She leaned against the wall while I struggled with the knife. Talking to herself, maybe, but also to me. "I'm gonna have a huge garden. And I'm gonna be one of those fucking rich people with their fucking cars. You know?"

"Look."

I motioned for her to move closer. She did so and covered her mouth with a hand.

someday... you'll be mine

"You're a dork," she said, now looking deep into my eyes and stepping closer. Lucy placed both arms around my neck and cocked her head. She chewed on her lip and blushed. "You know what you should do next?"

"What's that?" I felt my palms growing sweaty and my shoulders stiffen.

Lucy pushed against me and leaned her back against the doorframe we'd just carved. "Fuck me on this wall."

o o o

I thought about that night from time to time. Whenever I drove by the old house where it happened. It was falling apart now. In complete disrepair. But I can remember a time when it was finished and grand. An even better time when it was just bare bones and a carpet. All of that was gone, though. Just a dilapidated, forgotten frame left.

There were no houses anywhere near it. It stood alone, and one day it'd be gone completely. For now, it was a monument. Or maybe a memorial. To everything we had and everything we'd lost.

Laurie and Henry got together a few years later, once Henry started farming and decided to stick around Little Rush for the long haul. Things went better the second time around, since he'd smoothed out some of those rough edges. I stayed friends with the dude throughout everything. I remembered his brash and aggressive youth, but I also saw that he'd changed. Maybe that's why Laurie took him back. Or maybe we were all just settling for the best available.

Lucy and I started working soon after that incident at the house. She kept a job for a few years, but once the pizzeria made a profit, she quit to help me. First as a waitress, then a manager once we had enough help. We talked about buying that house, with the carved door frame and the gravel driveway, but decided it was too expensive. Too far from town. In the end, it just didn't work. We settled for something easier.

A few years later, she stopped working entirely. Once I hit it big with the stock market, bought up so many rental properties, she didn't need to. We got a house in the real nice neighborhood, started a family, and she stayed home with Mason all those years. I don't know if she ever regretted it. I always meant to ask her. Just slipped my mind. After a while, those conversations were impossible. Just have to let them die off.

The old house stood out there for a long time, falling apart more and more as the decades passed. I wanted to visit, just once, but never did. I wanted to step in that room and dance around and smile. But never did.

I wanted to own that house. We settled for something, and I told myself I'd stop settling. Start doing things that I wanted, that Lucy wanted, no matter the cost. But never did.

2
WILLOW

Mason and I were sitting inside the cabin, watching reruns of Family Feud, when the truck pulled into the driveway. We were both seated on the couch, Mason in a tank top and myself in a nightgown still. The wooden interior of the cabin, the log walls, the large fan spinning overhead, it all gave off the sort of cozy vibe that made you reluctant to get dressed for the day. This had become a ritual of ours anytime we spent the night here. I'd wake up late, roll out of bed in the loft above, and descend the narrow staircase to this room. Mason often had breakfast waiting and the television on.

Hudson's truck came to a stop behind Mason's car. When it appeared, Mason popped up from beside me and rushed to the front door. I watched him go, huffing, and jumped up from the couch to change into something less intimate. The front door swung shut behind Mason just as I ascended the stairs and went to rummage in my bag, which lay beside the untidy bed.

A solitary candle burnt on the side table, masking the smell of smoke from the night before. Mason and I had stayed up late, smoking joints that he bought from some older kid in town. It still felt weird to be alone here, just the two of us, when so many nights before Hudson had joined. But he'd had that date to worry about, and now so much more. It had only been one night since his dinner with Layla, but what an eventful one.

I dressed quickly and then hurried to the fridge for drinks. Through the kitchen window, I saw Mason leading Hudson around the house, toward the back porch. Their voices were too faint to make out the conversation, but it sounded casual, unimportant. I grabbed a few soda cans from the fridge and headed in the same direction, meeting them out back.

"I planned on sleeping 'til noon, just so you know," Mason remarked as he took a seat on one side of the table. He winked at Hudson and extended his hand toward me. I filled it with a can.

"Sorry," Hudson said meekly, taking his own seat. He glanced over the forest hillside splaying out in broad daylight. He always did this whenever we came here. Looked toward that creek, as if it would supply answers. "I appreciate you... letting me come over."

He directed this at Mason. In fact, his eyes and words completely avoided me. If I hadn't existed, the conversation so far would've been no different. This didn't surprise me, though. Not after the text he'd sent me last night.

Higher than I'd ever been in my life, alone in the darkened living room, I'd spent at least an hour on the floor. With the television playing music and my back against the soft carpet, I stared at the rotating fan high overhead. Only Hudson's text broke my reverie. Mason, fast asleep in the bed upstairs, had no clue. He still didn't. But Hudson knew. Even if he'd been drunk out of his mind, he remembered sending the text. I could tell from the way he avoided me, especially with his eyes. Oh, he remembered for sure. He'd probably read it over since then, full of regret.

"Anytime, man." Mason popped the tap on his drink and took a long draught. Then he cleared his throat, shot me a sideways look, and focused on Hudson. "So... your parents, man. That's... that's tough."

Hudson stared at his own can without opening it. He touched it with one finger and let the perspiration drip onto his skin. "It sucks. My mom turned up in the kitchen this morning. Dad's at your house, I guess."

"My dad and him are coming out here tomorrow. Staying at my house tonight, I guess," Mason said. Again, his eyes turned to me, maybe for support. I already knew the information he was relaying. "They'll probably just... shoot guns or something out here. And my mom's going on a weekend trip with some friends. So, you know, house to myself tomorrow, and maybe the next, too."

Hudson furrowed his eyebrows, still focusing on the can of soda, refusing to meet either of our gazes. "Are you inviting me or telling?"

"Inviting, for sure." Mason laughed, but it sounded hollow and out of place. "You, me, Willow. Like old times."

Hudson smirked at this, and I knew he had the same thought as me. "Old times" meaning just a few weeks ago. Before that party. Something shifted in our dynamics after that. A gradual canyon opening between him and us. Mason, apparently, remained oblivious to the change. Only we felt it. Me and Hudson.

"Maybe." Hudson's eyes rose to Mason now. For just a second, I thought they passed over me. "You two have fun here last night?"

"Got another joint, if you want it," Mason offered. "It's inside."

"I always say yes to illegal substances." Hudson's lips flickered with the hint of amusement. He opened his soda at last and took a drink. "You have no idea how drunk I got last night." He said it like an afterthought, just floating from his tongue.

Only I did have an idea. Although, to be honest, hearing him say it aloud comforted me in a way. At least, if Hudson had been black-out drunk, I could make an excuse for him. Maybe ignore the text, or at least take it less seriously. What he'd sent me... This made it, just maybe, a little more understandable.

"Well, share the love next time," Mason said. He leaned back in his chair and sighed, facing me. "You're awful quiet today, babe."

"Just got a headache," I lied. "Think I hit my head or something last night after you went to sleep."

This piqued Hudson's attention for some reason. I assumed that he only now realized Mason hadn't seen the text, since he'd been asleep already. Hudson could be fairly certain that only I knew his dark truth. And judging by his expression, that offered some relief.

"Ah, yeah. Best sleep of my life." Mason chuckled and finished off his soda can. With one hand, he crumpled the aluminum and chucked it at the back door of the cabin. "Oh, how'd your date go, man? You never texted me." He added quickly, "Not that I blame you, of course."

Hudson moved his finger around the sharp opening of his drink. His eyes were thoughtful, lost. "I... doubt we'll be going out again. If that's what you mean."

"Sucks to hear." Mason drummed both fists on the arms of his chair and leaned back. "Oh, well. What can ya do? Some girls just don't get it, you know?"

"What's that supposed to mean?" I asked, my vision now trained on him. "And maybe it's Hudson that doesn't want another date, not her."

"Hey, just thinking out loud!" Mason threw up his arms in defense and pushed out his chair. "I'm gonna grab another soda. Anyone want something?" When neither of us answered or even shifted, he shrugged and moved around the table. "Alrighty, then." I felt his fingertips brush through my hair and then heard the backdoor slam shut.

Our eyes locked immediately. Hudson bit his lower lip and ran a hand over his face. "Look, Willow..."

"You remember what you sent me?" I asked. I didn't want to waste any time. Mason would be back in a minute or two. And I needed this question answered. I needed to understand, at least partially.

"I... Yeah." He gulped, averted his gaze. "I'm really sorry to put you in this situation."

"No, Hudson..." I took a deep breath and then finally asked what I'd been turning over in my head for hours. "Is that really how you feel?"

"Honestly..." There was a pause. A brief, sad smile danced across his lips. "I don't know anymore."

At that moment, Mason exited the cabin once again, holding a can of soda and a Pop-tart. He let out a massive burp and then groaned, lowering into the chair he'd left. I glanced at him, trying to express in a kind way that he should shut up, but it didn't work. He immediately cracked open the beverage and finished a third in one go.

Mason gestured at Hudson with one of the pastries in his hand. "So, what's your day tomorrow look like?

"A hangover," he said. His eyes glanced at me now, for the first time in Mason's presence. "I'll text you if I can come."

Text me? Or text Mason?

Mason didn't notice the slight difference in tone. He simply agreed that this would work and continued to gnaw on his late breakfast. He told Hudson that he'd give him the joint tomorrow night, if he could come, and maybe they could raid his dad's liquor cabinet, too.

Within a few minutes, Hudson had taken his half-filled soda and made an unspectacular exit. Mason followed him to the truck. We both wished him luck and told him to call if something happened with his parents, any news. Good or bad.

I heard his truck roar to life and figured Mason would be back in a moment. Or maybe not. He might drift inside, back to the couch, and leave me out here. Processing.

Whatever the case, I drew out my phone and read the messages once again. The first one, at almost three in the morning.

Hudson: I can't just be a third wheel. i can't just sit there while you two fuck around all day in front of me. i'm a human being. i'm not a fucking third wheel and you know what? if this is how it's gonna be then... well, nobody even needs me, willow. not you, not my parents, not Layla, not anybody. If this is how it's gonna be i'll fucking kill myself! and i don't care! why not? answer me that. just... fuck it.

My reply, feeble and shaky, had been a request for him to call. I said that we should talk things over on the phone, asked if he'd also texted Mason, that kind of stuff.

It took him ten minutes to answer. Ten minutes where I lay on the living room carpet, holding my breath, waiting for a phone call that would never arrive. Wondering what that meant. With each passing second, thinking that he might've actually done it.

What would I do if I'd been the last person he'd texted? The last one before... he was gone?

Then a second message came.

H: i just need you to know i'm not okay. and i don't know if that's ever gonna change. goodnight, willow. i'm sorry.

3
BRUCE

Standing at the sink in my kitchen, I stared out at the cornfield just beyond the cemetery. It had grown now, so tall that the stalks were probably above my head. I could have gotten lost in that endless expanse. On the road next to my house, infrequent visitors would round the corner, smashing their brakes, wary of cars from the opposite direction. The bend in the road was so sharp and the corn so tall that you had no hope of seeing the other driver before they crashed into you.

I leaned against the counter and pressed my forehead against the window pane. I could imagine him in this exact position. The man I'd never truly known, always wondered about. That summer, long ago, when I'd stayed here for a few months. He always loved this view. I would sit at the kitchen table with a cold glass of milk, and he would lean against this same window. Tell me stories of his own childhood and of my grandma. Explain how the crops grew and the farmers harvested. I'd forgotten all of his wisdom by this point, but still I could remember his face.

If only I knew what he had, what I was still lacking. Capture that missing puzzle piece and become, in some way, more like him. Then, maybe, I would be happier. I would be a more complete, comfortable person. Sure of myself, of my legacy. I hated to think that in life and in death, he would always be the better man.

I thought of the photograph hidden in the bedroom, away from prying eyes. I wondered if anybody could understand what it meant to me. Should I set it on the coffee table again and take the chance of somebody noticing? No, likely not.

A sharp rasp of knuckles on the front door.

I jerked around and stared for a moment. Then it came again. Somebody knocking.

Setting aside my hallucinogenic nostalgia, I limped toward the front door. My knees were aching worse than ever, and it felt like the small of my back had been torn apart and set on fire. Still, I grasped the door handle and pulled backward, revealing the last person I expected to see on a random July day.

"You need something?" I asked, not trying to sound rude, just surprised.

Hudson shifted on my doorstep and looked past me, maybe checking for anybody else in the house. As if I would ever have visitors.

"I just... I don't have anyone to talk to." He glanced at my face then. His eyes were narrowed, almost suspicious. Most people were in awe whenever they addressed me, but on the contrary, he spoke with a hint of vitriol. His eyes darting around the room, sometimes glaring into my own. But he went on, "I don't... I didn't even wanna come here. So, if you can't—"

"Say no more." I moved back from the doorway and gestured for him to come inside. "Got nothing at all to do. Need a drink? Tea or something?

He hesitated to answer. The kid had a funny look in his eyes. I remembered that feeling when I first stepped through that door. I'd been more reverential, maybe. He glanced around the place more with disgust than admiration.

"Don't drink tea," he said.

I entered the kitchen, watching from the corner of my eye as he stood awkwardly next to the closed front door. He'd barely moved a foot since I let him in. His gaze settled on the couch, which he stared at intently.

"All I've got is beer," I called, opening the fridge and rummaging through it, hoping to find a stray soda.

"That works."

I hesitated, my back on fire from hunching over. It took serious consideration, but I decided to grab two beers. Standing up straight again, I fought back a groan and kicked the door shut behind me. As I reentered the living room, I gestured to the folding chair leaning against the window. He didn't react.

I moved to take a seat on the couch, but an idea came to mind. Maybe it was his expression, peering out the window now. Or my own desire to be free of this living space, full of memories and pain. Whatever the reason, I set down both cans on the small table and reached for my most shoddy sandals.

"My back could really use a stretch. How about we... go for a walk?"

"Not that damn path again," he said, raising an eyebrow.

"Just around the cemetery." I opened the front door and stepped outside, gesturing for him to follow.

He didn't smile or speak. Hudson continued to watch me and follow tentatively. I got the feeling that he regretted coming here, but now he couldn't turn back. Or at least wouldn't. I knew that much, even if I couldn't read his overall mood.

Once we both stood outside, I closed the door behind us and turned away. As I started toward the cemetery, he paused, looking back at the house. He raised an eyebrow.

"You don't lock the door?"

I shrugged. "Nothing much to steal."

He opened his mouth but then closed it again. Without a word, he followed my lead around the building. Hudson shuffled along beside me as I led us between two rows of tombstones. Again, I got the impression he regretted coming here. That he didn't want to start whatever conversation he'd come for. Instead, he danced around the subject.

"Where we going?"

"Nowhere in particular." I slowed my walk as we traveled deeper into the cemetery. Without explanation, I began to move the same way a person might in a museum. Taking a few seconds to read over the gravestones, to think about the names, maybe calculate a person's age when they died. Through this slow process, we progressed through the field of stone.

"How often you come out here?" he asked, sounding almost concerned.

I couldn't help but grin. Hudson, himself, seemed like the kind of person who might spend hours among the eternal sleepers. Maybe he didn't realize it.

Ignoring his question entirely, I asked, "Why'd you come here? To ask questions or get answers?"

Hudson groaned, barely audible. Since I'd called out his stall tactics, he grumbled into what he really came for.

"Well… my parents. They're having… problems."

"Mm." We stopped beside a Jenny Ostraman. I reached down and ran my hands over the grass under which she lay. There was still dirt visible under the sparse green. She must've been buried not long ago. A matter of months, rather than years. "Divorce?"

"Yeah. Something like that. I got a text from my dad out of the blue. I was on a date with a girl, and that's another thing!" His voice rose a fraction and filled with emotion. An edge to it. "I *swear* to god, every person I talk to asks about you. Even that girl. She just asked about… you, and I got mad. And then I got that text from my dad and…"

We arrived at a tombstone with three names on it. An entire

family, dead on the same date. A tragedy that had been lost in time, the only remnants right here. Almost a hundred years ago to the day. And how had they gone? A house fire maybe, or a murder? These thoughts consumed me until Hudson cleared his throat, and I remembered our situation.

"You can't always control what people do, y'know. Especially parents," I said as if this wasn't common knowledge. "My own... well, wasn't a divorce." I started walking again. Hudson followed suit, like a dog on a leash. "Dad left when I was... say, five or six. Then Mom, she got sick before long. Never saw him again. Not even at the funeral. It's an awful thing, y'know. Losing someone." I turned and focused on him. Tried to really make him feel it. "I lost somebody. Someone real important to me. Right in that house. You remember when I said I moved here by chance? I lied. This place, this town..." I took a deep breath and pointed at the cornfield. "Even that mess means something to me."

"I don't get what this has to do with me." Hudson, at this point, stopped walking and folded his arms. Defiantly unmoving. I narrowed my eyes and thought about traveling on, forcing him to follow, but decided against it. He wrinkled his nose and added, with some pride, "I'm not you."

"No, but are you much different?" I couldn't help but chuckle at his irritated expression. "When I lost somebody, you know what I did? Tried to kill myself. I can see it in your eyes, Hudson, and in the way you talk. You're not much different at all."

"I don't want—"

"I won't tell you what to do," I interrupted him. This time, I turned my back to him and headed for the edge of the cornfield. "I'm just saying. Think about the pain you'd cause. If your parents lost you."

He sped to catch up with me, until we were matching strides

once again. Everything about him was like Deja vu. The way he huffed, the way he mumbled to himself. A spitting image of what I had been. A more innocent version, maybe. Just as pessimistic. And maybe that's why I kept him around, in the end. Some people ask what you'd say to your younger self. In this case, I wanted to know what he'd say to me.

"That's some real shitty advice, if that's what you're going for," Hudson snapped.

I merely shrugged. "The way you're thinking, you're only gonna hurt people. You know that's true."

"You don't know a thing about me, old man."

We arrived at the edge of the cornfield. Like an impenetrable wall, separating this graveyard from some outside world. I could smell the aroma wafting toward us, the tilled dirt and sun baked stalks. The kind of atmosphere that you never really forget. It strikes unexpectedly and proves all over again why a place like Little Rush is so magnetic. It has a certain, unnamed magic. Even this corn.

"There are some things that advice doesn't fix," I said without looking in his direction. "Only time."

"It's fine. I guess I didn't expect you to help. Just to... distract me."

"Sorry, kid." I shrugged. "Are you busy tomorrow evening?"

Hudson raised an eyebrow. "I might go to a friend's, but I don't know yet."

"In that case..." I cleared my throat and tried not to think how this proposition could go south. "Well, how's about me and you grab dinner tomorrow? I wanna eat what you locals enjoy. And maybe learn a bit more about... everything."

He took a minute to answer me. I let the conversation drift into silence, let him compose himself. I could see the idea churning in his brain, all the pros and cons. Whatever anger he'd come with must have fallen away, because he agreed to my offer. I tried not to watch as he processed, but there was no denying that expression he wore. Shock. Excitement.

All traces of annoyance were gone from his posture and his tone. We stood by that cornfield for a while longer, gazing into the wall. Admiring the way cut grass morphed into a dirty field, all at once. Once his fingers were still, no longer fidgeting with the bottom of his shirt, I decided to strike up our talk once again.

"I'd like to ask you something," I began after a minute, "and I want you to answer honestly. Okay?"

"Only if I ask you something in return."

I nodded. This, at least, was one person I could talk to confidentially. One who I didn't mind spilling secrets to. He was a younger version of myself, after all. Not much different than talking to a reflection.

"Fine, then." I went on. "I wanna know… do you really think your parents are getting divorced?"

Hudson kicked at the loose dirt under our feet. He reached out and touched the coarse texture of the stalks, running his hands along that unique plant. I didn't interrupt his thoughts, as I hoped he wouldn't to me.

"No, I don't," he said finally. "I'm just… uncomfortable with them being flawed, I guess. Being vulnerable. Money's been tight, and I know that. My dad had to ask Jed for a loan, which never happens. I don't like thinking about that kinda stuff. Or my mom crying, like this morning."

I didn't press into what that last sentence meant, but I couldn't let one aspect slip by. "Jed?" I probed. "Who's that?"

"My friend Mason's dad. The one who I said owns a buncha stuff."

"Ah, right." For now, I registered the name *Jed*. I knew there were two major players in this town, one by the name of Cooper and one of Blough. "Is that Jed… Cooper?"

"Yeah." He didn't seem shocked that I guessed right.

I remembered the name, Jed Cooper, and decided that I would get in touch with this figure. Learn more about him, about the town. Possibilities abounded.

"My question," Hudson said, breaking into my thoughts. "You said that you... lost somebody. Who lived in that house." He jerked a thumb back toward the small home, a graveyard away. "I wanna know who."

"He's buried right here. Walked over his grave a few minutes ago." I sighed and rubbed at my chin. "And he may be the most important person I've ever known."

"That's not an answer," Hudson pressed.

"Fine." I turned away from the high schooler, staring back at the home. Its low roof, grimy windows. Like a large rock in the middle of an ocean, it stood alone with no other houses in view. I gave in to the pressure. If anybody deserved to know, maybe he did. It only seemed fair. "My grandpa. Years and years ago, he lived right there. And then he died."

4
JED

Henry threw his duffle bag onto the bright blue, twin bed. It bounced once and then lay still. He rotated, taking in the sights. Wallpaper that matched the bed's offensively bright colors. A tan carpet splayed out, with heavy curtains masking the window. A long-forgotten toy chest had been pushed to one corner of the room. In much the same way, this room itself, one corner of the second floor, hadn't been used for years.

"The guest room," I announced, as if it needed explanation. "And then tomorrow, you and I'll have the cabin to ourselves."

"I really appreciate this, Jed." Henry shook my hand with a tight grip, thanking me for probably the sixth time since he'd pulled in the driveway. "You're a real good man."

"Don't mention it," I said, although the compliment did touch me. "Also, try to avoid Lucy, if possible. She's, uh... taking Laurie's side, you might say."

Henry shrugged at the mention of his wife and took a seat on the bed. The springs creaked under his weight, but he didn't comment. Nor did he register the miniscule size of the mattress, at least compared to his wide shoulders. Instead, Henry just sighed and cradled his head, shoulders slumped.

"I don't know, Jed." He glanced up, the hint of a smile, but not a happy one. A lost expression. "I just don't know."

Never before had I seen him like this. A wandering soul, trapped in a child-sized room. His body giving way to pressures of marriage, work, debts. Those broad shoulders had never lost before. Never crumpled with all the weight, no matter how extreme.

"It's alright, Henry. Things'll work out."

I thought about sitting on the bed, wrapping an arm around his frame, but held myself back. Maybe I should've done the unthinkable, the emotional. But I didn't.

"You ever think about our high school friends, Jed?" He asked the question with innocent wonder. I couldn't have guessed at the intentions behind it. Just an honest remark. A dream, maybe.

"Not often. Not except Blough, and that's because I'm forced to." I cocked my head to the side. "Why?"

Henry leaned back on the bed, bumping his head against the wall. "Everybody else got outta this town, didn't they? Gary's out west. The twins are stock market geeks or something, right? Hell, even Jason is... what's he do?"

I grinned and propped an arm against the door frame, leaning on it. "He's a contractor in Indy or some shit."

"That's right." Henry sat up again and extended a hand. "Just gotta wonder what we'd be like if we'd... gone with the herd, you might say."

I helped him to his feet, groaning, and we stood in the dark room for a moment, almost uncomfortably long. Henry looking into my eyes, his own so full of confusion and hopelessness that again I wanted to hug him. Instead, I stepped into the hallway, and he followed.

As we were about to descend the stairs, Lucy called from just below us, "Heading out, Jed. See you later."

I held out an arm to stop Henry and called back, "Love you."

"Love you too," she replied.

Our never ending game of Marco Polo. Nothing but forced replies.

When the front door shut behind her, I took the first step and ran my hand along the railing. Moving down the stairs, I felt the pull of gravity stronger than ever, my own weight threatening to drag me down. These old knees weren't holding up well, not with so many days spent behind a desk. There was a reason I never visited the second floor.

"I'm glad you two are doing well," Henry commented as we reached the base.

I choked on my laughter. "Us? Doing well? Oh, Henry." I reached out and clasped him on the back. "For a while there, I thought I'd be the one sleeping at your house."

His eyebrows rose. "Really?"

I led the way into the kitchen where I gestured for him to take a seat at the table. With Lucy gone and Mason off with his girlfriend somewhere, we had the house to ourselves. I dug around in the fridge for a moment, extracting two cans of beer, and passed one to him.

Then I elaborated. "Just stress, you know. She kinda wants to move on from Little Rush. Even as a teenager she did. I just can't seem to let go." I popped the tab on mine, and a crisp snap echoed from his side of the kitchen. With my elbows propped on the countertop, I took a long drink and observed him. "We aren't so different, you and me. I do think about the guys from high school."

"Figured." Henry pulled out another chair from the table, scraping it against the tile floor. I wondered if this was an invitation to sit, but then he plopped both feet on it. "I love Little Rush, honest. Just have to wonder... what else's out there."

"I know what you mean. It's not like either of us got to see, huh?"

Henry grinned in a sly manner. "I took a honeymoon to

Florida and all, but I didn't see much outside the room."

I rolled my eyes and took another sip. "So, are we getting drunk tonight or just hanging out? It's your decision. You're the guest."

"You know what?" Henry again smiled in a way that suggested a kind of mischief. "I think we should call up the guys. Maybe... maybe hang out in a week or two. What d'ya think?"

"I think that's the only good idea you've had in a while. And you know what else I think?"

Henry sighed and leaned his head back against the chair. "Yeah, I can imagine."

"I think you should call your wife and apologize for being such a goddamn *asshole*."

We made eye contact, mouths curved, and took a sip from our drinks in unison. Henry had a twinkle in his expression and nodded, acknowledging the truth in my statement.

For a few hours, we reclined around the house. The kitchen for a while, and then the more comfortable living room, with a baseball game playing. We ordered a pizza just before nine o'clock and ate the entire thing. It was, in essence, the closest we'd ever gotten to being college-aged bachelors again. And for just a while, we forgot about the debts, the pressure, the marital strife. We were men again, tough, drunk, and carefree. When the baseball game had given way to a late-night comedy show, we even dialed Gary and made an arrangement to go out for drinks that next weekend.

With the pizza box and numerous beers in the trash can, Henry and I stood by the staircase. My bedroom was down the hallway, not up there. He would make this journey alone.

"Thank you again, Jed," he said, a satisfied expression now plastered on his face. His words were slurred, but the emotions were genuine. "For this. For the loan. All of it. You're a real great guy, and I hope you know that."

"If I'm honest..." I paused, steadied my words. And then from an untapped vein of honesty, I went on, "I've always looked up to you, Henry. And hearing you say that is... is really something."

Then he wrapped both meaty arms around me and squeezed. It was a tighter hug than any I could remember. When he pulled away, I could've sworn there were tears in the corner of his eyes.

"Call your wife," I reminded him, as he started to ascend the staircase.

He glanced over his shoulder at me and said, "You, too, old man."

For a while, I sat in front of the television, paying no mind to the cheap jokes or the laugh tracks. Lucy would be home early the next morning to grab some clothes. Then she'd leave again, this time for the whole weekend. I intended to stay up all night, just waiting for her. I had no idea if it would really help. Our issues felt deeper than something this simple, the kind of emotional baggage that not even conversations and late-night tears would heal. But if nothing else, I wanted to make an effort. She deserved that much and so much more from me.

Though she wasn't the only person I'd been letting down. I also owed him better, so much better. Mason.

But how do you fix a relationship when you don't know why or how it's broken?

5
HUDSON

My truck idled in the parking lot for about ten minutes before Bruce's car pulled next to me. His unspectacular Hyundai nearly brushed against my mirror as he parked beside me. Bruce's expression was focused, and the car jerked a few times before he shut off the engine and made to exit.

I got out of my own, taking a moment to glance at the restaurant. This was one of the nicer dining establishments in Little Rush. It was the kind of steakhouse that served fresh bread before meals and had silverware wrapped in dark blue cloth. I'd suggested it to Bruce when he called, assuming he wanted something less greasy than Allen's and more indicative of the region than Chinese or Mexican food.

That phone call itself was odd. The house phone rarely ever rang. When my mom picked up, her eyes darted immediately to me. For a second, I wondered if the cops had seen me drinking or smoking somewhere. That would've been just wonderful. But no, she'd merely said "it's for you," and handed me the phone. Then, with an inquisitive glance, Mom left the room.

The house phone didn't fit my palm quite right and the corners were odd. Much bulkier than any cell phone. Almost ancient. I held it to my ear and asked meekly, "Hello?"

"Hey there, kid. Sorry to call like this, but I never got your cell." Bruce's voice. I chuckled in relief and forgot to answer him. "You there?"

"Yeah, I am. What's up?"

"Dinner tonight, yeah? Just calling to see where at."

At that point, we smoothed out all the details. Time, place, what sort of food they served. Bruce, I knew, would pay for the meal, but I brought my wallet anyway. At least I would try to, and then eventually give in. Right before he hung up, I interrupted his goodbye.

"Wait, how'd you get this number?"

He laughed loudly, and I could tell he moved the phone away from his face. Once his heartiness died down, he said simply, "Phone book, kid. Heard of it?"

I ignored this slight. Thinking back on it as Bruce maneuvered his way out of the car, parked way too close to me, I couldn't help but crack a smile. He sidled awkwardly because the door couldn't open all the way without bumping into my passenger side. I waited for him. Once we'd merged next to my car, I gestured at the restaurant ahead of us.

He eyed it, stroking at his chin. I noticed that he'd shaved, at least partially. There were a few rough patches. In all honesty, his appearance didn't seem quite right. Rather than his typical homeless-man attire, he wore the tailored-jacket-over-t-shirt look, with slacks and deep brown shoes filling out his lower half. Bruce, to his credit, had clearly given his outfit some thought, even *tried*, you might say. But the haphazard shaving, almost paranoid eyes, and shaggy hairstyle all maintained that out-of-place, LA-old-man type.

"They've got a great twenty-dollar steak," I suggested as we approached the main doors. I stepped in front to hold it open for him, aware that my own clothing didn't match up to his. I donned an Arctic Monkeys shirt and jeans, although both were clean and void of wrinkles, so I guess I had tried in my own way.

After exchanging words and more than one ogle at Bruce, the hostess led us to a booth near the back of the restaurant. She bustled away, forgetting to take our drinks. Bruce simply slid into one side and chuckled good-naturedly. I moved into the other, set my phone on the seat beside me, and glanced up.

"Good people," he murmured, more to himself than me. He grabbed a menu and scanned it. "Good people here. That's what I like about it."

The restaurant had a slightly muted atmosphere as I glanced around. It was a spacious place, all the tables spread out and the lights dim. There were deer heads perched on the walls, as well as a few more exotic animals, like a bear and a fox. Whether or not they were real, I didn't care to wonder. Dust clung to the animals, to the decor in general. This was the kind of place you'd expect in Little Rush. The nicest dining we could conjure, but nothing amazing to Bruce, I felt confident.

In a minute, the blonde-haired girl returned, apologizing profusely for missing the drinks. She took Bruce's order for a beer and turned to me.

"Oh, Hudson! I didn't see it was you." Her mouth dropped open a fraction, looking back at Bruce, then to me. "Um... sorry, your... what to drink?"

"Dr. Pepper."

She scribbled it down and moved away, back toward the kitchen. As she went, fumes of baking bread and sizzling grills filled her place. I watched her go and noticed other patrons peeking in our direction from their own unfinished meals. Even though it was nearly eight o'clock on a weekday, the restaurant had a dozen or so seats occupied. It felt like each one had focused their conversation and eyes on us.

"You know her?" Bruce asked me absent-mindedly as he mulled over food options. I guess the extra attention didn't unnerve him like it did me.

I swiveled my head to face him again. "Yeah... graduated two years ago." I focused on my own menu, if only to avoid those beady eyes from every direction. "I actually didn't know she stuck around. Thought she... went to college."

"Oh, neat." He chuckled at something he read and then flipped the page, as if pouring over an amusing cartoon section. "These prices, I tell you. Wouldn't buy a hamburger in LA, I swear."

I found it hard to focus on my menu. My mind kept drifting away. Thinking about all the other patrons, with their gawking and whispers. About our waitress, that vaguely familiar face. I'd seen her roaming the hallways so many times, back when she was an intimidating senior. Back when she'd had dreams. And now... stuck here. Just like so many, she never got out of the cage we were born in.

"That girl..." Deep breath. Composing my thoughts. "That's kinda what I mean about this town." I lowered my voice and menu. I tried to catch Bruce's eye, but he focused only on potential meals, apparently. "Nobody gets out. Even if you plan to, you end up... end up working a job like this for years. You should see the older ones. Fifties, maybe. I bet they... bet they planned to go to college, too. They just settled for... this trash." I straightened up once I realized I'd been leaning over the table.

Bruce dropped his menu a fraction so I could see him peering over the top. The corners of his lips crinkled at some joke I couldn't spot. "My grandpa never got out, either. Died on that very couch I have."

"Oh..." I caught my breath, tapped my foot under the table. "I'm... sorry, I didn't mean—"

"You're right about one thing. People don't get out." He went back to searching for a suitable meal, lowering his eyes. "But maybe that's okay."

I considered this for a while, as the drinks arrived and she took our dinner orders. I stuttered over mine, lost in thought, and ordered the wrong side to go with my steak. It didn't really matter. Pretty much any combination here would make for a good meal.

Bruce watched me for a while. I felt him staring into my forehead as I scrolled on my phone. I didn't have anybody to text. Mason and Willow were probably fucking at his house now that they were alone. So instead, I explored Twitter and tried not to see myself in the reflection.

"I came here, you might say, to chase a ghost." Bruce planted an elbow on the table. I didn't raise my head. Chin against my chest, I waited for him to go on. "I'll tell you something, Hudson. This isn't my first time in Little Rush."

At this, I looked up. My expression must have shown confusion because he smiled, shrugged, and then nodded his head. I tried for some eloquent response but instead spat out a "Really?"

"One summer. Feels like forever ago." Bruce closed his eyes and rubbed them with two fingers. "I lived in that house with my grandpa. That was... the best summer of my life. Not long after, I started down this road... toward acting, toward Hollywood. Did you know he played guitar, my grandpa?" At this, a wistful expression touched his features, and Bruce ran a hand through his slicked-back hair. Individual strands flew out in wild directions. "Played it real good, I remember. Back then, I only ever wanted to be a musician. Hell, I wanna be now. But I can't play an instrument, never could. Can't sing, not a lick. I only ever wanted to be *that*, not an actor."

"But you're... good at acting," I offered. A dull kindness but no answers.

"I don't *create* anything," he went on. He pressed both palms against the table like any moment he would push through it, destroy the wood with just his hands. His muscles tensed. "I'm a fake. I just pretend to... to be more interesting people, and I hate it. Making music... goddamn it, Hudson, that's *real*. That's what I want." His arms relaxed, forearms dropping to his lap. As if a crushing blow struck his head, he folded. When he spoke again, it was with a weaker voice. "It's still sitting there, you know, in the corner of the bedroom. That guitar. The guitar I'll never... play."

It took me a minute to think of anything worth saying. I thought about changing the subject, but that might come off as rude. I figured the next best thing was to ask a question. "Do you... do you think you're similar to him? Your grandpa, I mean."

Bruce chuckled at this and picked at his silverware, not meeting my eyes. "If only you knew, kid." He let this phrase drift away, before raising his head and continuing. "I'll tell you one thing. I don't look like him one bit. I got a photograph back at the house. Maybe I'll... show you sometime." And this time he smiled wide, genuine.

Restaurants have a tendency to serve food right at the climax of conversation. This one proved no different. The meals arrived, aromas of warmth and cooked meat and seasoned potatoes. I could feel heat spreading from the dishes as she set them down. I thanked the waitress, now an older lady I didn't recognize. I wondered if they'd drawn straws to choose who would deliver food to the great Bruce Michaels, sitting in their very building. At any moment, I thought a photographer would crawl out onto the floor and snap a photo of Bruce with his heavy steak. Great for advertising.

For a few minutes, we cut into the meat as a silence fell like dense fog. I realized that my accidental side order resulted in Bruce and I sharing identical meals. Same sized steak, identical potato wedges and tiny bowl of chili. Only he drank a beer and I resigned myself to soda.

"Hudson, can you promise me one thing?"

I'd been slicing my steak and stopped at this question. While chewing a mouthful, I nodded and motioned for him to continue.

"Don't ever..." He dropped his fork. It clanged against the plate, and he scratched at his chin. A jerky movement that gave the impression of desperation, a constipated thought. He groaned, picked up the silverware again, but then set it down. "Don't ever believe that... you're meaningless." His hand, now hovering above the table, curled into a fist. "Nobody knows better than me how fragile life is, how easy it is to just... die one day. Be gone. And it's terrifying."

I smirked. "This isn't very comforting," I pointed out with a wave of my knife.

"I know, I know, just..." The emotion in his voice silenced any snide comments I'd been thinking. His expression had turned intense, and his throat constricted with every word, like he pushed each one out in a painful process. "Just don't forget that, to some people, you're important. And they're not... they're not somewhere out there. They're here." He stabbed the table with an extended finger and then settled back in his seat, bashful. "I'm sorry. That's just... something I wish my grandpa would've told me. Back then."

After this brutal honesty, the meal turned more lighthearted. Bruce told me a few stories about his time in Little Rush, talked about how things had changed. It was some of the same material that my father liked to parse through but spoken in a different way. Bruce even mentioned one of the closed-down factories, but rather than focus on the melancholy aspect, he explained how he and another boy would throw stones through the window. They used the factory as a place to impress girls, a solitary place to smoke, even an arena where they beat up one of the older kids. A nostalgic joy spread as he went on, and I couldn't help but feel it myself.

By the time we left dinner that night and said goodbye to the comfortable atmosphere, I had the visceral sensation that I'd never been happier. Bruce Michaels, the actor, an honest-to-god friend of mine. Living just down the road. We'd enjoyed a night of great conversation, of friendship, of maturity. I drove home, not worrying about my parents or even my frayed relations with Mason. Instead, I just savored my heart swelling. Felt it pumping harder against my chest cavity. And music soared in my head.

What kind of music would Bruce have made? I wondered. Such an introspective, curious guy. Just a guy with a guitar. An interesting old man. Even a good one, I might dare.

A small piece of me, somewhere inside, wondered if I put too much into this idea. That I had built my house on unreliable ground. It could split any moment and swallow me alive. But for the time being, such thoughts were buried under good food, intellectual conversation, and a future so much brighter than the past.

The moon hung in the sky, a full orb. I stared for just a moment, car keys in hand, my back to the still-warm engine. And appreciated that I was, for now, happy.

6
WILLOW

I curled my bare toes so tight that it hurt, feeling the carpet underneath and between them. My eyes were straight down, blank. I could barely hear the shower running just down the hall. It had been something like twenty minutes now. Longer than Mason ever took. Then again, nothing about this felt normal.

With a loose sweatshirt and running shorts that felt too tight now, I remained in that position for almost an hour once we'd finished. My arms crossed, head down. My skin felt gross, like a layer of sweat dried over everything, even though the room itself couldn't be warmer than 65 degrees. The curtains were drawn, the sky outside pitch black. I longed for any inch of sunlight to stream in, to touch my skin.

Every time, I thought about it, I squirmed uncomfortably, felt myself on the verge of tears. But I wouldn't cry, not here. I would just manage.

Goddamn it, Mason. I couldn't quite distinguish the feelings in my body, just like I couldn't exactly remember what'd happened. Alcohol does that, I guess. He'd been more drunk than me. Not that it was an excuse. Not for something like this.

The emotions coursing through me were some godawful mixture. Anger. I'd never been this angry at Mason. Also regret, even remorse. And just a general disgust. At myself, at him, at the two of us for letting this happen. But especially right now, especially the summer before our senior year.

God, those images in my mind. How would this change everything? What about senior prom? Even graduation itself? Not like this. Please, not like this. I didn't need this right now.

I didn't know anything for sure. It could all be an overreaction, I told myself. Just a scare. But something inside of me said otherwise. A sort of instinctual punch to the gut. A cringe. That's the right word for what I felt. An hour-long cringe.

Even after the stream of water died, Mason took his sweet time coming back to the room. Thirty minutes, at least. He smelled of shampoo and body wash. Wore new clothes, fresh ones, while I sat here in filth.

"Hey, sorry about that," he said, strolling into the room bare-chested, towel-drying his hair.

Sorry about what, I wanted to ask. The long shower or the fact that I could be fucking pregnant?

"It's fine." I stood from the bed, refusing to meet his eye. "Gonna shower."

He didn't respond. I didn't want him to. I trudged down the hallway, toward the bathroom. Never in my entire life had I felt so awful after sex. Not a single time. Not even the very first one, as awkward as it'd been. No, this sensation would never be topped. Could never, ever be beaten.

I hadn't even brought clothes to his house. I realized this with my hand on the bathroom doorknob. Even if I managed to scrub my body clean and rid myself of this bile, I would have to slip into the same underwear, the same shorts.

Nevertheless, I marched inside and locked the door behind me. The air still thick with steam and the odor of his body wash. I gagged for a moment and thought I would puke. I opened the toilet lid, just in case, and closed my eyes.

Images flooded me. Pregnant at family Thanksgiving and

Christmas. How would I explain this to my mom? To my brother?

Pregnant in a prom dress. Would I even be able to wear one?

Would I be still pregnant at graduation or a real mom by that point?

Oh, god.

Then I did puke, over and over again into the toilet. I thought, for a moment, how ironic. Would morning sickness be like this? Did that even really happen? I kept my eyes closed the whole time, not eager to see the disgusting pool just below me. On my knees, elbows on the seat, shaking my head back and forth.

Mason didn't have to deal with this. Maybe he didn't even know. Hadn't realized yet. The dumbass would be too hungover to talk in the morning. Too stubborn. He might not even remember.

A condom. That's all it would've taken. Just a condom. Just one of us remembering.

"Fuck!" I screamed as loud as I could. The word echoed back to me. I drowned it with more vomit. Induced by alcohol or panic, this went on for another few minutes. With each time, I grew more thankful that his parents weren't home and wouldn't be for a day or two. That I could shout to my heart's content, knowing nobody would hear me. Even for hours and hours on end.

Mason would hear me. And he would have no idea what to do, say, or think. I hoped it bothered him. I hope it fucking ate him alive.

Once I'd started the shower and felt it scorching my hand, I stood in front of the mirror, completely naked now. Eyeing myself, I noticed the hickeys just below my right cheekbone and gritted my teeth. My eyes dropped to my stomach. They stayed there for a moment.

I covered my mouth with both hands so that he wouldn't hear me crying. I didn't want to. I didn't want to start this. But I couldn't stop, and once the sobs had begun, they wouldn't ever end.

For an hour, I sat in Mason's shower and cried. The scalding hot water turned my shoulders and back bright red. My hair hung like a mop curtain around my crumbling frame. Mason didn't have to deal with this. No, he wouldn't ever understand. Not really.

It's impossible to explain why, in those moments, my thoughts turned where they did. Maybe it was the text from him, the brutal honesty. Or something about those words that I connected with. I'm not okay.

Hudson. If anybody would talk, or at least be honest with me, he would.

I didn't want to make the effort. I didn't want to start this. No, I just wanted the aching to be gone.

The shower beat down on my head, relentless. My body started shaking, and I threw up again. I watched as it swirled down the drain and imagined myself doing the same. Just... gone.

7
LITTLE RUSH
THE ROBBERS

Curtis shoved his notepad in the glovebox and slammed it shut, not terribly hard but enough to get Randy's attention. When the man turned with an expression that could start a fire, Curtis folded his arms and slouched deeper in the passenger's seat.

"How come I ain't get to drive? Always you!"

Randy rolled his eyes and turned away once more. He leaned forward until his chin almost touched the top of the steering wheel. Curtis observed for a moment, then groaned. Reluctantly, he focused his own attention on the house up the street.

They were parked on the side of a country road. A thick, expansive corn field lay to their right, and Curtis's door would've stuck on the stalks if he tried to open it. The front half of their car lined up with a curve in the road so that they could peer around the bend without the target noticing them. Randy had spent five minutes positioning the car, gritting his teeth the whole time. Methodical placing, even genius if you asked *him*.

"Think he's seen us yet?" Curtis asked, voice cracking.

Randy shook his head but didn't grant a verbal answer. He pointed at something straight ahead, near the house they were watching. Curtis leaned near him for a better view.

Bruce Michaels stood in the shade behind his house, facing the brick wall. He paced back and forth, from one corner to the other, occasionally touching his forehead.

Almost like them praying nuns, Curtis thought to himself with a chuckle.

Hunched at the shoulders, his hair wild and unruly, Bruce Michaels behaved like a man with an ungodly hangover. This explanation didn't fit, though, because he willingly stood outside where the heat and sunlight would worsen such a condition. Perhaps, then, he was merely a man who'd lost all control. His scampering eyes, darting from brick to grass to sky; his heaving chest. That analysis fit slightly better, in Curtis's opinion.

"So… which one'a us 'as to… to go in the back way?" Curtis asked, face oddly pale.

Randy raised an eyebrow. "Neither of us. That's June's job."

Curtis clicked his tongue and nodded. "Got'cha."

They observed for another minute. Bruce lashed out at the wall, swinging his foot like a furious pendulum. As soon as his shoe struck brick, he winced, hopping backward. Curtis and Randy shared a chuckle over this. For all his wealth and his undeniable fame, Bruce Michaels didn't *look* like a rich Hollywood actor. Nevertheless, the plan was the plan, and they had to execute it perfectly. These scouting trips — this being their second of three planned— would be vital to the outcome.

June had given them specific instructions on what to look for and jot down in their notebooks. Curtis' remained in the glovebox, rarely used. Randy scribbled on his from time to time. For the most part, their reports were delivered verbally and half-serious, often during a late-night baseball game. This irritated June to no end, but Curtis didn't see the issue. *They* weren't the brains of the operation. Although, to be honest, they weren't the brawn either.

"Oh, shit." Randy stretched, raising his hindquarters from

the seat an inch, and rummaged in his pocket. He furrowed his brow in concentration, finally extracting the buzzing cell. With a serious, shut-up glance at Curtis, he put the phone on speaker. "Hey there, June. About to call you."

Curtis sighed and went back to staring at the cornfield only a foot away. Leaning against the glass, he peered into the endless depths and dreamed of a day when he wouldn't have to live so close to corn. When he could have a real nice place, maybe even his own house. And he and Randy would stay near each other and have fancy dinners together from time to time. This pleased him, so he went on dreaming.

June snapped over the speaker, "How 'bout you get your ass back here. It's past time."

"We're just... getting real good stuff here. Didn't wanna leave." Randy bit his lip, and Curtis felt the same anxiety as she received their lie.

"Whatever." She sighed, exasperated. Sounded on edge, in his opinion. "Just hurry up. We need to discuss a day. Few weeks from now."

"Few weeks!" Randy exclaimed.

At this, Curtis gaped, his jaw hanging open. Almost comical if not for the gravity of what she'd said.

"Yeah. I'm gonna move it up to three from now. I'm tired of sitting around. We gotta act sooner." June cleared her throat, maybe to mask some anxiety of her own. "Point is, we need'a get going. Just hurry back."

"You got it."

Randy moved to hang up the call, but before he could, Curtis yelled out, "This guy's a real whack-o, June! You sure he's got money?"

Randy shot fire at Curtis as they waited for June's response.

"He does," she promised.

"Just looks unstable, you know? Even dangerous."

June paused for a moment. Static filled the line. Then she asked, "Randy, is this true?"

Randy gulped and took the chance to hit Curtis hard on the shoulder. The bigger man squealed and pressed himself as far away as possible from the assailant.

"Yeah, he's not looking right," Randy answered. He mumbled, "Probably could kill this fucking—"

"Doesn't matter," June interrupted him. "Doesn't matter. He can have guns for all I care. Won't matter to me."

Curtis raised an eyebrow. The almost-insult had flown over his head.

Randy stared at the phone before sputtering, "What?"

"What, you think we're going in unarmed?" June laughed, a ruthless sound. "I'm not afraid to spill some Hollywood blood. Maybe see if it sparkles, huh?"

Again, that joyless sound. It turned their blood cold.

8
HUDSON

Everything moved so quickly over the next few days, I couldn't process what happened with my parents. My father moved back into the house as if he'd just been away to see family. After only two nights away, he returned home, a duffle bag slung over his shoulder and sheepish grin on his face. I just happened to be in the kitchen when he arrived. Dad opened the door and poked his head inside, looking around.

Our eyes met. He grunted in surprise and asked, "Your mom... here?"

I shook my head and leant against the counter. The microwave next to me counted down, that faint whirring sound from the motor filling our empty spaces. "You staying at the Coopers' again?"

Dad shook his head and opened his mouth, but it snapped shut just as fast. "I'll explain later. Gotta... talk with your mom."

For another moment, he stood halfway inside, watching me. I didn't feel much like talking. There was no room for it. I only felt bitterness, a general disliking. While he watched me, I tried to remain as expressionless as possible. I didn't want him to know how I truly felt. That I couldn't stand him at the moment. If he *did* deserve to know, he would come and ask, talk man-to-man. This, I knew, would never happen.

"I'll just call her." He sort of nodded and then backed outside again.

The microwave beeped and I took out my popcorn. From the kitchen window, eating my dinner, I observed him. He paced for a minute, phone to his ear, before jumping into his truck and speeding away. Leaving me alone once again. I wanted to know where he'd gone but didn't care to ask.

Over the next few days, my parents behaved like nothing had changed. Around me, they were their old, happy, carefree selves. Dad, stressing over payments for the farm and new chickens, rarely spoke to me. Not that Mom did either. But she had an air about her, a certain peppiness, that showed just how glad she felt about his return. They clearly held their own catalog of conversations, ones I wasn't privy to. Whatever they discussed over those few days, it did the trick. Things returned to a sort of normal, whatever that meant.

While my parents' relationship blossomed anew, I felt more and more alone. Their reunion didn't affect how I felt, but I also couldn't ignore the coincidence. Each time they glanced at each other from across the living room or I caught my mom snuggling into his chest on the couch, I saw myself more estranged. On an island, perhaps, that had broken off from the mainland. Now, the ocean between grew with each day.

Mason and Willow hadn't spoken to me since that morning when I visited the cabin. I'd texted him, once I had plans with Bruce for dinner. Besides that response — *Sucks you can't make it, man. Next time!* — no word from those two reached me. Not even a call, a text, a tag on an Instagram post.

Well, that wasn't entirely true.

One particularly miserable night, when my parents were gone on a "date," I'd finished off the bottle of vodka in my underwear drawer. There had been just enough to get me drunk. With Netflix droning in the background of my life, I got a wave of inspiration.

The weather outside, being a typically perfect July night, lent itself to my plans. I slid the bedroom window open, as much as possible, and then flicked off my room light. Unsteadily and over the course of a minute, I climbed onto my windowsill and sat there. Feet dangling over a two-story drop, leaning out so I could feel the breeze on my head. I'd chugged the rest of the bottle right there. Without thinking, I chucked it as far as I could. The empty plastic container, snatched by the wind, carried to the corner of the house. It dropped in a bush. I told myself I'd fetch it later.

Just as I thought, *I need to text Mason and get alcohol from his plug,* my phone chirped. I'd forgotten all about it, laying beside me in darkness, until the screen lit up and blinded me.

I expected a text from Mason. It would've been another weird coincidence in this weird week. Instead, the message came from Willow.

Willow: hey, i don't really know why i'm texting you. i was just... i've been worried about you, since your message on Tuesday. if you ever need to talk, Hudson, i'm here for you. just want you to know that.

I read the message twice more, the words slightly fuzzy in my drunken stupor. The phone light, even at its lowest level, hurt my brain. Without thought, I stored the phone away for a different time.

Willow texted me twice more that week, each on different days. On the third occurrence, I finally messaged her back and said I didn't feel like talking, that it had just been an awful night. I would be okay, I promised, and thanked her for being "a really good friend," bullshit to make her feel better. I certainly didn't tell her that I thought about killing myself once or twice a week. I didn't mention that the night of my text, I'd honest-to-god gotten in my truck and intended to never return.

This type of honesty... people just couldn't handle it.

I often considered a visit to Bruce's house. He would have advice about this whole situation, for sure. Especially the part with Mason. Bruce definitely had wild, douchey, unreliable friends in the past. Ones even worse than mine, probably a lot of them.

The parts of Mason that irked me had grown more intense that summer. For whatever reason, I started to hate the way he talked to and about Willow. I'd never known somebody so eager to bring up his sexual prowess. And in the most gag-worthy of ways. The Mason I'd known all through high school had been a bit cocky, sure, but more on my level. He thought the same things, asked the same questions. Like our late-night, philosophical conversations in the bed of my truck, surrounded by beer bottles. Those days were long gone and so was that version of my best friend.

Apparently, he'd decided that senior year Mason would be wildly different. Would really lean into the douche stereotype he'd resisted for years, despite his genetically good looks and toned body. This new version stood up to and became the bully. Mistreated his girlfriend, ignored his best friend. No, not ignored. He just didn't *care*. He'd become entirely self-centered. That really bothered me. I figured that also caused the tension between him and Willow. Just a self-centered piece of shit.

People who only think about themselves are the worst. I hated the lot of them. And *I'd* never get like that. My vocabulary extended beyond "I" and what "they" could do for the all-powerful "me."

Bruce would've known what to do, what to say to Mason. At least Bruce still talked to me. He even called me once on my cell, now that we'd exchanged numbers. We talked for about half an hour, and I hadn't thought to bring up these issues plaguing me. I wanted to tell Bruce how right he'd been about me. "Don't ever feel like you're meaningless," he'd told me at that dinner. Suspiciously poignant. Almost like a mind reader. If only he knew how much I needed him to stick around.

Dad asked me toward the end of that week if Mason wanted to come over on Saturday and bale hay. He'd been planning to run through two of the fields —the ones we typically baled in squares— and needed my help. We also could use a second "strong, young man," he suggested. I begrudgingly texted Mason, praying he'd decline. I mean, I'd asked earlier that week if we could hangout and he'd refused that invitation. Why accept this one?

Naturally, he said he would be there by eight. So, I waited all of Saturday for him to show up. The narcissist I couldn't get ahold of but couldn't completely avoid.

o o o

The process of baling doesn't lend itself to small talk. My father would drive the tractor in strips through the field, over the hay that he'd cut down earlier. Strewn all around, as if some giant had taken a sickle and knifed through fifty-foot-tall grass. I suppose that analogy wasn't far off from the truth.

Attached to the back of the tractor was the actual machine, a short, stumpy little devil that ate up the loose hay. Through some complex, incredible process, the noisy, sputtering beast would release a rectangular bale of hay. Tight and compressed, the twine would cut into your hands as you lifted the bale off and threw it behind you. A wagon, the kind I would take haunted hay rides on as a kid, waited for every block we threw at it. It was my job to stand, precariously balanced, at the back of the baler and chuck these heavy objects behind me.

Doing all this for no money, no benefit at all. Not super fun.

At this stage, Mason would prove helpful. With him standing on the wagon and stacking the bales as I tossed them, we could torch through the fields at a much quicker rate. We might get one field every ninety minutes with his aid. Without having to organize the bales alone, the whole process felt a lot more relaxed.

On the night in question, Mason and I hardly spoke to each other. We shared a few moments of laughter, such as when one bale toppled off the wagon and we had to shout incredibly loud at my father to stop. The combined noise of the tractor's engine and the baling machinery made this difficult.

For stretches of five to ten minutes, we worked like dogs. With stinging lungs and trying to ignore the biting cuts on my palm, I sent the bales toward Mason as quickly as possible. By the time I took a breath, another one appeared. After about three-fourths of the field had been scraped clean, the wagon could hold no more. Dad ushered us off and drove away to retrieve a second wagon. He had three of them, identical in every way, because we never had time to move the bales inside the barn. Instead, they would loiter on the wagons for two or three days before we worked up the nerve to go at it again. Moving bales off the wagons and into the barn was a much simpler process but no less time-consuming.

"I'll never understand how it does that," Mason commented as we slouched against the exterior side wall of my house. My father had driven off a moment earlier to fetch the second wagon and now disappeared from view. "The baler," he explained.

"It's pretty cool," I said. "Cool," a calloused and nonchalant description, was our way of avoiding genuine feelings.

"My hands hurt so goddamn bad." He chuckled and then rubbed a finger along his palm, wincing at the touch. "I always forget how much it sucks until we do this."

"I can't believe this is the first time and it's already July." I didn't look at him, but knew he agreed. "Usually we've baled three times by now."

"How'd he do it without us?"

I shrugged. "Hired some local guys. Amish, probably."

"You should tell him to do that more often." Mason glanced at me from the corner of his eye. He took a deep breath. I thought, for a moment, an apology was coming. At least an explanation for his behavior in past weeks. Instead, I noticed something over his shoulder and gasped.

I ran past him and rummaged in the bushes. He called out, but I didn't pay attention. After some riffling, I extracted the empty vodka bottle from earlier that week.

"Thank god he didn't see this," I said. We shared hearty laughter over that for a minute.

Until my father returned and beckoned us to hop on the wagon, I stared across the fields, acknowledging the difference from just an hour ago. Without grass, either tall and waving or dead and layered, these stretches of land were bald. Horrifically so. Like in the dead of winter, they were an ugly scar on the land. A reminder, I suppose, that while everything out here would die one day, some did seasonally.

It only took us a quarter-hour to complete the first field. Once Dad had passed through it for the final time, he drove toward the house and the barns. The wagon was barely full, so I didn't understand until he parked the train of equipment next to the house and hopped off the tractor.

"Break time," he called out, gesturing for us to follow him.

Five minutes later, Mason and I reclined against the hood of my truck, water bottle in one hand and Payday in the other. My father's silhouette moved around the kitchen for a minute and then into the depths of the building. Mason shot me an inquisitive look but didn't ask anything. I expected that he'd gone in to see my mom. Ever since his humble and unexciting return from exile, he liked to take breaks such as this and have a quick word with her. Some kind of assurance that he hadn't run off, I guess. On days when he worked at the power plant, he would call once or twice, and they'd chat for about ten minutes. My mother always conversed in a hushed tone and occasional giggles, like some kind of virgin school girl.

The sky had morphed from its cloudless, blue expanse of earlier to a deep purple. In the far distance, where the sun had disappeared an hour ago, the horizon still glowed with an eerie, red distinction. For the rest of the heavens, they were like a misty, purple marble, and we were trapped inside. I guess in some ways, everything is a cage.

That scent of hay would stick in my nostrils for hours afterward. Even when I first woke that next morning, it would cling to my mind. Putrid and earthy, I'd always compared the smell of bundled hay to rotting vegetables. A barn full of that stuff could knock someone down flat, which was part of the reason we procrastinated from storing the bundles in their proper place.

For the time being, though, I drank in the fresh air, back against my reliable truck, and tried to make out constellations in the stars. Little specks of light peeking through our purple marble. I never could find any pattern. They were like the work of a haphazard artist, one who throws their paint against a background and hopes for the best. If you got lucky and watched a long time, some star would eventually fall in fantastic colors, ending its descent in the middle of nowhere. At this thought, I couldn't help but smirk. Bruce Michaels, it could be said in the most cliche of phrases, had been a shooting star. And this, Little Rush, his obscure landing spot.

"You been doing alright, man?"

I turned to look at Mason, whose question had come from nowhere.

"Yeah, why?"

He shrugged. I wondered if Willow told him about the texts.

I hoped not. If there was one person I didn't want to know about my inner turmoil, it was Mason.

"We should hang out sometime," I ventured, watching for his reaction.

Mason picked at something on his palm and nodded vaguely.

"Maybe a party or something?"

"Nah." His response, so quick and acute, caught me off guard.

I twisted my torso to either side, trying to crack my back. In reality, I just wanted to get a better look at his face. Standing in the shadows of my home, it was impossible to make out any emotion. His eyes were as barren as the fields stretching around us.

"It was pretty fun, honestly." I said this unsure whether or not it was a lie. Perhaps the party itself hadn't been fun. Maybe it even started this downward spiral for our friendship. But the closeness to Mason, the proximity to humans... that had been nice.

"I don't think I'll host another," he said. Though the sentence started in ambiguity, his tone served as the seal on a decree. No more parties, indeed. That was that.

"That's a shame..." A moment slipped by. "Everything alright?"

"Just leave it alone, okay?" He let out an aggressive, pent-up huff of air and then moved away from the truck. "Y'know, it's late. I think... I'll just head home." Without even turning to look at me, he raised a hand in the air and started toward his convertible. "Got shit to do," he murmured, barely audible.

"What the hell, dude?" Taking a few steps after him, I moved in front of his convertible. Even as he opened the driver's door, I rested my hands on the front. Our eyes met and I saw, now free from the shadows, that his were narrowed, nostrils flaming.

"Move, Hudson."

"No." I crossed my arms and hoped that my father wouldn't come out at that second. I didn't want any interruption. I wanted this and wanted it now. "What's up with you lately? You've been a real piece of shit ever since that party, and now you're just ditching? I just want... answers."

Mason worked his way into the driver's seat and started the car. Now staring through the windshield, he raised a hand and flipped me off before slamming the door shut.

"You're so *fucking* dumb," I yelled at him, hoping it wouldn't carry inside the house. I punched the hood of his car as hard as possible. Instant pain shot through the cuts on my palm and up my forearm. But I didn't flinch, didn't even grit my teeth at the sensation. I just let it pass through me like fire whiskey. "Get out of the car and talk!"

Mason revved the engine, as if to threaten me. Still, I held my position and refused to shift.

He rolled down the window and stuck his head out just enough to yell, "Fuck you, Hudson. Get outta the way."

I punched his hood once again, the contact hard enough that I expected it would leave a dent. My hand burned pretty good after that. Clenching both fists, I drilled him with an expression that could've killed small animals. "You motherfucking —!"

I jumped out of the way just in time, my words cut off. Mason sped past me, throwing up gravel behind the car. I stood in the darkness, shoulders heaving, and watched him speed away. The red taillights shrinking to little pinpricks before they were gone entirely. His car swerved onto the country road, and his engine sounded like a lion as he raced away.

With my rough and blistered hands, I grabbed at my face and focused on not crying in the middle of the driveway. My father would exit the house soon, and I'd have to make up an excuse for why Mason left. Then the work would commence.

Would go on until nearly midnight.

Those taillights were burned into my mind. Every time I closed my eyes, I could see them. And his words, his voice, tearing into me.

Mason. What a...

There are no words for when your closest friend has become somebody else. Just a numb feeling, an empty crevice that fills with boiling hatred, stomach-churning rage. But for the time being, a nothingness that threatened to make me puke.

9
LITTLE RUSH
THE JOURNALIST

Gina hunched in her chair, fingers paused on the keyboard. She strained, trying to crack her neck, and ended up gazing out the window to her left. Outside, the downtown streets were wrapped in a late-night fog. Or perhaps early morning. A slight rain fell, almost like a mist from the sky, and mingled with the fog across Little Rush. She'd grown used to this aspect of the city. Nearly every morning, the streets would fill with a cool, soothing cloud. Something about the river, she assumed. She'd had her share of fog in California, just nothing this... cold.

Her face cracked in a smile, thin and wistful. Gina sighed, leaned back from the computer. She closed her eyes and tried to imagine that day, when she would leave Little Rush. Would they know her name by that point, as well as they did Bruce's? The story in her back pocket... it would explode onto the national scene in just a few days. Carry her to new heights.

The email she'd just sent held the final version of her article. A lengthy, five thousand word answer to that question she'd initially started with. The question, scrawled on a post-it note, stuck to the back of her laptop this very second. In her scribbled writing, it asked, "What exactly happened, and what does he remember?"

That question had been the basis for her investigation, research, every interview with applicable people. Madeline had been shy about the process. Even after the initial accusation, about Bruce Michaels, the girl rarely opened up. Gina herself had to coax more information about the story after Madeline began. The place, the time, the context. Gina had written down everything, sifted through it, and then got to work.

Such a remarkable, heart wrenching article to write, and yet it had led her to Little Rush. This quaint, amusing town. Her home for the last two months and for another week at least. But then everything would be over. All her efforts published. The truth revealed. And her status... elevated.

In a day or two, she'd receive an electronic copy of the piece before it hit the presses. Gina stood from her computer and stretched like a cat. In the meantime, she would sleep. The world, soon enough, would understand what she'd uncovered. All the secrets of Bruce Michaels. Wildly popular actor and generally good guy. Not a bad bone in his body, they said.

Gina chuckled and glanced in the direction of her computer once more. Eager for that email. The finished copy of her article.

Like an atomic bomb, she thought to herself, staring out the window once again. Deep, calming breaths. *And I get to watch it fall.*

For the time being, everybody would sleep, unaware, absent-minded. The threat of truth perched above their heads. Ready to kill.

Poor Madeline, she thought, closing the laptop and leaving her in total darkness.

Guilt gnawed at her sometimes, but she'd learned to block it out. This was all for the good of the masses. Her audience. Madeline was just one young woman with a troubled history and a dark future. Especially after this article. Especially when her name got out.

These things have to happen. Gina readied herself for bed and tried not to think about the ripples. Focused on the stone as it dropped into the lake. *It's all worth it.*

10
JED

I noticed him first, sitting alone on one of the benches that lined the downtown sidewalk, staring out at the river. His eyes were glazed over, hands folded in his lap. The man's frame, once buff and proud, slouched in the seat. His arms were wrinkled, almost sickly, and his skin even paler than my own.

Approaching him by myself, I couldn't help but notice the groups of people walking by. Some of them glanced at him, but not all. I got the impression that everyone had seen him in person once or twice before, so the shock didn't register now. He was, more or less, just an old man inhabiting a bench by the river. And there were plenty of those kind around.

For myself, though, seeing Bruce Michaels in the flesh did a number on my breathing. I had to stop and compose myself.

What an absurd setting. This little river, our local gem, like a masterpiece of art that's been forgotten in the garage. We'd all grown so accustomed to it. The picturesque curves and the postcard-worthy bridge. Even on today, when the sky threatened storms and you couldn't see any blue past those angry clouds, it held a charm that I often forgot to appreciate.

This man, from the bright lights and noisy streets of LA, appreciated Little Rush. Its natural beauty, its intrinsic peacefulness. Maybe I had something to learn from him. Maybe we all did.

"Mr. Michaels?" I approached him and extended a hand.

His chin rose ever so slowly, scrutinizing my appearance. I'd worn one of my nicer, summer suits. It might look out of place down here by the river, but I suppose this qualified as a business meeting. Bruce Michaels, himself, had dressed in shoddy jeans and a wrinkled button-up, which only made me regret the suit more.

"Cooper," he said, voice like gravel. Then a chuckle. It sounded like the noise got caught halfway up his throat. "Call me Bruce."

"In that case, call me Jed," I assured him. Without dancing around the subject, I gestured at the sidewalk and asked, "A meeting, then?"

Bruce staggered to his feet, leaning heavily on the sides of the bench. A group of boys ran by, half of them shirtless and sweat-soaked. The local cross country team, most likely. Once they'd passed, I started down the sidewalk at an agonizing, methodical pace. Bruce kept step with me fine, but on the off chance he had knee problems or something, I didn't want to push too hard.

"That bridge up there." He pointed ahead of us where it crossed over the Ohio and touched down on the Kentucky side. His eyes were on fire as he stared, transfixed by the appearance. Surely, he'd seen loads of bridges in California, even the Golden Gate probably. "Can we cross it?"

"Technically, yes, but with this weather" —I jerked a thumb at the sky— "perhaps it's not the best idea."

He grunted and we went on, following the river's path. I brought up an advertisement campaign once or twice, but Bruce seemed reluctant to dive in right away. He wanted to tease out this conversation, really press my patience. Maybe on purpose, or maybe he just felt sociable. People like him, their productive days running out, always talked more. At least it seemed so to me.

As we passed couples and families and lonely walkers, a barge emerged from under the bridge. When the conversation lulled, our eyes were drawn to the massive, low ship as it glided. It moved, from our perspective, just barely faster than we walked. Bruce pointed this out to me and looked on with wonder at the wide boat, indiscernible black mounds carried on its five linked ships. Almost certainly coal. We only ever saw that and metal scraps on the barges nowadays.

"You all make good money off the river?" Bruce asked me at one point. We were a few blocks away from the public swimming pool, where I suggested we should turn left and head up to Main Street. For the meantime, I would indulge his river questions. Everybody had them, all the new people.

"Not really," I said. "Not for decades. Helps for advertising, a bit of tourism. Mostly it's just... there."

"Always loved rivers," Bruce said, taking a deep sigh and rubbing the back of his neck. We maneuvered our way past a small family with a stroller that had stopped for the moment. Then he elaborated. "Always coming and going... the endless flow of water... It's perfect, if you think about it."

"Sure is." I agreed without really thinking, moved my feet without walking. My mind had drifted elsewhere. Back to Mason. I wanted to buy him something from a shop on Main Street but didn't know what exactly or how to play this off to Bruce. If I could appear vulnerable but strong, it might actually help my chances of landing an ad deal with the guy.

"These kids, they just don't get it, Jed." Hearing him use my name sent a jolt down my spine, but I managed to hide it. Bruce scoffed at a couple who shuffled by us, holding hands and locked in conversation. He seemed to take this as a sign to continue. "Just... just lookin' at their phones and stuff. But there's nothing on there —nothing!—like this goddamn river."

"You're right." I thought of a way to interject here and went for it. "I got a son of my own. Teenager."

"Oh, yeah?" Bruce raised his eyebrows. "Tough age for boys. Both raising 'em and being one."

I nodded my head and gestured up the road at one of the empty factory buildings. "Me and my friends at that age, we were running around those empty places and throwing rocks and getting into all sorts of stuff. You know?" I stopped for a moment and pointed across the road at the sidewalk perpendicular to our own. "That'll take us up to Main."

We crossed, a slow but determined pace. There were no crosswalks or stop lights down here. Not enough traffic to warrant them, but just enough to make you nervous. Once on the other side, I stared at the incline. These streets ran to Main, all slanted at probably a thirty degree angle with some bend. It made them a real pain to lumber up. By the time we reached the top, I'd be struggling for air.

"I know what you mean," Bruce assured me. "It's not the same now. Real shame."

On that journey uphill, I tried to bring up an ad campaign once more. This time, my own out-of-breath and raspy voice did me in. Bruce smirked as I faltered. He didn't comment when we crossed the nicest street in town, the one just up from the river where the wealthiest downtowners lived. Nor did he mention the next one, with shabby apartments and foreclosed houses. No, Bruce simply drank in the sights of Little Rush. His eyes wandered with the same attitude he surveyed me. Thoughtful, silent, contemplative.

"Looks the same as back then," he mumbled when we emerged onto Main Street. He peered around, shading his eyes from the sun, and a twitch in his lip hinted at some unseen emotion. "That theater, there. Just the same."

"You've been here before?"

He shook his head. "Nah. Seen pictures."

I accepted this and led the way down Main Street. We chatted for a while about the different buildings. I told a few stories I knew, like about Allen and his burgers, or the coffee shop not far down. Whenever we passed one of my own properties, I curled up into myself, reluctant for any sort of self-promo. Things were different with this man than others. I didn't care if townies judged me. That's what they were here for. But a new person, one from LA... his opinion mattered to me, and not just because of the name and dollar signs attached.

"I'm thinking dinner at Allen's," I suggested after we explored the area for twenty minutes, "and then maybe we can get to talking about this advertisement?"

"Sounds fine." I knew this was for the first part of my question, not the latter.

We passed by a storefront, one that sold antiques and baseball cards mostly, along with a slew of pawn-shop objects. I stepped toward this building and said that I wanted to pop in for just a second to pick something up.

"Just a minute," I explained, opening the door to enter

I emerged minutes later to find him leaning against a light pole, brows furrowed. He wore a thin smile and crossed his arms when I appeared.

"What'd you get?"

I held up a pocket knife and then stored it away. "Just this." Without another word, I started to stroll away from the building and down the sidewalk, passing through a small crowd that had gathered.

"For your kid, right?"

I turned back to face him and stopped moving. Bruce watched me with a sad, compassionate smile that felt entirely out of place. We stood like that for a moment, sizing each other up, but not for a fight. Just to see who cracked first.

"I'm not…" My voice trailed off and with it any resistance.

Bruce nodded to himself. "Kid's gonna get in trouble with something like that." Then he motioned to the restaurant across the street. "Let's head over. Getting hungry."

I shuffled along beside him after that, head bent. We reached the crosswalk and waited for just a moment before heading across.

"I might be too harsh on 'em," he admitted, clasping me on the shoulder with a firm but gentle grip. "Can I tell you just one thing? I had somebody once, a parent of sorts. That kid don't want stuff, Jed. Just wants you."

Those words rang in my head for the rest of the evening. All through dinner, a general blur, they were torturing me. Advice that called me out, cut me from the inside. Yet I knew it was the truth. For the next hour, I tried not to meet anyone's eye.

Bruce spent most of the meal chatting with other patrons of Allen's Burgers, swapping stories and occasionally name-dropping a celebrity that set the crowd on fire. I'd never seen a man so charismatic, so aware of his charm. It unnerved me a bit, to be honest. If he could put on a show this mesmerizing over dinner, what could he do to a person over weeks, months? Maybe even to a whole city.

When I drove away from downtown not long after, Bruce stayed behind in the restaurant. He assured me on the way out that I would get my advertisement deal, sooner rather than later. But for the time being, he just "wanted to enjoy life here," he said. This perfect equilibrium he'd found. Something about him felt off when he said this, like it was neither a complete truth nor a total lie. Either way, he stuck around while I returned home.

One thought played in my mind like a broken record. The entire way home… *Just wants you.*

o o o

Those steps were some of the most difficult, most awkward I'd ever taken. The carpet underneath my bare feet, hugging myself with both arms. I approached the bedroom door foot by foot and longed to turn back with each step. Wanted to hurry away and join Lucy in our bed, the warm comfort of her body and familiar pillows.

Nothing about this felt familiar. I'd not done anything like this in a long, long time.

I stood facing that plain, white door for probably a full minute. One hand on the smooth hallway wall, the other scratching at my chin absentmindedly. From inside the room, I could hear noises. It sounded like quiet, desperate crying. I shivered at the thought.

Then I raised my hand to the wood surface and knocked twice.

"Yeah?" Mason called out. It sounded like he'd been crying, for sure.

"Can I come in, just a second?"

Mason cleared his throat and I heard him moving around. Then, "Yeah."

I twisted the doorknob and opened the door just enough so I could step inside. Mason sat criss-cross on his bed, back against the wall, staring at his toes. Across the room, his computer hummed, but the screen was dark. A lamp on the desk, next to the monitor, emitted the room's only light. Rather than snooping around, I stood straight and took a step near the bed.

"I... got you something."

I dug into my jeans for a second, noticed his quizzical expression. Then I extracted the pocketknife and held it up.

"Here... here ya go." I tossed it onto the bed, near his leg.

He picked it up and turned it over. Our eyes met, and I knew he wanted to ask, "why?" but held back. I appreciated that. Because I didn't really know the answer.

We stood that way for another few seconds. Mason touching the pocketknife, inspecting it, but I could tell he was waiting for me to either continue or leave.

"Talked to Bruce Michaels today," I told him, hoping this would elicit some kind of reaction. I added, "Might be coming over for dinner sometime. We'll see."

Mason nodded, still rigid like a board.

"Anyways, well... goodnight, man." I started to back away, out of the room. Felt the moment slipping from my fingertips. I'd let it fall away so many times before. I gripped the doorknob so tight that my knuckles were turning pale. Just in time, I choked out, "Love you."

He didn't respond. Just stared at me in disbelief. I finally understood the expression he wore and had since I stepped inside. One of sadness and fear. Anxiety, even. But when I spoke those words, the tiniest flicker of a smile passed over him.

I would've liked for him to call after me, "I love you, too." But this, of course, didn't happen.

Instead, we took our own paths for that night. But at least I knew that somewhere down the line, maybe we would cross again. For now, that would be enough.

11
WILLOW

Each summer in Little Rush and the counties around us, the last stages of summer break were marked by an extravagant, delicious, greasy festival. The entire plot of land couldn't be more than a few acres. That didn't stop the spectacle. Anywhere you turned, there were pop-up arcade games, food stands that came from nowhere and were gone in a day, not to mention the permanent structures of the 4-H ground itself. The animal smells mixed with scents of cinnamon donuts and caramel apples. Everything and everybody fried. A delicate balance of odors and noises and emotions. The reckless abandon it took to ride one of the shaky, spinning amusement park rides.

The county fair. An elaborate, beautiful, unique aspect of rural Indiana life.

For kids my age, the county fair was often a lot more. Our first date, our first kiss, holding hands at the Ferris wheel's peak. Throbbing headaches when we stepped off the worst rides, only to get back on soon after. The ever-present rumor of "oh, somebody lost a leg on this ride over in Ohio," but everybody rode it all the same. If we didn't, we risked standing alone in the middle of a sweaty and sun-burnt crowd, watching friends soar overhead.

Mason parked the car in an allotted spot, at least a football field away from the nearest ride. The cars in front of us were an endless sea, broken only by a few feet. They were all sorted into rows, spread across a grass field. As Mason shut off the engine and climbed out, I couldn't help but think if it rained hard enough, we'd all be stuck in this mud trap.

After a walk across that makeshift parking lot, we snuck between two of the rides and emerged on a dirt stretch. The fairground was organized, roughly, into two long streets. These were more dirt than grass, densely packed with crowds and food vendors. This first stretch had fair rides on one side and carnival games on the other. Mason and I exchanged a look and a grin. This might be our last time here, and I wanted it to be perfect.

"How many you wanna ride?" he asked me, weaving through the crowd. He reached back and held my hand as I followed. "If we're doing a lot, we should just get those wrist things."

"Bracelets?" I offered. "Yeah, that's fine."

"I'll pay," he said, more a declaration than a question.

They weren't cheap, by any means. Especially not when dinner would cost an extra fifteen. Altogether, we usually spent thirty bucks each. Now that we were older and our parents didn't drop us off, they'd also stopped lending us cash.

Someone bumped against me, and I groaned. Mason looked back, eyebrow raised, and then faced forward again when I didn't comment. I'd been more sensitive to contact recently. The explanation was pretty simple, but I hated thinking about it. The fact that I couldn't tell anybody only made me feel worse.

I'd waited five days after it happened to take the test. Buying the pregnancy test went easy enough, though the cashier gave me a weird look when I did so. I hate old men. Once I had it, I couldn't bring myself to actually *use* it. A few days before my period was due, I finally came around and the answer... didn't thrill me.

Even though I hadn't yet missed a period, even though I felt no different physically, even though my only catalyst for *taking* the test was that Mason hadn't used a condom... the damn thing had confirmed it. I was pregnant. I didn't know a hundred percent, of course, and I wouldn't for a week or two. Even then, I'd heard stories of false positives or close calls. Maybe I wouldn't truly believe it for a while. But at the same time, I had no doubt. I'd convinced myself, already, that a baby lived inside of me. Our baby.

And I still hadn't told him.

"Two bracelets," Mason said, raising his voice over the throng of people.

In the tiny, sweltering booth, an overweight man rummaged through a drawer and then snatched Mason's credit card. In a minute, he returned the card, two bracelets with it. "Put 'em on 'r left wrist," he barked at us before shooing us away for the next customer.

With our left wrists adorned in cheap-but-stubborn Tyvek material, we moved away from the booth and faced the expanse of redneck consumerism spread before us.

After a brief discussion, we settled on the most vomit-inducing ride to start us off. The one where I'd stand up, strapped to a wall, inside of a circular shape. Then the object spins around like crazy and forms a sort of anti-gravity chamber. Mason always loved it, and I managed, so that's where we stood in line.

I knew that the rides were safe, since I was only two weeks pregnant. But I couldn't help thinking about it. In just a matter of months, I couldn't do this anymore. My body would be wildly different. And I really didn't wanna think about that just now.

The sun beat down, relentless, and I found myself praying for the next few hours to go by quickly. Once that torturous globe descended, the fairground would light up with all sorts of beautiful colors. The last few hours, the fair in pure darkness, formed the best memories of my childhood. The rides all whirring late into the night, only the teenage crowd left. I wanted to experience that one final time. Before college and life and the lifelong chase began.

"Look at this," Mason spoke up, digging in the side pouch of his cargo shorts. He pulled out a sleek pocket knife a moment later and flipped open the blade. "Dad got me it."

"That's nice of him." I leaned against the rail which boxed us into line. There were at least two more ride cycles ahead of us.

"He's an idiot." Mason shrugged and pocketed the tool. "Thinks he can just... buy me over, you know?" He scoffed and his face morphed into a cocky smirk. "Like with my mom. They're all good now. He just... just bought her some shit, I bet."

I frowned but didn't speak up. Mason's relationship with his dad had always bugged me. According to Mason, Jedidiah was "never really there for me" and "spent all his time working." He definitely held some sort of grudge, and his mom giving in had annoyed him beyond belief. But at the same time, shouldn't he celebrate his parents working out their issues? Did he *want* to experience divorced parents? No, he didn't. He just didn't know any better.

"Nice knife, though," he murmured, feeling the spot in his pocket where it'd slipped to.

I couldn't help but grin, turning away to mask it.

The next hour passed in a literal daze. By the time we passed through five of the rides, doing them each multiple times, I could barely walk straight. I threw an arm around Mason's shoulders, like two weary soldiers returning from the war, and suggested we go eat. It was a short walk from this dirt stretch to the other one, where real food awaited, along with free water stations and always some kind of entertaining demonstration. Last summer, I'd witnessed a young karate school perform, with one of the kids my own age splitting a dozen bricks with his bare hand.

On the way, Mason stopped and chatted with a few other kids. He always knew people, no matter where we went. Even one adult tried to butt in with a comment about Jed, but Mason brushed this off. I stood by, silent, uncomfortably aware of myself. It struck me that I didn't have many friends, apart from those acquired through Mason. I knew this wasn't healthy. After all, my parents were similar before their divorce. In their case, my mom had all the connections, leaving Dad irritable and friendless. He hadn't developed much in that sense.

We chose to eat at a setup near the fairgrounds' edge. A few tables stood in a rectangle shape, with a canopy overhead. The servers would come out into the center space with our food and their own small talk. The building adjacent to these tables smelled of grease and deep friers. Through the two windows, I could see people bustling around with trays, holding up baskets, and causing a general clamor that lent itself to a peaceful dinner. The commotion inside only served as a foil to the peaceful atmosphere around the tables.

When we'd placed our orders and received a bottle of soda each, Mason slouched forward, elbows on the table. He turned to me and smiled cheekily. "You look gorgeous, babe."

I rolled my eyes and hit him on the shoulder playfully. "Whatever."

This conversation went nowhere. Mason pulled out his phone and messed around on that for a few minutes. We shared small talk with the waiter, a woman in her thirties with rosy red cheeks who liked to sigh a lot. She asked Mason about Jed and then told me how lucky I was to have myself "a keeper." That phrase didn't align quite right with his personality.

"Hey, honey…" I tapped my fingers on the plastic table and took a deep breath.

He powered off the phone screen and turned. "What's up?"

Then his eyes went beyond me, to the crowd of people walking by. I saw his shoulders tense, almost imperceptible.

"You okay?"

He nodded and shook off whatever it had been. "Yeah, fine." His lips parted, showing white teeth, a smile that I didn't believe. At least his eyes were focused on me, now.

"I need to tell you something," I began.

At that moment, the food arrived. The waitress stuck around after she dropped off our chicken tenders and supplied copious amounts of ketchup. Mason thanked her, paid with his card, and then she left us alone for good.

Through this whole encounter, I bounced my leg under the table, trying not to show just how anxious I felt. I could feel sweat dripping down my back and from my armpits. *Deep breaths,* I reminded myself.

The crowd around us was thinning now. The time for dinner had passed, and most of the vendors would close up within two hours. The fairgrounds were open another two hours from that point, until midnight. But those hours were filled by wild teenagers clinging to their last remnants of childhood. Or else sneaking off to make out in their dark cars, ducking when headlights passed on the way out. I remembered those days. I remembered everything about this place.

"So what'd you need?" Mason asked me now, his mouth full of breaded tenders. He took a sip from his drink and dug into another piece of chicken before I could even answer.

"I'm…" How many times had I imagined this scenario? The horrific look in his eyes, the realization we'd have to tell our parents, the way it changed *everything*. And yet, I didn't feel awful when I spoke the next words. I felt… in control. For the first time in a long time. "I think I'm pregnant."

I expected the chicken to fall back into his basket, the soda to bounce off the table and spill onto the ground. That he would stand up, eyes wide, hands clasped against his mouth. He'd start crying or at least show emotion.

None of this happened. He just narrowed his eyes and ravaged the food in front of him.

"Pregnant? For real?" He blew a raspberry and shook his head. "Damn. That night at my house, huh?"

"Yeah." I faked a cough so he couldn't hear the crack in my voice. The pain. He remembered the night after all, "huh?" But hadn't once mentioned it or asked why I spent an hour showering. Screaming at the torrents of water, puking in the toilet. No, he hadn't bothered to even ask.

"I mean… I guess wait and see if you get your period in a few weeks or something, right?" He gave me a kind of half-smirk, two fries dangling from his fingertips. "You feel any different?"

I ignored the fact that he didn't know when my period was. I didn't expect him to, but maybe he could get somewhere in the ballpark. Not "a few weeks" off. To answer his question, I just stared at my food, still untouched. I grasped the bottle of soda and thought about prying it open. Instead, I lost myself in the color of it.

"Just… let me know if you do one of those tests, alright?"

The conversation died off, and we soon buried it under a mountain of general observations. The weather, passing people with weird hairdos and shirts. The way the sun hurt our eyes. Stupid shit that we didn't really care about, but it was useful to ignore the topic we'd just killed.

I took our food baskets to the trash can, mine still mostly full. After Mason's initial reaction, I couldn't find any appetite. It only took me thirty seconds to walk over and toss them into the metal trash can. The edges were all rusted, and strange colors marked the base of it.

I turned back and saw Mason, still in his seat. Gazing

straight ahead, into nothing. One hand pressed to his forehead. He looked lost, defeated. But right when I noticed this, he sprang out of the trance and pushed back his chair. I lowered my eyes to the ground and hurried over like I hadn't seen a thing.

"I wanna see the animals," I announced, joining his side.

Mason stuck out an arm for me to loop my own in, a proper old-fashioned couple. "Sure thing. But first, we should get caramel apples."

"Oh, you're eating desert this month?" I teased. "In that case, I'm gonna order some of those donuts, if you don't mind."

The talk of the town all week long had been the wildly delicious donuts at the fairgrounds. The biggest Methodist church in town set up in one of the empty buildings and served sugary donuts in a few different flavors. Like everything else around, these were also fried. All year long, people in Little Rush waited to get their hands on a dozen, for the "family." I usually restrained myself, but in this instance, I wanted a full dozen.

Mason waited, sitting on a bench in the shade while I approached the building. I ordered through a small window and told them I'd be back in an hour or so, at least before they closed down. With that taken care of, Mason and I set off again toward the ride, where he could find one of the food stands with caramel apples.

I thought I saw him glance at my stomach once or twice. His expression was something foreign to me, abnormal for him. I didn't say anything at the time, because I didn't want to embarrass him. The longer we stayed there, the more convinced I became. Mason did, in fact, have emotions, even if he'd buried them under some faux layer of steel. Maybe he'd even expected the pregnancy, been worrying about it in silence since his condom slip-up. I'd bring it up in a day or two, I decided, and really talk it through. For the time being, somebody finally knew. That's all I needed.

He knows and he cares. I think.

That would be okay for now.

"Do they have those... those big rabbits?" Mason asked me.

"Probably, babe."

We were holding hands now. He swung mine back and forth playfully as we passed under a tiny, covered bridge. It spanned a little indent in the earth, one easily stepped over, but I loved the cute, colorful bridge anyway.

"And the pigs?"

"Oh, honey." I squeezed his hand and kissed his shoulder. "I didn't really mean I wanted to see the *pigs,* but whatever works. Hey, look." I pointed up ahead. We'd arrived at a small patch of grass in between the two dirt avenues. Through an opening between the skee-ball game and the dart-toss, I could barely make out a vendor. One of the signs read: "Caramel apples."

The alley filled, in that instant, with a group of three boys. Their leader took long strides ahead of them. He wore a wild smirk and stuck out his chest so much it was almost comical. I heard Mason groan beside me as the three of them advanced toward us. The two behind Blough were cracking their knuckles, grinning wickedly. I thought I could smell a hint of alcohol, and it didn't shock me. Kids like them were always sneaking out to the parking lot for drinks.

"Hey there, good pal." Blough moved so quickly, I thought he would lash out immediately and punch Mason. He stopped, though, just inches from my boyfriend's nose. "Been missing you lately. Ever since our tango downtown."

Mason, to his credit, didn't back down. He crossed his arms and raised his chin a bit. A different kind of confidence than the one I'd seen before, when he'd dumped frozen yogurt on an unsuspecting victim. This version of Mason held his ground with cool confidence and a snarl.

"What d'you want?" He looked right into Blough's eyes.

"Get outta here. I don't want any part of this today."

"*Oh,* I didn't realize I had to have your consent." Blough took a step backward, jerking a thumb at his two pals who were cackling like hyenas. "These two won't hurt you, buddy, no worry. Not a big, strong boy like you. Bet your mom calls you that when she's sucking you off every night."

Mason raised an eyebrow and still didn't flinch. "I'm not sure you understand the whole 'your mom's a whore' type joke."

Blough smirked and moved closer again. He shoved Mason hard in the chest, who huffed as the air left his lungs. Blough advanced, even while Mason tried to retreat. The other two boys started inching closer to me. I recognized them from the party and wanted no part of this. Now that they were closer, I had no doubt about the alcohol. All of them smelled strongly like beer.

"One of these days, pal." Blough cracked his knuckles and licked his lips, eyes never leaving Mason. "Mm, mm, mm. I'm gonna rearrange those pretty teeth of yours."

The other two were close to me now, and I had nowhere to run. Just a few feet behind me, some tiny shack blocked my only possible exit. They were both angled to cut me off from running.

Mason was still nose-to-nose with Blough who gestured at me. He cackled, "How's your slut doing?" and stepped even closer to my boyfriend.

Without thinking, without really knowing why, I brought my hand back. In a quick movement, a wide arc, I slapped one of the dumbasses next to me. I hit mostly the back of his head but felt contact with his jaw too. I heard the loud crack more than I felt it. My palm just went hot. They both growled and faced me now.

For a moment, I noticed the crowd of teenagers starting to gather, almost all of them touting cameras and a few even taking pictures. Blough stepped aside from Mason and moved toward me. With all three of them pressing me into the wall, I started to panic. Who knew how drunk they were. What they might actually do.

"Ah, here's the cunt," Blough murmured. Then they all moved in unison.

One quick blow to my stomach and I toppled backward, now firmly against the shack. My head smacked the board, and my vision went fuzzy. I felt hands pressing against me, holding me upright against the wall. Felt their hot breath coming closer. I couldn't see anything past them now. Couldn't even breath. I tried to squirm against their grip, tried to scream.

I could see it in their eyes. What they would do. And I'd never been more afraid.

"You fucker!"

When Mason screamed, he came back into my focus. As he charged forward, pure anger, I saw him digging around for something. Then he extracted the pocket knife and leapt at Blough. The blade slid neatly into his deltoid, and blood spurted out.

Chaos erupted then. I dropped to my knees as the hands released me. Head aching, eyes burning, I could barely register what happened.

There were screams from everywhere, bystanders who'd witnessed the assault. Blough himself started yelling, his voice shrill and panicked. Mason extracted the pocketknife and stared at the bloody weapon. His eyes shifted to me, still on the ground.

"I'm so sorry," he whimpered. Again, he looked at my stomach and I understood what had caused him to snap. The stomach-punch. The attempted rape. It had pushed him over the edge.

"Somebody call the fucking cops!" Blough screamed, clutching at his shoulder. Blood soaked the sleeve of his shirt. His face had gone extremely pale. Both of his friends had run off, shouting for help. Blough chased after them, stumbling along.

He pointed back at us, screaming "Mason Cooper! He tried to kill me! Help!"

Mason knelt beside me, a hand on my leg. He whipped his head in all directions. People were moving closer, foot by foot. Some of them were confused, others horrified. He kissed me, and I tasted salty tears on his lips.

"I'm so sorry, baby."

He stood at that point and sprinted away. Toward the rides, toward the vendors he wouldn't eat from. I watched him for a moment before it clicked in my brain. He'd stabbed somebody. What did that really mean? Jail time? Would it hurt his dad's business? His own future?

I felt the tears welling up inside of me, so I sprang to my feet and ran in the opposite direction. Mason would take the car and speed away. Somebody would call the cops, no doubt. Probably Blough himself or one of his dad's many friends. The same people Mason knew, had even talked to all around the fairgrounds.

That look on his face swam in front of me as I sprinted. My legs carried me to the place where we'd eaten dinner, where I'd told him about the pregnancy. I stood in the middle of the dirt street, people moving by on either side. They shot me weird looks, but I didn't care. Not now.

How long would it take until the cops got here? How much time did I have, if any?

I did some breathing exercises, ten seconds in, five seconds out. Then I walked. It had to be the most unnatural I'd ever looked doing something so instinctive. One foot after the other, a very conscious effort to not look insane. To the donut stand, where I fished out a twenty-dollar bill and paid for the fried blueberry treats. With the bag in hand and my mind unnaturally blank, I left that place, too. I didn't want to stay anywhere for too long. I knew the cops would be here any minute. For a family like the Bloughs, they were always on call.

When I found a shady area under a tree, I pulled out my phone and tried to call Mason while I ate the first donut. He didn't answer. But I seriously needed a ride out of here. Those damn cops were gonna show, and they'd have all sorts of questions for me. Even in the fading sunlight, they'd easily find me.

That thought brought a tear to my eyes. I would never get to see those fair lights, the Ferris wheel spinning at dusk, the darkness broken only by laughter. Then the sobs came, and they ravaged my body like nothing had in over a week. I hadn't cried this intensely since that awful night at Mason's house. I wondered if it was possible to feel so much pain and for my body to convulse so violently that blood would flow from my eyes instead of tears.

With a second and third donut in hand, I made my way to the animal shacks. If I was going to cry uncontrollably, I might as well do it in the company of these adorable animals. I reached the horse barn and noticed the smell, but I could barely register anything now. I couldn't stop thinking of Mason, of the cops, of what that Blough kid would say. He could make up any story, say Mason just attacked him out of the blue. Could they even say it was attempted murder? Wasn't that… years in prison?

"Oh my god!" The words were shattered, like a broken window, and barely understandable through my sniffling. "Please, no."

I stumbled out of the horse barn with considerably more attention on me than I had going in. I looked all around for somewhere more isolated to go. The rabbits, maybe, like Mason had wanted. At this thought, I checked my phone again but no call from him. I did get an idea. A way out of this fairground, maybe.

I pushed the call button and waited for the ringing. After five agonizing seconds when I didn't think he'd pick up, I finally heard that baffled, soothing voice on the other end.

"Willow?" Hudson asked, his voice slow and disoriented. "What's up?"

"I need you to come get me," I said through pieces of donut and the tail end of my emotional hurricane. "Fairgrounds, now, please. Hudson, right now, I need—"

"Okay, okay. On my way." I heard him moving around right before he hung up.

In the meantime, I wandered the different animal barns. Feasting on donuts that would give me a horrible stomach ache the next day. I managed to stabilize. Though I knew my makeup had been wrecked and my eyes were probably like strawberries, I didn't really care what people thought. It felt nice, the independence. But I would've given anything to be a self-conscious mess in Mason's arms instead.

Where'd he gone? Where would he stay? Did he tell his dad what happened? Were the cops, even now, racing toward that neighborhood of nice houses and expensive cars?

These animals weren't so different from me, I decided. They were all trapped in these cages. Their eyes held a kind of sadness. That thought cheered me an increment. I tore off a piece of the donut and tossed it at some of the chickens, but this didn't help them as much as it did me.

Then again, maybe their squawks were thank-yous, and somewhere in those little beaks they were smiling back.

12
HUDSON

From Bruce's house, where I'd been ever since lunchtime, it took about ten minutes to reach the fairgrounds. Even driving at outlandish speeds, I couldn't get there any quicker. Driving this quickly in the dark always made me nervous, but especially in a panicked situation like this. With each passing tick of my internal clock, I worried about Willow and hoped she would be alright. Running toward her, the engine thunderous.

We're all just running.

I drove along the state road for a while until the 4-H fairgrounds were in view. The parking lot, only half full, loomed closest. It wasn't easy to see in the waning light. I almost turned in to park there until I spotted the figure. On the side of the road, about a quarter-mile ahead, a teenage girl jumped up and down. I recognized the outfit as something Willow-esque and silenced my turn signal.

As I passed by the fairgrounds on my way to collect her, I noticed two cop cars parked near all the other vehicles, those red-blue lights still flashing. It formed a weird sort of disco ball now that darkness had almost taken over. About a dozen cars were pulling onto the road at the same time, leaving the police vehicles distanced from the others. It felt like I'd never seen so many headlights all jumbled together.

The fair definitely had a sort of beauty to it, especially at night. It'd always been a dream of mine to take a girl here, run around with her in the darkness. Things never worked out, though. The few girlfriends I'd had were never over the summer, which meant fair dates were out of the question. Maybe if things had gone better with Layla...

I pulled over on the side of the road. Since the fairgrounds were on the left, Willow hurried across the two-lane road and around to the passenger's side. When she hopped in, brushing wild hair back, I granted her a moment to collect her thoughts. While I pulled back out into the road, just driving straight, I couldn't help noticing the dark makeup smeared beside her nose, the general redness of her eyes and cheeks. This brought its own set of questions, but the biggest one had nothing to do with her appearance. Where had Mason gone? What were the cops doing out here?

"Thank you," she muttered after about fifteen seconds.

"We going anywhere particular?" I asked, drumming on the steering wheel.

Willow leaned back against the headrest, taking breaths so intently it unnerved me. Then she said curtly, "McDonald's okay?"

"Sure."

I made the necessary turns and drove back toward Little Rush. Willow adjusted the dial on the radio, where my phone played through the Bluetooth. Something by the National at the moment, a melancholy and rambling song. I offered her my phone, a chance to switch the music, but she declined.

"This is fine," she said. Her breathing had almost returned to normal.

She reached for the floorboards and then picked up a plain white bag I hadn't noticed before. Out of it, she pulled one of the "holy donuts" that people around here were so obsessed with.

They just made me feel sick. Nevertheless, she bit into it and closed her eyes. The relief washing over her confused me and amused me. People looked for and found comfort in the oddest of places.

We're all just looking.

On the way back into town, we passed by Mason's neighborhood. I glanced in that direction, out of a general curiosity more than anything. I saw Willow do the same, only she craned her neck as if searching for something specific. When she noticed me watching, she straightened back in her seat and stared ahead.

"So… you okay?" I finally asked. I turned onto the four-lane road cutting through the center of town. McDonald's waited about three miles away, and I wanted some kind of answer before I sat down with her.

"Mason… stabbed that Blough kid."

"What!" I almost pressed on the brakes, and for a moment the truck swerved dangerously into the other lane. I readjusted and tried to ask more, but my mind blanked. Mason stabbing somebody? What the hell caused that? He'd definitely been more aggressive lately, but that was… out of his usual character. I hadn't known he even owned a knife. Rich kids didn't usually carry those around.

"Blough shoved me. Mason had a pocket knife and stabbed him in the shoulder. Blough called the cops, Mason ran off. I went and hid until you came." She recited this like some English class assignment, zero emotion.

"Oh my god. Are you okay? Is he?"

I tried to focus on the road ahead of me. The last thing we both needed today was a car accident. It proved difficult, though, and I nearly ran a red light before Willow snapped at me to slow down. Once that crisis had been averted, we sat idling in silence, the truck stationery. We stared at the bright red orb, neither willing to speak.

"He hasn't called," she said. I could hear her voice falter, the threat of more crying, perhaps. "And I just... I'm so scared, Hudson."

I wanted to reach out and put an arm around her. Or at least grab her hand, promise her things would be okay. But I didn't. It wasn't that I felt uncomfortable, because I didn't. I'd always thought of her as *my* friend, not my best friend's girlfriend. And yet, I held back from that show of support.

The truck rattled to a stop in the McDonald's parking lot. It was nearly ten, and they would close in two hours. I didn't feel particularly hungry, and Willow, with her bag of donuts, couldn't have been either. But sitting in a truck outside of McDonald's felt even more pitiful than going in. Begrudgingly and together, we opened our doors and stepped out into the humid air.

I held the restaurant door open for her. Willow shuffled through, head bowed, cradling the white bag in her arms like a child. I didn't think the workers would tell her she couldn't bring it in, but then again, I wouldn't have been surprised. She made a bee-line for a booth near the rear of the dining room. I approached the counter, quickly ordered two large drinks, and then left.

"Don't let me see her eating no outside food," the cashier warned as I turned away.

I didn't bother responding.

When I approached the booth, I found Willow slumped against the dark window, staring outside. Her features, reflected on the glass, were so dismayed that I felt my heart sink. She hadn't specified how badly injured Blough had been. From the way she'd been acting, I almost expected he would end up in the ICU or something equally serious. That wouldn't be good, not for anyone. I didn't know what cops did to teenagers who stabbed their peers, and I didn't want to speculate.

"What do you want?" I asked, holding up the large drink to show her what I meant.

"Hudson, I'm pregnant." She turned to face me slowly, pale and terrified, like she'd seen a ghost out there in the vacant parking spaces. "I am."

I plopped down in the seat across from her, trying not to gape. Our eyes met and her lip quivered. So many questions bombarded me. How long had she known? How far along was she? When was the baby due, would they want to know the gender, what did their parents think? So many more, everything rushing around. My brain, suddenly a tornado, picking up loose objects and throwing them against the interior of my skull.

"You are?" I felt myself breaking out in a ridiculous grin, the kind of toothy nonsense that scared people away. But I couldn't help it. "Oh my god, Willow. That's... that's..." I reached a hand across the table and grasped one of hers. "That's so amazing!"

She looked up at me, chin still lowered. I noticed a flickering happiness, like a lightbulb that's almost gone out. I squeezed her hand tighter, but with no response. Then again, this time a little harder. She obliged and rotated her own until our fingers were entwined.

"I'm so happy for you two," I went on, pressing the point. "I'll do anything to help. Honestly. If you need... a babysitter or a... a cooked meal or—"

"Hudson, shhh." She placed her other hand on mine and rubbed the back of it. "You're sweet, but it's okay."

I refused to let it drop and leaned closer to her. "Willow, I'm serious. I'll do anything. This is just... just so good. It's amazing. God, you're gonna be a perfect mom. You know that?"

Her eyes started to well up. She released one hand and used it to cover her mouth, mumbling through her fingers, "A mom. Oh my god."

I felt something in my own eyes, almost like tears, or the threat of them. I stood up from the table, and she cocked her head. Then I sidled into the booth next to her, still grinning like an idiot. Everything felt so right. I had clarity like never before.

"You're gonna be perfect. All three of you." I threw my arms around her then, embracing her tighter than I had anyone in a long time. Willow buried her head in the crook of my shoulder and cried silently. Her entire weight pressed against me. I stroked the back of her head and caught my own reflection in the window beside her. Genuine tears trickling down my face.

In the face of my own nihilism, something worth living for. In the wasteland of this little town, a beautiful event. Something unmatched by anything out there. Only here, in Little Rush, could I find such a friend, an amazing couple that would form an even better family. With Willow in my arms, I had no doubts. They'd be okay. They really would.

"Don't give up on him," I heard myself whisper, barely a voice. "Him and you... you may not be perfect right now, but you're good together."

"I know we are," she mumbled into my shirt. It stuck to my chest in one area, soaked with her tears.

"You two are gonna be such good parents," I assured her once again. "Just don't give up on Mason, please."

Maybe I begged her to stay with him because I didn't think I could. The rift between us had grown to its widest point. He didn't want to speak or even see me. At least, if Willow stuck around for him, I knew deep down they'd end up okay. They'd get along without me. Mason had found his lifelong partner. They had a kid on the way. Wherever they ended up, even if I only saw him in passing, these two would live complete and meaningful lives. What could be more meaningful, after all, than a baby?

She pulled back for a moment and reached for a donut. The

bag had slipped under the table. She extracted two and handed one to me, which I took despite my distaste for them. We ate them together, in the McDonald's booth, with our backs to the cashier. The entire restaurant empty around us. Sitting close enough that our legs were touching, her hand resting on my knee, I felt more connected with someone than I ever had. To be here, alone, in such an intimate, platonic friendship... I'd never experienced that before. Never thought it was even possible.

"I want you to know..." Willow held up a finger and swallowed the food in her mouth. Then she went on, "Hudson, I want you to know we all love you."

"Thank—"

"No, I mean it."

Willow turned in her seat and grabbed my shirt aggressively. I felt scared more than anything. She'd really punch me if she wanted.

"Hudson, we all love you. *I* love you. And even Mason. No, he really does, shut up. And I..." A moment's silence. Then she shrugged and kissed me on the cheek, blushing as she pulled away. "Don't give up on yourself, either. Okay?"

We spent another twenty minutes in that booth. I thought back on my conversation with Bruce that day, all the stories he'd told, the photograph he'd shown me. It felt good, felt right, to be in this place. Just Willow and I, the only ones in an empty McDonald's. A thing of mundane beauty.

Sitting in that restaurant, neither of us spoke, neither of us suggested leaving. I couldn't help but feel ashamed, because the longer we sat there the more I realized how awful I'd been. Mason had certainly been a dick, but I had as well. Overly angry, self-centered, full of vitriol. Everything I accused him of, I'd managed to emulate. Not that I said this out loud. It was just a deep realization, an aching regret.

The hour wore on. We waited for a sign or somebody to kick

us out. The time dragged by, as it always did in Little Rush, only now I tried to savor it.

We're all just waiting.

13
WILLOW

The week after the fair might've been the hardest I'd ever gone through. Even after the brief rendezvous with Hudson and our intimate McDonald's experience, that night didn't pass easily. Mason never got in contact, not until the early hours of that next morning. I spent the entire time lying awake in bed, hands over my eyes or against my stomach. Just staring. The ceiling my only company.

He could be in jail right now, I told myself. I didn't want to think about that stuff, but the harder I tried, the worse it went. I gave in, after a while, and tasted all of my darkest fears, let them wrap around me like a constricting snake. Did any of it matter anymore? Any of the college classes I'd taken, the fight we had about moving away, all the plans I made for myself. All of that anxiety, as real as it was, took a backseat to this. Me, probably pregnant. Mason, probably in jail. What a way to start this next chapter of our lives.

Despite the lengthy hours in bed, my mind racing at the speed of light, I couldn't figure out what I truly felt. I didn't know, when the sun rose that morning and I met its glare with puffy eyes, if I blamed Mason for what happened. If I hated him for stabbing Blough. Just like I didn't know if I hated him for getting me pregnant. If he hated himself. So much hate in my life, just then, so much absolute bleakness. *Is this what Hudson thinks of daily?* I asked myself in the quiet of my bedroom.

I had no doubt anymore that those texts he sent me were real. That side of him, living in a dark and twisted reality, was the more honest one. Our best friend in the world, drowning right beside our boat... Maybe even under it. But the mystery of Hudson, the complexities of his moody and brooding behavior, would have to wait.

Mason called me that next morning around five o'clock. When I picked up the phone, voice scratchy and broken from lack of use, he said he was surprised I'd still been awake. Without any hint of amusement, I simply asked the question that had been cutting into my mind for hours on end. No chit-chat, no jokes, not even a "I love you, are you okay?" None of that mattered to me. I just wanted to know what had happened.

"I'm so sorry for leaving you," he started by saying.

"Save it," I interrupted, not masking the fire in my voice. "Just tell me what happened. You think I'm... I'm not used to you leaving me? You've been a real asshole for weeks now, Mason. Tell me what happened, okay? And then I'll... I'll decide."

His words didn't come for a minute, at least, but I knew exactly why he'd paused. Even saying it myself, I'd been shocked at the words leaving my mouth. A decision, I told him, but on what? Whether to stay together? Whether to run away somewhere else, forget about this whole town? Mason wanted to stay; I needed to go. He wanted to be this tough guy, do the cool kid things, act like he didn't care; I needed somebody who wouldn't and who did.

So, yes, when they choked their way out of me and into the phone, I knew the words were true. He had been awful. Obnoxious, self-centered, indifferent. Not just to me, but to Hudson. If nothing else, our conversation at McDonald's last night made that extremely clear. I knew both Hudson and I weren't completely free of blame, but right now, I wanted Mason to know how *I* felt. That I had *seriously* considered dumping him that morning. What kind of person stabs somebody, even in self-defense, and leaves their girlfriend to deal with the mess? Their *pregnant* girlfriend? What a... a fucking coward.

Mason told me then what happened the day before. He explained that he'd been seriously unnerved by my news about the baby. This I'd already guessed. But he didn't stop there. He said that when Blough had shoved me, he saw it as an attack on me and our child. He thought about everything built up between Blough and himself, the arguments, the schoolyard fights, that beating he'd taken at the party. In that moment, with the pocketknife weighing against his leg, he decided that enough was enough. It only made sense in his mind. To lash out in that way, to attack. Only once the blade had slipped in and out of the muscle did he realize his mistake. And flee.

He drove around for a few hours, Mason told me, and thought about calling Hudson. Apologizing, even begging. Something held his tongue, though, and he didn't understand until hours later that he still felt legitimate anger toward his distant friend. Hudson, with his bipolar mood swings and his sudden friendship with Bruce Michaels. Hudson, well-respected and never attacked for being "a rich boy." So many things, he realized, that Hudson possessed. And he wanted them.

"I'd trade places in a heartbeat," Mason had said, almost sending me over the edge again.

"And what about me?" I interjected, trying to maintain composure. I'd crawled to the floor and now lay next to my bed, face pressed in the carpet. I pushed my forehead so hard that it burnt a little. Eyes closed, heart thumping against the floor, I waited for his answer.

"You think people don't hate me because of you?" He

groaned, and there was an awful, staticky sound as he moved around. I still didn't know where he'd gone. "Everybody does. They all want you."

This didn't strike me as a compliment, and it hadn't been one. I didn't think painting me as a burden really helped his case. I'd only ever been good, or tried to be. I thought of myself as an excellent girlfriend, actually. Definitely above average. That might bring criticisms or even disapproving glances from other boys, but it should be a net positive to him.

Mason went on, saying that he'd returned home a little after midnight to find his parents waiting in the living room. Both his parents had dark bags under their eyes and weren't relieved by his sudden appearance. They addressed him, stern but gentle, and explained that Blough's parents weren't going to file charges.

"But why?" I asked, my tone still short. "You... stabbed him?"

"Those kids videotaping," Mason said, "one of them posted the whole damn thing on Snapchat. A bunch of others took it and shared on Instagram. It shows... everything. The boys pushing you against the wall, holding you down. And so I... well, it makes Blough look awful."

"And you like some hero," I finished for him.

"Well... yeah."

He finished by stating that his parents were concerned, but not overly angry, and that in the end, everything had turned out fine. Only instead of comforting my fears, this made me even angrier. Fantastic, things were good for him. I still felt like absolute shit. I was now the girlfriend to this *great* hero. A real damsel-in-distress. I just wanted to scream at him. But I held back.

With his story concluded, Mason waited for my response.

I held back tears, which had returned in full force. Just when

I thought the well had dried. And out of a boiling rage came meek words, a broken question. "Do you understand how... how much you've hurt me?"

This was about more than the knife incident. This was about the child inside of me. The weeks I'd spent alone, dealing with this on my own, struggling with the weight of parenthood. so much more than just the ruined fair trip.

Mason answered with the shaky, lip-biting tone I'd only heard a few times. The kind of voice that tells you somebody is on the edge of crying themselves, even a complete breakdown. "I'm so sorry, baby. I am."

"Mason..." Then I said it. I went for it. Laying on my floor, an elbow covering my face. "I need to think about it. Goodnight."

And I did think. Goodnight, at five in the morning, served more as a goodbye than anything. I didn't leave my room until noon, but I also didn't sleep. Just more of the mindless reclining that had gotten me to that point. I texted Hudson, just updating him that Mason wouldn't go to jail or anything. He never answered. Apparently, the beef between them hadn't been fully squashed. Even still, I knew he'd want the assurance.

Mason and I texted sparingly over the course of that first day. Nothing important, just words for words' sake. At around eight o'clock that night, after maybe twenty texts combined through the entire day, I said that I was going to bed and would talk in the morning. This lie passed easily, because neither of us wanted to continue the excruciating pretenses anymore. Acting like nothing had changed, with full awareness that it would never be the same.

On the second day, we met at the old smoking spot. The forest by the old baseball field had grown wilder since we'd last ventured there with Hudson. As the summer wore on, the boys sort of gave up smoking, and I did so on my own. Mason agreed to show up there around ten in the morning. I arrived earlier and had already burned through two cigarettes by the time he trudged in my direction.

Surrounded by forest, gazing up at a downtown park covered in fog, I opened my mouth to let the thin trail of smoke float away. Mason shifted, hunched over awkwardly, and jerked his head in either direction. Peering at anything but me. I sat on the tree log where I had many times before, gazing straight ahead, as if I hadn't noticed his arrival.

"Hey," he murmured. Still not looking directly at me.

"Places are so beautiful without people." I turned my head so I could see him and blew in that direction. My voice had grown colder since we last spoke. All the tears were gone now, and with them most emotion. "Don't you think?"

"Are you still mad?" He met my eyes for just a split second and then wavered. His arms were hugged around his chest like a child against the cold. Hair disheveled, like for the first time in months he hadn't methodically prepared his appearance.

"I'm not... as much," I said. He breathed easier. I continued, "But I'm not happy. And it's gonna take time. To forgive... everything."

"Just say it."

"You got me fucking pregnant, Mason, and you didn't even care." I took a deep inhale from the cigarette and held it for a few seconds. I watched his reaction, my own expression stoic. "You just fight people all the time now, huh? You... you don't care about me or what I want. You don't care about Hudson, your best friend. It's just a lot. It's hard to explain."

"I'm working on it!" he exclaimed, rapidly taking a seat on the log next to me. Pleading, now, with his bottom lip trembling. "Just give me time."

"I will." Another deep breath. I exhaled the smoke into his face. "As long as you are."

"Of course." He placed a hand on my leg now, gentle. "I'll do anything for you."

I kissed his forehead and then pulled him against me, the cigarette dangling from my mouth. I held him against me with both hands and spoke from the corner of my mouth. "We're gonna have to tell your parents."

And then I laughed, because after two days of no sleep, that was the only way to deal with things. Truthfully, though, I did feel a bit like the Joker.

There weren't many answers for us, not right away. All that conversation did was reunite us. It didn't explain what we'd do about college, if we would stay in Little Rush or move away. I only hoped that things would evolve naturally, that we'd find some kind of middle ground. The future remained in fog, only showing a few feet at a time.

We waited for another five days before taking our next step into that fog. After another positive pregnancy test, I called Mason and told him I knew for sure. In reality, I'd known ever since that moment when he hadn't used a condom. Just intuition. But we were in the thick of it now.

I spent that day alone, after the second pregnancy test, but not necessarily in sadness. Something about the way Hudson had reacted brought a shift to my thinking. A child wasn't a mistake. If somebody as bleak as Hudson could see the beauty in new life, then so should I.

Mason, upon hearing this news, said immediately that abortion wasn't an option. Even though I'd decided this on my own, it felt good to hear him say it. And to do it without prompting, either. We had this conversation on a phone call, so I could hear his voice and not just read his messages. I think he started crying toward the end, happy tears. When I hung up, we had a time for that next day. I would meet him at his house, and there, together, we'd go into his dad's office and... break the news.

Every horror story I'd ever heard about hateful parents and teen pregnancy filled my brain that night. I imagined how awful it could go. How terrible the reaction might be. But through those nightmares and through the early morning, I told myself everything would work out. Mason and I... we could do this, one way or another. Unexpected? Of course. But not impossible. Not unwanted.

o o o

Mason knocked on the door to his dad's study. I waited behind him, looking around at the walls of his home. A beautiful house, a great place to live. The hallways were wide and everything clean. This house had become familiar to me now. Would it be the last time I ever set foot in here?

I could feel my own heart threatening to break a rib or something. I placed a hand on Mason's back. His shoulders shook as his dad called out for us to enter. Mason turned the knob and pushed it open. Shuffling forward, we passed into the danger zone. I shut the door behind us.

I couldn't see his expression as we entered, but Jed's face lit up in a wide smile. He set down the document he'd been reading. The desk itself didn't have a square inch of free space. Papers upon folders upon professional-looking books covered the surface, a computer sitting to one side. One day, maybe even that would be under this mess. He certainly looked like a man drowning in business.

"Hey there," Jed said, directed toward me. He looked confused now but pleased, nonetheless.

I waved back a little, just raising a hand slightly from my jeans. Then I moved into a spot near Mason, my head bowed.

I remembered the story he'd told two days ago, about his dad coming into his room that night and saying, "I love you." Hearing Mason recount this, how it had really shaken and perplexed him, I'd been struck by the absurdity. My parents and I, while not super close, always said we loved each other. Almost daily. But the way Jed and Mason stared at each other now, the older man brimming with joy, I got a glimpse of how fresh this connection must have felt. How dead their relationship had been for so, so long.

"Dad, we have something to tell you."

Jed's eyes were as big as bowls right away. Maybe he understood, put two and two together. I'd never come in before, rarely even spoke with him. Mason didn't initiate conversations much with Jed, I knew, and the two of us together could only mean a few topics this serious. Marriage, of course, but as not even seniors yet, that would be improbable. The only other reason for this dramatic meeting, then, was a pregnancy.

"We're…" Mason reached down to hold my hand. "Well, she's pregnant."

Jed's gaze didn't shift to me, however. His eyes were focused on Mason. Maybe he blamed him, maybe he would yell. I really wanted to leave at that point. But no, I would stand here beside him. We were a couple. We were gonna be parents. I wouldn't leave his side.

"This isn't a… prank or anything?" Jed looked at me now, then back to his son, as if hoping one of us would pull out a kazoo and scream "surprise!" When neither of us did, he placed both hands flat on the desk and lowered his chin. He murmured something under his breath, closing both eyes. At this point, I expected him to erupt in fury. But he looked up and smiled ridiculously wide. "You… wow."

Mason fumbled with the next part of his planned speech. His dad's mixed reaction had caught him off guard, as well as me. I took up the mantle and carried on our script.

"We're definitely keeping the baby," I said, giving Jed the side of my face. I stared at Mason, leaned my head against his shoulder for a second. When I spoke next, I squared in Jed's direction, squeezed my boyfriend's hand, and spoke with determination. "I don't know if you're okay with that or not, but we're going to. We'll figure it out, and we'd love your help but if not... We love her. Or him. Our baby."

"We do." Mason beamed.

Under the weight of our intense joy, his dad shrugged and stood from the desk. "You two... you've always been a little crazy." He raised an eyebrow and smirked. "Don't think I'm completely in the dark about the cabin."

Neither of us confirmed or denied whatever info he had. We just held hands, facing him, and refused to budge. Jed shook his head a few times, a wide grin, almost incredulous. I didn't know how to respond, so I hoped one of these two would continue.

"Thank you for telling me," Jed said, standing behind his desk now with hands clasped together. "And... well, congratulations, of course." His head swiveled around the room, as if looking for something. Both hands uncurled now, and he began to tap on the desk. "Myself and Lucy... we'll be more than happy to help you two."

I opened my mouth to speak, hopefully put an end to this awkward stand-still, but before I could, Mason cleared his throat. He took a deep breath and, to my surprise, turned to address me.

"Can you... step out for just a minute?" He squeezed my hand. "I wanna talk to him."

I obliged and left the room without hesitation. As I pulled the door shut from the hallway outside, Jed's eyes were trained on his son once again. When the handle clicked into place, I walked to one of the recliners and sat alone for a few minutes. Mason's mom had been gone when we arrived, and he said he'd tell her that night himself. My own task, then, would be breaking the news to my parents. I actually thought about taking Mom along to talk with Dad, just in case he… disapproved.

She would be okay with it, I already knew. Definitely supportive. And my younger brother, maybe he'd even be excited. Maybe he'd even like the baby, once it came. I didn't know for sure, but I felt optimism. That was something new.

Those minutes in the chair were full of relief and wonder. Imagining what our kid would look like, what names we might choose, how awful senior year would be. Pregnant in my prom dress. A mother for graduation. My nightmare, honestly, but now… those felt like brief stops on the path to something so much happier. Something worth all of it. The puking, the nausea, the cramps, the pain. Mason would stand by me in the hospital. I had no doubt of it. No doubt anymore.

He emerged from his dad's office about ten minutes later. Both him and Jed were wiping tears from their eyes, grinning through all the emotion. I rose from the chair and tried to catch something from Mason's expression, but he walked past me. Jed reached out his arms and embraced me tightly, full of his old-man deodorant scent. First Hudson and now Mason's dad. Two people I never expected to hug like this. Funny what a pregnancy could do.

Ten minutes later, I sat outside in my idling car and conversed with Mason, who leaned through the open window. His mom would be home soon, and I didn't have any reason to stick around. Not when I had to break the news to both my parents.

"The real question," he said with a mischievous chuckle, "is when to make it Facebook official."

"Oh, shut up." I planted my lips on his for a moment and then pulled back. "Hey, you really should text Hudson."

"I know." All the air deflated from his chest. "I just don't know what to say yet. I feel…"

"It's okay." I reached out and stroked the stubble on his

cheek. "You'll find the words."

"We haven't talked in two weeks." He rested his forehead against the top of the car door and closed his eyes. "It'll take a miracle for all this to just... disappear. You know?"

14
BRUCE

I never expected it to happen.

That's not entirely true. The honest truth, if there was such a thing… well, the honest truth was harder to explain.

Ever since it happened, ever since that awful mistake, I knew it would eventually come out. Stuff like that didn't stay buried. Not for somebody like me. Not when the action was so real, unbelievably sordid.

No, I *had* expected it. I'd just hoped it would happen after I passed on. Or even that I would disappear from public view enough for them to forget me. If people erased me from their minds, then it wouldn't matter as much. If only the story broke a year or two later, once I'd fully vanished. No, it just happened too quickly. They still thought of me as an eccentric actor, a wild old man, searching for something out there in the wilderness beyond LA's lights. If only they knew.

It happened too quickly and not soon enough. If I'd been unmasked right after that fateful night, years ago, maybe I could have suffered through the consequences and forgiven myself. I would rather be in prison, I realized now, with a clean conscience. But I never came forward. I could've, really. Could've admitted to my sins, unearthed my own dirty secrets. I didn't. And so, I deserved whatever came down the line.

Those damn lawyers had been no help after all. Not when Madeline refused a settlement. That would've been easier to explain. This... not so much.

The cruelty in coincidence never struck me like it did that evening. I stood in front of my mirror when the news broke, straightening my tie. Dressed in my finest, most pretentious suit, the kind that made it clear I wasn't from around here. The kind that shouted, "I am not one of you!" and attracted them like magots to rotting fruit.

Just minutes later, I was going to leave out that front door and drive into town, where the mayor of Little Rush waited. He said we could meet a little after ten, once the restaurant had closed and we had the whole place to ourselves. Back at the steakhouse with dusty deer heads and the overwhelming aroma of grills. He wanted to meet me, at long last, and talk about my future in the town. Probably make sure that I wasn't going anywhere before he really took time to know me. I understood all of that, even appreciated it. And I really looked forward to the dinner.

This first step. The moment where I felt like a future here could really happen. It had been a dream of mine, one that I would make happen. Those folks at Allen's Burgers had been so kind and the conversation so enthralling. I wanted all of that again. I wanted it nightly. Hell, I might have bought an old bar downtown and opened it up myself, just to sit there and chat with locals. Just to feel like one of them, to drink their drinks and taste their personalities. That's all I wanted. That's all I goddamn wanted. To be normal, like them.

I could picture it in my mind. An old actor who held court at the bar a few times a week. Who kept the place going out of his heart's kindness and his bank account's swollen stomach. Trading stories with locals for years to come. Really *becoming* one of them. Goddamn it, I swear that's all I wanted, all I fucking *wanted.* But even that perfect, innocent picture shattered as soon as I saw the news.

Broken into shards. Glass scattered on the ground, cutting into my hand.

It's not my fault that I punched the mirror. It's not my fault that I continued punching it until my knuckles couldn't stand anymore. And it's not my fault that life teased with the promise of a real future.

"Damn."

I sat rigid on the couch, holding my phone gingerly. Reading. Scrolling. Bleeding profusely.

The vacant television screen looked on as I scrolled through Twitter that night. Right around ten o'clock, just as I'd planned to leave, the article started to circulate. Rumors flying left and right. TMZ had something go viral. All of this hit in waves when I opened the app. Saw the shares, saw my name thrown around in all directions. I imagined the hell-storm for whoever ran the Bruce Michaels account. The mentions, the replies. Well, fuck them, at least they got paid to deal with it.

I never read the actual article, the one written by some Gina Roberts. That name popped up three times as I scrolled through my feed. I googled her and found, among all the random faces that surfaced, a few pictures of an attractive, intimidating woman with sleek glasses. I recognized her in an instant. And my fears were confirmed. She'd been here, in this very house. Well, fuck her too. I guess this really was the end.

I propped my feet on the small table and leaned back on the couch, groaning loudly. Unsure what I felt. Unsure what any of this meant. What did allegations alone even do? They had no proof, apart from the story she'd told Gina. No other women had come out yet. I realized the absurdity, that I didn't even know Madeline's last name. Until I clicked on one of the TMZ stories, that is.

Gina Roberts, a well-respected if somewhat obscure journalist, had done the legwork, the interviews, the research. And yet, her story didn't even break the news. TMZ got a hold of it, one way or another, and their own recount turned out to be much more salacious and disturbing, more to the public's interest. Madeline's name showed up multiple times, even her home city. And it had a last name now. Suso. Madeline Suso.

Five beers and three shots in, I could barely make out the words on my screen. I read the TMZ article over and over again. Saw the public response, the instant backlash, the "cancel Bruce Michaels" threads. And then the hashtags started. By the time I looked away, the story had three separate hashtags, all of them trending. All of them incredibly damning.

"Is this what I deserve?"

I stood from the couch and ripped open the curtains. Not a single light out there. No stars tonight, no moon. Just a black canvas stretching as far as the universe itself. I placed a hand on the cool window and noticed that I was sweating. Remembered that my knuckles were ripped to shreds, blood running down my forearms. But I couldn't even feel it. My whole body was ravaged by a fire more painful than any alcohol or cuts.

All I wanted here was a quiet life. I just wanted them to forget me. I just wanted to visit a nice little bar and tell stories to the locals, hear their own in response. I just wanted to be *him*. That's all I ever wished for here, and this stupid fucking town couldn't even grant me that.

"Is this how it ends?"

I turned back toward the couch. The photograph rested on the coffee table. I picked it up and gritted my teeth, staring into the image. Without a thought, I hurled it at the wall. The frame broke, glass shattered, and the entire mess dropped to the ground. At some point, I bent over it and extracted the Polaroid, carrying it gingerly into the other room. Blood dripped onto the photo and I hastily wiped it clean. Then I stuck it back into my hiding place. Maybe I would never look, ever again, at that frozen memory.

I drank more that night than I had in years, maybe ever. Enough to kill me, I hoped. Enough to end it all.

Nothing to live for. Not anymore. No chance of redemption, no hope of forgiveness. I didn't even want it. I knew, on some level, that I had earned everything coming. I'd tied myself to the track and waited for the train to arrive. I wouldn't escape. I wouldn't even try. Just lay there, ropes cutting into my flesh as the roar of the engine hurled closer.

I did deserve it, the ensuing train. But I couldn't bear to watch, so I closed my eyes.

15

LITTLE RUSH
THE ROBBERS

June stood with a pistol in hand, aiming it right at the sleeping man. She motioned to her comrades. With eager but anxious grins, Randy and Curtis stepped forward out of the shadows. Curtis held a metal bat in his right hand, while Randy gripped a cold knife. They glanced back at June, eyes wide, as all three approached the man asleep on the couch.

"Go ahead," she hissed.

The sitting room around them held very few items of furniture. This couch, where their unwitting captive slept, and then a television on a cabinet across the room. June stood behind the coffee table, her back to the window, curtains drawn. The entire house waited in pitch darkness as they'd approached, snuck in, and finally crept into this room. From the first look around, it didn't have much potential. No expensive watches or elaborate golden lamps. Not even a wallet on the table, stuffed with bills. But she held out hope.

"Hey, you!" Randy shouted all of a sudden. His voice cracked the silence like an atomic bomb. He kicked Bruce in the ribs to ensure he woke up.

Curtis flicked on the lights, blinding them all momentarily. Bruce groggily sat up, shielding his eyes, still half-closed. Like a corpse rising from the grave.

"Get up!" Randy snarled, hitting him in the back lightly. "Get up, I said!"

Bruce covered his face with a hand and began sobbing. She noticed that the back of his hands and forearms were caked in dried blood. His hair, an unruly and sweaty mess, hung in his eyes now. It was matted against his head in places, a real disgusting appearance. The tears rained with great, sniffling snot globs. Randy and Curtis both looked back at their leader, uncertain. June paused, her gun still trained on the old, frail man.

She hadn't expected Bruce to be... this. Just a year ago, he'd taken part in an action movie they'd all enjoyed. And now, simply an old man on the edge of the world, a fraction of his former self, a ghost.

"Straighten up, you!" June snapped, unsure how angry to sound.

Bruce glanced up in surprise at the woman's voice. He fought back the crying and squawked, "What d-do you w-want from m-me?" He wiped his eyes with the back of his forearm and hugged himself. His eyes locked on the gun barrel, and his bottom lip started to quiver again.

"Money, riches, everything you got." June flicked the gun toward the bedroom. "Get us everything you have, or I'll shoot you. Please try me."

Bruce bowed his head and stumbled in that direction. Curtis moved out of his way, holding the bat at ready in case the old man tried anything. Rather than fight back, Bruce held up his own hands in defense, starting to mumble again as he stumbled into the bedroom. When he disappeared into the dark room, they all three looked at each other.

"What the hell?" Randy whispered to June. "What's... his problem?"

She shrugged and followed Bruce into the room, still holding her gun up. The other two copied. June couldn't fight the nagging sensation that they'd made a mistake. If this man didn't have any wealth here, it would all be for naught. What would they get, a single credit card? But maybe, just maybe, something in the bedroom would make it all worthwhile. She sure as hell hoped so.

This next room, also furnished sparingly, only had a bed against one wall, a dresser next to it, and a desk across the room. This might have been the least-cluttered desk she'd ever seen. It looked almost completely unused, if not for the small box on top of it. The black square, a keyhole just visible on the side, was thick, compacted. Some kind of safe, maybe fireproof. June grinned at the sight of it. The answer to their prayers. Who knew what might be inside. Diamonds? Actual gold?

Bruce fumbled in one of the desk drawers and pulled out a key. Glancing over his shoulder at them, he inserted it and twisted. The lid clicked, and he opened the box.

"This's all I got," he said, voice shaky. He turned around, holding a stack of hundred-dollar bills. "It's all I got, I swear."

"Go count 'em," June commanded. She motioned at Randy, who stepped forward to retrieve the money.

As he counted, June kept her eyes on Bruce. The old man folded his arms and stared at the ground. He hadn't quit sobbing, and every so often his body would shake violently. He looked like a man who had lost everything, only he didn't seem to have much to lose. The entire house might have belonged to a poor man who tended the cemetery outside, if not for this mysterious black box.

"Anything else in that box?" she questioned. She moved her gaze for just a second to the black box but couldn't make out the answer.

Bruce shook his head.

"Sure is!" Curtis announced, shoving his way past Bruce.

"No, stop!" Bruce lunged at Curtis, who eagerly swung his bat. It collided with Bruce's knee. He screamed and toppled onto the ground, clutching at his leg. As he writhed on the ground, tears flowing, he watched helplessly.

Curtis reached inside the box and extracted a photograph. Waving it back and forth, he grinned, clutching the black-and-white Polaroid print between his grubby fingers.

Bruce lowered his head and clutched at his shirt, more distraught than ever. His crumpled frame on the ground, like an extra piece of furniture. Curtis handed June the image. With the gun still firm in her right hand, she held up the Polaroid with her left and frowned.

It showed a young boy dressed in overalls and a patterned shirt. Next to him, standing beside a thick tree trunk, was an older man. He didn't look too different from Bruce himself, just rougher at the edges. He had a thick beard and a carefree smile. His arms, wrapped around the boy, were traced with scars and patchy bruises, but his expression couldn't have been happier. They were stuck like that forever, a moment in time, just the two of them. Posing next to a thick tree.

June narrowed her eyes and looked down at Bruce.

"Who is this?"

Bruce's body began to shake. He rubbed at his nose. "Nobody."

"Got about eight thousand dollars here, June." Randy waved the money around, half in each hand. "Not bad for a night's work, eh?"

"Shut up," she snapped at him. Her attention shifted back to Bruce. "Who *is* this?"

"My…" Bruce collapsed on the floor again, wailing harder than ever. His tears soaked the carpet, formed a small pool in the fabric. His knees and arms were curled under him at uncomfortable angles. He managed to choke out, "My gr-

grandpa."

The two men retreated and stood closer to June, almost fearfully. She lowered the gun and pocketed the money from Randy. There were no sounds in the house except for this old man, his sniffling and coughing and moaning. She held up the photograph, tried to see the connection between the little boy in the image and this wretched mess.

"Let's get outta here," she snapped at the others, throwing the Polaroid.

It fluttered to the ground inches away from Bruce's face. He lifted his nose from the carpet just a moment to stare up at them. Like a dog who has been kicked and stabbed, left to die, he snatched the Polaroid and stuffed it into his pocket.

"Real freak, huh?" Curtis chuckled, heading for the bedroom door.

Bruce scuffled across the carpet, grabbing June's wrist and bringing the gun to his forehead. She wanted to recoil but held her stance for fear of losing the weapon. His eyes were wild and face pale as he pressed the barrel to his wet skin

"Kill me," he whispered, making eye contact with her. "Please. Shoot me now."

She kicked him in the ribs hard enough that he fell back. The three of them moved toward the doorway. She raised the gun again, this time in self-defense. The other two were gone right away, hurrying out and tripping over each other. But she advanced slowly, almost reluctant to leave.

"I won't," she said after a pause.

"Now!" Bruce screamed, clawing at the walls. "Do it now, you *bitch!* Do it for *him!*"

o o o

And then they were gone. The three of them riding into the night, eight-thousand dollars richer. They would soon read the stories, the truth about Bruce Michaels. As soon as they checked social media, it would all come rushing back. The cripple in the corner of the room. The way his body writhed and his voice begged for death.

It didn't even pay for a year of her mother's insulin. It didn't give her the normal life she'd been craving or the opportunity to settle into a regular job. In the end, Bruce Michaels was just another job for her, a small success. And still, she couldn't shake that image.

June never forgot the night they'd robbed Bruce Michaels. She never forgot the moment when she decided not to end his life right there and then. If only because of what happened next.

16
WILLOW

His hands were the only warm thing around as we crested the bridge. Its elongated arc across the water rose high enough in the air that the winds would chip away at your bones. The drop to our right made me feel nauseous. Not that I felt surprised anymore. Nausea had become a part of my daily life. Pretty soon, the morning sickness would also show up.

Mason grinned at me, his smile petrifyingly white. The sky overhead had turned a deep, endless color. There were no stars visible, no moon. Just a melancholy darkness. It couldn't have been later than ten o'clock, but it didn't matter. Night had gripped our sleepy town in a cold claw and wouldn't let go.

"I can't wait to bring our baby up here," I said, misty-eyed.

Mason leaned over to kiss me on the cheek. "Me either."

Everything felt at ease in the world. The river hundreds of feet below us, moving gently through the foggy valley. That fog, only visible on the river's surface, would soon rise up and cover the whole downtown. I would wake that next morning to its cool embrace and drink in the beautiful sight. A town meant to raise children in. A town that should be called home.

My parents had both taken the news okay. Not as well as Mason's, perhaps. His own were fully on board with the thing. Didn't even ask questions, didn't judge us. Then again, Mason suspected they were just playing it cool to try and reconcile their relationship with him. This certainly seemed the case for Jed. But my own parents, they were brutally honest. When I told my mom about the baby, her first words were, "That wasn't too smart of you, huh?" Her and dad eventually came around. Accepted this new reality. But I was, truly, a little disappointed. I hoped that in time, my mom would support me fully in this part of my life. Would offer help and advice and wisdom. I hoped.

"Look at that, baby." I peered back over my shoulder toward Little Rush, down below us. "It's beautiful."

Mason smiled and turned around to see. We stood there for a moment, gazing at the streets. The lights lining each side of the road, the downtown shops in their waning hours of business. Cars passing this way and that. Some of them climbing the hill, some descending. The whole city abuzz, but not in a big city kind of way. This place, alive, but peaceable. A city asleep but with vivid dreams.

"I don't think I wanna leave," I said out loud for the first time.

Mason wrapped an arm around me and pulled me against him. "Honey, I don't want you to just—"

"I'm not doing it for you," I stopped him. I turned my chin up to gaze into his sparkling eyes. The city lights reflected in their smooth color. I couldn't help but kiss him. When I pulled away, I said, "Maybe I'll change my mind. But I just... I wanna have our baby here. I wanna... try it out. Give Little Rush a chance."

He embraced me fully in a hug and breathed into my ear, "I love you so much."

"I love you even more."

We turned to continue our walk across the bridge. On the other side, there was an old-fashioned Dairy Queen that stayed open late. It had always been a dream of mine to walk across the deep, dark river and then back, an ice cream in hand. Mason started to pull away from me, but I didn't budge. He turned back, confused.

"What's up?"

I held my phone now. One hand gripping the object, the other covering my mouth. The screen brightness hurt my eyes for a second, but I couldn't turn away. I'd gotten a notification and clicked on it absent-mindedly. Somebody had shared an article with me on Twitter, one of the girls from school. But now that I read, the headline gripped me. This idea tore at my reality. When I shifted the phone so Mason could read it, he had a completely different reaction.

"Oh my god." His own eyes were as wide as mine. He ran a hand through his hair, messing it up, and then looked back to me. "Hudson... Does Hudson know?"

"Let's head back," I said at once, stuffing the phone in my pocket and starting off at a brisk walk the way we'd come.

Mason hurried alongside me, muttering to himself. "No... no, no, no... Oh my god, Hudson..."

I reached for his hand, but he pulled away, chewing on his nails in distress.

"Babe, it'll be okay," I assured him. "I—"

"No, it's not." He met my gaze with a serious expression. With one tiny movement, he shook his head. "He can't handle this. He'll..."

The sentence died off, but I knew what he meant now.

He'd almost done it when his parents were fighting. I still remembered those texts viscerally. And this... this could push him too far.

Little Rush had never been a place where time moved fast. One of the best parts about life in those sleepy streets, really. High school dragged. The summer, even, took forever. But I had a feeling —as we raced across the bridge and back to the town we'd almost left— that things were about to change. This city, with the pause button forever stuck, had begun to fast forward. We were stuck, for now, in a place of passing moments.

PART 4

A PLACE OF PROFOUND UNCERTAINTY

1
BRUCE

I'd never been in a truck so fast, felt wind smack me across the face quite like that. An exuberant, fourteen-year-old with an exuberant smile. I got the window seat, something that rarely happened with the three of us, and seized the chance. As the speedometer rose, I stuck my head farther out the window. The wind threatened to tear out my eyeballs, it rushed so hard. But I kept them open. Watery marbles that drank in every moment.

Danny drove, like usual, only this time he had a death wish. I would say so, anyway. He fixated on those blurring yellow lines, biting his upper lip. His knuckles were white against the gray steering wheel. The engine thunderous, all around us. The truck seats vibrating, out of control. He pushed harder and harder on the gas. Pushed it to a breaking point.

"Let's fucking go!" yelled Jon, the boy in the middle. His long, straw-colored hair flew around like a tornado, sticking out from the back of his head. But Jon didn't care, he just smacked me in the shoulder and hollered again. "Yessir, floor that motherfucker!"

Danny, a seventeen-year-old, had him beat in age by a year, but not by excitement. Jon became a regular cheerleader anytime Danny did something cool. Like the time when he smacked a hot bikini girl's ass just as she climbed out of the public swimming pool, still dripping wet. I'd watched in amazement. That'd been my second day hanging out with them, and already Danny left me dumbfounded.

"Gettin' there," Danny growled, chewing as he did so. Danny had a nasty habit of taking a dip right before he did something like this. He also took it other times, but it caught my attention most in situations that were dangerous.

I leaned back into the soft, foam seat and glimpsed at the speedometer. The arrow moved farther across the dashboard than I'd ever imagined. Almost all the way now. His truck speedometer went up to 110, and we were inching closer. I held my breath as the speed ramped up, afraid to look forward now. All of a sudden, I wished Jon had taken the window seat and I could hide in between them.

"This is so bad, dude!" Jon yelled, his voice barely audible over the shrill engine. That noise did *not* sound okay, but Jon covered it with a wild, hooting laughter. He thumped me on the back again. Apparently, neither of them noticed my fear.

I forced myself to stare wide-eyed at the road. The lines were moving so fast, they became impossible to watch. It made me sick. Out the side window, fields of soybeans whooshed by so quickly that I didn't wanna look there either. Instead, I planted my gaze on the hood of the truck. It rattled and shook with the force of Danny's driving, but at least it didn't scare me.

"Hundred!" Danny hooted, smacking the dashboard with a palm. "Oh, baby!"

My eyes wandered to the rearview window. The highway stretching out behind us, endless, going on for miles and miles. How long had it been since leaving Little Rush? How many miles were already back there? I only hoped that on the way home, Danny wouldn't be so reckless.

Any second, I expected a cop car to peel out from one of the side roads. Lights flashing, horn blaring, probably sirens too. But it never did. I almost wished for it. At least then, we'd have to stop. Or maybe not. Danny said he'd escaped the cops before. Whether this was truthful or not, I believed him.

"Hundred-ten!" Jon bounced up and down in his street, head-banging to some song nobody else could hear. He pumped a fist in the air, actually punching the ceiling a few times. "That's it, dude, that's the stuff!"

Indeed, the speedometer had reached its max point. Danny let the truck glide to a slower speed. He didn't push on the brake at all, simply removed his foot from the gas. I took a deep breath, leaned into the cushioned seat. I focused on the ceiling now, frayed and browned from cigarettes. As the truck slowed and we returned to normal speeds, the wind rushing through the cab also slowed. I could once again smell smoke, that stench ever-clinging to the inside of Danny's truck. I didn't hate it. It felt kind of nice.

"You want one, kiddo?" Danny asked.

I turned to him, saw a cigarette extended toward me. His eyes, completely off the road by this point, traced the lines of my face. He chuckled and tossed it into my lap.

"Give'm a light, Jon-boy."

Jon took the cigarette from me and touched the end of it with a lighter he'd extracted from a pocket. Then he handed it back and lit one for himself. I tried to copy his actions, ended up coughing the first few attempts. But after a while, I got the hang of it. By the time we were en route back to Little Rush, a few hours later, I thought of myself as a bonafide expert.

Still no cop lights in the rearview mirror. I watched for them the rest of that day. And none ever showed up. I breathed a deep, woodsy sigh of relief as we passed by the "Welcome to Little Rush" sign. Wondered if my grandpa would smell it on me, these nicotine devils. Wondered if he'd even care.

Something about that memory always stuck with me. All those years later, returning to Little Rush, I couldn't shake it from my mind. Of all the people from that summer, only my grandpa was more vivid in memory than Danny. I thought of the older boy as a wild stallion. That redneck, truck-driving, hard-skinned son of a bitch.

Danny took up painting houses the next summer, I heard. From a mutual friend, I found out Jon and him got into a fistfight, so Danny up and left. To Florida. The most exciting, most daring man I'd ever known. Relegated to the exterior wall of someone else's home.

I thought back on that memory with fond emotions. The danger, the rush of blood, the adrenaline, the truck and cigarettes. All of it. But most of all him.

Danny, with his new profession, became a heavy drinker. Spent all his money on it. Some say he got himself in a bar fight, shot right between the eyes with a 22. Others say he washed up on the beach one isolated morning, caught in a rip tide.

I never knew what to believe. Only that I missed him. That I wished we could speak again, one last time.

Something about that truck ride always stuck with me. Just couldn't quite pin it down.

2
JED

When the news flickered across my Facebook feed, I didn't believe it at first. The guy who'd shared it — an old school friend who still lived downtown— had a reputation for sharing fake news. The local gossip group, which I'd joined for a source of grassroots local news, picked up the story and ran with it. Somebody located the original TMZ article and shared that, too.

At that point, I started to worry. I glanced up from my phone to Lucy, who lay on the couch underneath the open windows. All the lights were off in the house around us, save for the kitchen light and the sitting room lamp. This was her typical setup for late-night reading, while I sat in a recliner messing with my phone or watching TV. She held a Kindle in one hand, an oatmeal cream pie in the other, oblivious to the breaking news. For the moment, I didn't disturb her. I kept digging, my heart sinking deeper with every subsequent sentence.

Not Bruce. Not now. The man who'd given me advice about Mason... who'd brought with him a sizable economic boom, at least for a few weeks. This hallowed actor, this star of my childhood... Not Bruce. It couldn't be true. TMZ had been wrong about this stuff before. Surely they were again.

The sitting room lights felt dimmer than usual on that night. Outside, a hollow night had settled on the neighborhood. Mason had been gone a while, and who knew how long he might stay out. If he'd even come home. Not that I cared. The worst that could happen? You might say it already had. Willow, that poor girl, pregnant. I'd seen it in her eyes when they told me. She hadn't expected this. And the way she looked at Mason, such hope and dedication in her expression... I hope they made it. I really did. She was probably too good for him in a lot of ways.

I flicked on the television and turned to the local news channel, if only to check. Had they heard yet? Had they run anything on it? But to my dismay, or perhaps relief, they were talking about the weather. With this in mind, I settled back in my chair and clicked on the TMZ article. Time, at least, hadn't run out. I still had time to make my own conclusions. To think.

Lucy yawned from the couch, covering her mouth. "When's Mason gonna be back?" She then lowered the Kindle and focused on me.

"Dunno."

"You alright?" she sat up a little, like doing a crunch.

I granted her a weary, half-smile and nodded. "Just reading an article."

"Oh, yeah? Anything interesting?"

I shrugged, focusing again on the column of words against a petrified white background. "Dunno yet."

The allegations were pretty damning, and I could see why the locals had snatched it up so quickly. The idea that Bruce Michaels had come to Little Rush was wild enough. That he had done so running from a potential scandal made it all the more compelling. To my surprise, though, the TMZ article hinted at even more.

Madeline Suso. That girl's name, whoever she was, popped up multiple times throughout the short read. It couldn't have been more than five paragraphs, just a blip on the radar that promised a bigger storm ahead. And yet, by the end of it, she'd become as engraved in my brain as Bruce Michael himself. They even had a picture of her from about fifteen years ago, some high school in Illinois. A skinny, blonde girl, huge smile across her youthful features. But what really mattered, in this instance, was her age. Sixteen years old. Younger than my own son.

"Damn." I brushed a hand through my hair, blowing a raspberry. "There's no way..."

"What is it?" Lucy perked up, sitting straight on the couch now. Her eyes locked on me, as if they'd never really left. "Is something wrong?"

I groaned and said simply, "Check Facebook. I'm sure it's somewhere on your feed."

As Lucy reached for her phone and then navigated to the app, I read the article a second time. Made sure of all the key points. She'd accused Bruce of sexually assaulting her at a party about fifteen years ago. He was in Illinois to film a movie. She said they'd both been drunk, and she wasn't strong enough to resist. Something along those lines. Reading it again, my heart thumped painfully against my chest cavity. They used the word "rape" twice, placed selectively in the paragraphs. When I scrolled to the top of the page, I saw an image of Bruce from not long ago, right before he announced his move, in fact. A handsome, well-groomed man. A sly grin on his face, wearing sunglasses and slicked-back hair. The actor I'd grown up adoring, wanted to be like in many ways. And yet, if this was all true...

"What a... what a..." Lucy gaped at me, letting her phone drop beside her on the couch. It lay there, the screen dark now. I stared at it, if only to avoid her. "That's awful. I never thought he..."

"If it's true."

"Babe..." She shook her head and watched me closely. "Babe, that poor girl... There's no way it's a lie. You know that, right?"

I nodded, slowly, gripping the fabric of my armrests like it alone could save my life. "I do." And it was true. I did know. Bruce Michaels. A Hollywood legend. A monster.

At that moment, the front door flew open, and I heard footsteps on the kitchen floor. Mason dashed into the sitting room, panting like he'd just run a quarter-mile sprint. I hadn't even heard the car pull in or seen the headlights outside. Hadn't heard him approach the house.

Our eyes met, and I knew that he'd already seen it. Maybe the news, so visceral and sudden, is what caused him to come running home. I imagined him taking off at a moment's notice from whatever date they'd been on. Speeding toward the house, eager to talk. With me. If not for the present circumstances, I might have smiled. But happiness didn't feel right, not tonight, not here.

"Dad... Did you see?" he asked between breaths, both hands on his knees. His shoulders shook, but from effort or shock I didn't know.

"Yeah." I turned to Lucy, who watched him with a hint of confusion. As sure as she'd been that the awful story was true, I felt equally certain she didn't understand the magnitude. For me and for Mason. "I'm sorry, man. It's... it's just terrible."

Mason nodded, arms wrapped around his midsection. "Our favorite actor. It's just..."

"I know what you mean." The way he said "our favorite" killed me. I stood from my chair and moved toward him. He didn't react, didn't look up from the carpet, so I hesitated. "Even bad people can be good at their jobs."

"You think he's a bad person?" He lifted his chin now, and I saw a glimmer in his eyes, a solitary tear. Such longing in that expression, the slight quiver of his eyelashes. Desperate for an answer. A firm answer.

"I have no idea." I crossed my arms now, noticed how similar we looked. Myself balding, a lot less impressive physically. But for the first time in a long time, he again looked like a kid who needed help. Just a kid, questioning everything. I thought about telling him that Bruce had met with me, given me crucial advice. I wanted to mention how Henry described Hudson, the positive changes since he spent more time over there. How Bruce had changed that young man's life. But I held my tongue, if only because I didn't want to confuse him even more. "I don't know if we'll ever, truly, understand."

"I need to..." Mason took a deep breath. Another tear threatened to fall, but he wiped it away with a subtle movement. Then, in a movement so fast and fierce I almost toppled over, he sprang forward and embraced with me a hug. His muscular arms, tight against my back, clinging for dear life. I just had time to pat his shoulder before he pulled away. "I need to go."

I frowned and cocked my head. From behind me, Lucy spoke up. "You just got here, baby."

"I need to talk to Hudson." He scuffed at the carpet with his foot, avoiding both our curious expressions. "I'm just worried. If anything's wrong, I'll call you, okay? Be back later."

Then he ran out of the house, just as quickly as he'd come. I took a few steps toward the door, but it had already shut. Standing with my bare feet on the carpet, I watched, helpless, as he went. From that position, I saw the headlights pop on and heard the engine rumble. Then he pulled out onto the road, and two tiny red dots vanished into the distance. His convertible, the roof down, speeding away on a mission I didn't understand.

"You okay?"

I felt Lucy's hand on my shoulder. When I turned, she wore a pitying smile and threw both arms around my neck. "I know how much he means to you."

"Mason? Or... the actor?" I shuddered. The way I didn't

even want to utter his name. To think about him, what he'd meant to me. Is this what it felt like in those moments before a cult burns to the ground, when the followers realize they're wrong? The man leading them, no longer a god. Mortal after all. Except... no. Bruce Michaels hadn't become mortal. He was worse.

"Both, baby." Lucy hugged me, her embrace warm and inviting. Her lips brushed my cheek before her bony chin settled in the crook of my neck. "It's gonna be okay," she whispered, the words sweet on her tongue like honey. "Life goes on."

My phone buzzed against the table next to my recliner. I turned to look as it vibrated against the wood. It bounced around, this way and that, illuminated screen. Caller ID confirmed my fears. It was Mason.

3
HUDSON

I barely even felt them. That flat, stale liquid bubbling down my throat and to my stomach. Those four beers were probably the least I'd ever enjoyed alcohol. Usually, I could dive right into the drinking, but that night I struggled to get started.

When I saw the headline, I... well, it was impossible to describe that feeling. I should've felt anger and disgust. I should've been depressed, and I knew all of that. But instead, it was like an electrical wire bouncing around, shooting sparks. A lightning bolt hit me. Like some stirring of guitars, building louder and louder, I felt it growing in me. As I read through the article, as the words passed across my fuzzy vision, I knew what came next.

Earlier that day, I'd been sitting at the kitchen table downstairs. My father bustled around, throwing together a sandwich and fitting the meal into a plastic bag. He looked at me, and I raised an eyebrow, but he didn't respond. For another few minutes, he hurried around, cursing under his breath. Ran the sink over his outstretched hand. Then he finally straightened up and smoothed his hair with a wet palm.

"Goin' to work," Dad murmured, hand on the doorknob. He shrugged at me, a kind of "what can you do." Then he opened the door and started out.

"I love you."

I'd blurted those words out of nowhere. I didn't expect to say them. But I did. I might've thought he didn't hear if not for the slight stutter in his footsteps. Just as he closed the front door behind him, leaving me alone in the kitchen, he stumbled. A stiffness in his neck. No, he'd definitely heard me. And he chose to ignore it.

This scene played into my decision. Once the fourth beer had emptied inside me and I finished reading the article, I had no doubt.

It had been weeks since I'd talked to Mason. Every once in a while, I thought about him. I even chatted with Willow from time to time, but she had other things to worry about. A baby on the way. School coming up in a matter of weeks, no longer months. I couldn't even imagine her stress, so I tried not to impose too much. Her and Mason, they had their own life now. Something far apart from me. I'd learn to live with that.

I tried getting to know my father better, tried opening up. He never really listened. His eyes were usually glued to the television screen, baseball ever-present in our house during those July evenings. Even though I needed him more than ever, no miracle happened. He didn't suddenly become more present. If anything, he distanced further. Mom was around, but busy. I didn't blame her. These two, also, had a life apart from me. Working, farming, surviving in Little Rush. I didn't have anything to do with that.

So I fell even deeper into Bruce Michaels. The strange relationship we had. I spent a few evenings there every week, sometimes five or six. We talked, we had beers, even smoked occasionally. It was the kind of relationship I longed for. An older, wiser man who had been everywhere, done everything. He had so many stories to tell. Some of them took place right here in Little Rush.

I loved hearing about how the city used to be, decades before I was born. I admired the way he painted that setting, the descriptions he used. Much different than my father. He understood it on a deeper level than I ever had. I couldn't get enough of his life. From Little Rush to LA, all around the globe, so many women. Every bit of it, I savored.

Maybe that's why the breaking news hit me how it did. The fact that Bruce Michael could be so... such a bad person. The fact that he could hide it from me. I should've known. Should've never trusted him. Just another dirty celeb. Another worthless piece of shit that I devoted myself to. To think, at one point, I had given up on him. Then gone back. Another mistake.

I moved with abandon around the house. Throwing on shoes, a shirt, grabbing my keys and wallet. My mom, in the living room, didn't even notice when I left. Her eyes were fixed on the television screen. Outside, the sky had grown pitch black. I met it with a snarl and determination. The deadest of nights.

I wondered how long it had been since I read the news. How long I'd sat in my bed, thinking, wondering. Starting to understand what I needed to do.

Once I'd situated myself in the truck outside and started the engine, I took a moment to breath. To decide. There were a few options.

I knew what everybody would expect. They'd expect me to kill myself. And I couldn't blame them. It did have a nice irony to it. Maybe it was a fitting response to Bruce and what he'd done to me. All the lies.

I leaned my forehead against the steering wheel and took deeper breaths, like I was trying to suck in the truck itself. I must have been in that position for twenty minutes at least. The world didn't look quite right anymore. I could feel it coming on, an intense burning. I had to find more alcohol, for sure. But I also had to drive.

Not to the bridge. I didn't want to kill myself. I didn't want Bruce to have that much control. If I let this push me over the edge, then I would've lost, and that's not what I wanted. At least not yet.

So I pushed my foot against the pedal and maneuvered my way down the gravel driveway. There were two options. There always had been.

I could run away. I could leave Little Rush forever and create a new life somewhere else. With people who needed me and wanted me. Maybe find a girlfriend somewhere out there. A place with better weather and better people. A place without Bruce Michaels, without Mason and my family. I wanted everything that place had to offer. I knew I could find it.

Little Rush held nothing for me anymore. But out there... somewhere, I'd find what I needed. A place with sunshine that didn't burn your skin and a place with rivers that weren't so cold. I could start over. I could be who and what I wanted. I just had to make it there. So I would drive, non-stop, through a full tank.

At the end of my driveway, I turned right on the country road and made my way toward the nearest gas station. I would fill up there, get some food. Maybe steal some beer. I just had to make it somewhere. That's all I needed.

As the sky emptied and the clouds lost their shape, I started to think of an alternate ending. Something even more beautiful. A different kind of somewhere. The trees were hazy, and the cornfields blurred, just a mesh of colors that meant nothing. But downtown Little Rush, with the brilliant lights and parallel streets and hum of peaceful life...

I could drive off the hilltop. I could plummet toward that world, crash somewhere in the trees, maybe even into a building. A unique suicide. The ending I'd dreamed of.

With each mile of road that flew under my tires, I knew my

future less and less. I started to wonder how it would go, which direction the wheel might turn. If I even controlled it.

My phone lit up, and I glanced down, easing up on the gas. Mason's caller ID. I didn't answer. It went to voicemail, and I didn't listen to whatever message he left.

I don't want that to be the last thing I hear, I told myself. *I don't wanna talk to him.*

o o o

The lights were everywhere, blinding me. My head started to ache from all the senses. The sky brilliantly dark one moment and then flashing with headlights the next. Raindrops beating against my windshield as the stereo bass pounded a rock song.

I started yelling, and I don't know when I stopped. The world a blur, but I navigated the mess. I always could. The key was to lock onto certain objects. Like a tree or a stop sign, just focus on the car's relation to them. I managed by speeding through gray areas and pumping on the brakes from time to time.

Swaying, tears gliding down the windshield and my own cheeks, I found the gas station. Only then did I stop screaming.

4
JED

Those minutes felt like hours, every possibility weighing on me. I thought so intently on any warning signs I could've missed. Situations where I should've helped. But the truth was, I didn't know a thing about suicide prevention. I didn't know what teenagers like Hudson went through. And I didn't know if I held the blame or not.

At the end of the day, I would feel grief. If he was truly gone. But it would be nothing compared to what Henry went through, or his wife, or even Mason. It was all just too much for me. Enough to overheat my brain.

"Does it matter which flavor I brew?"

I could hear Lucy moving around, opening cabinets, rummaging in the drawers. She cursed under her breath as something fell to the floor, a thud on the tiles. She flitted from one side of the kitchen to the other, restless. In contrast, I was motionless, staring out the large window at our driveway.

"Umm... don't think so."

The neighborhood had fallen asleep for the most part. There were a few houses where pale, blue light still flickered in the main room, the ripples of a television broadcasting through curtains. I observed the whole street, particularly the homes I knew well. Remembering Carl from just across the street. He'd lost his own son two years ago in a summer camp accident. At the time, I hadn't been able to comprehend that feeling, that gut-wrenching and all-consuming agony. I realized, now, that I still couldn't. Not even for Henry's boy.

"How much do you think we'll need?" Lucy asked me, her voice calm and focused. She continued work at the Keurig. Only last month we'd purchased this newer version, the kind that could brew a whole pot instead of one serving at a time. Thank god we had.

"Dunno." I folded my arms. Thinking I should turn from the window to help my incredible wife or at least offer support. But I didn't. "Henry, Laurie, maybe Willow? Who else is there?"

At this point, I did turn from the outside, if only to gauge her expression. Lucy had paused to stare at me, frowning. We both knew the answer to that question. In certain relationships, if you fall off the radar, other people will get together late at night, drink themselves sick with coffee, and pool every resource to find you again. Hudson, the poor kid, didn't have many to do that for him.

"He'll be okay, though," I said, scratching at my head. I moved across the kitchen toward her and leaned on the counter, elbows flat against the cool surface. I stretched my back cat-like and groaned. "Long night ahead of us. I'll have to cancel a meeting tomorrow."

Lucy didn't say anything. She nodded, moving her lips slightly, and then returned to the Keurig. With the lid closed and the machine gurgling, she walked over. We stood on opposite sides of the counter, watching each other. Without a word, Lucy reached out and ruffled my hair, sighing.

"Did Henry say when he'll be here?"

I shook my head. "No. Just soon."

I'd called him right after getting off the phone with Mason. Henry, his voice weary and on the edge of sleep, answered with a yawn and that familiar farmer-drawl.

"Henry here. Who'm I talking to?"

"It's Jed." I hadn't moved from the spot when Mason hung up. Still sitting in my chair, phone in hand, I leaned forward so far that my forehead almost touched my knees. Curled up like a man experiencing stomach cramps for the first time.

"Oh, hey." Henry chuckled over the phone. "Didn't expect t'hear from ya. Everything alright?"

"Is Hudson home?" I asked, getting straight to the point.

"Hmmm. Just got back from the plant. Hold up, I'll ask Laurie."

Power plant, he meant. Must've been another long shift. He moved away from the phone, left it on the counter or something. I could hear him faintly. While they conversed in the background, I groaned, hand to my temple, and asked Lucy if she could get the Keurig started. Full pot, I told her. There'd be people here soon enough.

Henry returned at last, yelled into the phone across whatever room he'd left it in. "Left 'bout twenty minutes ago. Why? You need 'im?"

"You and Laurie need to get over here," I told him. I rarely ever spoke to Henry with so much command. He was bigger, stronger, rougher. The kind of guy who intimidated scrawny businessmen like me, not the other way around. "It's about Hudson. Just... trust me here."

"Alright, Jed," Henry spoke into the phone directly now, his voice wavering a little, "but can ya let me in the loop?"

"Just worried about him. Something's happened. You... just get over here. And check Facebook. It's about the actor."

Henry's reaction made me think back on my own, how stupid it had been. Compared to something like that, some piece of celebrity gossip, Hudson took center stage. I shouldn't have been surprised that a Hollywood actor turned out to be a scumbag. It didn't matter right now. Not with Hudson gone, somewhere out in the darkness, alone and unstable.

They had some system at the house in case he came back. Henry told me in the past about a security system that gave him phone alerts whenever somebody came to the door. I assumed they would use that to watch out for Hudson, since the both of them would be here at my house. I didn't think any of us expected him to go home. Maybe ever again.

That's what Mason had implied, anyway, on the first phone call. When it'd buzzed, bouncing around on the side table, I had let go of Lucy and jumped for it. One swift movement of my thumb, and then I took a seat in that recliner. Held the device to my ear and spoke into it, shaking. I knew from the first second, even before the caller ID, that it was Mason. That something had happened.

"He didn't answer my call," Mason said. I could hear his breathing grow more frantic as he drove. The engine roared so loud he must've been speeding, and by more than a little. "Dad, Hudson won't answer his phone."

"It's okay, son. It's okay. We're gonna—"

"No, Dad..." Mason took a deep breath to calm himself. "I'm... I'm scared."

I'd glanced across the sitting room at Lucy, who waited in the doorway, eyebrows raised. She mouthed, "What's going on?" but I just shrugged and shook my head. Then I spoke into the phone, "What do you mean, Mason?"

"Bruce. Hudson adored him. They were kinda close. And I'm just scared he'll be... This is the kind of thing that could send him over the edge." His words were broken at this point, spiderweb fractures.

"What exactly do you mean?" It started to dawn on me then, and my eyes locked with Lucy. She must have seen it. A deeper understanding we shared.

"Dad, I think he could kill himself."

After all the phone calls, after all the coffee brewing, we set five cups on the table and waited. Together, Lucy and I stared out the kitchen window, holding hands with loose fingers. I expected her to tear up or something, but she remained stoic. Expressionless, even. No, not that. Just determined.

I'd already drained one cup by the time his truck drowned our house with the pale glow of headlights. I stood from the table right away and rushed to the door. Lucy beside me, arm around my waist. The familiar grip that I'd relied on so many times for so much. I thought that I should thank her for the coffee, that I should kiss her hard and never break away, but I didn't. Because when Henry climbed out of the truck from the passenger's side, there were tears streaming down his cheeks. And Henry never rode shotgun. And Henry never cried.

I wanted to remember, in that instant, what I'd done when Carl had told me about their kid. What the funeral had been like. A tragic accident. Nobody to blame.

I could see in his watery eyes, as Henry lumbered toward me, that he blamed himself. How he put the pieces together, I'll never know, but he understood from the news about Bruce Michaels that his own son was in grave danger.

"Henry..."

Lucy moved ahead of me and embraced him, then threw one arm around Laurie. The three of them, hugging each other in the shadow of my front porch. I couldn't move. Couldn't even speak. I just watched in awe, dreading every moment that the phone call would come. That Mason would ring, or worse yet... the police.

The body. Would they ever find the body?

I stuck out my hand as Henry approached me. He ignored it, and thank god he did. The wide man threw his enormous arms around me and squeezed tight. I smacked his back, pounding sympathy into his spine. He wept on my shoulder, that shaggy beard scratching against my cheek.

And in his despair, Henry mumbled the words I'd been dreading. The thought that crossed every person's mind when someone they love could be lost.

"I saw it in 'im," he said between heaving sobs, the words cutting me like physical pain. "Them last few weeks... I knew he didn't look good. Just... not all here."

"Henry, it's gonna be okay. We're gonna—"

He pulled away to stare into my eyes. His own features so accentuated by the shadows that he could've passed for the devil himself. A terrified, blubbering devil.

"He told me he loved me this mornin'. Right when I left for the plant." Henry shook his head violently, as if expelling some terrible memory. "I... I just walked away."

"Mason's looking," Lucy assured him, placing a hand on his shoulder. I could see Laurie behind her, leaning against our outside table, staring into the distance. Lost in her own way.

"But what if...?" Henry hesitated. "What if he's already gone?"

I realized, in that moment, that we would all be guilty if Hudson was lost. To some degree, we'd all let him down. Over and over again.

5
HUDSON

Parked next to the gas pump, my headlights reflecting on the glass door of the Circle K, I turned my music up as loud as possible. The slashing guitars and messy drums threatened to tear the roof off my truck. Every person who strolled by raised an eyebrow, but I stared at them with cold, dead eyes. They would all turn away, nobody bothering to ask questions. I sort of hoped they would. Hoped somebody would stop me from the next part.

If even one person had asked, I would've turned back. If just one.

I'd been lucky enough to find a partially empty twelve-pack of beers in my back seat. There were five cans on my floorboard now, all of them dry to the bone. That made nine total beers, enough to get me pretty fucked up. Just enough liquid courage to do this.

I shut off the engine and felt a void in my brain where the music had been. It took me a few minutes, but I filled up my tank. Then I moved toward those glass doors. Rain sprinkled my face like a pleasant memory. There were ten people around, a few of them smoking in a group nearby. They were situated just under the ledge of the Circle K, rain falling not more than a foot from their smoldering tips. I desperately wanted a cigarette but didn't have the courage to ask. I had more pressing business to take care of.

I entered the gas station with my head bowed. In a drunken stupor, I became very aware of how my feet worked and of my appearance. I probably just looked sleepy, but then again, gas stations were probably used to inebriated customers. It took me a few minutes to locate the vodka stash. Tucked into one aisle, not far from the beer. I would've preferred a twelve-pack, but those were harder to steal and didn't get me as drunk.

Two bottles of vodka. That's all I had to grab.

I placed my hands on them, gently grasped the plastic. I couldn't even read the labels, but it didn't matter. They'd be fine. I couldn't feel my mouth anyway. The bottles felt comfortable in each hand. I closed my eyes to focus, regain a bit of strength. I'd almost made it. Once I had these, I just had to drive. Just had to escape.

I chanced a look at the cashier. It was a young, pretty girl, not older than twenty-three. Blonde hair, a casual expression. Only she frowned in my direction, eyebrows furrowed. Did she know what I planned? Would she call the cops when I left? I mean, if she did, they'd definitely arrest me. My blood-alcohol content had to be off the charts. If I got lucky, I'd pass out behind the wheel. They'd find my coma-induced body in a ditch of rainwater and blood.

I just had to go for it.

"Fuck it," I muttered. Then I grabbed the bottles and took off sprinting, stumbling.

Whether or not somebody chased, whether she even cared, I would never know. I pounded against the pavement, nearly running into a parked car. I reached my truck, out of breath, cackling wildly, and threw myself into the driver's seat. The vodka bottles sloshed on the passenger's seat. Without second thought, I dug my key into the ignition and turned. Then I raced away, distancing myself from that Circle K so fast it almost scared me. I did run over the curb on the way out, but whatever.

"Fuck you, rednecks!" I screamed again, smashing a fist into the steering wheel, hysterically happy. I thought it was a line from a movie, maybe even something Bruce had yelled once. Not that it mattered to me either way.

o o o

About a mile from the Circle K, I pulled over on the side of the road just for a moment. I unscrewed the lid of one bottle and chugged for a solid five seconds. The putrid, burning sensation torched my throat, and I almost threw up right away. I couldn't taste much, but it sent shockwaves through my body. I shivered, felt an ugly warmth in my stomach, and coughed for a while, beating on the steering wheel.

The music thundered so loud around me that I couldn't hear a single thing. Car Seat Headrest cutting through fog, right into my brain. The irony wasn't lost on me. That particular song, droning on with thumping instruments and wild vocals, spoke about drunk driving. And yet here I was, hoping for a drunken crash.

"Awful..." I said to myself out loud, grinning. "Awful people, aren't we?"

Bruce Michaels, of course, didn't answer, because he was probably getting drunk himself in that stupid house across town. I wanted to see him. Wanted to cuss him out, maybe punch him, but I didn't want to drive that way.

There were only two options. I could head straight, get away from Little Rush, try to find a better place. I could avoid all of this. Drink and drive and fly forever. With this in mind, I pulled back onto the road and pushed hard on the gas.

The speedometer became so blurry that I couldn't tell how fast or slow I might be going. The numbers were nothing, the hands moving clockwise now invisible. I couldn't see a thing, just shapes, just shadows, colors. An aesthetic palette of night. My eyes squinted, focusing on the road. I couldn't be sure where I was headed now.

Away from Little Rush? Or careening toward the hill, a drop-off that would kill me? Might I fly down, into the Ohio River Valley, and meet my end there?

I'd been born here. It only made sense.

"If you're gonna kill me, do it now!" I screamed over all the music, over all my thoughts. Straight on. Straight on forever. "Do it now! Fucking kill me!"

Straight. The ground bumping underneath me. Lights swirling by. The moon somewhere overhead, looking on. Trees on either side were an invitation. How easy would it be to veer off that way and split myself open on a trunk?

The yellow lines were shaky, wobbling. Headlights in the distance zoomed closer, passing by, their own lives and worries. Their own families. How bad would it feel if I killed someone? Someone loved and cared for? What would I do if I trashed their car, ended *their* life, but survived without a scratch?

I already knew the answer. I'd simply head for downtown and drive off the road. Fly over the edge, into those beautiful city lights. The ending I deserved. The great descent.

A good place to die, I thought. *Maybe the best.*

6
WILLOW

"I'm going to Hudson's," Mason had explained as he dropped me off.

"Call me once you find out what's going on, okay?"

He nodded. "I will. Love you."

Standing on the sidewalk, hands in my pockets, I said, "Love you too." I wanted to push back, demand to go with him, but hesitated. And in that moment of hesitation, he roared away in his convertible.

Now I stood in front of the mirror, hands on my stomach, staring at my reflection. It was probably a trick of the mind. Well, that's exactly what it was, because I knew that I couldn't be showing already. It had only been a couple weeks since the fair. It's not like my stomach could change in that time. And I still went to the gym a few times a week. The doctor said to be "as physically active as you were before." So I did try.

In front of me, the toothpaste and brush rested on the laminate countertop. The faucet dripped, an annoying quirk that we couldn't fix. Watching it would drive me crazy after a while. I'd been exhausted all day, and now, finally, I could lay down. Darkness had fallen about an hour ago, and still no update from Mason. I could only assume him and Hudson were now deep in conversation. I'd have to catch up with them both in the morning.

The bathroom light flicked off above me, rousing me from daydreams. Five seconds later, it popped on again. It'd been doing that for a few days now. Each time, I thought to myself, Shit, he didn't pay the electric bill, but then the darkness fled as the lightbulb came on. Dad had forgotten bills in the past or lost them altogether. I wouldn't have been surprised.

He'd been super anxious ever since I told him. Like, driving me up the walls. Each morning asking if I felt alright, if I needed money for lunch, what groceries did I want that week. He kept patting me on the back as he passed. Other times, he would grin sheepishly whenever we made eye contact. I didn't know what to make of it. He had this buzz around him, maybe excitement.

My dad's attitude had completely changed since our first conversation, where he'd acted bitter and downcast. That next morning, with a radiant smile, he made pancakes for the two of us, a skillset I didn't know he possessed. Over the empty plates coated in syrup, we had a long talk. I didn't usually sit at our table for that long. When he asked what I would do now, my future plans, I tried to answer honestly.

"I'm thinking about staying," I admitted, lowering my eyes to the maple ocean. "I mean, in Little Rush."

"And school?" He took a sip of water from a coffee mug with the side chipped.

"Maybe I'll do some more online college," I said, shrugging. "I don't know, Dad. I didn't plan on this either, okay? And Mason... he wants to stay for his dad's business."

"They do got a mean pizza joint," Dad said, winking at me. When my expression didn't change and I didn't smile even a little, he went on. "You do what you want, okay? College? That'll be around. Who says..." He fell into a coughing fit, holding up a hand to pause the conversation. When it subsided, he took a gulp of water and resumed. "Who says you need it? You're a tough, smart young woman." He made a movement like tipping an imaginary cap at me. "Can't take none of the credit. That's all your momma."

I couldn't help but grin and reach for my own cup. We only had three glasses, all from a McDonald's promotion years ago. This one, the only option without smudges or little cracks, might've been the nicest kitchen-item my dad owned. And he always let me use it for meals. Insisted.

"I think I'm starting to get this town," I told him when I set the drink down. "Is that... bad?"

"No, sweetheart. It's a real good place to be." He leaned back in his chair and observed me with a wistful, curious twinkle. "After all, your old man didn't stick around for the..." He chewed on the inside of his lip, thinking of the appropriate phrase. "Career opportunities," he concluded with a flourish of his hand. I was reminded of his personality from years ago, before the divorce. An extremely insightful man

"Oh, yeah? You just loved this place too much to leave?" I teased him, propping my elbows on the table.

He shook his head and pulled a cigarette pack from the pocket of his rugged jeans. "You stick around for the people you love," he said, watching my expression. Dad lit the end of his cigarette deftly and inhaled. As the smoke trickled from his nostrils, he offered me one from across the table. "And it works out in the end."

Now preparing for bed, days later, I studied my own reflection in the mirror. I reached into the pocket of my sweatpants and pulled out the cigarette. I'd been carrying it with me ever since, refusing to smoke it. I didn't even smoke now, since the pregnancy overrode my nicotine addiction, but I wanted to keep the gift anyway.

If my dad could make a McDonald's glass something special, then I could do the same with a cigarette.

Maybe by staying here, I was letting other things go. I was settling for an average life. But that was okay. My dad had done the same with me. And I would do it with this new baby. In the end, like he said, it's not the place that makes you stay, it's the people. I just couldn't let go of all these people, not yet.

Just as I opened the door to leave, my phone buzzed against my thigh. I pulled it out and saw Mason's name. A shockwave tore through me. I'd almost forgotten about this situation, since Mason dropped me off after our trek on the bridge.

Answering, I started across the hallway. Dad glanced at me from the living room, and I mouthed "Goodnight" to him. Then I hurried into my bedroom and closed the door behind.

"Mason?" I spoke into the phone. "Is everything okay?"

"It's Hudson," he said. "He's not home, and he won't answer my calls."

I sat on the edge of my bed, and all thoughts of sleep were instantly gone. Things hadn't gone as planned, then. I'd been praying that Hudson would just get drunk at his house, but now I seriously worried. Sure, Bruce Michaels meant nothing to me. But to Hudson... I should've expected this. The worst.

And now, I had no doubt about the next step. My next step.

"Oh my god, Mason." I gripped the phone with two hands and turned it on speaker mode. With the volume low, I held it in front of my face and spoke in a quiet voice that wouldn't disturb my dad. "I... What are you thinking?"

"I have no idea, Willow." He took deep, intent breaths, but I could hear the anxiety underlying it. Almost feel his rapid heartbeat against my own. "Dad called Henry. I dunno what they're doing. I just..."

"Do you need me to come with you?" I asked, standing up from the bed. I could hear the engine now and understood that he must be driving around, looking for Hudson. Like you search for a lost dog, I thought, disgusted at myself for the comparison.

"No, no." Mason paused. The noise around him calmed, no longer just the rushing sound of wind. Maybe at a stop sign, then. Definitely in the convertible. "I'll call you if I need help. I just wanted to tell you."

"I understand. I'm sure you'll find him," I lied. I knew I had to move. Sitting here, waiting for the phone to ring with either good or awful news... That would be hell. Sensing the conversation had come to an end, I added, "Mason, I'm really sorry about Bruce. He seemed like a... an okay guy. I feel bad for you and—"

"It doesn't matter," he said through what sounded like clenched teeth. The engine roared louder as he pressed hard on the accelerator. "I just have to find Hudson. I can't... I can't let this..."

Then the phone went dead.

I sprang up immediately and retrieved my keys from the stand beside my bed. I threw on a bra, a different shirt, and my shoes. The phone didn't change. No texts from either of them, no phone calls. I half-expected Mason to call back, but also knew that he wouldn't. He didn't want to say what we both knew.

If Hudson did it, if he actually took his own life, well... for the last month, him and Mason had been locked in some kind of fight. And for Mason, if that's how things ended with his best friend... I couldn't even imagine that weight.

After a quick lie to my dad and nearly soaring face-first down the stairwell, I sprinted to my car. Each second felt incredibly precious now. Any minute could be the one. The engine roared to life, and I made a swerving, illegal U-turn into the other lane. A few violent turns later, I pressed hard on the gas. Within minutes, I raced uphill, the headlights leading me to Little Rush's hilltop.

The city I'd fallen in love with. The city that threatened to take my closest friend.

I found myself idling at a red light with no other cars in sight, cursing whatever gods had decided to play with me. Of course I got a red light now. Just perfect. So I grabbed my phone and noticed a new text. I hoped it would be Hudson, but no. Not so lucky. Nor was it Mason bearing news.

Jed: Have coffee and will be up all night, if you need to come over & talk. Need anything, let me know. We're here for you. We're deciding how to look for him right now.

I punched in a response text and dropped my phone into the passenger's seat. The light still hadn't changed. With a sudden fury, I punched the steering wheel three times as hard as I could. My hand ached afterward, but the rush of adrenaline tore through my body like nothing before. A wild determination.

I retrieved the phone just as the light burned green. I pressed my foot on the gas and kept an eye on my screen. In just a moment, I'd pulled up Mason's "Find my iPhone" location. We both had each other's, but rarely-if-ever used it. Now, though, I wanted to watch him. See where he drove. See if he ever stopped. Two of us could look for Hudson, but I didn't need to retrace his steps.

My answer to Jed had been simple, to-the-point, and true.

No thanks, I texted him. Don't worry. I'll find him.

7
HUDSON

I couldn't explain how I got there if my life depended on it. All I knew was that I found myself hunched in an awkward, painful position, face buried in deep grass. Rain pouring down on me, soaking my clothes, my cut-up appendages. I opened my ears and wobbled for a moment, unsteady on my feet. Just trying to regain some sense of life.

The field around me looked all too familiar and normal. Tall, looming trees on three sides. A pleasant rainfall dotting the place with sparking droplets. Behind me, there were no trees, just a country road. I turned in all directions, confused, aching.

I could feel the alcohol in me still, complicating my thoughts, blurring my vision. It felt like a sledgehammer smashed my forehead over and over. Like a hot, boiling liquid poured into my stomach and my lungs. I couldn't move right, couldn't see. My breaths were all over the place, slow and then fast, irregular.

Just barely, I could hear the familiar chime of my truck. The noise it always made when a door was left open. I turned back, searching for the source. And then I saw it. The lights still on, doors wide, and memories flooded back at the sight.

I remembered loud pops and shattering glass and the world turning on its head. But the moment of impact, I'd forgotten. I could only stare at the wreckage beside the road. Drop to my knees and cover my mouth with both hands.

"Fuck!" I started to cry, burying my face in the soft grass for just a moment. Sobbing, my whole body shaking. Then I got to my feet and wobbled toward the wreckage.

The truck lay in a twisted, mottled heap. Parts were smoldering, others putting off steam from the rain on hot metal and burning oil. It smelled like hell, like the worst parts of life all mixed together. I stumbled that way, hardly believing what my eyes could barely see. My truck. Reliable, constant. So many nights spent in that bed, drinking. So many mornings in the cab, on the way to school, music pumping. Now, just a mess of broken glass. Flattened tires, crushed hood. My truck, totaled. Laying in a field that I remembered.

Mason and I had been here not long ago in that very truck. One of my last memories with him. One of our final laughs. Before everything started to change.

"Fuck you!"

I lunged forward, fist careening through the air. It shattered one of the windows. I felt a surge of red-hot pain shoot up my arm but shook it off. I punched out the last intact window and pulled back, blood gushing from my knuckles. I lashed out at the beat-up doors, kicking and bull-rushing them. After two minutes of assault, they were as wrecked as they'd ever get. I stumbled away, back into the field, tears streaming. My entire body like fire.

Without much thought, without any feeling except for those jagged cuts on my fists and arms, I shed my clothes. I struggled out of my jeans and shirts, throwing them away. They landed somewhere in the tall grass, lost. With only underwear, I hobbled to the center of the field and just started yelling. As loud as I possibly could, all sorts of obscenities and profanities. The worst things I ever said in my life. They just came pouring out like hot venom, like an evil spirit. I threw my head back and roared like never before. Over and over, screaming at the top of my lungs, until I started to choke.

I doubled over, coughing up blood. And I knew I couldn't scream anymore.

"Just kill me." I dropped again and punched the ground with the last of my energy. The realization dawned that I wouldn't die tonight. But that I wanted to. That I would give anything for a gun or even a razorblade.

The crash hadn't done it. I'd managed to escape that wreckage or maybe fly through the windshield. I couldn't remember a damn thing. I could only stare at the aftermath. Feel the alcohol ripping through my insides. I wished I was sober. I wished I was dead. The two weren't necessarily unrelated.

Alcohol poisoning could have killed me, and so I waited in the field for this slim chance. Praying that it would happen. Praying for the end. There was nothing left here. Nothing but a town I wanted to leave, a family I didn't care for, friends who were absent. Nothing at all. No good people. No good men. No good places. Just death and burning alcohol and gut-wrenching pain. That's all I had.

I understood now. I wanted to die because of Bruce. Because I would do something terrible one day, just like him. After what happened with Layla, after what happened with Mason, my parents, all of it. If I didn't die, I would become like him. And the people around me would suffer because of it.

The headlights caught my attention. I picked up my head just enough to see the convertible pulling off the road next to my truck's remains. Then he got out, whipping his head in all directions. I felt happy that he'd come. I couldn't explain it. I just knew it was a good thing. One of the last good things in the world, maybe.

"Hudson!" he yelled, running through the field. His white shoes now muddy, his shirt and hair soaked. Mason's eyes were wide, petrified, so scared. The most scared I'd ever seen him.

I rose to my knees and felt too much agony to rise any farther. I doubled over and started to puke, hot venom inside me spilling over. Two or three times, I heaved and felt like my eyes were going to pop out. The worst kind of vomiting I'd ever had. Pure fire in my throat, and the aftertaste like flaming shit.

"Oh my god! Are you okay?" Mason stood in front of me and placed his hands on my shoulders. He knelt down to my level and stared into my eyes.

I couldn't help but grin, vomit still on my lips. My eyes bulging, throat blood-coated and raw. "I'm really not, man."

Mason hugged me, and it hurt like hell, but I didn't pull away. I threw my arms around him too and started to cry again, all of a sudden. My tears soaking his shirt. I realized I was naked, that he'd hugged me with abandon, pushed himself against my bare torso. And I appreciated this. I closed my eyes and let myself fall apart.

"There's nothing good left in me," I whispered, even just those words stinging my throat.

"I love you, man." He pulled back, a stupid smile on his face.

I sunk to the ground again and held up a finger. Vomit spewed everywhere as I turned my head just in time, sending it to the ground beside us. Mason backed away, covering his mouth with an elbow. When I faced him again, we were both laughing.

"You need to go to the hospital," he said, shaking his head. "Jesus Christ, how much did you drink? How did you total your truck? What are you even doing?"

I shook my head and shrugged. The rain started to feel cold against my skin. I thought maybe I would sober up, but knew it was impossible. I'd only stopped drinking twenty minutes ago. If anything, I would be worse off in an hour than right now. He was right about the hospital, too, but I just couldn't yet.

"I want to kill myself."

When I said the words I'd been avoiding, I expected him to have some drastic response. To gape. He didn't, though. Mason just blew a long raspberry and stared into my eyes. He nodded, slowly, and sat on the ground. Like two wild animals, we both rested in the middle of a rainy field, a smoldering wreck not far off. Maybe we had become the deer that we used to see run across.

"I know you do," he said gingerly. His hand twitched, like he wanted to move closer to me, but held back this impulse. "I want you to get the help you need, Hudson. I want you to... to feel better."

"Feel better..." I chuckled, ruthlessly, and lowered my head. My speech slurred, but understandable. "What a phrase."

"You know what I mean." Mason paused and glanced up, letting the raindrops fall in his eyes. "I need you around, man. I've got this kid coming... and I just need you. I'm so scared, you know that? I don't know... I don't know what I'd do if you... And I know that's maybe not a good thing to tell you right now. But it's the truth."

"I've wanted to kill myself for years," I said, holding back another torrent of crying. I clutched at my throat, where a sharp pain built up, and took deep, shuddering breaths. "I don't wanna live another day."

"We're gonna get you help." Mason stood up, and I thought for a moment he would actually just leave me there. But then he extended a hand. "I just need you to take the first step."

I grabbed his hand and struggled to my feet alongside him. It occurred to me that my leg might be broken, or at least one of the bones might be. But I couldn't feel too well, and I couldn't tell for sure. I wrapped an arm around his shoulder and winced with each step as we advanced toward his car.

"I love you, too, Mason," I said at last, my voice faint, almost nonexistent.

"I know you do," he said, his own arm wrapped around me tight and supportive. "And I'm sorry how things have been lately."

A new pair of headlights joined Mason's at that moment, and I recognized Willow's car. Mason looked surprised to see her, but I just smiled. After everything, I realized she was the person I'd miss most. The one I didn't want to hurt. And as she advanced toward us, her expression sent a wave of emotion through me.

I didn't know what would happen next as I struggled into the passenger's seat of Mason's convertible. But I knew that I didn't want to die anymore, not at that moment, and maybe that was the first step he'd mentioned.

Little puddles had collected in the seats of his car since he hadn't put the top up still. I asked him to leave it down, just for a while, so I could feel the rain. He obliged and started the engine. I sighed, but even that hurt.

"Hospital, right away," Willow urged him from the back seat, her hand gently on my shoulder, grip soft and comforting.

"For sure." Mason pulled onto the road. "Right away."

"I love you both," I said, raspy voice barely held together. Leaning my head back and closing my eyes, something like sleep washing over me. Rain touched my face, and I felt okay. I knew it wasn't death, and I didn't want it to be. I could get used to waking up.

8

LITTLE RUSH

THE REPORTER

Gina threw her clothes into a suitcase haphazardly, pausing only to glance out the window of her apartment. The lights were all off, and the sun had just risen outside. Light glinted off the Ohio River and illuminated the fog that swallowed downtown Little Rush. She heaved another pile of clothing into the suitcase and sat on the lid while she tried to zip it shut.

This was always the worst part of an assignment. The moving back. The leaving everything behind. No matter where she went, leaving was never easy. Little Rush, though, might've been the hardest place yet to abandon. The brief stay in a place so quiet almost made her forget the big cities. But now it rejected her. She was too loud, and they were too sleepy.

Just small things, but she noticed them. The hushed conversations in stores. The people with their backs to her on the sidewalk, chattering like chipmunks, words all a blur. The community caught off guard, like the rest of the country. Only these people had to deal with it firsthand. For people in Louisville, only an hour away, they could read the articles and chuckle quietly. Appalled, sure, but also intrigued. Here in Little Rush, they had to deal with Bruce Michaels personally. The buzz he'd brought to their city now turned into a dark cloud. The man who had used them as an escape became an exile.

Gina glanced at the laptop sitting open on her bed. Her email pulled up, stagnant. It had been days since she'd received any updates. Just a week ago, her boss had called and told her to come back. "Time for the next assignment," he said. And she agreed. But that week of packing, planning, plane tickets had taken a toll. She didn't really want to go yet. She wasn't ready.

Madeline Suso had emailed her twice. Both angry. Furious that her name had been used. Outraged at the effects it had on her life. She couldn't hide in anonymity any longer. She'd quit her job because of coworkers asking questions, some even teasing her. Crude remarks. Telling her she should've kept quiet. Consequences in a man's world.

Not only that, but she'd been harassed by other reporters ever since word got out. Ever since that TMZ article. Not that it mattered. Gina's article, when finally released, didn't at all resemble the piece she'd written. Fragments of it, sure, but the whole thing had been sensationalized and colored in black-and-white. Bruce Michaels, a Machiavellian villain. Another old, rich, white, perverted man.

Madeline had suffered. She'd been thrown into a fire because of the story. The story that Gina had written. It was meant as a character study of Bruce, as a question. What makes a man do what he did? And what compels somebody to run away? But in the end, through a combination of editors, and maybe her own mistakes, the story turned out wildly differently than she'd imagined at the onset.

And for Gina herself? No fame. No critical lauding. Nobody even knew her. All they cared about was the story, the salacious details, the gossip. Not the journalist integrity she'd been aiming for. Just the dirt.

Gina grabbed her suitcase and threw it into the main room. She opened another one and started to pack the rest of her stuff.

Everything but the laptop. She left it on the bed, email open, hoping for news. Of something better. Maybe something from Madeline. Offering forgiveness rather than furious, scrambled messages.

You promised, Madeline had written. *You promised not to use my name. You promised not to involve me. But I guess that's all you fucking reporters do. You just fuck people over for clicks and stories. I didn't take a settlement because of you! I could've had a million dollars! And now I'm jobless.*

It was true, no other women had come forward to stand with Madeline. Maybe that's why she took the full brunt of the public interest. And also true, it had cost her a million dollar settlement. But could they really blame Gina now? The whole thing was out of her control. Out of everyone's control. And nobody knew where it would end.

Gina closed the laptop and collapsed on the bed next to it. Staring at the ceiling, wondering if anybody would remember here. If Little Rush had a place for her in its memory, or if she would simply be forgotten. There were worse things than being forgotten, she supposed. Just a few.

9
WILLOW

The cicadas were obnoxious as we pulled into the driveway. I'd never driven Mason's convertible before, but he'd insisted. Once he knew what Hudson and I had planned, he'd practically begged me to take it. I guess it was another one of his peace offerings. I'm pretty sure Hudson understood.

I parked beside the quaint house and stared for the first time. It stood next to the cemetery like a rock in the middle of a great, stormy ocean. A country road on one side, the same one we'd driven up. On the other, a cornfield spreading out for miles and miles. Hudson had commented, as we approached the driveway, that he loved how you could see the water tower from here at daytime. It had gotten too dark to make out that distant horizon, but I took his word for it.

With the car parked and the headlights bathing Bruce's house in a dead light, I turned to Hudson. "Are you ready?" I asked, reaching for his hand.

He nodded, biting his lip. He looked like hell still, even after a few days in the hospital. It had been two weeks since the crash, since the huge storm blew through. Little Rush had no rain since. An endless, thirsty drought. The start of our senior year was coming, a matter of days now. But it still felt like a long way off, mainly because of this. Because we had to do this.

Hudson had told me so, laying on his hospital bed, hooked up to a few machines. The kind of hospital wing where you don't *want* to be there, of course, but you're not super scared. There aren't people crying around every corner. The nurses can smile sometimes. And Hudson, he drank in everything. He seemed to thrive in the hospital. I couldn't explain it. But he looked at home.

We had one really tough conversation there on the first day. He divulged a lot of the regret and pent-up hatred stuck inside of him. Like spoiled milk, it oozed out in nasty chunks. He told me the realization he'd had a few weeks earlier.

"I'm a self-centered, entitled piece of shit," he said, eyes downcast. There were no tears, just a desolate acceptance. "I've been just as awful as Mason."

"That's the past," I told him, reaching out to run my fingers through his hair. "This is a chance for all of us to start over. That's what matters now."

That conversation lasted for about an hour, but afterwards he found new life. His grin lit up the room, though it was a rarity some days. I spent more time by his hospital bed than I ever expected. Sitting in an uncomfortable chair, I became a piece of the furniture, a constant presence. But we talked for a long time. A few conversations were rehashed over and over, but for the most part, it was fresh and interesting. I couldn't help but stay. I couldn't leave him there. And in the meantime, I'd learned more about him than ever.

Mason stopped by often, but not every day. Him and Hudson were still working things out, and I appreciated this. Their relationship had been so deep and had fallen apart so quickly that a simple confession in a rain-soaked, lightning-bolt field couldn't fix everything. They were working through stuff that I couldn't understand. But most importantly, they were working. Piece by piece, restoring what had broken.

Henry and Laurie showed up pretty much every day, but they didn't always stay long. Henry couldn't get off work as much as he liked, and Laurie had her own stuff going on. (I tried not to pry.) I'd say they were around for maybe five of the six days. The first four and then one absence. Once he'd really stabilized, dried out. Once we could be sure that nothing else dramatic would happen.

There were other guests, of course. People from the high school. Teachers, the principal, all that. Hudson's elementary teacher who doted over him so much it made me hate her a little bit. She just didn't have a great bedside manner. Also Jed and Lucy, who came in twice and were on the verge of tears each time. After every guest's visit, Hudson and I would rate them on a scale of five stars. He seemed to really enjoy this game, not in a cruel way. Just the way you need distractions when you've almost died.

I couldn't tell for sure, but I don't think those people knew what really happened. I got the impression, from the conversations they brought and the looks on their faces, that they didn't understand. In their mind, it was just a scary car accident. They didn't know about the underlying mental health problems or the work still to be done. Just like the whole deal with Mason, things weren't perfect yet. And in Hudson's case, only he knew what came next.

"I brought you this," I said one day, entering the room around lunchtime. It was the second day, I think, because Hudson looked better, and he was more talkative than at first. "Here you go." I handed him the iPod his dad had sent with me and headphones.

He raised an eyebrow at me. "Why?"

"Your dad said you might want music. And your phone... didn't exactly make it in one piece." I cringed and took a seat beside the bed. "Anyways, he said it's all on there. All your songs. I already got the Wi-Fi connected."

Hudson thanked me and stuffed one earbud in. He started scrolling through the songs on the iPod, absent of expression.

"I think I know why I like music," he said, clicking on a song. He powered down the screen and let the iPod drop to his lap. Hudson turned, clearly expecting me to ask.

"Why's that?"

"Because they can kinda yell and all that." He grinned sheepishly, as if this was something he didn't quite feel comfortable admitting. His neck scrunched down the way he always did when embarrassed, like he was trying to be a turtle. "They can... have emotion. Let their voice break. The way you can't if you're just talking."

"I suppose that's true." I leaned my head back against the wall and closed my eyes. "What're you listening to? Anything I'd like?"

"Bon Iver?"

I shrugged and moved from my chair to the bed with an exaggerated groan. Sitting next to his legs, I leaned closer and he put the free headphone into my ear. A falsetto, soothing voice greeted me and almost-wild guitars.

"I've already heard this song," I teased him. "You always listen to it. Play something new."

Our days in the hospital passed like that. Hudson introducing me to music, and I would often return the favor. Our preferences overlapped enough that it really was an enjoyable time. He didn't have many female artists, so I showed him tons of alt rock with women leading the band or else being solo acts. Every day there passed in a blur. It felt like we were in a time capsule, just the two of us. The world outside spinning, but we were stationery. And of course, we'd have to break out at some point. For now, though, I would introduce him to Phoebe Bridgers, and we would judge his hospital guests too harshly.

It was the day before last. That night would be his final one in the hospital. I would leave for dinner around six-thirty and come back at eight-thirty for the last time. Just like every other day, only this time it felt a bit more serious. Like the end of our time bubble. Like stepping back into the real world.

When I left a little before seven, I was surprised to find a new visitor coming to take my place. I recognized the girl barely, one of those faces I'd seen at school and everything, but Hudson grinned wide as soon as she entered. I left the room with an eyebrow raised. When I returned a few hours later, she'd already gone.

"Who was that?" I asked, entering with a fast-food bag to gift him.

"Layla," he said, blushing.

I chuckled and sat down beside him, handing over the bag. There were moments I wished we could stay like this forever. Or at least stretch out for an extra few days. But everything had to pass, especially the good stuff.

Hudson and I were chatting around ten later that night. I had thirty minutes or so until the nurse started badgering me to leave, and I'd been talking with him about the next steps. What life would be like outside the hospital. He told me his plans for therapy, for dealing with school, for talking to his parents. Stuff that he'd been dwelling on since arriving in the hospital. Maybe even longer.

I stared into his eyes, barely visible in the dark room. Only the flickering television offered any light. "We gotta leave here pretty soon, Hudson. Now that this is all over," I said, resting a hand on his leg, "I just want you to know I'll still do anything for you. Once we're out there, in the real world... If you need to talk..."

"I do need something." He cleared his throat and stared at the television. He often did this to avoid meeting my eyes. "I need to see Bruce."

"Hudson…"

"No, don't. Don't try to stop me." He faced me now, and his expression couldn't have been more serious. "It's not over yet… I have to see him one more time. And then I'll be done with it."

"Closure?" I frowned and shook my head a little. "Are you sure that's…"

"I've gotta try."

And so, in that way, we found ourselves standing on the porch at nine o'clock at night. We hadn't set a date, hadn't decided anything, except that Hudson wanted to go and I would go with him. I didn't know why he wanted support, but I didn't question. It made sense, in a way. And I knew he would choose me, not Mason, to go with him. Our bond had become something unexplainable, something meaningful. Him and Mason were still building. It just made sense.

A few days after he left the hospital, Hudson texted me at dinnertime asking to go that very night. I obliged and told him I'd be around to pick him up in a few hours. Since I'd been with Mason at the time, he'd asked me to take the convertible. Mason didn't give an explanation, but I knew he wanted Hudson to realize he was still trying. I told Mason, every day, that things were going to work out. He just had to give it time. Let Hudson get used to therapy, to this sober life. Once school started, things would seem different anyway. New beginnings. For all of us.

"I guess… knock?" I suggested.

Hudson tapped his knuckles three times against the door. I noticed the window to our left, curtains drawn. They fluttered just a little, like somebody had been peering out moments earlier. I faced the door again and heard the deadbolt grating as it slid open. Then the knob turned, and it swung inward, revealing a haggard, wild, rough man.

Bruce Michaels had dark bags under his eyes. His skin was

drawn tight against his bones, and his shoulders looked incredibly rigid and uncomfortable. He hunched over like a beggar and leaned against the doorway, staring at us.

"I thought you'd come," he said, voice gravelly and slurred.

Hudson shook his head and stared straight into those dull eyes. I was impressed with the way he maintained that gaze, crossed his arms, stood straight. The two of them watching each other for a moment, taking deep breaths.

"I couldn't believe it." Hudson bit his lip and sighed. "I guess I should've known. I can see it now."

"There are no good people, Hudson." Bruce shrugged, still resting against the doorway. "I hope you get that now."

"I don't care about your excu—"

"They aren't excuses," Bruce snapped. It felt like he was only moments away from lashing out. He frowned. Those eyes flicked to me for a moment, and I recoiled. Just the way his head moved. His lips quivered, like a man on the edge. "I came here to chase my grandpa." He looked at Hudson now, narrowing his eyes. "I came here to be better."

"I don't care."

Bruce straightened up and backed away into the house, gesturing. "If you'll just sit down and give me a—"

"No," Hudson snarled, his words cutting through any doubt. "I came here to say... I'm not coming back." Then, without warning, he started moving back from the house, dragging me by the hand. I went without hesitation, watching Bruce from the corner of my eye.

Bruce nodded and placed a hand on the door. "I hope, one day, you'll forgive me. Hudson." He started to push it closed but paused with just an inch of space remaining.

We were a few feet away from the porch at that point, but I glanced back over my shoulder to see his eyes peering through the gap. Hudson reached for my hand and squeezed it as we approached the convertible. At last, I heard the door slam behind us.

Hudson collapsed into the passenger's seat, closing his eyes. I started the engine but didn't back out right away. I just stared at him, his expression of pain. Hudson gripped the door handle so tight that his knuckles were turning pale, but a smile crept along his face.

"It's over," he said, now looking at me. "It really is. The first time I heard him say my name… it got me. But now I didn't even flinch. I don't need him. Not anymore."

The engine purred as I pulled onto the country road and started away from the cemetery. Hudson turned to look back one final time, and a content wave washed over his face. He settled back into the seat, his vision flicking in the direction of the water tower. I still couldn't see it, but maybe that didn't matter.

"What do you think'll happen to him?" I asked as we zipped past trees and farmhouses.

"No idea. Whatever he does, it's not part of my story anymore." He threw his arms into the air and yelled, hair flying all over the place. A resounding shout that didn't hold any anger or pent-up aggression. Just the sound of being alive.

10

LITTLE RUSH

When they found his body, it had been decomposing for two weeks. The blood-splattered wall had dried completely, like a grizzly coat of paint. The couch sagged under his weight. The corpse alone since that instant when he pulled the trigger. The gun itself had fallen onto his lap and remained there until the police collected it.

Nobody came to look for him, because nobody had a reason. Townspeople assumed he had fled once the news broke. National news didn't want to interview him, didn't want to ever broadcast his face again. Little Rush, collectively, turned their back and tried not to think about the man in their midst. The man they'd welcomed with open arms and clamored for his approval. The man they'd been so eager to see, and now couldn't bear to think of.

Teenagers got in the habit of driving by the house and flipping him off. This escalated to throwing things at the house. Eggs, empty bottles. His only interaction with the town came via these trouble-seeking high schoolers. And as the days passed, they got even more daring with the pranks.

It was a few angsty teenagers who discovered his body. They had been throwing stones at the house but grew tired of this sport. The four teenagers, two boys and two girls, inched closer and closer to the house. Mischievous grins spreading over their adolescent courage.

"Let's go break the window!" one of the boys said.

"Can we just leave…?"

"God, can you even imagine what he'd do?"

They started toward the house after that, glancing around for any cars or any potential witnesses. Nobody disturbed their mission. Not even Bruce Michaels seemed to notice. So when they reached the front door and peered in the window, it was no surprise they all jumped backward and one of the boys screamed.

Bruce Michaels, slouched on the couch, blood crusting the side of his head. Brain matter and blood adorning the wall behind him and the cushion to his left. His lifeless corpse frozen, staring right at them, skin as white as paper. Tongue sticking out, head leaning back against the wall. His eyes like a vacant motel.

They called the cops a few minutes later, and within an hour, the news had broken. Everybody in town heard. Everybody conversed in low voices, almost afraid to be heard talking about the man. The local paper ran a story. The national news picked it up, and Bruce Michaels had his final hours of relevance.

Most of them were astonished, but not necessarily saddened. The man had already died in the public's mind. He had become less than nothing. He had become the antithesis of all those acting roles. No longer the deep-thinking, rugged, wilderness man, or even the high-class art thief with a penchant for love. He had become Bruce Michaels, rapist. Bruce Michaels, villain.

Little Rush cast out the national media soon after Bruce's dark secrets were revealed. In the same way, his own body was cremated and shipped away. To an ex-wife, the locals said, or maybe sold to the few fans who clung to his memory. Whatever the case, the man was gone. At long last.

Hudson, upon hearing the news, took it harder than most.

Sitting in his room, headphones playing a Phoebe Bridgers song, he stared outside in the vague direction of Bruce's house. And with a hand over his mouth, he cried silently for a few minutes. Struggling to comprehend. Struggling to make sense, still, of the fallen god he'd worshipped. The mortal man who had caused so much pain and also so much joy.

Hudson knew that he had done it on the couch, because it was the only thing that made sense. Where his grandpa had died. That's what Bruce said in one of their many conversations. He, of course, would die in the same exact spot. Always chasing a legacy he could never obtain. Maybe, Hudson decided, that was the real memory of him. A man who tried to become more. A man who had done awful things and attempted to run from them. But in the end, there's no field big enough to hide in.

"Gone..." Hudson wiped his eyes one last time and cleared his throat, standing up from the bed. "I guess it's over for us all."

Little Rush, the scene of such a brutal end, the home of a fallen god, would continue on as if nothing had changed.

11
WILLOW

I figured out the deal with alcohol that summer. It had taken me a few years and an unplanned pregnancy, as well as a best friend nearly dying in a drunken car crash, but I knew by the end. It's just a really simple cheat code. It's a shortcut to the highest peaks and lowest valleys of emotion we can reach as mortal humans. And it feels damn good.

But I've figured out that reaching those same peaks without it feels even better. It's just harder to achieve. When you get there, it's majestic. A hearty, full stomach laugh with friends or the moment when a strip of sunlight hits your frozen cheek. And the valleys, they aren't quite as low.

The three of us were seated around the table one last time. The cabin, shrouded in darkness, stood beside us like a barrier from the outside world. Just the three of us, slouched in our chairs, fingertips drumming on the table, a gentle forest breeze singing all around. There's something about the way an October evening touches your skin.

The boys didn't seem to notice, but then again, I've always suspected they aren't as in tune with the seasons. They weren't the ones wearing flannel and dark leggings and boots. My classic fall attire, maybe a bit basic, but ask me if I care. It's comfortable, and I look as good as I'm gonna with layers and layers on. Mason prefers crop tops or whatever in the summer, but those days were past. Not only was it cold outside, but I had a bump. A small one, not as cumbersome as I had expected, but a bump, nonetheless.

Mason held an e-cigarette between two fingers, the way he did with real ones. He inhaled it and blew out through his nose, a cloud thicker than any Marlboro.

"You look like an idiot with that," Hudson said, rolling his eyes.

Mason shrugged and offered him the device. "Tastes better, smells less."

"Just as likely to kill you." Hudson reached for it and sucked on the end. "I'm never getting one of these."

Mason smirked and gave him an "uh-huh, sure" expression.

The recently installed porch lights offered a clearer-than-usual scene out here. Over the past few weeks, there had been quite a few additions to the cabin. Weeds and brush around the porch cleared away, making it a bit easier to circumnavigate the house without contracting poison ivy. The driveway out front paved and expanded. Inside, numerous projects, like the upstairs floor and the kitchen sink replaced. It certainly felt different, less rugged, if a private cabin in the woods could ever be called that.

We all felt it that night. A slight shift in the world. This was the last weekend of the year suitable for relaxing outside, coming at the back of a curiously warm Fall Break. And it truly marked the end. The end of our time in the cabin. The end of break.

Senior year, after this, would hit full steam ahead. No more learning old material. No more dancing around those tough questions. Just a daunting wall we had to climb or shatter against.

"Can you believe about that football player?" Mason asked us both, shaking his head. "Shootin' up in the bathroom two weeks ago. I mean, what the hell? If you're gonna do drugs, at least—"

"Says the kid who got drunk in a stall during sophomore year," I interrupted, jabbing a finger through the air.

"That's right!" Hudson clapped his hands together and laughed, leaning back in the chair so far that it almost toppled. "You snuck him out, right? Or was that…"

"*That* was Dannielle." I scowled at them both and tried to hide my smile.

"Let ex's be ex's." Mason threw up his hands in self-defense. "Talk about something else besides my impulsive sophomore year."

Hudson folded his arms, and his eyes flicked toward me. Then, with a satisfied smirk, he cleared his throat and directed his attention to Mason. I recognized this as the buildup to some great punchline.

"You left all that impulsiveness behind, right?"

Mason nodded. "I'd say so."

"Would you say it's impulsive to… oh, I don't know…" — Hudson raised his eyebrows— "stab someone at the county fair?"

"Hey!" Mason lashed out across the table, snagging his e-cig from Hudson's grip. He settled back in his own chair, taking a smoke now, and laughed behind a hand.

The two bickered for a while about who had done the most impulsive things in high school. There were stories passed, of course, that would've gotten either in a wild amount of trouble, but senior year brought a willingness to admit some of our past mischiefs. Cheating on a test freshman year was suddenly the least concerning thing in the world. As was fooling around with someone during class or a well-laid prank on the teacher. Nothing they said, though, could ever touch my experiences over the past three years, not that I bothered to share just then. While they went on and on, I sighed and observed.

There were moments all through high school when I'd recognized why people called it "the best time of your life." Sparse moments, fleeting and fickle, but in their own way important. This brief escape from reality, a quiet night with friends, topped them all. The best time of my life...

Hudson held his Coke can with a familiar grip and slurped a third of it in one go. Mason, smoking whatever flavor he had for the week, had a soda in front of him too. I didn't touch alcohol, of course, and hadn't since the pregnancy test. But it struck me in that moment that none of us were drinking. None of us had in months. Not even Hudson. I didn't know if this was a choice recommended by his therapist or something he'd decided independently. But I felt happy for him, for all of us, the way that was only possible on a comfortable October evening.

"What about you?"

I sputtered to awareness and saw Hudson's eyes trained on me, his lips parted in a question.

"What?" I answered.

"Most impulsive thing you've done in high school."

Still on this, I thought to myself before scrunching up my nose and churning over a few ideas. "Probably... well, one time I threw old milk in this kid's trunk. Stayed there for a while, too." I beamed at the memory. "Oh, and I slashed Blough's back tires once."

"Jesus Christ!" Mason said, smacking the table with a hand. He threw his head back, laughing, and Hudson joined in. "That's a felony!"

Hudson leaned forward onto the table and rested his forehead. He held his stomach and took a minute to collect himself before managing, "I hope that's your worst."

"Not even close." I winked and brushed my hair behind an ear.

The night progressed, and the sky grew deeper purple until

it might've been mistaken for black. Somewhere behind those clouds, the moon and stars were hanging like shattered light bulbs. We traded high school stories for the next hour or so, played a few games of "Fuck, Marry, Kill," and forced Mason to decide which one of his ex's he'd hook up with. This took some finagling, and I pretended to be angry at times, but he finally settled on Danielle.

Just as I thought.

Mason quit smoking at around one in the morning, and we were all out of Cokes. The cooler, now full of melted ice, lay on the wooden porch beside us. The boys had given into a deep and unshakable silence, broken only by the songs of cicadas and treetops. Every so often, I thought I could hear the creek bubbling, just a short walk downhill away, but this might've been my imagination.

Every few minutes, Mason and I would exchange a meaningful look. Hudson didn't seem to notice. His eyes were locked on the trees, peering into darkness. I might've thought he'd fallen asleep if not for the occasional grunt and shift in his chair.

Mason gestured at me, but I shook my head and nodded back at him. He frowned and ran a hand through his hair. I shot him the sternest expression I could manage and pointed at Hudson, trying to be discreet. Mason bit his lip and shook his head rapidly.

I sat up straighter in my chair and sighed. "Hudson…"

He turned to me, eyes wide, curious. "What's up?" Seeing my face, his profile darkened just slightly. "Everything okay?"

"We haven't told anybody yet…" I smiled at Mason and reached a hand across the table.

"Oh god, it's twins, isn't it?" Hudson let his head fall against the chair's back. "Not double Masons. That's…"

"No, no."

Mason took over before I could continue, his voice deeper

than usual and unsteady. "We're... Me and Willow, that is... We're gonna graduate early. In December."

Hudson started to speak, but I held up a hand. "So we can get married in the spring before... everything." I rested a hand on my stomach.

"You're getting married?" Hudson covered his mouth with two hands and stared with owl-eyes. "Oh wow! Did you...?" He shifted to Mason and cocked his head. "Did you propose?"

"Last week." He beamed, clearly proud of this. I interrupted again before he could start on a story that Hudson wouldn't care to hear right now.

"We're gonna be around town, of course." I leaned toward Hudson this time and extended a hand. "Just not... at school."

He nodded, more solemn. As if it had just hit him. The three of us, no longer classmates. The great divide we'd been dreading, watching in the distance, and now it stood less than three months away. None of us spoke as his brain churned and soaked up the information. His smile didn't leave altogether, but it flickered and became something less.

"I'm happy for you guys," he said at last. His lips were tight, but he nodded fervently. "I'm... I really am."

"Have you decided what you're doing... after you graduate?" I asked him, if only to shift the conversation.

He shrugged and picked at the fabric in his jeans. "Think I might take a year off from school. Just work, you know."

"That would be great!" Mason exclaimed, banging on the table yet again. "We're gonna be..." He shot me a look asking if he should share the news. I motioned for him to go on. "We're gonna be here, too."

At this, Hudson's chin rose, and his eyes locked on me in particular. "But..."

"Online college," I told him, tapping the side of my head. "So it looks like we'll have at least one more year together."

12
JED

I heard, once, that there's a time in your life when everything is weddings and celebrations and babies. A time full of new life and relationships, hope and promise. But that shortly after, quicker than ever expected, there's a time of funerals and divorces and loss. Gut-wrenching, soul-crushing loss.

What I'd never heard explained was the time in between. Where your children and your friends' children are experiencing that first phase. The part where they're joyful and radiant and beautiful.

We never expected it to come so soon. Lucy and I weren't really sure about the pregnancy in the first place. What to think or how to act. And credit to Willow for being resilient and unflinching in the face of awkward situations. She was the one to always start conversations. One to push Mason in the right direction, to make the good and tough choices.

"We could graduate in December with just two extra classes this semester," Mason had insisted to me. "Really... free up the spring." Then he took a deep breath and stumbled on, "I wanna marry her in the spring."

There isn't enough said about the incredible willpower that goes into planning a wedding. On top of all that, the middle stages of pregnancy and the final semester of high school... I couldn't imagine handling all of that simultaneously. But somehow, some way, those two did it. Those marvelous, wild teenagers. Kids, really. Not much more than kids. And yet, so much more. So much older than I ever realized until that instant.

When I sat in front of that old barn, a picturesque setting for occasions just like this, I held my breath. I couldn't help it. Lucy, beside me, squeezed my hand tight, and our eyes filled with tears as they stood facing each other, the minister behind them. In all my years, I'd seen buildings taller than the mind can comprehend, artwork that touches the soul, heard music that seeps into your bloodstream and loiters there. But never, in all my years and moments, had I seen something like that.

The barn itself was a rather unremarkable scene from the outside. Situated along a winding, country road, only a sign at the front marked it. "The Old Barn," it said, matter-of-fact and unambiguous. Underneath that, "For weddings, birthdays, proms, and more since 1955." Just up a gravel driveway, across a freshly manicured lawn, there stood a large, unremarkable, red barn. The kind you might find in a children's book or a postcard of rural Indiana fantasies. But this place was the real deal. When we stepped inside for the first time and Mason introduced us to the man in charge of the arrangements, I couldn't help but grin.

Rustic and elegant at the same time, the wooden walls and sloping roof were a flawless picture. A beautiful frame for this happy day. There were smooth, white chairs in rows and rows, gorgeous tapestries on the walls, a blended scent of oak and perfume drifting through the air. Ornate lights hung from the ceiling and along the sides, the kind you could ignore if you tried, but they made the whole place come alive and the air dance. It smelled like the best parts of an apple orchard and looked like the final moments of a sunset. They couldn't have picked a better spot.

"I do." Mason, standing in his tuxedo, dark bow tie just

under his chin. His broad shoulders and straight back made for an intimidating posture, but the subtle tears glinting down his cheeks humanized the whole affair. His soft gaze completely arrested by the flawless bride.

Willow stared at him, makeup touched onto her beautiful features, her own cheeks dry but lips slightly parted. She wore a dress with short-cut sleeves and a loose midsection, no veil blocking her from the crowd. When the minister finished his section, she responded, "I do."

Then Mason wrapped her in his arms and they kissed. We all started in thunderous applause, and Lucy covered her mouth to hold back sobs.

o o o

"Beautiful ceremony, Jed."

Henry took a seat at the table, lowering his plate of food to the white tablecloth. He beamed at me and Lucy, tipping his head to her. When Laurie appeared by his side, Henry gently pulled out her chair and then took his own seat directly across the circular table from me.

I took a drink from my glass of water and nodded. "Sure was. Great venue."

"So is this, though." Henry motioned around with a hand. "You're not thinking about buying it, are you?" he teased, winking at me. "I know how you get."

I shrugged and sipped on my water again to hide a smile. The thought had, in fact, crossed my mind.

The wedding reception took place in an old, abandoned warehouse that I'd renovated for this occasion. Turned it into a pretty fine banquet hall, in fact. The walls were all lined with candles, and high windows allowed natural light to stream in. Circular, white-cloth tables were arranged throughout the expansive room, all decorated with the finest silverware, glasses, and flowers. Overhead, we'd installed a makeshift ceiling closer to the normal height so that the guests didn't *feel* like they were in a huge warehouse. From this hung drapes and tiny, sparkling lights, giving the impression of midnight stars overhead. Carpets were spread out and fastened to the ground, completing the elaborate makeover. Besides the wedding DJ's equipment just beyond a dance floor at one side of the room, the entire scene had been my undying labor for the past few months.

All of that, right beside the four-lane road that cut through uptown Little Rush. Close enough to see the smokestacks from the plant.

So yes, I had thought about purchasing the building. Already made plans to. This would be perfect for wedding receptions in Little Rush. I could rent it out at fairly inexpensive prices for any younger couples in town. That, at least, was my hope.

"They'll be moving to Indy or something, I suppose?" Henry bit chicken off his fork.

"Staying here, actually," Lucy answered him, not masking her excitement. "Online college for a few years and then the two of them might just take over the business."

"Businesses," I added, taking a deep sigh. I glanced around the room to find the married couple entertaining guests, every person wanting to shake their hand or have a quick conversation. "Everything will be theirs before long."

"Ah, coming to farm with me, are you?" Henry chuckled in his deep, throaty way and snapped again at his fork.

I didn't answer at first because this thought, too, had crossed my mind. It wouldn't be the worst thing in the world. Problem was, to truly let go of the businesses here, I'd probably have to move a bit farther away. Not that I wouldn't come back and visit often. Just that, for Lucy's sake especially, it might be time to hit the road and stay on it a while.

As soon as these two had the baby and got settled in, Lucy and I would take an RV and drive around. Maybe for as long as nine months. Travel to the coasts, spend week after week alone together. It's what we needed. What we deserved. These kids were doing alright. They could manage on their own for a bit. The two of them, they'd be fine.

Hudson exchanged a word with Mason, and they laughed. Then the former rushed off to a table with a plate of food and the latter continued greeting people. Willow watched him go with a content but slightly sad expression before her hand was shaken by a rough old man I recognized as a regular at Allen's Burgers.

When I refocused on my table, I found Henry sitting there alone, his eyes trained on me. A quick glance over his shoulder confirmed that our wives had left for the buffet. I would've taken that trip myself, if only my nerves would relax and my knees would stop shaking long enough to stand. I desperately wanted to break out the wine bottles, but that would have to wait. Later in the night, maybe. There were a handful of kids here, after all, and even more high schoolers. But without a doubt, as the night wore on, there would be drinking

"This place never does change," Henry commented, drumming his heavy fingertips on the table. His fork lay on the half-eaten plate.

"Suppose you're right." I grinned at him half-heartedly and made to reach for my glass of water. I changed my mind and let the hand fall to the tablecloth, like landing on a pillow.

"You leavin', another Cooper takin' up business." Henry clicked his tongue and wagged his head. "Never changes."

"I didn't say I was leaving."

He winked at me and pressed a finger against his chest. "I known Lucy, and I known her as long as you have, matter of fact. Point is, we both know you're leaving. Where to? God knows. But you're both going."

I smiled bashfully and ran a hand through my hair. "Guess you're right."

"So that girl's helping with the businesses, huh?" Henry gestured at Willow. He chewed on his bottom lip, furrowing his eyebrows.

Without turning to look at her, I answered him, eyes dropping to the three roses at the center of our table. "Sure is. She's wild smart. And passionate about it, to my surprise."

Henry fell silent after that with a content chuckle and started forking the plate's contents back into his mouth. I watched him for a moment, turning over my next words. He didn't seem to mind or even notice my staring. Lucy and Laurie were still at the buffet, had just now gotten their plates. Without pausing to consider, I cleared my throat and went for it.

"Henry... You think we made the right decision? By sticking around here."

With a mouthful of food and a hand half-covering it, Henry sputtered, "Turned out okay, didn't it? That's all y'can ask for, these days."

I knew what he meant, as I watched the new couple moving around the celebration. I could imagine grandchildren now, wrestling with them in the sitting room, a bonfire out at Henry's place. One for now, maybe more later. Growing up right in front of my eyes. And they would turn out okay, too. Because in my experience, everything does in Little Rush.

13
WILLOW

"I love you so much."

Mason beamed at me as he stepped away, gently letting go of my hand. His fingertips slipped away, and he backed toward the outside corner of the dance floor. From the crowd of onlookers emerged a man dressed in a shoddy suit with two distinct cuts on his chin from shaving. He stepped forward, and it took everything in me not to start crying right there.

I'd held it together pretty well through everything. The rehearsal dinner the night before, though tiring and incredibly emotional, hadn't brought tears. Just heartfelt thankfulness and deep hugs. Hudon's toast, especially, had been powerful. Worth every penny this wedding cost us. But not that dinner, not the wedding ceremony itself, not the moment Mason kissed me... none of it compared to this.

My dad took my hand and placed his own gently on the small of my back. I stared into his eyes and lowered my head onto his shoulder as the Tom Petty song swooned from speakers nearby. My pregnant stomach pressing against his beer belly just slightly, so I couldn't stand too close.

When Mason and I began our first dance five minutes prior, I had felt the eyes of everybody. Could tangibly feel them sinking into my skin and burning through the beautiful dress I wore. But with my dad, it was like nobody else existed. I didn't hear the "aw"s and the "so beautiful"s. I barely even noticed Mason with my mother, just a few feet away.

"You look gorgeous," my dad whispered, smiling. His breath had a faint smell of cigarettes, but it had been mostly covered by something minty.

"Thank you so much for... being here." I buried my head into his chest and took deep, shuddering breaths. Trying not to give in. "It means the world."

"Anything for you, sweetheart." His hand patted my back to the rhythm of the music. "You pick this song?"

"You know I did," I said, grinning into the worn fabric of his suit jacket. I closed my eyes and felt the tears seeping out anyway. Soaking into his attire, dripping down my face. Goddamn it, my makeup would be smeared or worse, but I didn't want to resist. I said, voice breaking, "It's your favorite."

o o o

The dancing went on for what felt like hours. Most of the adults were tipsy or altogether drunk. A sea of bodies mixing in sweat and laughter and hopefulness. New beginnings. I understood the emotion drifting through the air and tapping everybody on the shoulder. I could finally pinpoint this sensation of relief and trust and genuine love.

It felt the same way a sunset looks. Those goddamn sunsets. They always come back for you.

The sheer amount of people here wasn't something I'd expected or even wanted initially. Among the planning phases for the wedding, we'd had to make so many decisions. Mason and I spent countless hours talking about it. We preferred to hash over these conversations at the old smoking site, peering out at the baseball field. Not that either of us smoked now. I hadn't touched them for months, thanks to the baby, and Mason only did from time to time. No, that spot had become much more to us. A place of peace and innocence. The one thing from our childhood.

The location, venue, reception, food, music, expenses, all of it were difficult talks. But when it came to the amount of people here, that had really taken some work. Mason started off wanting to invite literally everybody in the town. I said *close* friends and family. In my head, this meant somewhere around ten people.

We met in the middle. There were a lot of people here, but not too many. The perfect number, really. It felt like the entire town had come out. This would've concerned me, usually, but Mason's dad had an unorthodox proposal that we'd accepted. Mason and I would make our list of guests that *had* to be there and that we could afford. Jed, for his part, would pay for the rest. The ones we were fifty-fifty on inviting or unsure if they'd squeeze into the budget.

When I asked him why, out of earshot from Mason, his answer surprised me.

"Little Rush needs something like this," Jed said, winking at me. "Needs to celebrate and drink and dance. We all deserve it, especially you two."

Months before wedding preparations started, Mason and I had come to the even-harder decision about our future past high school. College courses online, through the same site I'd used over the summer. Not only that, but we decided to stick around here for the long haul. To take over the Cooper businesses. All of them.

When we first came to this decision, I felt uncomfortable, like Mason had chosen the path for us. I had wanted to leave, initially, but the more I looked around, the more I wanted to stay. And when Mason brought up the businesses once again as his main reason for staying, I felt a sudden pin prick of an idea. That little spark grew and grew until I made the pitch, late one night, sitting in the living room of his house.

"I want to run a business," I said confidently, bracing for the feedback. "On my own."

Mason went along with this incredibly well, and the plans were set in motion.

While I didn't plan to stay in Little Rush forever, I did see a future here for the time being. Hudson was here, my best friend. The businesses, an incredible and once-in-a-lifetime opportunity, were here. The downtown walks late at night. The winding, scenic country roads. The endless farms and lazy evenings. All of it, here.

I could search out there for all of this. Or I could appreciate Little Rush for what it was and enjoy the first few years of my marriage. Mason, my incredibly sexy husband in that tuxedo, waited for me across the banquet hall. Hudson, seated at the table with him, was locked in their conversation.

As I moved from the dance floor and made my way toward their table, I pulled out my phone and took a very quick, subtle picture. Just something to keep in memory. And sure, we'd have tons of pictures from the photographer we hired, but I wanted that shot right there. All for myself.

Yes, Little Rush might not be my forever home. But for tonight, for now, it would be everything and more.

14
HUDSON

While Mason and Willow were still on the dance floor, I had the table to myself for a while. At this point, Layla floated toward me through the crowd. Like always, she possessed the kind of beauty that struck me dumb. To think I'd made out with her in the woods, had gone on a date. To think that a girl like her, so gorgeous and intelligent and independent, could want anything to do with me.

When I saw her moving across the expanse of tables, leaving the dance floor behind, I grinned a little and rolled my eyes. She had locked onto me and drew closer, maneuvering past other guests. In each hand, she held a small plastic cup of red punch. On her face, a dazzling smile.

"It's lonely over here," Layla said. She set a punch in front of me and then drew out a seat. Before I could reply, she'd settled into it, plopped one elbow on the table, and raised her own plastic cup. "Cheers?"

"To what?" I raised an eyebrow and my cup.

"The lonely table." She touched hers against mine and then took a sip.

I drank mine all in one go. "Doesn't feel so lonely anymore." I'd always expected that punch at a wedding would have alcohol, and yet, for many reasons, that wasn't the case. If there had been, I wouldn't have partaken. I'd sworn off that particular substance for a few months, maybe longer. Enough time to get my feet under me. Figure some things out.

"Beautiful wedding," she murmured, nodding toward the dance floor. "Everybody looks great."

"Including you," I pointed out. I folded both hands on my lap and stared straight ahead as we talked.

"I've missed talking with you." Layla sighed and leaned her head back. "You ever think about us? Why we... didn't work out?"

"Try not to," I said, chuckling. It was the truth, after all. "The more I think about it, the more I kick myself for missing those chances."

"Same."

Layla turned to me, and her lips were a perfect curve. She'd outdone herself for this event. The makeup, the colorful dress, all of it. I hadn't seen her in months, it felt like, not since she visited in the hospital. Even though we attended the same school, our paths never seemed to cross. Class schedules just didn't line up. I had assumed she'd forgotten me, like I'd tried for her. But something about her stuck in my mind. Her smile, her lips, all the time we'd spent texting. I missed it. Missed video-chatting and the way her eyes would sparkle with mischief. I just missed her.

"If you ever... feel like it again," she started, pausing to reach out and touch my leg gingerly, "I'd be happy to pay for dinner this time."

"I'm not sure I'm ready for that yet," I said, letting out a defeated sigh. "And I'm sure you've got plenty of other suitors waiting around."

"There's no rush." Layla reached for her cup and finished it off. "Looks like the groom is coming for you."

Mason had just appeared from the crowd and started toward

my table. I groaned internally, wishing for a little more time with Layla. As he approached, she rose from her seat and kissed me on the cheek, holding my head gently. With her flawless body just inches away and sweet perfume brushing against my senses, I couldn't help but imagine something with her.

"Text me, will you?" she whispered in my ear, before exchanging a word with Mason on her way.

I stared at the tablecloth, fully aware of the red color in my cheeks. Mason filled the seat she'd left and plopped another punch down in front of me.

"You and her?" he asked, reclining in the chair. His tie was a little askew and sweat slicked his forehead. Besides that, he was the same well-prepared groom as earlier. The perfect-looking guy, as always.

"Not sure yet." I strained my neck to look around the room and then eyed him curiously. "Where's Willow? You scare her off already?"

"She'll be here in a minute." He tapped on the table absentmindedly, as if playing piano. I recognized that his fingers matched the song playing at that moment. "You having a good time?"

"Of course I am."

At that moment, the sea of people parted again, and this time spat out Willow. In her flowing dress, professional makeup, the radiant glow of joy, I'd never seen a prettier bride in any movie or TV show. She moved exactly as expected, her face in a permanent, electric smile. And when her eyes landed on me, I couldn't help but return it.

I nudged Mason. "She's out of your league, you know that?" I grinned as Willow started across the banquet hall toward our table. "Take care of her."

"One-hundred percent." Mason rubbed his eyes with two fists and held back a yawn. Still, he nodded enthusiastically.

"Goddamn, Hudson, I'm tired."

Willow reached our table finally, drifting across the floor like a ghostly apparition of perfection. She took a seat next to Mason, propping one elbow on the table and collapsing onto it. The music continued over on the dance floor, with most people involved one way or another. The wine glasses around the banquet hall were empty, a surprising number of bottles stacked in a tub against one wall. They hadn't broken out the alcohol right away, but when they did the crowd chugged it. I chuckled at the sight and turned away.

"Hudson here was chatting up old Layla before I came over," Mason teased, addressing his new wife.

"And you interrupted?" Willow scolded him, punching him lightly on the shoulder. "Dick."

"Did not!" he protested, but she didn't pay attention.

Her head swiveled to me, wearing a "go on" expression. I sighed. "We *were* talking a bit, but it wasn't going anywhere. Maybe I'll text her in a few days. I dunno." I shrugged and avoided her eyes. "Doesn't feel like we'll ever be more than friends. I'm not ready for it yet, either way."

"I'm sorry, Hudson." Willow granted me a pitying look. "She doesn't deserve you, anyways."

"I guess maybe we shouldn't have invited half the school," Mason said thoughtfully, rubbing the back of his neck. I appreciated the change of subject. "It's a bit full, this place."

"I like it," I commented. "It's a great wedding, honestly."

Mason nodded in silent agreement and started picking at the flowers in the center of the table.

"Gonna be a pain to clean up," Willow said, frowning. Her eyes wandered around the banquet hall as she clicked her tongue. "Beautiful for now, isn't it? I wish this could last forever." Her eyes widened, and she groaned loudly. "Shoot, Mason. They want us back on the dance floor. Your mom's waving."

I didn't care to follow her gaze. I saw Willow put up a finger, prolonging the expectation just a bit. When I raised my head, our eyes met, and I nodded. She leaned closer and kissed me on the cheek, then reached across the table for Mason's hand. I felt a bit like a prisoner, with them on either side, but it would all be over soon.

"You wanna come over tomorrow?" she asked, her eyes pleading. "The cabin."

"What about the honeymoon?" I squinted at her and then Mason.

"Leaving Sunday night," he explained.

She nodded. "So, one night at the cabin. You wanna come? I'd love to see you before we go, Hudson."

I grinned and hit Mason in the shoulder. "For sure. I'll be there."

"How come I'm the one who always gets hit?" Mason grumbled, but he winked at me as he stood up.

"Thank you." Willow embraced me in a hug, the texture of her dress rubbing against my neck. Then she stood from the table and gestured for Mason to follow. They disappeared into the crowd as quickly as they'd come.

I wished that Layla would return. Wished for somebody to sit here with me. Nothing frightened me as much as the months stretching ahead. My two best friends, now a married couple. I knew things would be okay, if only because they were incredibly thoughtful people. The wedding would end, and things might return to normal, in a sense. But not exactly.

I would spend the last half of senior year alone. I'd make a decision for that upcoming autumn all by myself. While they were in community college, I'd have to get a job or join them in that online school. Unless I moved away to a physical campus. The closest one, an hour off. I had no clue what my own future held. Or who. Or where.

So, in a sense, things weren't okay. But I felt, for the moment, like I would be. There was nothing to do about it, not for now. Maybe I'd text Layla after all, just to see what her plans were for college. Just to talk with somebody else who didn't have it all figured out. That might help.

"You okay, kid?"

I felt something on my shoulder and recognized the voice. But when I turned in my seat, there was nobody. Just a collection of tables, mostly empty, with a few stragglers sitting alone. I decided that, if there were no answers in here, I might as well take my questions outside.

o o o

And so I found myself pushing open the doors with a red EXIT sign shining overhead. As soon as I moved through and stood outside, a cold wind cracked across my face like a whip. I took a deep, lung-filling breath of the icy air and heard the metallic doors clang shut behind me.

I stared across a desolate bean field, not yet planted. For the time being, just an expanse of dirt and mud. It hadn't rained in days, so I started walking across the field, unsure who it belonged to and not really caring.

The sky overhead was an intense and soul-crushing purple, but I found comfort in it. The crescent moon, a brilliant white against that dark background, reminded me of simpler times. Ahead of me, the ambiguous farmer's land stretched out for maybe a quarter-mile. Maybe a half. Everything was subjective when judged by the moon's shadow. Just beyond this expanse of dirt that I slowly crossed, a few trees towered. The strip of forest left only separated farmers' lands. It served no purpose other than getting in the way, but tonight I would push through it.

It had to be late. Later than I wanted to stay up. But sleep hadn't called to me in recent months. It had been so long since I felt tired. One night around Christmas, I'd realized that I didn't enjoy sleep anymore. Just didn't. I never pushed the snooze button on my phone's alarm. I didn't want to miss a moment of what I had left, whatever it would be.

As I crossed the landscape on my solitary mission, that beacon up ahead barely visible anymore, I could imagine the swarm of people dancing inside the banquet hall. Enjoying the dying fumes of a party thrown well and thrown lavishly. But I didn't find my answers in the mass of bodies that were breathing life into the world through movement. I found nothing there.

Tonight, after the highs of a wedding, I remembered a simple but solid truth. For the moment, I felt content. For the month, even. But it wouldn't last forever. There would be dark periods. There would be moments of self-loathing. For now, I felt okay. Right in that moment. And I could appreciate the subtle hope of it.

Therapy had helped me immensely. I no longer felt terrified, just aware. Aware that the future would be drastically different. Aware that Mason and Willow couldn't sustain me forever. That I would have to find other friends. Maybe even other best friends. At the same time, I shouldn't rush things. I should just let them be as they would be.

Too many dancers in the banquet hall of my brain.

I started running through the field, kicking up dirt behind me and spraying it onto the back of my dress slacks. Fumbling to unfasten my tie, barely keeping to my feet. After only a minute, I reached the forest and cut through it with ease, dodging branches and underbrush and thorns. One snapped at my cheek and caught flesh. A trickle of blood ran down the side of my face, but I persevered.

Across a smaller field and into a collection of houses. It felt like the longest journey I'd ever taken. I entered that neighborhood, still at a run, and cut through yards, ignored barking dogs. I fought against every instinct and every anxiety. I fought against myself, and at last reached the place I was meant to.

There it stood, just ahead of me.

"Got you now," I said aloud, flexing my hands at the sight of those many rungs.

The water tower, reaching high above, and that deck so far up. I couldn't even see it from down here, only a basic silhouette, but I knew it would be there. I just had to climb the ladder, the endless rungs of steel and endless feet of danger. Then I would finally see Little Rush as a whole. Then I could let it be what it would be.

It only took me a few seconds to jump the fence. Pain shot through my ankle as I landed, but that barely even registered. With my back to it, an expanse of fields and houses and people who didn't notice my absence, I decided it was time.

I approached the water tower warily, taking deep breaths. The closer I got, the more immense it looked. A task so improbable that I could die from it. Right here, right now. And while I no longer desired sleep, I had a visceral fear of the eternal kind.

One hand on the rung and then a foot. Up. Two more movements. Now six feet above the ground. My last chance to jump down. I stared up at the ladder ahead and imagined the platform so high, the place I had to reach.

I didn't stop climbing. I would reach it. Somewhere up there, the answers.

"You can't make it, kid." That voice again, now from just below me. I could feel his presence coming after me, reaching up for my ankles.

With each rung I pushed off and each grip on the cold bars, I bit my lip harder and furrowed my eyebrows. Sweat trickled down my cheeks, threatening to drip in my eyes. That burning, a momentary blindness, could lead to an eternal sleep.

"You won't make it."

I shook off those ghostly words and braced myself against the wind. Somewhere up there, I would find answers. No matter what forces tried to pull me down.

The higher I climbed, the less afraid I felt. If death would come, let it. I *could* make it.

Somewhere up there, a place of profound uncertainty. And that would be okay.

ACKNOWLEDGMENTS

Where to begin with this monster of a novel? The process and the finished product itself means so much to me, and I'm glad to finally share it with you. But more than anything, I need to thank the people who made it possible.

First off, there's some other authors who shaped the look and content of this book from day one. Fellow authors Jordon Greene, Theresa Jacobs, and Andrew Clegg were all incredibly valuable and have their own fantastic books you should check out. Rebecca Weeks of Dark Wish Designs created the fantastic cover, while Marni Macrae did the professional-level editing and improved the book ten-fold. Both of them write as well!

I had family and friends who also served as beta-readers, especially my dad who read the book first and in its entirety. Without his exhaustive notes and encouragement, the first draft likely would've been the last, and these characters would reside in a dusty box somewhere. Willow, at least, deserves better than that lonely fate.

My mom deserves a lot of praise not only for encouragement, but also for inspiring the book in a large part. As someone who has experienced firsthand the difficulties of small-town Indiana, my mom embodies all the tenacity, grit, and

ιcy required to live and thrive in a place like this, against
s and opposition. Without her raising me, I would have a
wildly different view of this rivertown I call home.

I made the decision to include part of W. H. Auden's poem
at the beginning because I think it reflects the tone and emotion
of this book. Not only this book, but also small-town life in
general. The sort of endless days that all blend together, and
everything is the same night after night. The three stanzas I
included are the most powerful and each one packs a special
punch. I hope you enjoyed that bit as much as I did.

This book is also the most up-front and honest about the
mental health struggles and substance abuse of people growing
up nowadays. While not everything is based on somebody real,
most of it is derived from my own life or from others I've talked
to. Mental health and suicide awareness are wildly important. I
hope this book can serve as a reminder or at least provoke
thought.

About Madison, Indiana, the town Little Rush is modeled
after, I can't say enough. Come visit for yourself or email me with
questions. There is life and death, grief and joy, celebration and
devastation. Each and every day, I fall deeper into the mystery
and intricate web of this town. It truly is magnetic.

Through the process of writing this book, I learned so much
about Madison and about myself. Hometowns, in general, are a
weird thing. The places we grow up are never quite how we
remember them, but always so familiar. No matter our
upbringing, the various people and places that surround us are
never forgotten or entirely cast off. Rather than fight this feeling,
I've tried to indulge it and appreciate my surroundings.

I hope this book made you think deeply, and I hope you
enjoyed the ride through my hometown.

ABOUT THE AUTHOR

David Kummer is a young author who grew up in Madison, a small, southern Indiana rivertown. He grew up in a large household with many siblings and studied English and Education at Hanover College. David has written books in multiple genres with many of the settings and characters influenced by Madison. When not writing, he enjoys listening to indie rock and watching sports, as well as spending time with family and friends.

Visit David online at
www.DavidKummer.com

If you enjoyed this story please
consider reviewing it online and at Goodreads,
and recommending it to family and friends.

CPSIA information can be obtained
at www.ICGtesting.com
Printed in the USA
BVHW081154150421
605031BV00002B/135

9 781087 937274